Praise for the DS Rick T

‘Murphy has always been an exciti
the tension to an even greater level. *Dead Man Walking* is a compulsive thriller with pace, brilliant plotting, and characters who are credible, despite the extraordinary situations in which they find themselves.’ **Ann Cleeves**

‘A terrifically tense sequel… featuring a vicious triangle formed of law enforcement, criminals and vigilantes’ **Daniel Sellers**

‘I loved this. An immediately gripping, compelling and emotionally wrought thriller where the high stakes and strong mystery never let up from first page to last. Clear your diary and get reading!’ **Gytha Lodge**

‘An unstoppable and addictive thriller. You’ll want to read this in one sitting.’ **Michael Wood**

‘Rich with tension and action, there are surprises at every plot twist.’ **Marni Graff**

‘Tension bristles on every page on this rollercoaster of a read. I couldn’t put the book down.’ **Sarah Ward**

‘Gripping and powerful’ **Simon McCleave**

‘I loved it!’ **T. Orr Munro**

Photo credit: E.A. Murphy

M. K. MURPHY writes internationally acclaimed and bestselling psychological thrillers under her own name, and forensic thrillers as Ashley Dyer and A. D. Garrett. She is a past Chair of the UK Crime Writers Association (CWA), founder of Murder Squad, and a former RLF Writing Fellow and Reading Round Lector. She's been a country park ranger, biology teacher, dyslexia specialist and visiting professor in creative writing. A Short Story Dagger, H. R. F. Keating, and CWA Red Herring award winner, she has also been shortlisted for the 'First Blood' critics award and CWA Dagger in the Library.

Also by M. K. Murphy
Dead Man Walking

Blood Debt

M. K. MURPHY

H|Q

ONE PLACE. MANY STORIES

HQ
An imprint of HarperCollins*Publishers* Ltd
1 London Bridge Street
London SE1 9GF

www.harpercollins.co.uk

HarperCollins*Publishers*
Macken House, 39/40 Mayor Street Upper,
Dublin 1 D01 C9W8

This paperback edition 2024

1
First published in Great Britain by
HQ, an imprint of HarperCollins*Publishers* Ltd 2024

Copyright © M. K. Murphy

M. K. Murphy asserts the moral right to be
identified as the author of this work.
A catalogue record for this book is
available from the British Library.

ISBN: 9780008618285

FSC
www.fsc.org

MIX
Paper | Supporting
responsible forestry
FSC™ C007454

This book contains FSC™ certified paper and other controlled
sources to ensure responsible forest management.

For more information visit: www.harpercollins.co.uk/green

Printed and Bound in the UK using
100% Renewable Electricity at CPI Group (UK) Ltd

For Murf

Chapter 1

February

DEPTFORD WATERS, A SPARROW-HOP FROM CANARY WHARF and just thirty minutes overground to central London – if you can believe the sales hype. The brand-new arty tower block reflects the setting sun in gold and blue and peach. The town houses and dinky retirement bungalows remain empty for one final night, but the last-minute finishing touches are done, and they are ready for release to the first lucky owners. In the dying rays of the sun the development seems almost to glow with pride, and even a brief shower seems calculated to add an extra shine to the scene.

Everyone has gone, save the developer who is full of excitement and nerves for the next day, when councillors, planning officers, academics and experts on the built environment will descend to admire his work and share their thoughts with press and media.

Too early for a first pass from the security firm, too dark for further sweeping and primping, the development quietly waits. Only the developer's fire red BMW remains, parked in front of the show house, and a dark Ford Transit van in one of the more distant bays. The sudden grind of a motor disturbs the picture of serenity. Nothing to cause concern, only a landscaper's van – the foreman no doubt – coming to make a final inspection of the work.

He parks in front of the show house, easing himself slowly onto the tarmac, his head bent, watching his step, waxed jacket on top of his overalls, his battered, broad-brimmed hat still wet from the recent shower. He limps around to the back of the van to retrieve a rake, then makes his way to the side gate.

The landscaper continues his slow shuffle around to the back of the house. The garden has been laid to gravel and decking, softened with perennial borders. The first snowdrops are already peeking through a mulch of bark. The security light comes on and he dips his head, holding his hand up as if to protect his eyes from the glare. The patio doors stand open. Odd, given the coolness of the night. The room is unlit, but the floodlight illuminates a sheen of water on the tiled floor, so the doors must have been left open and unattended for ten or fifteen minutes.

The man straightens up, shedding a good twenty-five years in the process. Shaking off arthritis with miraculous ease, he returns down the side passage and quietly leans the rake against the gate. It won't stop anyone, but it will warn him of their arrival. Returning to the open patio doors, his limp vanished, and the last remnants of his landscaper persona discarded, he steps lightly inside the house.

A whimper.

The man moves away from the glass doors, aware that while he's visible, he is vulnerable. Standing with his back to the outer wall, he waits for his eyes to adjust to the level of light and listens. There! Again, a faint whimper.

The man is standing in a kitchen-diner – open plan, but compact – no chance of anyone hiding in any corners. There are boot prints leading across the tiles into the hallway. A glimmer seeps through the open kitchen door: the lights must be on in one of the other rooms.

He unholsters his gun and, taking a suppressor from his jacket pocket, screws it in place, then flicks the safety off. The hallway is clear. He glances up the stairwell, pistol ready, then glides soundlessly to the front room. Doorless to increase the sense of space, this is where the light is coming from. It's empty. More boot prints muddy the carpet, and a lamp has been knocked over.

Returning to the stairs, he begins the climb, aware of muffled sobs. An oblong of light shows through an open door at the far end of the landing. Tiled floor – so probably the bathroom. This is the source of the sound, too, he realises. The threat from a whimpering individual is almost certainly less significant than the possibility of someone lying in wait in one of the darkened bedrooms, so he continues methodically checking each room.

Room one is clear. On to the second. Crouching low, he sweeps left, right, above. The wood-framed bed has linen spilling over the sides to floor level. He moves fast, lifts the bedding, finds nothing.

Back onto the landing, he heads towards the distressed sounds; this is where it could get interesting. There are clear signs that someone had come into the house uninvited ahead of him. The question is: are the frightened whimpers a reaction after the fact, or are the interlopers still on the premises – perhaps waiting behind the bathroom door?

He slams the door open, hears a stifled shriek as the wood bounces off the bath rim. Steadying it with one gloved hand, he swivels to check the bath. A man is bound with zip ties to the taps, tears coursing down his face.

Seeing the gun, he shrieks again, shaking his head wildly, begging through the tape covering the lower half of his face.

It *looks* like the property developer, but he needs to be certain.

'My God, what happened?' the man says.

Confusion is mingled with fear on the developer's face, now. He tugs at the taps, his eyes bulging, mumbling through the gag.

'Hey, it's okay.' The armed man raises both hands, gently placing the gun down on the floor. 'Here, let me . . .'

He peels the gag away, taking a few layers of skin with it and eliciting another shriek from the property developer. Yes, it is Jason Floren.

'What happened?' he asks again, his voice loaded with concern. 'Who *did* this to you?'

'Oh, thank God, thank God! I thought they were going to *kill* me. They—'

'They? Who are "they"?'

'I don't . . . I don't know. They made me—' He breaks down, sobbing.

'Look at me,' the man says, and the authority in his tone has its effect. 'I can help you, but you need to calm down.'

'Oh, God,' Floren wails, his eyes wild. 'You're police, aren't you?' The man's overalls don't exactly shout 'police', but Floren is traumatised, his judgement impaired, so his confusion is understandable.

This is Sam Turner – a man so far outside the law that the question is almost laughable. But he keeps a straight face and lets Floren make up his own mind.

'Fuck,' Floren groans, tears still running down his face. 'You're going to arrest me, aren't you?'

'Not necessarily,' Sam says kindly. 'Tell me everything that happened, and maybe we can work something out.'

Hope blossoms in the property developer's eyes. 'I have money. I can pay you – a-a lot.'

'Please, Jason, don't insult me,' Sam says. 'I've been paid. I don't want your money.'

Stricken, Floren stammers, 'I-I'm sorry, I thought you—'

'Just be honest and leave it to me to decide. But be warned – I will know if you're lying.' Sam doesn't really need to hear the details of Floren's ordeal; he'll do what he was paid to do no matter what he hears. But his curiosity has been piqued, and he's irritated that whoever was here before him has created an untidy scene. He would like to know why.

'Okay, but just get these ties off me, okay?'

Sam shakes his head, eyeing the zip ties binding Floren. 'I feel safer this way.'

Perhaps Floren has forgotten that his potential rescuer was carrying a gun when he came into the room. Anyway, he doesn't mention it.

'Okay . . . Okay, I'll tell you,' he says.

Sam listens for several minutes with increasing wonder. If he hadn't found the man in this position, he might have thought the entire story a fantasy. As Floren finishes, Sam hears a distant police siren and feels the first real pang of concern. 'They said they'd send police?' he asks.

The property developer nods shakily. 'I thought it was a trick. But then you came, and you said you'd listen.' He laughs, tears springing again to his eyes. 'I swear, I never thought I'd be happy to see the police.'

'You thought I was police?'

'You said—'

Sam shakes his head. 'No, Jason, I didn't.'

'You're *not* police?'

'Far from it.'

'Well, look, they'll be here any second. Get me out of here and . . . and we'll talk,' Floren says, avoiding a second, insulting offer of money but still negotiating like a true businessman.

'I think I've heard all I need to hear.' Sam stoops and picks up his gun from the floor, shoots Floren twice: once in the chest and once in the head. He checks for a pulse and – finding none – takes a few photographs to confirm death.

Sending confirmation to his client will have to wait: the sirens are close. He slips out through the kitchen; red and blue lights strobe at the front of the house. The van is of no use to him now, so he runs to the end of the small garden, leaping to grip the top of the fence. The drop on the other side is a good fifteen feet, so he swings over, dropping the last few and landing softly on the earthen pathway of the canal towpath. Treading quietly, light on his feet, he vanishes into the dark like an urban fox.

Thirty minutes later, safely distanced from the development, Sam sends proof of Floren's death to the person who commissioned the hit.

Payment confirmed, he is about to ditch the SIM when a message comes through.

—Did you have to make so much noise?

It seems that news has travelled fast.

—The razzle-dazzle is of someone else's making, Sam replies.

—Well, I don't like it.

Sam isn't interested in his client's likes or dislikes. The job is done, their business concluded. He turns the phone off and ditches the SIM card.

Back at his hotel, Sam completes his packing – he'll be gone from here in five minutes. But he recalls that there was another van, parked in one of the bays at the far end of the road at Deptford Waters – a dark Ford Transit. He'd driven past it on his way in, and his headlights picked up a dulled ghost in the shape of flames above the rim of the wheel arches – the remnants of vinyl graphics removed in a hurry, he surmises. And wasn't there a faint crease in the sliding door, too?

He takes a moment to set up alerts for any mentions of a van of that description in connection with the Met Police. Floren's story has him intrigued.

Chapter 2

Early April

THE WAREHOUSE WAS ABLAZE. Detective Sergeant Rick Turner stood at the inner cordon tape, mesmerised by the play of colour above the semi-derelict building. Shades of green, phantom, teasing, sometimes barely visible on the edges of his vision, then sudden flashes of apple green and vivid flickers of hot pink. The red and blue emergency lights of fire appliances added to the chaotic light show while two crews of firefighters, kitted out with breathing gear, aimed solid water jets at the flames. As steam and smoke rose in swirling vortices into the night sky the colours seemed to dance and shimmer, expanding and contracting, fading in and out in pulsating waves. The sound of the fire was an angry growl and the *taste* . . . Charred wood, burnt plastic and an almost vinegary acidity caught at the back of Rick's throat.

Another month of work, literally gone up in flames.

A group of three firefighters stood to one side of the action, helmeted, but without breathing apparatuses. One of them jerked his head towards the cordon and a tall man broke off from the group. A moment later, Rick introduced himself to the station commander.

'What do you know about this?' The commander had to yell to be heard over the drone of two fire engines and the answering roar as hot metal turned water to steam.

'Suspected drug warehouse.' Rick had been one of a team observing the building for over a week.

The commander nodded, as if he'd made that assessment already. 'Not a factory?' The question wasn't idle curiosity. If the occupants had been manufacturing the stuff, there would be a greater risk of explosion.

Rick shook his head. 'Unlikely.'

'*Unlikely.*' Rick was tall, but the commander stood five inches taller in his boots and helmet. He stared down at Rick. 'Is that the best you can do?'

The warehouse was being used by Ayaz Emin, and it had been set up only seven days before. Just a month earlier, the Met Police and other agencies had been ready to put him on trial for drug trafficking. Until witnesses disappeared, changed their stories, or blankly refused to testify. Then evidence went missing, and the case collapsed. But this was privileged information Rick wasn't authorised to share, so he said, 'My boss will be here in five – he'll be able to tell you more. Anyone inside?'

'Too dangerous to check just yet. But we found two men zip-tied and unconscious just outside the roller doors, and a fair number made their own way out. Ambulance crews have taken some to hospital just to be sure they're okay, but it looks like they were well clear before the fire got going. We saw at least seven legging it across the waste ground as we rolled up.'

Rick turned. Despite the late hour, lights were on in a row of low-rise apartments a couple of hundred yards away across a flattened desert of concrete building slabs, glass and shattered bricks – all that was left of what had once been a busy industrial estate.

'You must've got here fast,' Rick shouted.

'My guess is someone called as the fire started.' The commander must have seen the surprise on Rick's face because he added, 'Yeah, you don't often get that kind of civic responsibility when a drugs factory catches fire. They were very insistent that we should send hazmat units as well.'

'So, they knew what was in the building.'

'It would seem so.' The commander glanced over his shoulder to his two teams, clearly itching to get back to them. 'Tell your boss I need a word when he arrives. And you might want to move back to the outer cordon while you wait.'

Rick lifted his chin in question.

'See the green tinge in the flames?'

'It *is* there, then,' Rick stared at the shimmer of colours, fading now, as the fire crews doused the flames. 'I thought I might be hallucinating.'

'I wouldn't rule that out,' the commander said with a grim smile. 'The taste at the back of your throat?'

Rick worked his tongue against this hard palate. 'What *is* that?'

'Cat pee,' the man said. 'Oh, not literally – but burnt heroin can taste like it.'

'And the colours – that's drugs, too?'

'Adulterants,' the commander said. 'Cutting agents to make the stuff go a little further. Odds-on they've used rat poison, given the fetching shades of green in our mini-aurora.'

Alarmed, Rick looked again at the homes close by.

'We've got local police knocking on doors, telling residents to keep their windows closed,' the commander reassured him. 'Wouldn't want them blissed out on fumes now, would we? Meanwhile, you can see which way the wind's blowing, Sergeant – just take yourself off to the outer cordon and keep upwind of the smoke.'

Chapter 3

THE SOUND OF SUBDUED LAUGHTER rose from a small group gathered around a fire pit in the back garden of a house in Blackheath. Shielded from prying eyes by high walls and careful planting, four men and a woman were congratulating themselves on the success of the night.

Satisfied that they were well provided with beer, their host, Cap, had taken his station at the barbecue. He gazed at them with pride: six months ago, he would not have thought any of this possible.

Sooner, always the quietest, appeared almost detached from the chatter around him.

Living up to her name, Frosty seemed the most chilled, as if armed combat was all in a night's work. Out of tac gear, she was slim, almost slight in appearance. But appearances could deceive – Frosty had a wiry strength that should not be underestimated and was in fact the most battle-hardened of the six.

Brock sat facing him, firelight shining off his bald head, gold and yellow sparks leaping in his eyes. Taking a good swallow of ale, Brock set the bottle down on the flagstones to warm his hands over the fire. 'We *did it*, guys,' he said. 'Did you see those colours? Like green fire!' He kicked the foot of the man seated

10

next to him. 'Should've saved yourself the money on that Iceland trip, Prozac, mate – could've brought your missus along to see the light show for free!'

Prozac grinned obligingly, but his jaw was clenched tight, and the host knew that he was desperately trying to keep his teeth from chattering. He watched Brock's gaze flit from the younger man's face to his bobbing right knee – a sure sign that Prozac was agitated. During action, he could be as cool as any of them; it was the release of tension that the kid found so difficult – in the van on the way back, he'd been quivering like a nervous whippet.

'Loosen up, man,' Brock said. 'It went like a dream.'

Prozac didn't look convinced.

Cap felt he had a point, and to deflect Brock's increasing irritation he called, 'Food's ready,' and five faces turned to him.

Pug was first up. 'Nice one, Cap.' Despite his substantial bulk, Pug was light on his feet – a boxer from boyhood, most of the weight he carried was muscle – none of it for show. He piled burgers and buns, pork ribs and relish onto his plate like he was eating for two.

'*Oy*,' Brock complained, elbowing him out of the way. 'Leave some for the rest of us!'

Pug flexed his pecs in answer. 'Takes protein to keep this toned, mate,' he said, then picking up the mustard bottle in one giant paw, he squirted a generous gloop onto his burger.

'Schnoz like yours, you should go easy on that stuff,' Brock said. 'One sneeze, you'd blow us all from here to Greenwich.'

Pug gave his considerable hooter a tug. 'Had it broke so many times I don't smell too good no more.'

'You're telling me!' Brock chortled, and Pug wrinkled his forehead and feigned a coming sneeze.

Prozac laughed along with the rest, but Cap thought that he seemed relieved that the focus of attention had shifted away from him, rather than genuinely amused, and he wondered if Brock had been needling the younger man out of earshot.

For the next ten minutes, they ate mostly in silence and Cap sat with them like the good host he was. It was a cold, still April night and the fire crackled merrily, sending red and orange clusters of sparks skywards. The heat on his face and the sweetish scent of burning cherry wood made him almost sleepy. But a top note of petrol fumes clinging to his crew's clothing soured the fire's aroma, reminding him that he had less pleasant tasks to attend to before bed.

They'd earned their moment, so he let them enjoy it, waiting for the lulling effect of food and beer to mute the hum of adrenaline coursing through their veins. It wasn't till twenty minutes later, during a break in the conversation, that he brushed crumbs from his hands into the fire, sending up a flare of orange sparks.

'Anyone need another beer?' he asked.

The majority shook their heads, murmuring thanks, readying themselves for the drive home, but Brock leaned across Prozac and claimed a fresh bottle.

Cap waited for Brock to take his first swallow before saying, 'We need to talk strategy.' His voice was calm and low – he made sure of that. Even so, he caught a few uneasy glances around the fire pit.

Prozac cleared his throat. 'Will this take long? Only, I promised Livi I'd be home before midnight.' He sounded anxious.

Brock shot him a nasty grin. 'Sounds like you need to grow some balls, Cinderella.'

Pug laughed, always easily swayed by Brock's attempts at humour, but Prozac got on the defensive.

'No, it's just the baby. She's been cranky since she started teething and Livi's not getting much sleep, so I said I'd—'

Leaning one elbow on his knee, Brock feigned nodding off and Prozac started to bristle.

'You'll be home by midnight,' Cap soothed, his eyes fixed on Brock's smirking face. 'Why don't you start us off, Brock?'

Brock snorted. 'Pass.'

Cap stared at him, implacable. 'Don't be bashful. I'm sure we all want to hear what happened.'

'Whaddaya mean?' he slurred. 'They all got out, didn't they?'

'That has yet to be confirmed,' Cap said.

Brock glowered into the flames. 'We got the workers out.'

'Not *all* of them.' He waited, aware that the crew were mostly avoiding even a glance in Brock's direction.

Finally, Brock spread his hands, sploshing beer from his bottle. 'The office was dark – I didn't think anyone was in there.'

'But someone *was* there – the warehouse manager. Which was dangerous,' Cap said. 'For him—'

Brock interrupted with a sharp, 'Pfft!'

'And us. What if he'd been armed?'

'Well, he *wasn't*, so—'

Murmured exclamations of '*Fuck*, man!' and 'Jesus, Brock!' seemed to sober him a little. He leaned forward again, both elbows on his knees, and scratched the angle of his jaw with his free hand.

'Our tactical goal tonight was disruption,' Cap continued evenly. 'Any death in the course of these operations is a failure – even if it happens in self-defence. And a death resulting from a sloppy error from any one of us is unforgivable,' he added, forcing the point home.

'*Okay*,' Brock said. 'I get it. On the same page – won't happen again, Cap.' He ended with a mock salute.

Cap held Brock's angry gaze. 'Good to know. And – just so we're "on the same page" – if it *does*, you and me are going to have a serious problem.'

Brock blinked and looked away, but even this gesture had a measure of contempt in it.

Chapter 4

Morning debrief, a day after the fire

CHARGED WITH UPDATING THE TEAM, RICK TURNER took his place at the front of the meeting room at Hammersmith Police Station. The ten others seated around the table represented the Met, the National Crime Agency and Border Force.

'Can you start with casualties?' The question came from DCI Will Fenton, the SIO and case coordinator. Just shy of forty, the DCI had the round face and soft brown eyes of a spaniel, but Rick knew that looks were very deceiving when it came to Fenton. He'd seen the man flip from spaniel to bullmastiff in a second.

'Fire crews found three men in all. Two – probably guards – dumped outside the building, bound hand and foot with zip ties.'

'What makes you think they're guards?' Fenton again. Although this was an inter-agency operation, as the local force, the Met took the lead.

'No weapons found, but both wore holsters, and one had a thirty-round Magpul magazine tucked in his belt – fully loaded with 7.62 by 39 cartridges.' This was Russian ammo, deadly at over two hundred yards. 'So I'm thinking AK47s.'

Nods of agreement around the room.

'But residents in the apartment blocks nearby say they didn't hear shots fired,' Rick said, 'and there was no gunshot residue on either of the men.'

'So they were ambushed.'

'Pretty efficiently, I'd say. They'll live, but judging by their injuries, the medics think one man had been choked out, the other bashed over the head – he had a lump on his noggin the size of a duck egg.'

'Hm.' Fenton folded his arms. 'If this is all from the medics, I take it Emin's men aren't talking?'

'Tight as clams, both of them,' Rick said. 'But they're definitely Ayaz Emin's crew.' When the prosecution case against Emin had collapsed, the Met had made a show of stepping back from investigating his gang, but an inter-agency team had secretly continued to keep a quiet watch on his activities, albeit on a reduced budget and with skeleton staffing.

'Emergency services were quick to arrive on the scene,' Fenton said. 'Who made the call?'

'Not known. The third man taken to hospital was the warehouse "manager". The first crew at the scene managed to drag him clear of the building,' Rick said. 'He says he wasn't even aware there was trouble until he saw the flames from his office window above the shop floor – he collapsed coming down the stairs – overcome by fumes, apparently.'

Fenton's eyebrows shot up. 'He's cooperating?'

'He was sobbing with gratitude when he made that statement, but . . .' Rick raised one shoulder.

'Gratitude has a short half-life,' Fenton finished for him.

'Yep. His lawyer was at his bedside less than an hour after he arrived at the hospital.'

'Do we know what they had on-site?' someone asked.

'Forensic reports are pending.' Rick pulled up a video the CSU had sent from the warehouse. Windows, a narrow access personnel door and the roller door at the main entrance were soot-blackened. 'Product in the process of cutting and weighing had been laid out on trestle tables – most of that went up,' Rick explained.

'Were the tables the seat of the fire?' Fenton asked. All that remained of them was twisted metal and melted and charred plastic.

'The commander says multiple points of origin,' Rick said. 'They're still damping down, but he hopes to have a clearer picture by the next briefing.

'There was more product further inside the building,' he went on, as the camera zoomed in on sacks of a white powered substance and smaller, brownish blocks stacked in pools of greasy hose water and grimed with soot and tarry streaks.

'That'll help in prosecuting the men we have in custody,' Fenton commented. 'Although I understand that some of the cutting agents are highly toxic, so it's going to be a slow and difficult extraction process.'

Rick nodded. 'The good news is a lot of the packages are intact. And from a visual inspection, the CSU is confident there's heroin, cocaine and maybe fentanyl in there.'

'Not a very thorough job, is it?' This comment, spoken half to herself, came from an NCA agent, a square, sallow-skinned and solid-looking woman in her early forties.

Rick glanced across to her. 'Bethnal Green fire station crews were the first attenders. Their commander thinks someone must have dialled triple nine a good *five minutes* before anyone outside of the place would've noticed the flames.'

'Don't we have *anyone* who'll talk to us?' This plaintive question came from a Border Force representative.

Rick shook his head. 'Most of the locals say the first they were aware was when they heard the fire brigade sirens. And a lot of the factory workers who were taken to hospital disappeared during the night. The others are too scared.'

'The lower-level workers aren't likely to be able to tell us much, anyway,' Fenton said.

'What are we looking at – a rival firm? If so, there's bound to be blowback.' This came from a tactical support officer seconded from MO19, the specialist firearms command.

'Albanians, maybe?' someone volunteered. 'They've got the monopoly on cocaine across the city, and a stash like that would be tempting if they got word of it.'

The NCA agent spoke up again. 'That's unlikely; the Albanian mob avoid tit-for-tat rivalry – they're all about building relationships.'

'And anyway, they didn't touch the drugs by the look of it,' Rick added. 'That's weird, isn't it?'

'The Albanians ship their cocaine direct from Colombia. It's the cheapest *and* the best quality on the market. They don't *need* to go scrounging around for the stuff – in fact, Emin probably bought his supplies from them in the first place . . .' She tilted her head, considering. 'I suppose they might torch the place as punishment if Emin pissed them off, but as revenge attacks go, this was pretty mild. When the Albanians do get violent, they're *brutal* – you'd expect to see a body count – I mean, no shots fired? And the guards dragged to safety?' She grimaced. 'I agree – it doesn't feel right.'

'Okay, so maybe a smaller crew,' the tac support guy said, sounding on the defensive now. 'Someone wanting to build a rep for themselves—'

'Then why'd they burn the product?' Rick demanded. 'Why didn't they steal it along with equipment?'

'I'm sure we could argue the finer points from now till supper time.' The comment, in a rich, carefully moderated tone, came from the back of the room. Everyone turned; Detective Superintendent Ghosh had just entered. Satisfied that he had their attention, he went on: 'The press hacks have already made their minds up about the who and the why. Rick – can you do a web search for "Tower Hamlets drugs blaze", throw it up on the screen?'

He closed the door and Rick obliged, clicking through a few of the articles. The tone varied, but each questioned police effectiveness and speculated that gang warfare was being fought openly on the streets of London.

'We need to clamp down on this, and fast,' Ghosh said, taking Rick's place in front of the smartboard. 'Emin is bound to move his operation, set up elsewhere, perhaps even go to ground if he feels personally threatened. So the question is, do we sweep in now and take what we can get, or wait and see how this shakes out?'

Fenton said, 'We've got eyes on him. I say we watch, record, gather info, move in when we have something substantial we can hold him on.'

'We've got a warehouse full of drugs,' someone chipped in, 'three of his men in custody—'

'We need a direct line from Emin to the warehouse,' Ghosh interrupted, irritably. 'Do we have that?'

Rick had interviewed the property owner an hour earlier. 'Keyholder says he rented the place out three weeks ago to a "business type" with a bag full of cash. Didn't know what he wanted it for and didn't ask. There's no written contract – he says it was a "gentleman's agreement".' That raised a chuckle around the room.

'And was he able to provide a description?' Ghosh's words dripped with sarcasm.

'He was vague, but he did recall a name – Smith.'

'How original.' Ghosh locked his dark eyes on the detective who'd mentioned the men in hospital. 'And while I agree it's highly suggestive that three known members of Emin's crew have been found in possession of a significant quantity of drugs, we all know to our detriment that the man himself has very recently wriggled off the hook with far more compelling evidence against him. I have no doubt that he will deny all knowledge and claim police harassment.'

A dispirited silence followed. Failing to prosecute Emin twice in a matter of months would be hard to take – they had put too much work into trying to dismantle Emin's criminal network to let the case drop. And why – because of a random attack on his premises?

You might as well shut up shop now, tell the gangs that the city is theirs for the taking. This advice came care of Rick's older brother. Although Sam had been absent for almost half of Rick's life, it was always his voice Rick heard at times like these. Often gently mocking, almost always irritating.

Rick had worked with Ghosh before, and Sam-the-counsellor was right – the superintendent had his CV to consider – and with the possibility of promotion to his dream job just one high-profile result away, the Met's upper echelons would be watching. As a skilled politician, Ghosh would drop the Emin inquiry without a second thought – settle on the quick and easy prosecution of three low-ranking, expendable drones rather than risk failure in prosecuting the kingpin of the organisation.

Well, are you going to let him look the other way because he's worried he might lose face? Sam goaded.

'Emin doesn't know he's still under police surveillance, sir,' Rick ventured. 'And he's got to be feeling the pressure, right now – smaller crews looking to get a toehold,' he said, with a nod of acknowledgement to tactical support, 'foot soldiers hoping to impress the big boys with their initiative. He needs to restock in a hurry to keep his business viable, which means he'll put his own people under pressure, take risks. All it takes is one mistake, one careless move to give us the break we need.'

Ghosh scratched his eyebrow and sighed. Finally, he addressed DCI Fenton: 'Is he still at his house in Mayfair?'

'For now,' Fenton said, and Rick saw a flash of eagerness in his eyes. 'And if he does relocate, there's a better chance of getting access to the new property to install audio equipment. Part of the difficulty of establishing good surveillance on him is he's got that street pretty much sewn up – vehicles at either end of the road, men on constant watch around the perimeter of the family home. But if he sets up elsewhere, he'd need to spread his resources more thinly. Speaking of which—'

'I know, you need more warm bodies,' Ghosh said, pre-empting the request. He stared over the heads of the team, a furrow creasing his brow as if he were working on a difficult mental calculation. Maybe he was, because after a few moments he said, 'I'll see if I can wangle more personnel. But we can't wait till we get the nod – Emin, and anyone in his inner circle, need to be watched closely *right now*. I want to know where he's planning to set up before he lays cash down on the transaction – before he's even made his mind up that he wants the place. Okay?'

'Understood, sir,' Fenton said.

The room remained silent until Ghosh's footsteps could be heard retreating down the corridor, then the tension broke, and it seemed all ten in the room let out a collective woosh of breath.

Chapter 5

Midnight, a few days later

Two cars – a heavily modified Ford Fiesta hatchback in two-tone red and black, and a decidedly elderly Audi A3 in nondescript grey – pulled into empty bays near the down-ramp on the fourth floor of a largely empty multistorey car park just off the Fulham Road. Two men got out, leaving their doors open and engines idling.

The Fiesta driver was in his mid-twenties, kitted out in boy racer sports gear, a thick-gauge Cuban-cut silver chain around his neck, and a Rolex rip-off on his wrist. His car exhaust burbled and popped, and the Audi driver, a man in his mid-forties, eyed him scornfully. 'Keeping a low profile, son?'

The Fiesta driver scowled. 'I'm not your son.'

'And they say the art of repartee is dead,' the older man said, a smile curling the corners of his mouth.

'Well, I ain't, so . . .'

The Audi driver clutched a hand to his heart. 'Cutting. You just bloody cut me, boy!' He was laughing now, and the younger man rammed his hands in his pockets.

'Where the hell is he, anyway?'

'He'll be here – don't panic.'

'Who says I was panicking? I ain't panicking, I just don't see why we had to come here – I mean there's cameras on every floor.'

'It's the twenty-first century, mate – there's cameras on every bus, road junction, traffic light, pub, shop, and doorbell in the city.'

'Yeah – that's what I'm saying, innit?'

The older man sighed. 'The difference is, the cameras in *this* place are managed by my firm. How d'you think we got around the bank manager's home security?'

The younger man's brow crinkled. 'That was you?'

'Safely Does it Security, at your service,' he said with a bow. 'I knocked out the security cams remotely about fifteen minutes ago – from the barriers all the way to the top floor. By the time they send someone to fix the outage, I'll have 'em back online again – they'll think it was a glitch in the system.'

On the third floor of the car park, in an unmarked van, Prozac sat before a bank of screens.

'What're they saying? You getting it?' Cap's voice in his ear sounded tense but controlled.

Prozac's eyes flicked from screen to screen. 'Audio *and* visual.' He'd reinstated the car park's security cams minutes after they'd been disabled, and audio was being provided by wireless 'smoke detectors' on each level. 'I'm patching the live audio to you – *now*.' He tapped the 'return' key in time for the team to hear the boy racer through their earpieces:

'He'd better be here soon, 'cos I've waited as long as I'm gonna.' The audio was loud and had too much echo. Unhurried, confident – this was his domain – Prozac made the necessary adjustments.

'Ooh,' the Audi driver said. 'Does that mean I can have your cut?'

'That good enough for you?' Prozac said, grinning.

'You're doing great, but we haven't got 'em, yet,' Cap said, and Prozac heard the warning in his tone. 'We're not done till Target One is here and they've split three ways.'

'Well get your dancing shoes on,' Prozac said, "'cos Target One just drove up the ramp. White Nissan Qashqai.' He recited the registration plate.

'Wait for my go,' Cap said. 'No one moves before the exchange – clear?'

'Clear!' Five voices spoke as one.

'Stand by,' Prozac said. 'He's stopped on level three. He's parking up.' Prozac switched to a camera nearer to the incoming vehicle and zoomed in on the car.

The driver parked nose out, halfway between the up- and down-ramps, leaving a good ten or fifteen yards between his car and the next.

Cautious, Prozac thought. He held his breath, almost afraid to blink in case it alerted the driver to his presence.

For a full thirty seconds, there was no movement in the Qashqai, then the driver's door opened, and a tall man hauled himself out from behind the wheel. He checked up and down the rows. Perhaps a dozen cars were parked at uneven intervals on this level. The surveillance van was at the furthest corner, partly hidden by a defunct pay booth. The new arrival must have felt reassured because he walked around the back of his SUV and opened the boot, lifting out a large gym bag.

'Target One on way. He's heading up to you on foot.'

The response: 'All received. Stand by.'

Everyone heard what came next. Prozac alone, with eyes on the targets, watched as the tall man handed hefty carrier bags from his holdall to the two waiting men. The Fiesta driver began to rummage, but Target One stopped him with a sharp, '*Oy*, show some sense. It's all there – you can count it when you're home.' He followed up by issuing instructions as to how and when, as well as how much they could spend without attracting attention.

'The cops haven't given up on Blackfriars, yet, so hold back for a while, be cautious, pay cash – and *don't brag*.' He glared at the younger man as he said this.

23

The other two packed their cash into backpacks and hoisted them into their respective cars.

As Audi-man and Fiesta-boy dropped their packages behind the rear seats of their cars, Cap murmured, 'Go, go, go!' and Prozac felt a thrill run up his spine and into his arms, sending pins and needles into his fingertips. On the fourth floor, the fire escape doors either end of the level flew open, and five helmeted operatives in black gear piled out, screaming, 'STAY WHERE YOU ARE! STAND STILL! DO NOT MOVE!'

Prozac laughed, seeing the boy racer twitch like he'd got a cattle prod up the jacksy.

The boy racer clasped his hands behind his head and sank to his knees sobbing, 'Don't shoot! Please don't shoot me!'

'Uh-oh . . .' Distracted by the drama, Prozac hadn't noticed that the third man had ducked behind the Audi, then flipped over the ramp barrier, landing at the far end of level three.

'Target One's making a run for it!' he yelled into his mic. 'He's heading back to his car!'

Cursing, Prozac shoved his chair back, launched himself into the driver's seat, and turned the key in the ignition.

The engine caught for a second, then choked and died.

'Cap, do you read me?'

More yelling, no answer.

'Shit!' He tried the engine again. '*Start*, you bastard!'

The engine caught and he over-revved.

'Target One is running!' he yelled again then, abandoning any attempt at the agreed comms protocol: 'Fuck it, I'm going after him.'

Hitting the clutch and crunching into first gear, he floored the accelerator. The van jumped forward, clipping the edge of the pay station. Target One had reached his car. Two of the team were in pursuit – Frosty and Sooner, judging by their build and speed – but they'd lost vital seconds. Prozac accelerated, the engine screaming in first gear. He saw the man's eyes widen as the van bore down on him.

24

Then Target One reached behind his back.

'GUN!' Prozac screamed. *Oh, jeez, oh fuck.* 'He's got a gun!'

He turned the wheel sharply, simultaneously yanking on the handbrake, and the van skittered sideways. Staring through the passenger window, Prozac saw the man raise his right arm to shoot.

Jittering over the tyre-polished floor, the van skipped and slipped for three heart-stopping seconds, the chassis juddering as the wheels gained and lost traction. Then with a thud, the offside front made contact with the nose of the Qashqai, bumping it hard into Target One, jarring his elbow. The gun flew left, loosing off a shot with a deafening bang. It continued, clattering across the concrete towards the two in pursuit.

The van stalled, blocking the SUV entirely, and with a desperate glance over his shoulder, Target One came around the car towards Prozac.

Prozac scrabbled to lock the doors, but the man got there before him, reaching inside, ready to haul the tech out of the driver's seat.

Suddenly Target One jerked backwards, and with a yelp, fell hard to the concrete floor. Sooner's voiced boomed out, 'STAY DOWN! DO NOT RESIST!'

Frosty moved in with zip ties in hand and, seconds later, the gunman was trussed up and bundled into his own car.

Euphoria and tinnitus from the gunshot had put Prozac off-kilter, and it took a few moments to notice and then make sense of the noise in the background. 'Comms One – SITREP, OVER!'

Oh, Jeez . . . Cap! Prozac whipped around to check the screens. Pug and Brock stood, weapons at the ready, next to the Audi and the Fiat, where the other two were already secured. Cap, crouching at the barrier to peer down onto their level, repeated his command for an update.

'Sorry, Boss,' Prozac said. 'Target One secured, over.'

'Received, Comms One. Proceed per instructions.'

'Will do. Out.'

Bugging his eyes, he turned back to his two oppos. They wore balaclavas under their helmets, but he could see that they were grinning and, for once, he knew they weren't laughing at him. He watched from his wing mirror as Frosty slid the door open and she and Sooner swung inside. Cap, Pug and Brock were already running down the ramp from the upper level.

Laughing softly to himself, Prozac started his van and reversed to steer around the SUV. Driving slowly past, he saw the owner, zip-tied to the steering wheel and staring at him with pure hatred, which only made him laugh louder. Zooming to pick up the rest of the crew, Prozac allowed himself a whoop of triumph.

Chapter 6

Eight-thirty, next morning

RICK TURNER HEADED INTO THE OFFICE, anticipating another day following up NCA suggestions of possible warehousing for Emin's drugs operation – dull, but necessary grind. Recent experience had proved that the most unpromising lead could be the one that blew a dead-end investigation wide open, so he made it a rule never to prejudge the day's work.

As he crossed the threshold, an ironic cheer went up from a huddle of detectives and admin staff in the far corner of the room.

'Wassup?' he asked, shrugging off his jacket.

DC Joe Cossio glanced over his shoulder. 'Take a look, Sarge.'

Rick strolled across to the gathering. They were watching a BBC news bulletin recorded at night outside a multistorey car park. Grey concrete in the background, police tape to the fore, a bank of mics on stands behind which gathered TV reporters and press, while others held up audio recorders and mobile phones. The whirr of camera shutters was audible over the hum of traffic noise. Camera flashes and the red-and-blue flicker of emergency vehicle lights animated the normally immobile features of DCI Kevin Anstell.

The crawler at the bottom of the screen read: 'Blackfriars Bank Heist . . . three arrested.'

'Wasn't Kath Steiner leading that inquiry?' Rick asked.

'Oh, *yeah* . . .' Rick heard the chuckle in Cossio's voice. He tapped the computer operator's shoulder. 'Wind it back, mate.'

Anstell was framed at the centre of the press gathering, hands apart, palms down, patting the air, waiting for silence.

'Today, I am pleased to announce that we have made three significant arrests in the inquiry relating to a robbery at Blackfriars Bank in Fleet Street,' he began. 'As many of you will recall, three months ago a gang of robbers abducted the bank manager's wife and child and the assistant manager's fiancée. Using threats and coercion, the robbers gained a haul from the bank estimated at two-point-five million pounds.'

A reporter on the front row raised her voice. 'Have you recovered the money, Inspector?'

Anstell's slab-smooth cheeks and narrow mouth betrayed no emotion. He looked around the people behind the tape, taking his time before finally turning his slate-grey eyes on the questioner. 'I can confirm that we have on video the division of a substantial sum of money – and that money *was* retrieved during the course of the arrests.'

Rick winced. 'Bit reckless, isn't he?'

Cossio glanced at Rick, his brown eyes twinkling with malicious glee. 'Keep your eye on the bottom left of the screen.'

'Is Gary Quinn in custody?' someone called out. Quinn, a former employee at the bank, had been arrested on suspicion at the time of the robbery, but released on bail.

'Mr Quinn—' Anstell broke off as a blur of movement caused a stir among the reporters, then DCI Steiner's blonde bob came into focus. She'd ducked under the tape. Straightening up, she tugged her suit jacket into place and smoothed her hair, then performed a fast pirouette, finishing next to DCI Anstell. She looked flushed and annoyed.

'Detective Chief Inspector Kath Steiner,' she said, raising her voice as if her colleague had continued speaking. 'That's all we have to say for now.'

'Did you get a tip-off, Chief Inspector?' The question came from a dark-haired woman holding a mobile phone up.

'My team has been working tirelessly behind the scenes, following up multiple leads,' Steiner said, clearly ad-libbing. 'We're grateful for the strong public support we've had in investigating this crime. This is a dynamic situation in an ongoing inquiry.'

'Do you expect to make more arrests?' the BBC reporter asked.

'We have no further comment to make at this stage, but we will provide updates when we are able to do so,' Steiner said firmly.

The dark-haired woman thrust her mobile phone at arm's length towards Anstell. 'Chief Inspector Anstell – have you anything to add?'

'Please address your questions to me,' Steiner said sharply.

Anstell's expression seemed to shift from frozen stoicism to something more emotionally charged.

The mobile-wielding reporter was not easily deterred, though. 'Sir?' she insisted.

Antsell ducked his head and murmured, 'No further comment.'

'Looks like a depressed undertaker, don't he?' Cossio chuckled.

'So would you, if you'd just been kicked in the jocks on the BBC,' Rick said. 'Can't say I blame Steiner, though. I mean, what's he playing at?'

'He's known for it, Sarge,' Cossio said. 'That's just Anstell doing his credit-grabbing thing.'

Rick knew Anstell's reputation. 'It's a bit bold claiming credit for this one, though, isn't it? As far as I know, Anstell's been working on a spate of tourist muggings and laptop thefts for the past few weeks.'

'Note his careful use of the royal "we" when he announced the arrests,' Cossio said. 'And he didn't actually say *he'd* recovered the dosh, did he?'

'Well, it looks like the gang *and* Anstell caught Steiner on the hop,' Rick said. 'So, who *did* make the arrests?'

'MO19,' Cossio said, clearly enjoying himself hugely.

Rick shook his head. 'You're not making sense, mate.' MO19 was code name for the Met's armed response unit. 'That lot don't investigate.'

'Maybe not,' Cossio said, grinning, 'but they're still claiming the collar. They got a shout at eleven-forty-five last night, to "bring into custody an armed gang, restrained, but possibly dangerous" at that precise location. Mate of mine at MetCC says the caller identified himself as Job.'

'So how come the hero of the hour didn't step up to claim his share of the glory?'

'That's a mystery – 'specially as every other bugger's tried.' Cossio jerked his chin towards the frozen image of Anstell looking decidedly shifty on the computer monitor. 'The call sign was fake, but who cares if the intel's good? Word is, there's audio *and* visual of the money share going down. Looks like they got the Blackfriars robbers bang to rights.'

Chapter 7

BROCK WAS GROUCHING about the police press briefing. Cap could hear him going at it in the next room, railing against the announcement of 'significant arrests'.

'We do their jobs for them, and they parachute in and take the credit,' he fumed.

Cap sighed inwardly – getting the others wound up was not going to help. Time to defuse the tension.

'There's hot drinks in here, if anyone wants them,' he called, deliberately breaking into Brock's barrack-room sound-off. In a varied career, Cap had found refreshments and a change of setting very effective in de-escalating potential flare-ups.

The crew appeared at the kitchen door moments later – Pug first as always. He swooped on the plate of biscuits with a murmur of appreciation and grabbed the first mug to hand. Sooner came second with Frosty taking up the rear. She sent Cap a look of amused sympathy as she added a splash of milk to a mug of coffee and moved to the far end of the island, then watched the men dig in. Her light brown hair tied back in a ponytail, she was dressed in boots, walking trousers and hoodie, as though ready for a hike.

A full minute later, Brock came through the door, clearly aggrieved to have been abandoned by the rest.

'Did you see what that *knob* did on the news?' he demanded, directing his outrage at Cap.

'I saw it,' Cap said. 'Help yourself to tea or coffee – there's more biscuits if you want them.'

Brock surveyed the offerings with obvious disdain. 'Got any beer?'

'Plenty,' Cap said. 'But it's eleven in the morning, Brock.'

'And?'

'*And* . . . there's tea or coffee. Water, if you prefer.'

Brock's eyes burned with suppressed fury and a hush fell over the gathering. Cap remained calm and implacable and finally, ignoring the steaming mugs, Brock returned to his theme: 'They used our hard graft, claimed it for their own, and . . . what? You don't mind, 'cos it's all for the common good?'

'I mind,' Cap said, and meant it. 'I'm as angry as you are—'

'Oh, well I'm glad we got that straight,' Brock scoffed, glancing around at the others in an attempt to recruit support, but they remained intent on their food and drink.

'I know it's infuriating,' Cap said, still trying to be the peacemaker. 'But on the positive side, no one got away, and every crew member did an excellent job.'

Prozac spoke up: 'It was fricking slick, like a wolf pack or something.'

'Yeah, well, no one asked you, *Twilight Saga*,' Brock sneered.

Prozac visibly shrank, but Cap grinned. 'I like that – very apt,' he said. 'It *was* slick – you should be proud. And we achieved our objective: these men *will* be held to account.'

'Yeah, so step up and take a bow, Chief Inspector *Dickhead*.' Brock shook his head angrily. 'Is that what we are now? The Met's PR men?'

'And women.'

Everyone turned to Frosty.

Brock threw her a contemptuous look. 'Yeah, yeah – don't get your knickers in a twist, luv.'

Cap looked to the one female member of the crew, a question

in his eyes. The merest flicker from Frosty told him to stay out of it. Ex-army, she had fought in Helmand Province and dealt with more than her share of misogynistic machismo.

She set down her coffee and locked eyes with Brock.

'The last tiny penis who said that to me was talking falsetto for a week,' she said. 'Now, I know you're upset, and probably overcompensating,' she added with a glance towards his groin. 'So I'm going to give you a choice. You can take that back, or we can sort this outside, *mano a mana*.' She broke her gaze to ask conversationally, 'If that's okay with you, Cap?'

Cap glanced out through the patio doors. 'It's stopped raining. We'll clear the decks if that's what you need.'

Pug, underestimating the seriousness of the situation, laughed. 'Ooh-hoo-hoo, Brock's gonna get his arse kicked!'

Cap eyed Brock with genuine curiosity. He must realise that everyone in the room would enjoy seeing him flat on his back in the mud. If he was in any doubt, the look on Sooner's face should convince him. Sooner was the quietest member of the crew. He rarely expressed an opinion – scarcely spoke at all – but his habitually closed expression held such a level of dislike that surely even Brock couldn't miss it.

Colouring slightly, Brock said, 'Nah. We shouldn't be fighting among ourselves.'

Frosty agreed, her tone pleasant, but her famously chilly gaze unflinching. 'Didn't hear a retraction, though.'

Cap knew from training with Frosty that she was a competent fighter, but she was under no illusion that in hand-to-hand combat, men generally had the physical advantage – and Brock was a bull-necked gym bunny, so Frosty would need to use dirty tactics to gain the upper hand. From personal experience Cap knew that she'd have no qualms on that score.

'I spoke out of turn,' Brock said with a shrug. 'Nothing personal—'

Frosty cocked an ear, still waiting, and finally, he threw his hands up. '*Okay*, I take it back. God, you're such a ball-breaker!'

Pug pressed his lips together to stifle a laugh, his eyes bugging, and the rest looked to see Frosty's reaction to this fresh insult.

For a long moment, she stared cold-eyed at him, but at last she broke into a grin. 'And don't you forget it!'

The laughter that followed had a cleansing effect on the mood of the crew, but Brock hadn't finished.

'Seriously, though, Cap. We need to do something about this – I mean, what are we – *volunteer police*?'

The murmur of agreement from the rest told Cap that he would need to address this now, or risk losing authority.

'What do you propose?' he asked.

'We've got the bodycam footage. Send it to one of the broadsheets, tell them it's ours.'

Cap considered the idea. 'Videos can be faked – or leaked. The police could say we're crazed wannabes trying to claim credit for good police work.'

He saw that even an outside risk of being identified made the others uneasy, and that realisation seemed to get Brock worked up all over again.

'*But—*' Cap added, 'it's a sound premise. What are we doing this for? I mean, what do we *want*?'

'To make those bastards suffer,' Brock said.

'To bring them to justice,' Frosty corrected.

Brock twitched his shoulders irritably. 'Like I said.'

'And to demonstrate that gangs *can* be brought to justice, given the will and a little courage,' Cap added. 'If five committed people with limited resources can do it, then it begs the question: why can't the police?'

'How're you gonna get the message across – telepathy?' Brock demanded. 'I say we tell the press what we did and give them the recording.'

Cap shook his head. 'Mainstream news media journalists are dangerous. They have the resources to do background

34

investigations of their own. What if they make connections we don't want them to make?'

Brock swore under his breath. 'It's all very well saying what *won't* work – what are we gonna *do*?'

'I don't know, yet,' Cap admitted. 'I need to think it through. But it needs to be safe – we've got to protect our identities at all costs.'

Chapter 8

Later that day

RICK TURNER STOOD AT AN OPEN ROLLER DOOR, staring at the drab interior of an empty warehouse in the Limehouse district of London. He'd received a call mid-afternoon from SCO35 who were operating covert surveillance at Emin's new address. Emin had sent his right-hand man to look over this building.

The warehouse was brick-built, so probably more than a century old. Iron pillars stood at twenty-feet intervals along each side of the space. The walls had been painted uniformly white, perhaps to compensate for the lack of natural light, as the iron trusses and bracings that must once have supported glass skylights had been largely replaced by some form of corrugated material. A small office pod had been built against one wall, taking up a three-by-three-metre block of space. The floor was worn and pitted concrete. The space, dimly lit by old-style fluorescent strip lights, had been swept clean but black stains on the concrete and a faint whiff of engine oil suggested it had been used to store old cars in its recent past.

The building was tucked away in a narrow backstreet over-looked on one side by a 1990s-era block of low-rise flats, and its relative seclusion reduced the rumble of traffic on the nearby A13 to a muted drone.

Aware of the estate agent's scrutiny, Rick wandered inside and was struck by an overriding reek of damp mortar and rust.

Noting the surface-mounted sockets and few flyblown electric bar heaters lining the opposite wall, Rick asked, 'Do those work?'

Following his line of sight, the agent said, 'The main plug sockets are off at the mo – we're running the lights off of a generator – but I've got the energy provider coming in to reconnect within forty-eight hours.' He was a tall man, square-built with sharp-edged shoulders and large flat fingers, curiously like a Lego man.

Rick sniffed. 'Is that damp? 'Cos I'll be storing dry goods that need to *stay* dry.'

'It's just condensation with the cold weather we've been having, sir – the place has been vacant for a few months. Soon as the mains electricity's back on, we'll put a couple of heaters and dehumidifiers in.' The agent splayed his fingers in a way that made him look almost cartoonish. 'It'll be dry as drought in a few days.'

Rick shook his head doubtfully. 'Maybe I should call back when the power's up and running again.'

'Oh, I wouldn't wait too long, sir – we've had a lot of interest.'

'A lot?' Rick said, sceptical.

'Only this morning, I had someone giving the place a once-over.'

Rick's heart did a little kick then, as was often the case in moments of intense excitement, it slowed, and his head cleared. The covert surveillance unit would want to know all about that other viewing. Rick had learned a few tricks from his older brother on how to gain intel without arousing suspicion. *Put them on the back foot; they'll always tell you more than they mean to*, Sam would say.

So he cocked his head, a slight smirk on his face, and said, '*Someone*?' His tone deliberately needling.

Stung, the rep said, 'A catering start-up. Very keen, they are.'

Rick glanced around. 'The ambience is a bit soup kitchen isn't it? I mean, I can't see your average punter wanting to satnav his way through the rabbit warren of streets and alleys round here just for a burger and chips they could buy on the high street.'

The barb had its desired effect – the man physically bristled.

'I believe their speciality is burritos,' he said. 'And who needs ambience when you're selling straight into people's homes?'

Rick feigned a puzzled frown.

'You've heard of dark kitchens, haven't you? Virtual restaurants?'

Rick shrugged, and the rep took it for an invitation to explain, clearly feeling the need to defend the prime real estate he was representing.

'These places are *booming*, post-pandemic. There's been a massive rise in demand for premises like this one – and the other party—'

'I'm not in the eatables business, mate,' Rick interrupted, having established Emin's cover story.

A flash of white teeth in lieu of a smile betrayed the agent's underlying anger. 'So, what *have* you got in mind for the old place?'

'Storage of electronic goods, a bit of light assembly work,' Rick said vaguely.

'In that case, a lot of the positives still apply. Concrete floors, cast-iron supports.' He slapped one iron pillar appreciatively with the flat of his hand. 'If you're storing expensive electronics, this place is practically fireproof.'

Rick guessed that would be a major selling point for Emin, after his recent tribulations.

'Yeah, well, I'm a belt-and-braces type.' He jerked his chin in the direction of the roller door. 'Is that the only way in or out?'

'Funny you should ask that,' the agent said. 'The other party wanted to know the same thing. As it happens, there's an exit inside the office – leads into an alley. Too narrow for traffic, but head south, it'll take you to the riverfront – five minutes at a fast walk. North'll get you to the A13 in three minutes, tops.'

Rick nodded, letting the rep know he was warming to the property, and he guessed from the gleam of greed in the man's eyes that he was calculating the percentage to be gained from his two 'parties' bidding against each other.

'We're north of the river,' the rep said. 'Always a plus, as I'm sure you know. Easy access north, east *and* west – you wouldn't believe it, but we're just five miles from central London.'

'I've just driven it, so I suppose I would,' Rick said, letting him know he wasn't as green as he might look, but softening the rebuke with a smile.

'Well, there you are!' the salesman exclaimed, as if he and Rick ended up on the same paragraph of the very same page. '*Plus* the DLR's on your doorstep, if you're bringing staff in from outside of the city. This—' he pointed emphatically to the ground at his feet '—is a hub.'

Rick was more interested in the narrow back street. He hadn't heard a single car pass down it in the ten minutes they'd been talking.

If parking's restricted, it'd be easier for Emin to monitor comings and goings – making police surveillance harder, Sam's voice chimed in his head. In the thirteen years Sam had stayed out of his life, Rick's phantom counsellor had sounded like the East End rascal he'd been in his teens and early twenties, but when they'd reconnected last year, Rick had discovered that his brother's accent had softened, the cockney glottal stops becoming a distant memory. Now, when counsellor Sam whispered advice, he spoke with the rounded vowels and clipped tones of an Old Etonian.

'What about access?' Rick said, echoing the voice in his head. 'Parking restrictions?'

The estate agent strode to the wide roller door. 'No exit at this end, so it isn't used as a rat run for drivers dodging snarl-ups. Parking bay reserved for your exclusive use, so you won't have to compete with householders. And a mooring not two hundred metres that way.' He swung his arm to point south.

Rick's ears twitched. 'Oh yeah?'

'Not even half a mile by road,' the guy said, disguising the hastily revised distance with a change of units. 'I mean if you want to ship your goods along the river, it might be worth thinking about. It'll cost a bit extra for the mooring, if you're interested – which the other party is—'

I bet they are.

As if Rick had spoken aloud the agent said, 'Prime site, immediate availability – it's a no-brainer, right?'

Rick took out his phone and clicked off a few photos. 'How much?'

'Two thousand square feet, seventeen pounds fifty per square foot.' The agent paused, watching for Rick's reaction. Perhaps he imagined a hesitation, because he added, 'You won't get a price anywhere near that figure with the other agencies.'

'I'd have to talk to my team, get back to you,' Rick said. 'Is there a deadline?'

'The other party's gonna get back to me by tomorrow at three p.m. They plan to be up and delivering by the end of the month. I promised them full access by the weekend – if they make me a decent offer,' he added with a knowing smile.

'I'll be in touch,' Rick said, keeping his tone neutral, but buzzing with the certainty that this was the most promising lead they'd had in a week.

If I was Emin, I'd be on it like a shot, Sam chipped in.

Yeah, well nobody asked you, Rick sniped back. Sam was right though – the warehouse had everything on a drug distributor's wish list. The fact that Emin's guy had stipulated almost immediate access as part of the deal meant that Emin was in a hurry – and hurrying would mean he was liable to make mistakes.

Chapter 9

Next morning

SAM TURNER WAS BREAKFASTING in the Art Deco splendour of the Wolseley in Piccadilly when he received a call he'd been anticipating for weeks.

'He's out.' The tension in his informant's tone told him that this was not the routine call he had been expecting.

'When?' Sam asked.

'The official line was seven-thirty this morning,' the man went on, talking nervously and too fast. 'I had people waiting from four o'clock.'

'And?'

'He never showed up.'

'You're not making sense,' Sam said.

'I-I mean, he'd already gone.'

'He'd *what*?'

'He was released just before midnight yesterday.'

'What does your informant say about this?' Sam asked tersely.

'He can't explain it,' the man said. 'As far as he was concerned, the intel was good.'

'And now he's gone,' Sam said.

'Billy – my eyes on the inside – swears he saw him himself, in his cell as of ten-thirty last night. It's like Harry Houdini or something.'

'I imagine money, and not magic, was at the core of this vanishing act,' Sam said, curtailing an angry response. The man he was stalking had his own extensive network of contacts, informants and facilitators, after all.

'What d'you want me to do?'

'For your own sake,' Sam said, 'you should find out who fed your insider false information.'

'Will do, Boss,' his employee said humbly. 'D'you want me to let you know how it—'

'No.'

Sam disconnected – he would never use this man's services again.

Gazing up into the domed ceiling of the splendid building, he was already running through a range of approaches by which he might locate his quarry. Most of the ex-prisoner's properties had been seized after his conviction on multiple charges, but Sam was in no doubt that he'd taken advantage of many of the ways that enterprising criminals might hide wealth and property from the government and the law.

Sam understood the vanished prisoner better than most and he knew that the Crown Prosecution Service had confiscated only a fraction of his assets under the forfeiture rules. They would go looking for him when they realised that their model prisoner was not planning to adhere to the terms of his early release. But that would take time, and Sam at least had a head start on them. He intended to make the best of that advantage and bring the errant prisoner under his own jurisdiction before the probation service, prison service, or the Metropolitan Police had even raised the alarm.

Chapter 10

Morning briefing

RICK ENTERED THE MEETING ROOM HARDLY KNOWING what to expect. He'd reported back on the warehouse viewing at the evening debrief, where Ghosh had gnashed his teeth over the increased press coverage of the Blackfriars Bank arrests. He'd muttered darkly about needing better coordination but hadn't been willing to specify what that might look like in practical terms.

Glancing around the room now, Rick thought it looked like more personnel – representatives from the same outside agencies involved in the Emin inquiry, only more of them.

He definitely hadn't expected to see DCI Kath Steiner in amongst the others. Sharply tailored as always, she was wearing a chiffon scarf, perhaps in an effort to hide the red blotches on her neck which were a sure sign that she was feeling the strain.

Calling the room to order, Detective Superintendent Ghosh introduced the group to each other as the Met OCG Task Force. His announcement caused a shuffling and a metaphorical fluttering of ruffled feathers. Met Ops and the National Crime Agency – poorly labelled by the press as 'the British FBI' – were already tasked with investigating organised crime groups, and most of the other agencies with a finger in the OCG pie were already involved in the Emin investigation, so why the name change? Judging by an almost literal flexing of muscles around the table, some clearly felt that territorial boundaries were being threatened.

It's obviously a PR exercise. As always, the inner counsellor's voice belonged to Rick's older brother, Sam. *There's more suits in here than a Savile Row tailor's.*

The strong showing of senior press and media officers in the room suggested that Rick's superego was right.

Ghosh called on DCI Steiner to outline the arrest of the Blackfriars Bank robbers.

She arranged her papers and, glancing up from her notes, her eyes fell on Rick. He gave a nod of recognition, but she didn't return the courtesy.

'I understood that this was a briefing for senior staff,' she said stiffly. 'If DS Turner would care to step outside until after I've spoken . . .'

Rick hardened his gaze and did not move.

'I'm afraid you misunderstood,' Ghosh said, his tone firm. 'Detective Sergeant Turner is currently on an inquiry into one of the OCGs whose activities this task force is focused on disrupting, and he has a proven track record on that, as you are well aware.' He was referring to a case they had both worked on – DCI Steiner having been parachuted in to take charge as SIO after Rick had gathered enough proof that a death signed off as accidental was actually part of a major conspiracy. Uncovering links to two murders had pushed the investigation above Rick's pay scale, and he'd given way as graciously as he could, but the responsibility had proved too much for Steiner, and for some reason she resented Rick for it and seemed to hold a grudge against him.

She started to raise an objection, but Ghosh interrupted her again, distinctly waspish this time: 'We do have a *lot* to get through in this meeting, Kath, so if you wouldn't mind getting *on* with it?'

Her face flaming, Steiner reported the sequence of events, beginning with a triple-nine call reporting that the Blackfriars Bank robbers were in 'temporary custody' – disarmed, and bound with zip ties – but advising police to approach with extreme caution.

'Have you spoken to the caller?'

'We're trying to trace him,' she said, going on to explain that Anstell had been the duty DCI that night, and he'd delayed calling Steiner in.

Rick saw a slight grimace of disgust on Ghosh's face. He didn't approve of tittle-tattle, but Anstell was possibly more out of favour than Steiner just now, and Ghosh said, 'Speaking of Anstell – I'm sure we've all seen him making a spectacle of himself on social media.'

The carefully neutral expressions on the faces of Met staff and barely concealed amusement of their colleagues from external agencies said they had.

Anstell's apologetic head dip and mouthed 'No further comment' had gone viral as gifs in highly critical tweets, TikTok, and Instagram postings. Even BBC London had commented.

'We need a coordinated approach to this press assault on the Met,' Ghosh said, scowling at the team as if they'd posted the embarrassing clips themselves.

The Met media representatives nodded, frowning, and a suit at the far end of the table took a breath, ready to speak.

Ghosh held up a finger. 'Just a minute.' Then, to Steiner: 'Aren't you going to tell us about the recording?'

'I was about to, when I was interrupted,' she snapped.

A loud sigh from Ghosh brought her to the point.

'We have audio and visual of the three men discussing the money split from the bank, and referring to Blackfriars by name,' she said. 'For some reason, the evidence was relayed to DCI Anstell's inbox, and he falsely claimed that it was police surveillance.'

'I've read his statement and believe he said he'd "assumed" it was a police recording,' Ghosh said. 'I'm sure the disciplinary hearing will look into the subtle nuance between making a bold *claim* and an unwise *assumption*, Kath. But let's suspend judgement till then, *hm*?'

Steiner paled and then flushed again. 'I-I didn't mean to imply—'

'That he thought it was *clever* to claim bragging rights?' Ghosh said, his head cocked to one side, eyes wide in false innocence.

Rick had been on the rough end of Ghosh's character-demolition jobs, and he couldn't help feeling sorry for the chief inspector.

She began another stammered attempt to explain herself, which Ghosh waved away with a whisk of one long-fingered hand.

'Is that it?' he demanded.

Steiner gathered herself. 'Forensic tech support and the car park's security firm agree that their cameras must have been hacked – the system was down for about twenty minutes around the time of the incident.'

'Inside job?' Ghosh asked.

'One of the arrested men works for Safely Does It Security, which controls the cameras, so it seems likely. The odd thing is, that – judging by some of the angles – it seems the video recording of Quinn divvying up money came from the firm's *own* CCTV.'

'So someone *re*-enabled the cameras after the gang nobbled it,' Ghosh said.

She answered with a lift of her chin. 'They don't know *where* the audio came from – their cameras are visual only.'

'I needn't tell you that question needs answering as a priority.'

'Of course,' Steiner said, stiffly. 'We're looking into it.'

'What does Quinn have to say for himself?'

'Gary Quinn claims he ran when a gang of five masked men attacked them "without provocation". A van smashed into his Nissan as he tried to escape, and then one of the men dumped a gun in his car boot.'

'Quinn was the suspected gang leader from the very start, wasn't he?'

Steiner nodded. 'Although of course he's still denying all knowledge.'

'Well, you might want to point out that we've got him on camera handing out bags of cash.'

Steiner bristled, but Ghosh pushed on: 'I don't suppose any of this alleged chase was caught on camera?'

'The sequence we got was edited,' she said. 'And the "masked men" don't feature in any of it. But Quinn's fingerprints are on the gun, and he had gunshot residue on his right hand and jacket cuff. We're in the process of recovering CCTV in the wider area but surveillance cameras on that block were knocked out, and the car park's barriers had been got at, so no vehicles were recorded going in or out at the key times.'

Ghosh tapped the table impatiently and Steiner raised her voice, apparently anticipating another outburst: '*However*, we *do* have one promising lead – a blue or black high-top, long wheelbase Ford Transit van heading away from the area. It was caught on a traffic cam fifty minutes after the car park's cameras were disabled. Damage to its offside front panel is consistent with Quinn's statement that he was rammed.'

Ghosh became still and thoughtful. 'How have you actioned this?'

'I don't want to release it to the press, yet,' Steiner said. 'But we've issued a description of the van and registration to all patrols – the number plate is fake, but they might still be using it. And we've shared images with traffic police. An ANPR search is ongoing. With a bit of luck, we could find the vehicle before the attackers decide to torch it.'

'Good,' Ghosh said. Steiner was so startled that she seemed to lose the thread for a moment, and he was instantly impatient again. '*Well*, go on . . .'

'Oh, yes.' She riffled through her notes. 'Forensic teams are searching the houses and cars of all three men and they've already identified fibre trace from the Blackfriars victims. DNA evidence is in train.'

'Put a rush on that,' Ghosh said. 'We could use some good news in this bloody farrago.'

'Already done,' Steiner said.

'What have the other two got to say for themselves?'

'On the night, all three of the suspects claimed their presence in the car park was a coincidence.' This raised a murmur of amused disbelief. 'Since their arrests, only Quinn has answered any questions. The other two are giving no-comment interviews. I think we should hold Quinn but release the others on bail. Then we can hit them with what we've got when the forensic results are in.'

The senior media officer stirred, clearing his throat, and Ghosh warned him off with a glance. 'The recording alone is damning,' he said. 'And the forensic evidence against all three looks compelling, even without the DNA results.'

'Agreed, sir, but we've always known that Quinn wasn't working alone – the bank manager's wife was convinced she'd heard three different voices – and Quinn *wasn't* one of them – she'd have recognised his voice straight away. What if this was a revenge attack by a member of the gang who was pushed out? The other two could lead us to his door.'

'If this was revenge, it's weird they didn't take any money,' Rick said.

'We don't know that,' Steiner countered. 'Not all of the money stolen from the bank vault is accounted for in the bags the men had in their cars.'

'So it's possible that *some* of the money was taken. But a bank robber with a sense of fair play – I mean, does that stack up?' The question was genuine, but Steiner fixed Rick with a hostile gaze, refusing to answer, and Ghosh had to intervene:

'It's a fair question, Kath.'

'I'm sorry, sir, I'm not entirely clear what he's asking.'

Steiner avoided eye contact after that, and when it became clear that she wasn't going to back down, Ghosh turned to Rick. 'What's your take on this?'

'If this was bank robber number four, taking his cut of the haul, why would he bring in another five men to do the job? Six, if you include the van driver – wouldn't they want to be paid for their part in what went down at the car park?'

Rick saw a few nods of agreement around the room. 'Unless money *wasn't* the motive.' He raised one shoulder and let it fall. 'I'd be looking at family and friends of the banker and his assistant manager. They were most affected by the abductions.'

Steiner bristled. 'Are you seriously suggesting that the victims turned detective and rounded up an armed crew of bank robbers? I'm sure that'll go down well with the press.'

Rick spread his hands. 'I didn't say anything about the press.'

'No one is saying anything to the press *or anyone else* about the families,' Ghosh said. Then turning to Steiner: 'You can have another twenty-four hours to interview Quinn's accomplices. Make good use of it. Meanwhile, the FLO will be the best way to quietly establish the mood in the victims' families and to ask discreet questions.'

Steiner nodded, chastened. A family liaison officer would have been assigned in the early stages of the inquiry to explain procedures and keep the bankers' families informed of the progress of the investigation. As a sympathetic presence in the lives of traumatised victims, a skilled FLO could become a trusted confidante. Their role was to keep victims informed as far as an ongoing inquiry allowed. But they *were* police – so intelligence gathering was also part of their remit – and people often let their guard down in their increasingly familiar and reassuring presence.

Broadening his attention to the wider meeting, Ghosh continued, 'A serious error has been made. It would be damaging to the Met's reputation to admit to that error now, but Anstell's had a verbal warning and faces possible sanction after a formal review of his conduct. Who's speaking for Media and Communications?'

The senior media officer he'd silenced earlier introduced himself. 'Our approach will be to keep delivering the message that inquiries are ongoing. After consultation with all parties, it's been agreed that we will confirm that a man arrested on suspicion and released on bail at the time of the Blackfriars Bank robbery *is* among the arrests made last night. We will not name him as Gary Quinn.'

Ghosh looked around the room. 'As for the rest, we can*not* go public till we have a clearer picture of what happened at the car park. Right now, all we have is the word of three suspects in a kidnap-robbery case. We need a lot more than that. Who is responsible? What are their motives? Quinn is cooperating – see what you can get out of him,' he added, with a glance towards Steiner.

'Of course,' she said, crisply.

'That will be all.'

For a moment, Steiner stared blankly at the superintendent, then she realised she was being dismissed, and blinked rapidly. An excruciating silence followed as she gathered up her notebook and tablet and with one furious glance at Rick, left the room.

Jeez, Rick thought. *That was brutal.*

Ghosh returned to the agenda with cold-blooded insouciance. 'Next item, the Emin inquiry. We've had a lucky break. Rick?'

Rick gave the meeting a quick recap of the tip-off from SCO35 about Emin's man sussing out a warehouse in Limehouse, adding a few details of his own scouting expedition. 'I've got a few pics,' he said. 'Can I . . .?'

Ghosh waved him to the front of the room, and he pulled the first image – a view of the three-storey apartment block on the left, a high wall opposite across the narrow street, the warehouse dead ahead, almost blocking off the other end, except for a narrow alley on its left side, with a concrete bollard preventing vehicle access.

'The apartment building backs onto the access road,' Rick said. 'But there's no rear access to the block, and no public parking allowed, so a surveillance vehicle parked on the roadway would be out of the question.

'They're setting up a dark kitchen as a cover,' he went on. 'Likely specialising in burritos.'

He added an aerial map alongside the photo. 'Pedestrian-only access at the end adjacent to the warehouse,' he pointed out. 'And no direct line of sight to the warehouse doors.'

'They'll have lookouts either end of the road,' a sergeant from MO19 said. 'But it does mean that we'd be able to control access either end.'

'Emin's man was interested in river access as well,' Rick said, bringing up another slide showing the hidden exit inside the lean-to office, and a map showing the route down to the mooring. 'They might have a boat moored for escape, or to move goods in and out. And there's an emergency exit via the office pod onto the road at the far end.'

'How much time do we have before they move in?' Ghosh asked.

'The estate agent gave me the impression they were keen to make a start. The building's energy and water supplies will be reconnected in the next day or so.'

The NCA representative spoke up: 'We could get a couple of people in under cover of the utilities companies, put eyes and ears inside the building if he seals the deal.'

'Let's go ahead and just do it,' Ghosh said. 'You can always take 'em out again if Emin goes somewhere else.'

'The property agent gave me until this afternoon,' Rick said. 'I can call, ask for more time – he'll probably refuse, but it'll give me a chance to suss out if Emin's going to take possession.'

Nods all around.

'The warehouse will be under passive scrutiny from the apartments,' the blonde NCA agent observed.

'There's an empty second-floor apartment overlooking the access road,' Rick said. 'It's having a spruce-up after tenants moved out. Trades were coming and going yesterday afternoon. It'd be the perfect place to set up obs.'

The mood in the room became charged with controlled excitement. Ideas flowed from all parties as to how they could monitor Emin's communications and survey the warehouse without arousing suspicion.

Rick listened, a pleasant glow of excitement in his chest. Thrilled by the focus of thirty-plus minds bending their intellect and skills to a common aim. This was why he joined the police – local and national agencies, pooling resources, working meaningfully against the Emins of the criminal world. This was real policing.

Chapter 11

THE ESTATE AGENT HADN'T EVEN GIVEN Rick the chance to finish his plea for extra time to consider the warehouse.

'Sorry, sir – you're too late. The building's rented out, full price, immediate occupancy.'

'Immediate – they *must* be keen,' Rick said. 'Considering the damp and all.'

Sensitive to his needling tone, the rep's crowing quickly turned to defensiveness. 'I told you, there *is* no damp, just a bit of condensation. We have the dehumidifiers in tomorrow, soon as the mains is back on.'

A half-hearted attempt to interest him in a smaller property had ended with Rick making an equally half-hearted promise to talk to his firm, leaving the rep in no doubt that the ship had sailed on the prospect of signing any deal.

After relaying the information to his line manager, Rick was now heading home. It was five-thirty and he'd spent all day indoors from eight a.m. He knew from the complaints at shift changeover that traffic was snarled from Hammersmith flyover all the way down Fulham Palace Road. Since Jess was gone, there wasn't much waiting for him at home, and he wasn't exactly in a rush to get there. But the only options for his daily commute were to sit in a car, choking on exhaust fumes or plunge into the dark confines of the underground, so he often ran the distance. Tonight, he set his smartwatch as he headed to the river in a light drizzle, intending to take the Thames Path.

The National Crime Agency would ensure that when the utilities companies went to reconnect the property, someone from Special Ops would go with them, ready to install covert surveillance. Cameras hidden in light fittings and audio devices disguised as plug sockets – it all had a James Bond feel to it – but this was standard kit in twenty-first-century covert monitoring.

Five minutes into his run, Rick was off the main drag, finding his stride and making good time, passing terraced houses at millionaire prices. At Fulham Reach, apartment buildings rose either side and he knew that he'd entered the exclusive world of the seriously rich.

Turning left onto the pedestrianised riverfront, he splashed through puddles. At this time of the evening, the path was normally busy with cyclists and joggers, but the rain must have kept them indoors. At that instant, the sun broke through, dazzling off the paving and, pounding across the astonishingly pristine flagstones, Rick felt his spirits lift. They'd finally had a breakthrough in the case, and every agency involved was pulling together – although the jury was out on the Blackfriars Bank investigation.

Neil Ghosh was a canny political animal and it was widely known that he had his eye firmly fixed on promotion to chief superintendent in the near future, so why had he brought Steiner's case under his direct oversight? Since press and media were treating every criminal gang in the Greater London area as one cohesive group, Ghosh risked being tainted by Steiner's case.

Could it be that Ghosh didn't trust her? He'd dropped hints to that effect in the past. Rick shook his head in frustration, remembering the hostility to his suggestion that they should look into the families. His stride faltered, and he realised that he was getting breathless.

You're tensing up, old son. The voice in his head, dispensing advice, was superego Sam. The fact that he was right didn't make it any easier to accept.

Rick took a moment to shake out the tension in his arms and shoulders, then ran on. It wasn't his case. He needed to focus on Emin.

Because he'd been seen around the warehouse, Rick would need to stay out of sight. His job would be to observe, record and report back. The landlord of an empty apartment in the block overlooking the narrow access street had given them permission to set up in the back room of his property. Mid-afternoon tomorrow, Rick would travel by bus or Tube as far as Aldgate and wait to be picked up by a marked van borrowed from a legit painter and decorator and stocked with the cameras and tripods the surveillance team would need.

Across the river, trees in the wetland nature reserve were showing the first signs of leaf, so that the opposite bank was fuzzed with pale lemony green. A small flock of ducks flew in arrow formation over his head, making for the sanctuary, and a cormorant dived off a nearby piling as he passed with barely a splash. Rick ran on. The low-level boom of the city faded, so that he heard only the sound of his breathing and the steady tread of his running shoes. At last, he felt the tension and stiffness of the day release and drift away.

The path diverted inland at Fulham FC, cutting around to the front of the stadium before rejoining the riverside path at Bishop's Park, where daffodils pooled like sunshine on the wide expanse of grass, and vast, ancient plane trees overhung the pathway, reaching out as far as the riverbank.

It was here that Rick became aware of a sound that didn't fit. A dull thud that jarred with the softer squish of his own shoes. Someone running in hard-soled boots? Sam maybe? He hadn't seen his brother in months, though he'd been on Rick's mind. And it was just the kind of stunt he *would* pull, showing up without warning, seeing if he could ambush Rick as a kind of game.

He dodged into the park, away from the riverbank and, a few seconds later, heard the heavy thud of boots on the Thames Path. He turned, catching only a fleeting impression of man in a jacket – hood up – and tailored trousers. The man kept his head down, carrying on without hitch, apparently intent on his run. Definitely not Sam – too tall, for one – and he lacked Sam's swift-footed agility. Rick tailed the stranger until he turned left onto Fulham High Street, away from Putney Bridge, which was Rick's route home. Rick watched him jog on for a few hundred yards before losing sight of the man in the constant flow of people and traffic.

Turning again for home, Rick ran back to Putney Bridge, stopping only to pick up groceries. Maybe the booted jogger was just an office drone, desperate to stretch his legs after a day of drudgery, but he would keep a sharp eye out from now on.

Chapter 12

Later the same night

FROSTY, PUG, SOONER AND PROZAC WERE CIRCLED AROUND an impromptu bonfire in the remains of a nine-teenth-century factory on the eastern reaches of Greater London. Originally on three floors, part of the structure had caved in, showing the joists and boards of what remained all the way to the roof apex. The rain that had swept in waves from the west during the afternoon and evening had finally stopped, but the brickwork streamed with it and water dripped constantly from gaping holes in the slate roof. The temperature hovered a few degrees above freezing and the place was so damp that Frosty could taste the rot.

As night fell, a mist crept across the ruined landscape, seeping in from the Thames a quarter of a mile away, sinking into depressions and gouges, forming misty pools and creeping on, eventually spilling onto the factory floor.

Nobody felt like talking and the only sounds were the crackle of the fire and an occasional rustle of rats, nervous of the human invasion into their territory. Minutes later, the sound of a car engine roused the crew, and they lifted their heads. Pug went to investigate, peering into the mist from an open doorway.

'Brock,' he said, returning to the warmth of the fire.

The man himself swaggered in a minute later, a beanie hat pulled low over his bald head, and a large backpack slung over one shoulder. 'Where's Cap?' he asked.

Frosty warmed her hands at the fire. 'Dunno. Said he'd be a bit late.'

'I brought the rappels.' Brock shucked the backpack off his shoulder, letting it drop to the floor with a faint clink of metal. Prozac flicked an anxious glance at the bag; Cap had called them together to practise night manoeuvres and they were going to refresh their skills in climbing and abseiling.

Brock crouched next to Frosty at the fire. 'Did you bring food?'

'Do I look like your mother?'

He swivelled his head, and she felt the insolence of his gaze like a burn on her face and neck, knowing what was going through his mind – as if he'd spoken the obscene words.

She stood suddenly and clapped her hands, pleased to register a fleeting startle response. 'Let's see what you've got,' she said, gratified again to see confusion in Brock's face.

Pug chortled. 'She means what you got in the *bag*, muppet!'

'Well, why didn't you say?' Brock pivoted, snagged the bag and rose in one smooth movement, then tipped the contents onto the concrete floor with a clatter.

Hearing a scurry of movement in the darker reaches of the space, the crew turned as one. Brock bent to the fire, dragged a blazing piece of two-by-four from the edge and hurled it into the shadows. Frightened squeals, then a boiling mass of movement as a dozen rats streaked in all directions from the burning block of wood.

Prozac leapt to his feet as one panicked rodent almost blundered into his lap and, laughing, Brock reached towards the fire a second time.

Sooner was there before him, blocking him bodily, sending him staggering. Brock's boot caught the base of the blaze, raising a flurry of sparks, peppering his clothing with hot ash. With a cry of indignation, he steadied himself and turned to face Sooner, his fist clenched.

'*Enough*,' Sooner said, not raising his voice. He didn't need to. The very fact of his having spoken had its effect.

Brock stood frozen for a few seconds, then slowly lowered his fist.

With deliberate contempt, Sooner turned his back on the man and began sorting through the gear on the floor.

Some mistook Sooner's reticence for shyness, but Frosty knew him better than most, and they'd been friends long enough for her to see past his quietness. Sooner was reserved in a way that only those sure of their worth could be.

'What's the plan, Frosty?' Sooner asked a minute later. Their weapons expert had lived in Oklahoma, the 'Sooner' state, till he was sixteen years old, and he still spoke with a soft drawl.

'The staircase is sound,' she said, 'and we've got a couple of good anchor points on the second floor. We can practise ingress via an external wall or simulate a surprise attack on the interior via the stairwell.'

He nodded. By now the ropes, carabiners, belays and two harnesses were laid out neatly, ready for use.

'I'll go through weapons safety before we start. You know tactical rappel is real tricky.' Sooner ran the firing range where they practised their weaponry skills and had organised a couple of field trips to a tactical firearms training centre in Oklahoma City, but their last trip was three months ago, so it was up to him to keep the rest of them up to the mark.

Frosty risked a quick squint at Brock who had retreated to sulk on the other side of the fire. A slight movement behind him caught her attention – a disturbance in the slow swirl of mist – and she peered into it, trying to make it out. The mist thickened, obscuring the incomer. Then a figure emerged, moving with long, loping strides. She tensed. Male. Helmeted. Head bent. A grey wolf's head decorated the crown of the helmet, reflecting the light from the fire.

With a muttered curse, Pug scrambled for his weapon, tucked away in the sports bag he carried everywhere. Brock began to turn, and she saw him bare his teeth, ready to launch himself at the intruder. Sooner was first to deploy his weapon, but Frosty laughed, closing her hand over his, easing his pistol down.

'It's Cap,' she said.

Their leader raised his visor. 'Tensions seem to be running high,' he said, with an ironic twitch of his eyebrows. 'Did I miss something?'

'Nothing worth seeing,' Sooner said, and something passed between the two men that Frosty couldn't read, but Cap glanced at Brock, who had turned again to the fire. He knew that trouble had been averted.

'Okay.' He dumped a backpack on the ground. 'Gather round.'

When everyone was settled, he began. 'I've been thinking about what Prozac said. He's right – we are like a wolf pack.'

Pug's eyes widened, his mouth already curving into a smile, ready to laugh at the joke. Prozac struggled to make eye contact, confused, she thought – and a little panicked. Sooner and Brock were unreadable.

'As you probably know, wolf packs have an organised structure,' he went on. 'And as of now, during operations we'll be known by wolf pack designations.'

Pug's face scrunched up in question.

'Call signs, if you will,' Cap clarified. 'I'll be known as Alpha One. Frosty, you're Alpha Two—'

'How come *she* gets to be an alpha?' Brock interrupted.

'A wolf pack has an alpha male and an alpha female,' Cap said. 'Do you want to be the alpha female?'

Pug glanced at him, his eyes brimming with mischief, and

Brock twitched his shoulders, muttering something under his breath.

'Sooner, you're Beta One,' Cap continued, 'Brock, Beta Two.' As he went through their call signs, he handed each a wolf decal for their helmets. 'Pug, you'll be Beta Three.'

Prozac had brightened visibly now he was sure that he wasn't about to be made the butt of a joke, and his nervousness turned to excitement.

Handing over the last decal, Cap said, 'Prozac, you're—'

'I know,' Prozac jumped in. 'I'm Beta Four.'

Brock snorted. 'Nah. You're the Omega, kid.'

'What's the Omega?'

Brock laughed cruelly. 'The lowest in the pack, son. The one that stays home and looks after the pups. Rolls on his back and exposes his belly when any member of the pack looks at him sideways.'

Frosty glared across the flames at Brock. 'For God's sake – leave the kid alone.'

'Hey, come on,' Cap said. 'Everyone has a vital role in this enterprise. Everyone has their personal strengths and in the last op in Fulham, every member of the team worked perfectly within their roles.' He spread his hands. 'But it was a fluid situation, and it could have gone badly wrong when Quinn broke off and tried to get back to his car. It's no secret that Prozac doesn't like the physical aspects of what we do, but he did exactly what he needed to do to protect the rest of us.'

Brock looked unconvinced.

'When it's kill or be killed, two things kick in: training and instinct.' Frosty jerked her chin at Prozac. 'That's what happened with you at the car park.'

Prozac stared at her, round-eyed. They all knew her background: as an army medic she wasn't supposed to be involved in close combat, but she had been – she'd even killed a man in one exchange of fire.

'Yeah, well he wasn't the only one there,' Brock muttered.

'That's my *point*,' Cap said. 'We all worked together. *That's* why we're the wolf pack. It's not about status or rank – it's about cooperation.'

'Well, whoopie, we're officially the cool gang,' Brock said, staring morosely at his wolf transfer.

'I think we should stick with "pack" – Wolf Gang sounds more like a classical music appreciation society,' Cap said, with just enough humour in his voice to raise a smile from the others. 'Look, it's like you said, Brock. We can't let lazy cops take credit for our work. But the problem right now is our actions could be a series of random, unconnected events. We need recognition.'

'And this is *it*?' Brock held up the decal in his hand. '*This* is how we're recognised?'

Cap held Brock in his gaze. 'That's part of it.'

Insensitive that Cap might have more to say, Brock grumbled on, 'The police get it all their own way. They can *literally* say anything they want, and the media just pastes the press releases on their websites.'

Pug murmured sympathetically, and even Prozac nodded in agreement.

Cap seemed unfazed, and Frosty felt a thrill of anticipation – the man had a plan.

'Absolutely,' Cap said. 'The question is, what're we going to do about it?'

He took out his phone and showed them the video of the detectives blagging their way through a barrage of press questions outside Fulham Place car park after the pack had captured the Blackfriars Bank robbers. One woman's voice carried over all the rest: 'Did you get a tip-off, Chief Inspector?'

She was young, dark-haired, her only recording equipment a mobile phone.

A BBC reporter asked if they expected to make more arrests and the female detective improvised a response. Then the woman's voice rang out again, her mobile phone held at arm's length towards the prick who'd claimed credit for their arrests. 'Chief Inspector Anstell,' she demanded. 'Have you anything to add?'

Cap stopped the recording.

Frosty tilted her head. 'You're going to give her the story?'

'Are you crazy?' Brock demanded. 'I mean, is she even a journalist?'

'She is Pandora Hahn.' Cap glanced down at his phone and scrolled to an app. 'Her "Pandora Unboxes . . ." podcast has two hundred thousand followers on Spotify, and sixty thousand on YouTube.'

Frosty snatched her phone from her back pocket. 'She's on TikTok as well. Calls herself a "campaigner and activist".'

'At the end of last year, *Pandora Unboxes* focused on bad cops. Ten episodes covering excessive police powers, abuse of power, and lack of police accountability,' Cap said. 'This series it's "Hamstrung Law" – you can guess the gist.'

Frosty raised her eyebrows. 'Well, I *suppose* you could say she's likely to be sympathetic about what we're doing.'

'Judging by the small sample I listened to last night, she's all about building her audience,' Cap said dryly. 'And what we're doing is perfect material for her current hobbyhorse.'

He glanced at Brock. 'To answer your question, she is *not* a trained journo, nor does she have press contacts, as far as I've been able to establish. Which is good for us, because she won't have the resources to go looking into us as individuals, and that minimises our risk of exposure. But she does have a significant following, so we get the coverage we need, while *she* gets her fifteen minutes of fame.'

Frosty took stock of the men around the fire, sensing that the tide was about to turn in Cap's favour. A subtle shift of posture – heads up, a loosening of the shoulders, and direct eye contact – Brock included.

'It looks like we're all in, Alpha One,' she said. 'Now who wants first dibs on jumping off the top of a building?'

Chapter 13

RICK WAS SITTING AT HOME munching through a takeaway. He had BBC London news running on his flatscreen TV, while he googled major arson attacks across the city on his laptop.

The Blackfriars arrests left a lot of questions unanswered. Rick kept coming back to the fact that finding the stolen money at the scene had given the Met a much better chance of successfully prosecuting Quinn and his crew. What criminal would play to the police's advantage? What criminal would leave that kind of dosh untouched? He couldn't think of any he'd ever met – Sam included.

The people who had most to gain from such compelling evidence were the victims and their families. No doubt about it, Steiner *should* be looking at them. But Rick had seen the traumatised bank manager and his assistant on news briefings at the time, had watched with the rest of the country as the freed victims were carried from ambulances into hospitals. He couldn't imagine these same people stalking Quinn over several months, then ambushing three men – one armed – as they split the bank's cash. And after all that, coolly handing the criminals over to the police with recorded and physical evidence of their involvement in the robbery.

The whole set-up had the ring of professionalism about it – DCI Anstell had assumed that it was a police operation, after all, as had the news media. But whoever had cuffed and stuffed those lowlifes in their own cars with the contraband on them, it *wasn't* police – at least not *official* police.

Rick swerved away from that uncomfortable thought, circling back to it almost immediately despite himself. Was it pure luck that nobody had died in the fire at Emin's warehouse? If it *had* been a gang revenge attack, why had the arsonists left valuable drugs to burn? And who had called in the fire service before the fire had really taken hold? House-to-house enquiries hadn't come up with a name; Rick had listened to the triple-nine call himself. Experts said that the voice was disguised, and it didn't take an expert to say that the speaker had the calm control and crisp delivery style of someone who'd made similar calls many times before.

SCAS – the Serious Crimes Analysis Section – was set up to find common factors and identify patterns in apparently unrelated crimes. Their database could make connections and even map out incidents in specific areas, linking behaviours, vehicles, even language patterns if witnesses could remember what assailants had said. A request from Steiner for a SCAS analysis might give the inquiry a link they could investigate, but Rick knew she hated complications. Steiner would stick to gathering forensic evidence and focus on gaining a conviction of the three men who had fallen so conveniently in her lap. And if Rick's own investigation last autumn was a predictor, she would almost superstitiously avoid thinking about how or why she'd had this stroke of good fortune, terrified that her luck might change.

The problem was that Rick couldn't make the request. The rules were clear – it wasn't his case, and neither Steiner nor Ghosh would take kindly to him even making a few tentative enquiries.

Technically, the Emin warehouse fire wasn't his remit, either; DCI Fenton was SIO. But Fenton was increasingly being sidelined by Ghosh's continuing intervention. So he carried on, scrolling through story after story, making notes on the horrors criminals inflicted on others, hoping that he might find a connection that would persuade Fenton to ask for a proper analysis by people trained to do the job.

Limiting his search to arson attacks in the Greater London area, the worst incident he found was an arson attack on two multi-occupancy buildings out in Deptford. Three died, ten more were injured. Rick remembered the case – the landlord had suddenly found himself sitting on valuable property when a new extension to a rail line was announced. A property developer had approached him with a lucrative plan for redevelopment. What was the developer's name?

Rick clicked on the article and found it in the first paragraph: *Jason Floren*.

Greed overtaking common humanity, instead of paying tenants to move out, or helping them to relocate from his run-down low-rise apartment blocks, the owner had tried strong-arm tactics to force them out. They'd dug their heels in, and when they'd organised, he'd lost patience and torched the place. Skimming reports of the trial, he learned that landlord was currently serving a minimum twenty-year sentence, but Floren had walked free.

How the hell did he manage that?

Tapping through a few more links, Rick finally landed on the Dream Schemes Property Development website, Floren's shop window, and found himself staring into the face of a well-groomed snake-oil salesman. Next to his smiling face, a shot of two run-down low-rise blocks, and a retouched image of a glossy high-rise, towering over a street of mixed housing. It took Rick a moment to realise that he was looking at before-and-after images of the development that had resulted in three deaths by arson. The web designers hadn't included pictures of the old buildings as burned-out shells after the arson attack.

But how had Floren bagged the job when a hundred other

property-hungry developers must have been baying after the rights to Deptford Waters?

Scrolling down the page, his eye snagged on a black-bordered image of Floren and he read on:

'Since Jason's tragic death, we at Dream Schemes Corporate Trust have taken on the day-to-day running of Dream Schemes property developments, ensuring continuity and commitment to delivering Jason's vision of creating premium homes that offer quality of life and personal well-being at affordable prices.'

Floren is dead?

Rick opened a new tab and searched for 'Jason Floren, death'. The top three headlines were:

CONTROVERSIAL DEVELOPER FOUND DEAD AFTER TIP-OFF

PROPERTY DEVELOPER KILLED IN "TARGETED" SHOOTING

FLOREN KILLING – ARSON VICTIM SPEAKS OUT

There were dozens more like it.

Earlier reports were fuzzy on detail, but as Rick scanned the pages, it quickly became clear that Floren had been alone at Deptford Waters on the eve of its grand opening. An anonymous triple-nine caller had reported a 'disturbance', at the development's show house.

His attention was drawn to the TV. They were running a clip of DCI Steiner standing in front of the car park in Fulham Palace where the Blackfriars Bank gang had been arrested. Rick turned up the TV volume, but they must have muted Steiner, because it was the presenter's voice he heard.

'Knifings, machete attacks and even shootings have sadly

become an accepted fact of life across the capital,' he intoned solemnly.

The programme switched to the studio, where a stern-faced female anchor stared into the camera lens. 'The Met has had little to say on the arrests in Fulham a few days ago. They have stated that the arrests were made in connection to the Blackfriars Bank abduction-robbery,' she said, 'and that Gary Quinn, who was questioned and released shortly after the robbery, was *re*arrested at the car park in Fulham two days ago.

'At a press conference this evening, the lead investigator, Detective Chief Inspector Steiner, declined to comment on Quinn's rearrest,' she went on, 'but a surprise question from the floor has fired new speculation.'

The next frame showed a bland room that could have been a meeting room anywhere but was probably somewhere inside New Scotland Yard. Most reporters were packing away notebooks, cameras, mics and stands when a dark-haired woman in her mid-twenties pushed through the crush. A camera kept her in frame, following her progress to the side of DCI Steiner.

Holding her mobile phone on the flat of her palm, the young woman said, 'Pandora Hahn of "Pandora Unboxes" podcast, Chief Inspector.'

BBC London's sound recorder must have been one of the bank of mics that stood abandoned at the front of the room, and it must have been left on, because Pandora's voice came over loud and clear.

Steiner eyed her loftily. 'The press update is finished,' she said, rising to leave. 'No more questions.'

The woman stood her ground. 'Have you tracked down Bert Wickstead?' she asked.

Steiner stared at her. 'Bert Wickstead?'

The remaining media representatives must have realised that something important was going down, because a few drifted back to their seats.

The podcaster was clearly enjoying herself. 'Bert Wickstead,' she repeated. 'Pandora Unboxes has discovered that the person who called in the police that night identified himself as Bert Wickstead.' She paused. 'Did you find Mr Wickstead, Chief Inspector?'

Steiner looked ready to flee. *But if the triple-nine caller had identified himself as Wickstead, surely she would have tried to track him down?*

'The caller didn't provide contact details,' Steiner said lamely.

'It's unlikely he will,' Pandora said. A silence fell in the room, as every person present collectively leaned in to hear what the podcaster said next.

'There was a famous superintendent in London Metropolitan Police in the 1970s,' Pandora said, and Steiner licked her lips. 'His name was Detective Superintendent Wickstead and he was known as "The Gangbuster".'

A shuffling and some suppressed laughter followed, and Steiner shot a furious glance towards the Met press officer at her side. The look said it all: *How the bloody hell didn't we know this?*

'Was the caller *mocking* the Metropolitan Police, Chief Inspector?' Pandora asked.

Steiner swept up her papers, murmuring, 'No further questions,' and a moment later, she was gone.

Returning to the studio, the newsreader struggled to suppress the glee in her stern expression. Turning to her co-anchor, she asked, 'What do you think this means, Alex?'

'It means you lot have got your headline for tomorrow,' Rick muttered, turning off the TV in disgust.

Chapter 14

Next morning

SAM TURNER WAS SAVOURING A FLUFFY MUSHROOM OMELETTE in the Foyer and Reading Room at Claridge's. At this time of day, the room was awash with pale, greenish light – a cleverly contrived illusion of daylight. At night, the Deco features of this opulent place glowed bronze and pink and gold, but Sam wouldn't linger to see the transition – he had a specific goal in mind. He ordered a macchiato to follow, pleased to see it served with an exquisitely restrained dot of milk foam. He breathed the nutty aroma of roasted coffee beans and smiled at the waiter. 'I swear, Julio, even the *smell* of it raises my IQ twenty per cent!'

'That being the case, we really should have an endorsement on the website, sir,' Julio deadpanned.

'Fetch me a pen and paper, I'll write it immediately,' Sam said stoutly, though in reality, he knew that his current alias would carry no weight with the hotel's wealthy, celebrity-skewed clientele. Which was how Sam liked it.

His phone buzzed in his pocket, and he glanced at the screen. 'Might you bring me another of these delightful pick-me-ups in the lobby?' he asked Julio. 'And the bill, please. Regrettably, I must take this call.'

With his customary discretion, Julio melted away and Sam opened the clamshell burner phone as he walked across the chequerboard marble of the entrance hall to a quiet table. Settling in the club chair, he said, 'I'm listening.'

'He was picked up at the prison gates by a black guy and big bruiser in an SUV, according to my contact.'

'Errol and Mercer,' Sam said. 'I take it they've vanished, too?'

'Like they never existed. Of the other names you gave me, Sean Green and Rory MacKinnon walked out of their council flats ten days ago – no one's seen them since,' the caller said.

Gathering the faithful around him, Sam thought.

'I've approached any of his old professional contacts who can be bribed, got a watch on those who can't – including phone taps. If he goes anywhere near them, I'll know.'

Sam watched a famous actress sashay down the gentle declivity of the staircase, barely grazing its sumptuous balustrade with the pinkie finger of one delicate hand.

'*I* need to know immediately, and *precisely* where and when,' Sam said.

'I'll do what I can.'

'I don't pay you to do what you can,' Sam said coolly.

Fascinated, he watched as a man rose from one of the lobby chairs and strolled across the gleaming floor. They kissed, and the man – another actor, Sam now realised – took her hand and drew it through the bent crook of his elbow. They walked towards the foyer as if their movements had been carefully choreographed and cameras were rolling.

'I pay you to do what I need you to do.'

The sound of his informant's breathing at the other end of the line was like static on a bad radio connection, and Sam waited for the full import of his words to be felt.

'I—' The man cut himself off and began again: 'Understood.'

'Good. I'll expect an update by the end of the day.' He snapped the clamshell shut and slipped it back into his pocket, smiling as Julio approached with fresh coffee and his bill folded discreetly inside a leather holder.

'Could you spare a moment, Julio?' Sam asked, his question a genuinely courteous acknowledgement of the busy time of day and the effect on the waiter's workload.

'For you, sir, always.'

Sam sifted through his wallet, extracting a large sum of paper money, which he slipped into the bill holder, and a three-by-four-centimetre photograph, which he handed to Julio. 'It's a while ago,' he said, 'but I wonder if you recall . . .?'

After a careful examination of it, the waiter gave him a knowing look that had no more than a twinkle of humour. 'I rarely forget a face, sir.' He offered Sam the image.

'No, you keep it,' Sam demurred. 'There's a number on the back, should you need to reach me.'

'Thoughtful as ever, sir,' Julio said, spiriting the useful aide-mémoire into the coin pocket of his uniform trousers and, with a slight nod, he retrieved the bill holder and sped on his way.

Chapter 15

ON HIS WAY IN TO WORK, Rick picked up a copy of the metro newspaper from one of the racks at Putney Bridge Railway Station. The headline: GANGBUSTER COP TAUNT. Ghosh would not be happy. Officially, Rick was off duty until two p.m. when his first surveillance shift would start over at Emin's new place of business, and he intended to stay well out of the superintendent's way.

Skimming the newspaper text, he realised that Steiner would be another one to avoid – they couldn't have been more critical of her inquiries into the bank robbery. But since he would be riffling through the files on Jason Floren's murder, leaving the bank well alone, he should be able to fly under her radar.

Unauthorised use of the Police National Computer could get a cop in a lot of trouble, but Rick's nominal role on the new gangs task force gave him some scope to snout out connections, so he was able to do a broad search. For the first hour he acquainted himself with the arson attack in Deptford.

Although the police reports were couched in forensic terms and avoided emotive language, details of the three deaths and life-changing injuries to the survivors were harrowing. Moving to the public sphere, he saw that the tabloids had no such scruples, showing images of the two blocks of flats ablaze, alongside disturbing images of bodies being carried out of the buildings. They mentioned Floren's name, but only in the context of his role as a property developer. The quality nationals generally weren't interested in local London news, though they did cover the verdict of the trial.

The local free press had made no accusations, instead taking the safe route of posing questions and relying on readers' comments to make their point for them. Although on the day of the trial verdict, one news site did a two-column feature on the Deptford Waters development, complete with an artist's impression of the proposed new housing, placed alongside a report of the jury's verdict. The landlord, Terrence Gillies, had been found guilty on all charges.

It seemed everyone suspected that Jason Floren was mired in guilt from his Gucci loafers to his Burberry beanie hat, yet the free papers had been unusually circumspect, as if trial by media had suddenly gone out of fashion.

Around lunchtime, Joe Cossio's voice carried across the office. 'Aye, aye, Sarge – you're in early, aren't you?'

'Catching up on some reading.' Looking around him for the first time since he'd sat down at the computer, Rick found himself surrounded by largely empty desks. 'It's a bit quiet in here today, isn't it?'

'Everyone's out doing "busywork",' Cossio said, sauntering across to him. 'The shit really hit the fan with that gangbuster headline. Did you see it?'

Rick tapped the bin next to him with the side of his foot.

'Best place for it.' Cossio peered over Rick's shoulder. 'What you squirrelling after then?'

With a quick movement, Rick switched off the monitor. 'What the hell?'

'Come on, Sarge,' Cossio said, unabashed. 'Cops and insider intel – it's the stuff of life.'

'It's "staff of life", Joe, and this is confidential.'

'I'm discretion itself – ask anyone.'

'Joe,' Rick said, 'you do know they call you Gossip Guy?'

Cossio hooked his thumbs in his side pockets, looking unreasonably pleased with the nickname. 'Well, we wouldn't *be* police if we didn't love to *know* stuff.'

Rick sized the detective up, working out his options. He'd got as far as he could on the PNC database, but widening his search any further could raise red flags on the system, and Joe Cossio's extensive scrapbook of idle gossip might provide the information he needed without compromising himself.

Cossio was watching him from under half-closed eyelids. 'Go on . . .' he coaxed, 'think of me as an intelligence resource – a kind of wetware database.'

Rick grimaced, and Cossio drew down the corners of his mouth. 'Yeah, that sounded better in my head.'

'All right,' Rick said. 'What d'you know about the Deptford arson case?'

Cossio showed no signs of recognition, and Rick began to explain. 'About two years ago – fire destroyed two blocks of 1960s flats—'

'Yeah, yeah. Three dead, ten injured. I just wasn't expecting you to bring up the Gillies case – I mean, didn't you get the gen on it back when it happened?' His tone was an unmistakable dig in the ribs.

'What's that supposed to mean?' Rick said, ready to play along.

'Well, you might call *me* Gossip Guy, but you've got a bit of a rep yourself, mate.'

'A reputation for what?'

'Dr Pritchard calls you "the sin eater", 'cos of all the death scenes you turn up to.'

It was true. For years, Rick had snuck into scenes of sudden deaths, bothering pathologists, police, CSIs, and mortuary staff with questions he strictly had no right to ask about every thirty-plus white male in the Greater London area who'd ended up on a mortuary table. He'd been looking for his brother, and Dr Pritchard, a pathologist whose scenes he'd haunted perhaps more than most, had indeed called him a sin eater.

But Rick had found Sam very much alive last autumn, and that sad chapter of his life was behind him.

'Ancient history, mate,' Rick said, with the smallest twinkle of humour.

'Is that right? Find what you were looking for, did you?' Cossio shot back with sharp perceptiveness.

'Jeez, do you *ever* stop?'

'Just curious. I mean—'

Rick gave him a hard stare, and Cossio held up a placatory hand. 'Not ready to share – got it. But that fire was the talk of the East End at the time – all over the local news, an' all. I would've thought you'd already have the granular details.'

'I was working out of Richmond and Twickenham when that lot went down,' Rick said. 'And you do realise that I'm a detective sergeant and you're just a lowly constable, pushing his bloody luck?' he added, only half joking.

'Oh, I'm a good climber,' Cossio said. 'It's only a matter of time. Anyway, you and me's whatjamacallits – peas in a pod, twins under the skin.'

Rick laughed. 'You reckon?'

'No question, Sarge. So, what d'you want to know about Deptford Waters? Ask me anything.'

Cossio had got quite loud by then and, seeing a sudden movement on the edge of his vision, Rick peered around Cossio, catching the eye of a geeky type of about the same age as him.

'You can lower your voice, for starters,' Rick hissed. 'And who's that messing around at your desk?'

'See, that's why you need me,' Cossio said. 'That is Tim Jennings, Tech Support – I got a computer problem that isn't fixed by turning it off and then on again, apparently.'

The techie gave a shy smile and a little wave.

'Now ask me something interesting.'

'Joe, you weren't on the inquiry.'

'*He* was,' Cossio said, with a nod towards his desk, but the tech had disappeared under it, so maybe he was trying the turn-it-off-and-on-again technique after all.

A dull *thunk* and a muffled 'Ow!' then Tim the tech appeared, again, testing a tender spot on the crown of his head. 'Awful, what happened to those families,' he said. 'I heard—'

'No offence, mate,' Rick said, 'I don't want hearsay, I want facts. From someone who was actually there.' He could have added that he also didn't want his questions broadcast all over Hammersmith Police Station.

'Please yourself,' Cossio said, sounding less chirpy.

'Come on,' Rick cajoled. 'I know you can point me in the right direction.'

Incapable of withholding privileged information, Cossio relented. 'You want to have a chat with Alan McGuinness. And far be it from me to spread hearsay, but you might want to ask him about the Floren death scene as well. Definitely iffy.'

Rick thanked him and Cossio answered with a huffy shrug.

As he stood to leave, Cossio added, 'Only don't say I sent you.'

'Why so suddenly coy?' Rick asked.

Cossio was uncharacteristically close-mouthed on that subject, but Rick soon found out the reason.

It turned out to be a good-news, bad-news scenario. The good news was DS McGuinness had been recently assigned to Hammersmith and he was on duty. The bad news: he was on the Blackfriars Bank inquiry, and as soon as he introduced himself, Rick knew that it wasn't just DCI Steiner who considered him *persona non grata*.

Chapter 16

ALAN MCGUINNESS WAS SLIGHT and sandy-haired. Rick doubted if he'd spent much time on the beat before being promoted to CID, and he didn't look like the kind of cop who enjoyed knocking heads together, but right now, his brown eyes held a real threat.

He examined Rick's offered hand as if it might harbour contagion. 'What d'you want?'

'A few words, that's all.' Rick pulled out a chair.

If McGuinness had seemed unfriendly before, he was unmistakably hostile when Rick sat opposite, uninvited.

They were in the canteen. Laid out with tables in pale blonde oak veneer, the area was divided by trellis screening to offer diners a degree of privacy. It reminded Rick of a department store restaurant.

'I'm working on the gangs task force,' Rick said.

McGuinness returned to his lunch, chewing slowly, showing no sign of interest.

'The investigation went belly-up when someone burned down the drugs warehouse we were supposed to be watching.'

Some of the anger went out of McGuinness's eyes. 'I heard about that – lit up the night sky like a kaleidoscope.' He focused on his plate again. 'What's that got to do with the Blackfriars Bank robbery arrests?'

'I dunno. Nothing, probably.'

'Good, 'cos I'm not talking to you about that.'

'Understood. It's an arson attack on two blocks of low-rise flats in Deptford I'm interested in.'

McGuinness glared at Rick. 'Is this a wind-up?'

'I promise you it isn't.' It wasn't entirely honest, either. Rick *really* wanted to quiz him about the Blackfriars gang, but he'd have to tread softly if he wanted answers about the car park arrests. 'There's something *off* about the warehouse fire, so I go looking for other arson attacks and I find the Deptford fire. Then I see this follow-up story two years on, saying the property developer who was questioned about the fire was found bound and shot in his own show house at Deptford Waters. There was an anonymous tip-off on that as well, and I just needed to dig deeper,' he finished lamely.

McGuinness carefully set down his knife and fork and considered Rick for a few seconds. 'Yeah, you've got a name for turning up at mortuaries uninvited, poking into closed cases.'

Rick winced. *Twice in one morning.* 'It has been said. But Floren's case isn't really closed, is it?' He quirked his eyebrows. 'I mean, they never found the shooter, did they?'

Something complicated was going on behind McGuinness's eyes, but he was a good cop, and whatever it was, he didn't give it away. He didn't make a move to leave, either, so Rick began with an easy question: 'The landlord – Gillies – was convicted on all counts?'

'We had him on camera buying the fuel. Thought we wouldn't be able to track him 'cos he'd travelled *all the way out to Essex.* Pillock. *And* he dropped one of the canisters when he caught some blowback on one of the stairways. Fingerprints all over it.' He smiled to himself. 'His eyebrows singed off as well – that was a bit of a giveaway.'

'But Floren was cleared.' Rick saw McGuinness stiffen and hastened to explain.

'Over the last couple of weeks, every paper, podcast and online news site has been flooded with speculation, rumour and downright libel against the Met. Yet during the arson trial, I gather they went all coy about Jason Floren.'

McGuinness gave a cautious nod. 'Yeah, they practically tiptoed around that slimy toerag.'

'So you *do* think he was in on it.'

'Up to his eyeballs.'

'He was never even charged,' Rick said. 'What happened? Did evidence go missing? CPS cock-up, or what?'

The barriers slammed down again, and the sergeant studied him, working his tongue between his teeth and lips. 'What's it to you?'

'Just trying to make sense of what happened,' Rick said.

'Now? Nearly two years later?' McGuinness waited. 'No answer.' He began collecting his crockery to move to another table. 'Okay, it's been nice talking.'

'Wait.' Rick glanced around to check they couldn't be overheard. 'The arson attack at the drugs warehouse – I'm struggling to see a motive. They burned the drugs, and someone called it in – anonymously – *real* sharpish.' Strictly, he shouldn't be telling McGuinness this, but it was already public knowledge that the drugs had gone up with the rest, so he wasn't exactly spilling state secrets. As for the tip-off – well, sometimes you had to give to get.

McGuinness shrugged. 'Concerned citizen. So what?'

'The building's a couple of hundred yards from the nearest dwellings. We haven't found a single person who claims to've seen the flames before the appliances arrived. I'm thinking whoever set the fire must've called it in.'

He gazed at Rick for a few seconds. 'What's this got to do with Floren?'

Rick lowered his voice. 'Look, I know that the car park security cams were down when whoever it was grabbed the Blackfriars gang. Yet MO19 was tipped off within half a minute of it happening.'

'And there it is. *That's* what you really want to know. Fuck you.'

'No, no-no-no.' McGuinness was half out of his seat and, panicked, Rick held up both hands to placate him. 'Wait. Listen, the MetCC call came in apparently before any of the locals even *saw* the warehouse fire. *You* got a tip-off seconds after the Blackfriars crew were cuffed and stuffed at the car park. And – look – I *really* shouldn't be telling you this, but the LFB commander I spoke to at the fire said the triple-nine caller specified the need for hazmat appliances. And that's out of the ordinary, isn't it?'

McGuinness lowered himself into his chair, frowning.

'The arsonists disarmed two guards, bound them with zip ties, and carried them outside, when they could have left them to burn along with the drugs,' Rick went on, talking fast. 'And why'd they burn the drugs when they could've made money out of 'em?'

McGuinness shot him a confused look. 'I don't know what you're trying to say, here.'

Rick's shoulders sagged. 'I'll be honest with you, mate – I'm not sure myself. There's a lot about these incidents that seems off to me, and I'm just trying to get it straight in my head.'

'O-*kay* . . .'

It was an invitation, and Rick took it. 'The Deptford Waters tip-off was anonymous, wasn't it?' he asked.

McGuinness jerked his chin in acknowledgement and reached for his coffee cup.

'How come site security didn't report it?'

'It happened before the first physical check of the night, and CCTV was out of action.'

'Out of action or nobbled?' Rick asked, thinking about the disabled cameras in and around the car park when the Blackfriars gang was caught.

'The security firm couldn't confirm they were hacked, but the system went down for a bit, then came back online as the first responders arrived.'

'Did MetCC get any details on the caller?'

'Male, mature. Local accent – wouldn't give a name. Number untraceable. "Disturbance at location," he said. He called back a few minutes later with the message: "Possible shots fired."'

Rick drew down the corners of his mouth. 'Doesn't sound like some elderly dog walker, stumbling on the scene, does it?'

'Nah, I heard the dispatch recording – he sounded calm – kind of . . . professional.'

'Like Job?' Rick said. 'Like it was all in a night's work?'

McGuinness eyed him sceptically, and Rick heard Sam's amused voice in his ear:

That imagination of yours, Rick. Are you really implying that police are mixed up in this?

He was about to apologise and withdraw the suggestion, but McGuinness's face clouded for a second and he checked himself.

'Come to think of it, he did give a grid reference,' McGuinness said. 'The first responders were glad of the info 'cos the development wasn't even on Google Maps at the time.'

Like Job. Rick thought, although he didn't say it aloud this time. Like whoever requested a hazmat fire appliance to attend Emin's warehouse fire.

McGuinness was watching him, waiting for him to comment, but Rick asked instead, 'You had no suspects in the shooting?'

'Officially, I haven't a clue. I got kicked out of MIT way before the hit on Floren.'

Rick stared at him stupidly. The Major Investigations Team were practically royalty in the Met, and getting shunted out must have been a devastating blow. He returned to the question of how Floren had been cleared of involvement in the deadly arson attack – had even won the development contract – and his mind leapt to conspiracy.

As if he'd read Rick's mind, McGuinness said, 'It's not what you're thinking. I just asked too many questions that could've got a messy case reopened after it had been put to bed.'

Rick had been in exactly the same position himself last year, after forcing the reopening of a hit-and-run inquiry. He'd scored a major victory against organised crime for the Met, but had made enemies in the backwash of that investigation.

'Wait a minute – you said "officially" you haven't a clue. What about *un*officially?'

McGuinness smiled for the first time in their entire exchange. 'Nice catch. I wasn't the only one who thought Floren had got away with murder, and I *may* have heard an odd detail about what went on at Deptford Waters that night.'

'I believe the scene was a mess,' Rick said.

'It was – the CSIs couldn't work out how much of it was the paramedics and how much the killer.' He frowned, remembering. 'Or killers.'

Rick tilted his head in question.

'There was rain that night,' McGuinness explained, 'and they found multiple shoeprints tramped through the house. And then there was the weird thing with the gag.'

He seemed to fall into a reverie, and Rick prompted, 'The gag?'

'When the first responders got to Floren, he was bound, and at some point, he'd been gagged,' the sergeant said. 'But the gag had been removed before he was shot.'

'You're right, that *is* weird,' Rick said. 'The papers said he was shot twice.'

McGuinness nodded. 'Execution-style. Head and chest.'

'Did your MIT contact tell you if they looked into the families?'

'I didn't need an insider for that. I got a couple of calls from a niece of one of the victims, complaining we were treating them like criminals. There was a lot on social media after that, accusing the Met of "victim blaming".' He shrugged. 'They were checked out anyway, and they were all in the clear.'

McGuinness froze, looking past Rick towards the food counter. 'Oh, shit . . . You'd better push off – it's Steiner, and she just clocked us.'

Rick said a few quiet and sincere words of thanks then stood, scraping his chair loudly on the linoleum. 'Yeah, cheers, mate. Thanks for *nothing*,' he snarled, keeping his back to Steiner and striding out of the door in a fair imitation of foul temper.

Chapter 17

AT ONE-FORTY P.M., RICK CLIMBED INTO THE BACK of a painter's and decorator's van near Aldgate Station. The uneasy feeling he'd had the night before that he was being watched had stayed with him, and he'd taken a few extra twists and turns on the journey, just in case. The business owner was driving, and Rick was accompanied by an expert from the Technical Surveillance Unit.

Fifteen minutes later, wearing borrowed decorator's overalls, Rick and the tech walked in through the front of the apartment building carrying surveillance gear hidden in cardboard boxes and paint-spattered canvas bags.

The apartment was on the second floor, the back room already finished, but the decorators had whited out the windows. The technician briefly opened the window casements either side of the fixed glaze, working out angles, before closing up again and carefully removing small patches of the glass whitewash and positioning the cameras. A separate team of trained officers had already taken care of installing Wi-Fi gizmos inside the warehouse – Rick's job would be to monitor the roadway.

The man was calm and deliberate, measuring, checking for reflections, focusing, adjusting, refocusing, chatting and explaining as he went. He set up two still cameras and a videocam, one of each pointing to the entrance of the warehouse, a still camera pointing back down the narrow backstreet towards the main road.

Finally, they were ready.

'You done this before?' the tech asked.

'A few times, yeah,' Rick said.

'Quick refresher: rule number one is don't mess with the settings on the video – it's focused right for the entrance.' He bounced a couple of times on the balls of his feet, then checked through the eyepiece again. 'This is a concrete floor, so you shouldn't get too much vibration – but don't touch the camera body or snatch up the remote – you could knock it off-kilter, okay? Take it slow and easy – all right?'

'Don't breathe near the gizmos,' Rick said. 'Got it.'

'I'm serious,' the tech said scowling. 'Normally, we'd have a tech on-site to make sure you don't break anything, but the situation being what it is, right now, we're pushed for time, equipment and staff. If you don't think you can handle it, now's the time to speak up.'

'I can handle it. And I'll be careful,' Rick promised.

After talking him unnecessarily through how to use the remote, and then insisting on a practice run on each camera, the tech left, but not before warning Rick not to turn on the lights.

Rick settled down to watch, while the real decorators carried on their work in the other rooms, talking companionably, occasionally raising their voices in laughter. His interrupted conversation with DS McGuinness left a number of unanswered questions, and he hadn't had the opportunity to quiz the detective on how Floren had won the bid for Deptford Waters. Why hadn't he been disbarred from even *trying*, after the fire? And why had McGuinness been booted out of MIT?

He put a call through to the police station's switchboard and asked for McGuinness.

After he introduced himself, McGuinness answered with a curt, 'Go ahead,' and Rick realised that others were listening.

'I'm guessing you have an audience.'

'Uh-huh.'

'There's a few more things I wanted to ask. I'm on duty over-night, but could we meet first thing? Breakfast, maybe?'

'All right,' McGuinness continued in a neutral tone.

'I've got a nine a.m. briefing, so I was thinking somewhere close but not *too* close to the station – at about eight?'

'That's doable,' McGuinness said.

'Great.' Rick named a corner café on King's Road.

The decorators knocked off at five and the apartment settled into stillness and silence. The warehouse was quiet, too. Only a couple of vans had come and gone in the three hours to five o'clock, delivering boxed items, backing up against the entrance, unloading and leaving. He logged each arrival, photographed number plates and the faces of the deliverymen. Others on the team would identify the drivers, but Rick suspected that they were regular white van men, earning a living from delivering for one or more of the national parcel delivery firms.

He was stationed in the living room, which the decorators had completed a few days earlier, so the headache-inducing reek of drying paint and turps had mostly gone. One wall had been replastered and coated with emulsion and the combined smell of drying plaster and chalky paint brought to mind the last time Rick had decorated the family home in Putney. That was four or five years ago. With a painful jolt, he remembered that last autumn, Jess had gently prodded him to update the colours and replace the sheer curtains in the master bedroom with something that would keep out the early-morning sun. Actors, like police, worked peculiar hours and snatched their sleep whenever the opportunity arose. He would sometimes come in at four in the afternoon and find her curled up in bed, 'catching up', as she called it.

In unguarded moments of tiredness and in the phase of unreality between dreaming and wakefulness, Rick would still catch a glimpse of Jess in profile against the backlit drapes or see her sleeping contours in the fall of the bedcovers.

There will be life after Jess.

It was Sam's voice he heard.

Life after Jess . . . Rationally, Rick knew it as a literal fact. Hadn't he gone on, these last five months without her? But logic couldn't assuage the dull ache he felt coming home to an empty house every night. He'd never been big on socialising, but after the things he'd done – the liberties he'd taken and laws he'd broken in searching for Jess – he'd have felt a hypocrite sitting in a bar with honest coppers. So, in the five months since, his days were a monotonous routine of work, the gym, the dojo, and home.

Could he really call that life?

Chapter 18

Next morning, eight a.m.

THE CAFÉ HAD JUST OPENED when Rick slipped inside. DS McGuinness came in a few minutes later, eyes on a swivel, looking for anyone he might know.

Two mugs of steaming coffee arrived as McGuinness settled himself at the table, and to save on time, both men ordered food before the server left.

'Sorry about yesterday,' Rick said. 'Did Steiner give you grief over it?'

'No, that was quite a convincing performance you gave.' McGuinness's mouth twitched. 'Almost had *me* fooled.' He took a sip of coffee. 'You might want to steer clear of her for a bit, though.'

Rick scratched his eyebrow. 'That's the plan.'

'So,' McGuiness said. 'Unanswered questions.'

Asking straight out why he'd been booted out of MIT would be tactless, so Rick asked about Floren getting off the arson charges without even a reprimand.

McGuinness shook his head. 'That fucker ... We couldn't find a one single thing to link him to the fire. No paper trail, no e-trail. We looked at his mobile phone, his computer, the satnav on his car – nothing. We even checked his dashcam flash drive, hoping he'd slipped up, said a few unguarded words. He didn't. And he was nowhere *near* the blocks the night they burned down.'

'But you're still convinced he was in on it?'

McGuinness gave a snort of disgust. 'Wouldn't surprise me if he nudged Gillies in the direction of the petrol cans.'

'D'you think that's why he was murdered?'

'I know he got what was coming to him.'

'To be fair, we did away with the death penalty last century, mate.' Rick smiled to show he wasn't entirely unsympathetic.

'Yeah, but Floren didn't just get away with murder, he made a bloody fortune out of it.'

'That's been bugging me – how *did* Floren get the development?'

McGuinness's look said, *You really have to ask?*

'Okay, so maybe he greased a few palms,' Rick said. 'But didn't—'

Their orders arrived and for a few seconds they remained silent while hot plates of scrambled eggs were juggled and room was made for sides of toast, and McGuinness began scarfing his eggs and potato waffles with a relish that was surprising in so slender a man. Rick leaned forward and began again, keeping his voice low. 'Didn't the victims' families lodge objections with the planning department?'

McGuinness chewed and swallowed. 'They tried every legal avenue open to them. When Floren put in plans to the council six months before the fire, they emailed objections, gathered petitions, held protests at the town hall – you name it. But he got his outline planning consent anyway, and the council planners were wowed by his detailed proposals. The scheme was finalised and approved the week of the verdict.'

'That's a bit cold, isn't it?' Rick said. 'You'd think the whole thing would have been put on hold at least till after the trial.'

'You would, wouldn't you? Except Floren was a charmer. Everyone I spoke to at the council said what a *nice* man he was.'

'But after the fire the families would have a strong case to stop the project. Why didn't they go back to the council?'

'Those people had been literally burned out of their homes,' McGuinness said. 'They'd been through hell – still are, some of them. God, some of the injuries . . .' He shook his head. 'But the NHS is broke, mate. There's millions on waiting lists and the survivors needed help *right then* – not eighteen months down the line. And where were they gonna get the kind of money they needed for a planning appeal? Not from Victim Compensation, that's for sure.'

'The Crown must've seized Gillies's assets?'

'As soon as he was charged,' McGuinness said. 'The land, his house, even what was left of the blocks of flats.'

'So they decided to sue Gillies for damages instead of launching a planning appeal?'

A brief nod. 'Most of them wouldn't want to go back even after the new development was finished. And a law firm offered to represent the residents on a no-win no-fee basis in a class action. It was the best offer they were likely to get, and they took it.'

'Well, at least that should be a big payout for the families.'

'Not as big as you'd think,' McGuinness said sourly. 'Floren had paperwork to show he'd already sunk a shitload of money into the scheme. He got every penny of that back from Gillies's assets on the basis that he'd been defrauded.'

Rick swore softly.

'Amen to that,' McGuinness said.

'So Floren got a chunk of cash *and* his application went through unopposed. What about competition from other developers?'

'You know how it is. Councils are always strapped for cash and opening the scheme to new investors would've meant going through the whole costly rigmarole of vetting new planning applications and new investors. Floren even said he'd cover the expense of cleaning up the site. It was almost inevitable he'd get the gig.'

Rick could see why the families might be motivated to take Floren out, but the families had been cleared. He tapped one finger on the tabletop, mentally shifting the scraps of information around, trying to make the pieces fit. 'If it wasn't revenge for the arson attacks, who *did* put the hit on Floren – Gillies?'

'He would seem the obvious suspect,' McGuinness said. 'But he hadn't a bean to barter with.'

Rick took a bite of the bacon and egg bap he'd ordered while he thought. 'Well, if the families didn't pay for the hit, it had to be some criminal Floren pissed off.'

McGuinness tilted his head in agreement.

Recalling Floren's website, Rick asked, 'Who runs the corporate trust that's taken over the day-to-day running of his property company?'

'I would love to know,' McGuinness scoffed. 'I'm told it was "looked into", but the inquiry didn't get far.'

'*Who* looked into it?' Rick was wondering if Dave Collins might have had more success than whoever the Met got to look into Floren's financials.

McGuinness wiped his face and hands meticulously with his napkin before answering. 'Trusts *are* the go-to for criminals wanting to shield money.'

Rick stared at him. 'You think Floren was a frontman for a criminal gang?'

McGuinness took a swig of coffee and Rick got the impression he was deciding how much he could safely say. He began slowly, as if weighing every word.

'When Floren got the development through planning, I went to the SIO on the arson inquiry, told him I wanted to talk to the planning officers. I got shut down.'

'By who?'

'The SIO. But he looked as sick as I felt telling me to lay off.'

'The order came from higher up the food chain then.'

McGuinness didn't reply, but the look on his face told Rick everything he needed to know. Someone had been bought off.

'Did he buy off the free press?' Rick asked. 'Is that why they didn't lay into him during the trial?'

'Look, I've got no proof that money changed hands – not between him and the council or the free press,' McGuinness said. 'But a pal of mine works freelance for the local rags. She said Floren had threatened her with libel action if she linked his name to Gillies or the arson attack. She'd been working on an exposé, asking questions. She's experienced – knew to keep it vague, didn't get specific. Passed it off as a touchy-feely human interest type story. The only person who knew what she was really up to was her editor.'

'So, *he* was paid off?'

'Or scared off.'

'By Floren? Or by whoever's behind this trust?'

'Back then, I thought it must be Floren – I mean, he *was* the face of Deptford Waters . . .' McGuinness raised one shoulder and let it fall. 'It was only after he was killed that the Dream Schemes Trust came out of the woodwork. Suddenly it all made sense: the money for bribes and lawyers, the chemical clean-up after the fire, muscle to put the frighteners on people – it all came from the trust. Must have.'

'So maybe they used Floren to get their investment capital back, and killed him when he outlived his usefulness?'

Before McGuinness could answer, Rick's phone buzzed in his pocket. Checking the screen, he mouthed, 'Superintendent Ghosh.'

'How soon can you get here?' Ghosh demanded.

'I just finished my shift, sir – I'm having breakfast.'

'That's not what I asked.'

Rick suppressed a sigh. 'Ten minutes, if I rush it.'

'Do that. My office.' Ghosh rung off, and Rick stood, tucking cash under his plate and picking up the bap to take with him.

'It's not even eight-thirty, yet,' McGuinness said.

'Well, you know what they say about the wicked,' Rick said with a rueful grin.

Chapter 19

RICK TURNER STOOD IN FRONT OF Detective Superintendent Ghosh's desk, waiting for him to finish tapping in something on his laptop.

'You can't go pestering investigators about inquiries you have no connection with,' Ghosh said, without looking up.

For a second Rick wondered if someone had seen him deep in conversation with McGuinness over breakfast, but Sam had taught him a thing or two in childhood about the art of dissembling, so he held back from commenting, instead gazing at his boss with polite interest.

Irritated by his silence, Ghosh shoved the laptop aside and glared at him. 'The Blackfriars robbery is none of your business,' he hissed.

Rick relaxed a little: they hadn't been seen; this was about his chat with McGuinness in the canteen the previous day.

'The task force *is* looking at gang crimes in the round, sir,' he ventured.

Ghosh shook his head. 'I won't have that. The Blackfriars crew isn't in Emin's league – Quinn is just a disgruntled employee who roped in a few friends to help him extort money from his bosses.'

'They kidnapped two women, held a bank to ransom, got away with millions.'

'They *didn't* get away with it,' Ghosh snapped.

'No thanks to us.'

Ghosh launched to his feet; his eyes bugged. 'I *beg* your pardon?'

'I'm just wondering who turned them in,' Rick said, backpedalling a bit.

'Again – not your business. *Steiner's* business.'

'Okay. But there's something off about the Blackfriars arrests *and* the Emin setback.'

Ghosh's long fingers were splayed on the desktop, as if he might spring across it at any moment, and Rick took the safe option of sticking with Emin. 'Take the warehouse fire. Two guards disarmed and bound with zip ties, then carried to safety. The production-line workers allowed to leave. The tip-off coming before the fire really took hold, the caller requesting a hazmat appliance.'

'Your point?'

'Why'd they let the workers just wander off into the night? Why let guards go? Why burn the drugs? Why would a rival gang *care* about firefighters breathing noxious fumes?'

Ghosh chewed on that for a few seconds. 'Valid points. But it still doesn't justify your intrusion into the Blackfriars arrests.'

'But there's parallels,' Rick said. 'They didn't touch the money from the robbery and the arsonists didn't touch Emin's drugs. They locked Quinn's firearm in the boot of the car before they called the police in. Warned them as well. Doesn't that look like concern for first responders' safety? Same as the caller who warned the fire service they'd need hazmat.'

Ghosh stalled for a second, folding his arms and frowning at a spot on the table. 'I'll talk to Kath Steiner and Will Fenton,' he said at last. 'Ask them to look into it. But you will keep your mouth shut and your nose out until you're invited to give an opinion. Clear?'

Rick hesitated, and Ghosh said, 'For God's *sake*—'

'I think there's another case we should look at again,' Rick said. 'The Floren murder.'

Ghosh seemed almost dizzied by the suggestion. He shut his eyes for a moment. When he opened them again, Rick saw his temper had risen. 'The consensus is that the *landlord* commissioned Floren's murder. It was simple revenge.'

'He was zip-tied. CCTV was down – knocked out, maybe.'

Ghosh fixed Rick with a flat stare. 'CCTV cameras fail all the time – usually at the exact moment you need them.'

'Who called in the police? The security cameras weren't working and the place was deserted that night. Why wouldn't they identify themselves?'

'People make anonymous calls to emergency services. And there's one striking difference between Floren and the other two incidents,' Ghosh added sharply. 'Floren was *murdered* – shot dead – probably by a professional assassin.'

'I think everyone's agreed on that, sir.'

'Well, that's very magnanimous of you, Sergeant.'

Rick ignored the snipe. 'But Floren was bound and gagged. What professional assassin takes the time to bind and gag a man? And why would he then *remove* the gag, then shoot him?'

Ghosh seemed stuck for an answer to that.

'There were two triple-nine calls – one to say there was a disturbance, and another a few minutes later to report shots fired. Same caller. Why would he call twice? Wouldn't the killer *know* he'd shot Floren? Or did he forget to mention it in the first call?'

You might want to dial down the sarcasm a bit, Rick, Sam warned.

Rick took a breath. 'The CSU found multiple footwear marks at the scene. Professional assassins usually work alone. Someone else was there, sir.'

'The CSU couldn't determine if the shoeprints were from the paramedics and police responders.'

'Couldn't rule out persons unknown, either,' Rick said, working the next part out as he spoke. 'But if there were *two* incidents at

Deptford Waters that night, it begins to make sense.' He saw that Ghosh was about to interrupt, so he talked faster, raising his voice a little. 'In the first incident, Floren was bound and gagged. In the second, someone *unconnected* with the first assailants shot him.'

Ghosh threw up his hands. 'Floren doesn't fit your so-called pattern because he's dead, so you just make up a story that'll fit!'

'That's not what I'm doing, sir,' Rick said, exasperated, but trying to remain respectful and reasonable. 'There was a van with fake decals on the development that night. Whose was that?'

'The assassin's, no doubt.'

'A bit absent-minded, leaving it behind, wasn't it?' As soon as he said it, he wished he could take it back.

Rick saw something slip behind Ghosh's eyes and knew that he'd lost the man – lost the argument entirely – and with it, any chance of convincing his boss.

Ghosh pointed a finger at him. 'You're like a puppy chasing leaves. Turning this way and that, constantly distracted by *irrelevancies*. That's not how police work is done!'

Rick experienced a cold wash of anger. 'Worked out all right last autumn, didn't it, sir?'

'Be very careful, Sergeant.' Ghosh's icy tone matched his own.

Easy, Rick . . . It was Sam's voice he heard. *The man's under pressure – the last thing he needs is his protégé turning on him.* Words like 'protégé' had only become part of Sam's vocabulary after Theo Lockleigh, dodgy lawyer, illegal moneylender and amateur art collector had made Sam his own protégé. That mentorship had led to the darkest days of Rick's boyhood.

From the set of his jaw, Rick knew that Ghosh was grinding his teeth. But he couldn't bring himself to apologise. He took a slow breath and said, 'I don't believe that the Blackfriars mob was turned in by a disgruntled ex-crew member, or that Emin's place was torched by a rival. And Floren's shooting looks a lot more complicated than a revenge attack arranged by his former partner.' Should he tell his boss the conclusion he'd reached?

No. 'Vigilante' was almost a taboo word in policing, so he stayed silent on that point.

Ghosh eyed him for a few moments longer, sucking his teeth. At last, he spoke: 'D'you think I don't know what you're driving at? Don't you know the potential damage that kind of wild rumour could cause?'

Rick had no real, concrete proof, so he chose his words carefully: 'It's true, I don't have all the answers, but surely, we should at least be asking the questions?'

Ghosh shook his head bitterly. 'Get out of my sight.'

Chapter 20

Nine a.m. briefing

ONLY A FEW MEMBERS OF THE TASK FORCE were present in the meeting room, the rest being actively engaged on inquiries. Rick picked a seat out of Ghosh's direct line of sight, sipping coffee and blinking away tiredness, focusing hard on what each person had to say. He'd been awake and active since seven a.m. the day before, and the room seemed to be spinning slowly. In moments of clarity, he gathered that Emin was moving fast at both the supply and processing ends of his business. He had left his temporary address in Dalston just after dark the previous night to meet with a Turkish Cypriot suspected of bringing large quantities of heroin into the country via the Balkan route.

'They met in a Turkish café on Stoke Newington Road.' This came from the sallow-skinned NCA agent. 'Interpol's got him tagged as moving large shipments – heroin and cocaine – people, as well,' she went on. 'I think we can safely assume that Emin is negotiating a restock after the fire that wiped out his main factory.'

Ghosh spoke up. 'Assume?'

'We couldn't get listening equipment anywhere near the place.' When Ghosh began to fidget, she said, 'It's a tight-knit community – we'd need someone of Turkish ethnicity to have any chance of getting in there unnoticed, and we just don't have the personnel.' She spoke with regret, though she seemed unruffled.

'So we have no idea *when*,' Ghosh said, irritated, now.

'Sooner, rather than later would be my guess,' Rick chipped in before he could stop himself.

The searing look Ghosh gave him made heads turn. Finally the superintendent jerked his chin and said curtly, 'Go on.'

'The warehouse was quiet except for a few deliveries up until six-thirty last night. White vans, single crew.'

'We checked the vehicle registrations you sent in.' This came from the tech who'd set up the cameras on Rick's surveillance the previous afternoon. Rick hadn't noticed him at the table, so maybe he'd joined them part way through. *Or maybe you nodded off for a second.* The notion was unsettling, and Rick made a mental promise to himself to get a few hours of sleep in as soon as he got home.

'. . . local and national delivery services,' the tech finished, and Rick realised he'd missed something.

'So they were all legit,' he said, winging it, hoping he wasn't contradicting whatever it was that had come before.

The tech stared at him as if he were slow. 'Well, yes . . .'

Well, it would seem that you just stated the bleeding obvious, Rick.

'Then box vans started arriving at seven p.m.,' Rick said. 'If you remember, the estate agent told me that whoever rented the place was going to set up a dark kitchen selling Mexican food? Well, these vans were marked "Papa Pepe's Burritos".'

'Hang on.' The tech clicked to an image Rick had taken of one of the vans.

The name was emblazoned in an arc of red and green lettering on a white background. Beneath this, images of dancing burritos wearing brightly coloured sombreros and a bold promise: 'Delivered to your door!'

'The vans were bought at auction a day after the warehouse fire,' the tech added. 'And the graphics look like cheap vinyl stickers.'

He nodded to Rick to continue.

'There are three vans. They showed up every thirty minutes or so in rotation,' Rick said. 'Two-crewed, same crew each time – and fully loaded, so they must've been picking stuff up from somewhere local.'

Ghosh turned to the NCA agent. 'Can we get GPS trackers on those?'

'We could *try* . . .' she said doubtfully. 'We know they've got someone watching each end of the access road, and it doesn't get much foot traffic, so it's a big ask. We'd probably do better with a combination of TfL cameras and mobile surveillance.'

They wrangled for a couple of minutes over personnel to crew cars and sit through hours of Transport for London traffic cam footage, then the technical surveillance expert gave a breakdown of what was in the boxes the vans were ferrying in. Hidden cameras inside the warehouse had sent live video of weighing kits, bags, tape, polystyrene fast-food boxes and clingfilm, such as a catering company would use. But any thought that they were catering only to food cravings was dispelled when he showed them stills of bulking agents unpacked and stacked on pallets in readiness for cutting the drugs when they arrived. Boxes of surgical masks, tiny click-seal baggies, pill presses and encapsulating machines had also been laid out on long metal tables in what was surely destined to become a production line.

'We got names for most of the crew,' the tech said, coming to the tail end of his report. 'Except this guy.' He threw a still on-screen of a short, thick-set man with a dark fuzz of five-o'clock shadow that extended from the top of his cheekbones to his T-shirt collar. 'They only referred to him as "guv" or "boss".'

Ghosh named Emin's right-hand man, getting there ahead of Rick.

'He wouldn't show up on-site just for a progress report,' Rick said. 'They must be expecting a consignment.'

'We'll put a team onto him,' the NCA agent said. 'We've already got eyes on Emin – and Border Force is on alert at Dover.'

The Border Force rep nodded. 'We'll let you know immediately if we believe a shipment has come in. We can track boats to the London ports without arousing suspicion.'

'And if they unload the cargo at Dover?' Ghosh asked.

'We'll enlist air support, if need be,' the NCA shot back. 'Rest assured, if they go by road, we'll have the shipment covered every step of the way.'

After a few more minutes of discussion on comms and staffing, the meeting broke up and Rick headed to the locker room. He stared stupidly into his locker at his running gear, wondering if he had the energy for a thirty-minute jog to Putney, deciding after a few addled moments that it might loosen the stiffness he felt after eighteen hours cooped up in one room. He was tying his laces when his work mobile buzzed in his pocket, and he fished it out.

'Where are you?' Ghosh asked without preamble.

'The locker room.'

'Well, get back up here – pronto.'

Almost the full complement of inter-agency personnel were already gathered when Rick walked through the door. The room was packed, and he wondered what could be so important that they'd dragged people off tasks they'd just been assigned. The arrival of a major drugs shipment was imminent – what could be more important?

Maybe sleep deprivation was making him paranoid, but heads seemed to turn as he edged inside, and he felt he was getting some funny looks from the more senior members of the team.

Ghosh rapped on the table and the room fell silent. 'This just went live on various podcast platforms.' He clicked a button on the remote and stood to one side, watching with the rest.

The screen lit up to reveal a woman with shoulder-length dark brown hair. She was sitting at a desk, with a microphone in front of her. Rick recognised her immediately. Pandora's podcast was designed to work on audio channels, but the video clips she used to make her investigatory points lent themselves to visual presentation, and she encouraged her followers to access her YouTube channel and her website for the additional material.

'My name is Pandora Hahn,' she began. 'And you're watching the *Pandora Unboxes* podcast.'

This caused some uneasy shuffling of feet.

'In this second season of *Pandora Unboxes*, we're digging deep into policing in the capital. Trying to work out why criminals can brazenly go about their illegal activities without consequences. Is it because our law enforcers are hamstrung? Are British law enforcement agencies *incapable* of carrying out their sworn duty to serve and protect because they're afraid of infringing the rights of those who *break* the law? If so, what about the rights of law-abiding citizens? Don't they have a right to feel safe on the streets of our capital?'

She paused, looking into the camera. 'In this episode of *Pandora Unboxes*, I will reveal the shocking truth of what really happened the night that London Metropolitan Police arrested three men in connection with the Blackfriars Bank robbery.'

The room was too crowded for everyone to take a seat, and Rick was standing at the back in a corner, with a good view of the rest. The looks on their faces bore an odd mix of avid interest and dread.

'Blackfriars Bank is an independent institution, based here in London. This case involved kidnap, threat and extortion. On the sixth of January, the wife of the bank manager and fiancée of the deputy manager were kidnapped in separate car-jackings as they drove home after the morning school run. They remained in the hands of the kidnappers until ten o'clock that same evening, after the manager and his assistant were forced to give the kidnappers access to the bank vault.'

Her image shrank abruptly, ending up in one corner of the screen, while an image of Quinn opened up.

'Police arrested this man, Gary Quinn, but released him without charge a day later. Three months on, he's back in custody, along with two other men, following a tip-off to police.'

Quinn's picture was replaced by the now infamous video clip of Anstell outside the car park in Tower Hamlets, prompting groans and eyerolls around the room.

'"Three significant arrests,"' Pandora quoted from Anstell's thirty seconds of self-glorification. '"A substantial sum of money was retrieved during the course of the arrests . . ."' Then, quoting DCI Steiner: '"My team has been working tirelessly behind the scenes."'

Pandora froze the footage at a point where Steiner appeared to have an unpleasant snarl on her face, then looked into the camera and said, 'Does it sound like the Metropolitan Police are claiming full credit for the arrests? Detective Chief Inspector Anstell says, "We have on video the division of a substantial sum of money," yet we now know that the police were not on the scene at the time the money was shared out between the suspects. They had a tip-off from a man named Bert Wickstead – and I revealed in the last episode of *Pandora Unboxes* that the name was fake – at least in the sense that Bert Wickstead is dead . . . He *was* a famous gangbuster of the 1960s and Seventies – a well-known and greatly admired detective superintendent at the Met. The caller even *identified* himself as a police officer, yet *nobody* at the Met made the connection.'

She went on to invite viewers to tune in to previous episodes and like and subscribe to the podcast.

'Do we *have* to sit through all of this?' The plea came from Kath Steiner herself.

Ghosh flicked a look in her direction. 'Context, Kath. Keep watching.'

'The police have backpedalled since then,' Pandora was saying. 'So what really happened that night?' She paused. 'You're about to find out. *Pandora Unboxes – Hamstrung Law* has exclusive video from *inside* the car park on the night of the arrests.'

A nervous shifting and a few murmured curses, then the room fell silent again.

The screen faded to black. Then, the dimly lit interior of a multi-storey car park in shades of grey. In the bottom right-hand corner was a stylised wolf logo. Rick thought the image was a photograph until one of the strip lights flickered. A few cars stood in the bays, but there was no sign of human activity. A sudden glare spotlit the concrete beams of the ceiling, then a light-coloured car appeared at the top of the up-ramp at the far end of the level.

Someone said, 'Is that Quinn's Qashqai?'

For a few seconds the full beam of the headlamps blinded the camera, until the car turned and reversed into a bay.

A long pause, then a man swung out of the car. It was Gary Quinn. After checking that he was alone, he hefted a large sports bag from the boot of his SUV and started walking.

A slight flicker indicated that the surveillance operator had switched to a different camera, then the screen split in two, showing the empty Qashqai on one level and Quinn on another, nearing two men, standing next to two cars.

The gathering watched as the spoils were divided, then Quinn said, 'The cops haven't given up on Blackfriars, yet, so hold back for a while, be cautious, pay cash – and *don't brag.*' The incriminating words were spoken with crystal clarity.

Suddenly five helmeted, masked, and heavily armed figures in tactical gear burst on the scene, bellowing commands, subduing two of the suspects in seconds. But the split screen remained on, and they saw the tall figure of Quinn fold himself like a paperclip and drop down to the lower level.

The next minute was a confusing blur of movement. A van appeared out of nowhere as Quinn tried to get into his car. He reached behind him as two of the tactical team came into view at the far end of the level.

A muffled scream, then the van skidded sideways, colliding with the Qashqai. Here, it was hard to make out what happened, but there was a definite muzzle-flash and a deafening bang, then Quinn came around the van and reached in to the driver at the exact moment two of the tac team appeared and dragged him back. They dropped him hard to the concrete floor, rolled him on his face, zip-tied his hands, and dumped him in his car in one fluid and practised action.

'Now, it's difficult to make out what was happening in those last few seconds,' Pandora said, her voice calm and objective. 'So let me talk you through.' She ran the end of the clip a second time, describing how Quinn had tried to shoot the van driver.

'Impressive, aren't they?' she said. 'But they are *not* police.' She paused for effect. 'Look at their jackets and helmets. No police logos, no chequer banding, no badging. You might think, well . . . maybe they're under cover – they *are* wearing tactical gear, and they *are* armed, after all. It's a thought, but I'm pretty sure it would be illegal.' She allowed herself a small flicker of a smile. 'And I say again, with *absolute* certainty they are *not* police, or any other law enforcement agency. I know this for a *fact*, because they told me.'

A gasp, then a buzz of conversation.

'Quiet,' Ghosh snapped and they subsided once more.

'I was sent this recording by the group that made the arrests,' Pandora explained. 'They accomplished in one night what the Metropolitan Police with their considerable resources have failed to do in *three months.*' Another pause. 'They achieved justice for victims, consequences for criminals. They even returned the stolen bank cash. Be sure to check back soon with *Pandora Unboxes*, because they assure me that the Blackfriars Bank robbers will not be the last.'

This provoked a more determined rumble of protest and muttered curses that Ghosh could not quell.

'They call themselves the Wolf Pack,' Ghosh said, muting the screen as Pandora started her wind-down to the end of the programme.

Animations and icons on the screen encouraged people to 'like', review and subscribe to her podcast.

'She didn't get anything from them about who they are?' the NCA agent asked.

Ghosh shook his head.

'They look police or military trained,' Rick said, and a murmur of agreement followed.

'I want her arrested,' Steiner hissed.

'On what charge?'

Rick recognised the lofty tone Ghosh often took before descending into acid sarcasm.

'Theft of evidence for one,' she said.

'Where's the theft?' Ghosh demanded. 'She claims she was given the recording by the people who claim to have made it.'

'Conspiracy, then,' Steiner said with an irritated twitch of her shoulders.

'Conspiring to do *what* – advance the course of criminal justice?'

Steiner hardened her voice. 'She's shielding perpetrators of crime. A gun was discharged. Those amateurs could have killed someone.'

'Yes,' he said. 'I know. But they caught the robbers practically with their hands in the till.'

She shook her head.

'Look, Kath,' Ghosh said, more conciliatory, now. 'I sympathise. But what *exactly* do you think it would do for the Met's image if we went after a reporter who is in communication with a group who claims to be cleaning up London's streets?'

'She's a *podcaster*, sir!'

'She got more information about what went down during the apprehension of the Blackfriars mob than we did,' he pointed out. 'She got a digital recording to corroborate it. And if what we've just seen is *amateur*, what does that make us?'

The DCI verbally flattened, Ghosh turned to practical matters

108

and in a matter of under five minutes the NCA had agreed to dig into Pandora Hahn's background and her podcast, while Ghosh allocated someone in the press office to ask her to come in for a chat.

The meeting dispersed and Rick was about to slip out of the door, when Ghosh raised his voice over the murmur of voices. 'Rick – a word.'

The room emptied faster, hearing the superintendent's tone, and soon all that remained were the senior NCA agent, the representative of Border Force, Rick and Superintendent Ghosh.

'So, Rick,' Ghosh said, after firmly closing the meeting-room door. 'There's now no doubt that we have vigilantism – at least as far as the Blackfriars arrests go.'

Rick glanced at the other players. The looks on their faces said he hadn't been paranoid – they were looking at him as though he'd prophesied the apocalypse.

'Sir,' he said neutrally.

'But you say that this "Wolf Pack" is responsible for other reprisals and attacks on criminal gangs.'

'No, sir.'

A flare of light in Ghosh's brown eyes warned him not to mess about, but Rick was damned if he'd allow Ghosh to put words in his mouth.

'Even if the Wolf Pack *is* responsible for the Blackfriars arrests, I can't know if they're implicated in the other cases.'

The other two swivelled to Ghosh to gauge his reaction.

The superintendent sucked his teeth. 'Oh, well, I'm sorry if I misquoted you,' he said with strained patience. 'Perhaps you would like to explain for yourself why you thought Blackfriars was linked to Deptford Waters and the arson attack at Emin's warehouse.'

Rick went through the similarities he'd laid out for Ghosh before the briefing: the drugs left untouched at Emin's warehouse, the money at the Blackfriars arrests; anonymous calls to emergency services *suspiciously* earlier than expected – and the calm, helpful, and *professional* way in which emergency services were informed. Also the interesting lack of casualties in what were suspected gangland reprisals. He finished with the tip-off at the crime scene.

'Wait a minute,' the NCA agent said. 'Jason Floren was shot. It looked like a hired assassin.'

'A professional killer doesn't bind and gag a man, then remove the gag and shoot him,' Ghosh said.

He stole your line, Rick – you're not going to let him get away with it, are you? Sam's voice in his head sounded almost admiring of the superintendent's audacity.

'As I said earlier, sir.' Rick glanced at the NCA agent and saw a twinkle of laughter in her eyes.

Ghosh saw it too, and knew he was rumbled.

'Yes, yes, gold star to DS Turner,' he said testily. 'Explain your theory on the Floren shooting.'

Rick outlined the unusual aspects of the assassination, high-lighting the removal of Floren's gag, the mystery van, and the second call to emergency services by the same caller.

'He doesn't think they shot Floren,' Ghosh added, unable to resist butting in. '*He* thinks they intended to hand him over to the police.'

'You think they got a confession out of him for the arson that destroyed the original properties at the development?' the NCA agent asked.

It took Rick a few seconds to make sense of her question and he shook his head to clear it. 'It's possible, isn't it?'

'*Possible*, yes,' she conceded. 'But what's your reasoning?'

Sleep deprived as he was, Rick wasn't sure he had the mental capacity to explain his rationale.

'Okay,' he said. 'There was something off about the warehouse fire and, digging around, I stumbled on the Floren shooting.' He shrugged, forcing his brain to work through a fog of exhaustion. 'I saw some common factors. But based on what we've just seen on the podcast . . .' He tailed off, trying to gather his thoughts.

Three pairs of eyes were fixed on him, and for an uncomfortable half-minute, nobody spoke. Then he saw a flash of spiteful glee in Ghosh's expression and, grateful for the angry spike of adrenaline that look had triggered, Rick began again:

'Floren, Emin, and Quinn have all recently dodged a bullet in legal terms.' He counted them off on his fingers as he went through each: 'Floren, cleared of involvement in the arson attack on his development, Quinn arrested on suspicion of kidnapping and extortion – released without charge. As for Emin – well, basically, Emin's Teflon Man – every case brought against him in the past three years has collapsed.' He stopped. 'I'm not sure if I'm making sense, but this Wolf Pack claims responsibility for the Blackfriars arrests – it must be worth looking at them for the other two, d'you think?'

The agent answered with a neutral tilt of her head.

'And, coming back to Floren – if the assassin *did* find him trussed up in the bath at the show house, ready for the police to bring him into custody, you could see why a vigilante crew wouldn't want to share anything they'd recorded in what turned into a murder scene.'

'Nicely argued,' she said, and Rick felt a surge of relief. 'But there's an awful lot of speculation and what-ifs in there, Sergeant.'

It wasn't said unkindly, and he laughed. 'You're not wrong.' Without looking to Ghosh, he added, 'So, I was thinking maybe SCAS could take a look.' Meaning the Serious Crimes Analysis Section's database.

Her eyebrows went up and she nodded, approving. 'Our analysts could do a deep-dive into the circumstances of the three cases Rick's highlighted, work up a behavioural comparison, see if the stats support the theory.' She looked to Ghosh for his approval; as the senior officer with oversight of all three investigations, he would need to agree the action.

He gave a brief nod.

'You *do* need to bear in mind that if there are other linked offences SCAS *will* fish them out.'

'I am *well* aware how the database works, thank you,' Ghosh said.

'Just warning you,' she persisted, unruffled, 'in the light of what the press is already saying about police incompetence.'

Now it was Ghosh who looked sallow. 'Yes,' he said tiredly, 'I'll talk to Media and Communications.'

As Rick staggered to his feet a minute later, he glanced towards the NCA agent, and maybe he imagined it, but he could have sworn that she dropped him a wink.

Chapter 21

Same day, six p.m.

SAM TURNER sat in a vintage Eames leather chair in the book-lined living room of an apartment in Maida Vale, TV remote in hand and a glass of very good Margaux on the table next to him, while his employees worked around him.

He'd watched the latest episode of *Pandora Unboxed* with great interest, and it seemed that it had alarmed the Met's publicity and PR machine. Since Ms Hahn had released her latest offering, every news bulletin had some pitiable police representative declining to comment on the video, and then announcing that the Met would give their response to the podcast in a press conference at six p.m.

Sam checked his watch: one minute before. He clicked the remote and settled back in his chair, lowering the volume to a murmur, not wanting to disturb the neighbours.

The conference room was filled to capacity and the excitement palpable. That the press and media were kept waiting for only a few minutes was an indication of just how rattled the police were.

Four senior officers, all in full uniform, filed in under a barrage of camera flashes and the wheezing clicks of digital camera shutters. An assistant commissioner, flanked by Detective Superintendent Ghosh and DCI Steiner. Intriguingly, the London Fire Commissioner was the fourth member of the panel. They took their seats at a long table, facing the media.

Neither confirming nor denying Pandora Hahn's claims, the commissioner spoke out against vigilantism, stating the danger that vigilantes were to themselves as well the general public.

'Quite right,' Sam murmured.

Asked about the attempted shooting during the car park arrests, the commissioner said, 'A firearm was discharged that evening. The weapon has been retrieved and is in safe custody. It is a miracle that nobody was seriously hurt in this incident.'

'Is it true that Gary Quinn's fingerprints were on the gun, Commissioner?' a journalist asked.

The commissioner fixed the questioner with an unyielding look. 'As I'm sure you will understand, this is an ongoing investigation. Therefore, I am not at liberty to comment.'

Sam laughed softly. The police hated when criminals gave 'no-comment' interviews, but 'not at liberty to say' was their equivalent.

Another member of the press wanted to know if the van seen crashing into Quinn's car on the recording had been found. The commissioner glanced at Steiner and she said, 'The search is ongoing, and we would ask for the public's support in finding this vehicle, which may contain valuable evidence.' She went on to give them a description of the Ford van, its registration number, and the damage done to it, telling the assembled media that they would find an image in the press pack, then she quoted the hotline number, advising those who preferred to remain anonymous to call Crimestoppers.

Sam shook his head. If these vigilantes were any good – and he believed they were – they would have trashed and torched the vehicle long before they'd released the video to *Pandora Unboxes*. Which was a pity. In truth, he had an interest of his own in the van, recalling that one just like it had been parked on Deptford Waters the night he'd dispatched Jason Floren.

For a few minutes, Sam listened with half an ear as he fielded questions from the team of three, who continued with their work, methodically going from room to room.

He was surprised to hear Ghosh introduce the arson attack at Emin's warehouse into the mix before handing over to the fire commissioner, who described in some detail the deadly poisons that had been released, putting hundreds of lives at risk.

A clamour of questions followed that little gem:

'Did the Wolf Pack set fire to the warehouse?'

'Superintendent, are you confirming that the warehouse was another vigilante attack?'

'Do you accept that communities are taking back control the police have lost over criminality?'

'What do you have to say to the Wolf Pack, Commissioner?'

This question came from the podcaster, Pandora Hahn, and she seemed to be relishing her newfound notoriety.

The commissioner waited them out and when he had the floor again, he repeated his caution on the theme of dangerous interventions.

'British law works on an assumption of innocence and due process with high standards of evidence and legal proof,' he said. 'We at the Met stand by those tenets—' A few groans and even some stifled laughter made him stop. When he continued, he spoke calmly, but his anger was unmistakable in the set of his jaw and the hard edge to his voice.

'Make no mistake, *anyone* who takes the law into their own hands endangers the very legal process they claim to support. They threaten the safety of the public *and* the police. And we *will* prosecute those who break the law, no matter how they try to justify their actions.'

Sam noted the careful use of generalities and avoidance of the Wolf Pack name. But it struck him as wanting your cake and eating it to ignore the pack as an entity while implying that they were responsible for the attack on Emin's drug factory.

An image of the van appeared on the screen, and he laughed, softly. It was the same make and model that had been parked in an out-of-the-way spot on Deptford Waters the night he'd found Floren trussed like a turkey in the show house bath. A Ford Transit van was not in itself distinctive – there must be thousands of them on the streets of London. What convinced him was a patch of dull paintwork above the offside front wheel arch. Judging by the shape of the ghostly imprint, the van had once been adorned with a decal depicting flames. This was no coincidence; it was the same van.

He jotted down the plate number. Interesting that the police made no reference to its presence on the Deptford Waters development. Had the van not been caught on security cameras, or were the police holding back the evidence? Of course, they didn't have the additional information he'd extracted from Floren. He had given the vigilantes a full confession of his involvement in the arson attack that had made him so rich. Had the vigilantes sent his confession to the police? Surely the police wouldn't have supressed such powerful evidence?

It came to him in a moment: Floren's death had been ruled a professional hit – which of course it was. If the vigilantes had released the recording of Floren's confession, they would have risked being accused of the murder, so naturally, they'd withheld it. And even if the Met *had* worked out the Wolf Pack's involvement by now, they would have to admit that they'd overlooked the fact that for some reason Floren's gag had been removed before he was shot. It would be crushingly embarrassing to admit that the same vigilante crew had done their job on *three* occasions. How would that reflect on their 'high standards of evidence and legal proof'?

Normally, such things would be only of passing professional interest to Sam, but the fact that he'd nearly been caught at the scene and had been forced to take an escape route he didn't want to take, made it personal.

He rang a number from one of his burner phones. 'The vigilante crew,' he said. 'What are your thoughts?'

'They seem legit. Didn't touch a penny of the Blackfriars stash.'

'The police seem to think they were involved in Emin's warehouse fire.'

The man at the other end of the line took a moment to ponder. 'An awful lot of valuable drugs did go up in smoke . . .'

'Seems wasteful, doesn't it?' Sam said. 'I'd like to know more. Can we make a few discreet enquiries of our own?'

'D'you want me to tap our police contacts?'

Sam tilted his head. 'I'm not sure they'd be much help. Did you watch the press conference?'

A snort of laughter. 'Red faces all round.'

'See if the locals have information on the fire at Emin's place – the take-down of the Blackfriars crew if you can get it, too.'

'I'll get right onto it. Anything else, Boss?'

Sam would very much like to know why the police had failed to mention the van parked on Floren's waterside development, but there were client confidentiality issues to consider, to say nothing of his own safety if he were to be exposed. So he injected some wry humour into his voice and said, 'Mobile phone footage would be marvellous!'

He ended the call and beckoned to the senior tech who was standing at a respectable distance, waiting for him to finish.

'How is it looking?'

'Clear as crystal.' He handed Sam a tablet.

At first it looked like Sam was staring at himself. Then he tapped an icon and the screen divided into sections – sixteen tiles in all – giving multiple perspectives on each room in the apartment. The tech had not exaggerated – the images were pin-sharp.

'Audio check?' he asked.

'Complete,' the tech said. 'We got audio in every room – including the bathroom.'

'Excellent.'

Sam looked around him at the men carefully clearing up snips of wire, dusting down surfaces, ensuring that any boxes, stray plastic wraps and other detritus were collected.

'Well, it's time we were on our way,' he said, handing his wine glass to one of the crew and getting to his feet.

'Want me to dispose of the bottle, guv?'

Sam replaced the cork in the bottle and tucked it into the backpack at his feet. 'I'll dispose of this myself,' he said with a smile.

Tapping through to the photo gallery on the tablet, he retrieved an image of the room as it had been when they'd entered, then placed the device where they could all refer to it. 'Be sure to leave things exactly as you found them,' he reminded the crew.

Although the apartment was registered as the property of a shell company that Sam himself had set up to shield the real owner, this was the home of his one-time mentor, Theo Lockleigh. His former boss was apparently avoiding his old haunts and had made no contact with his professional acquaintances – at least as far as any of them would admit. Which was to be expected, since Theo had effectively absconded from custody. If all he meant to do was flee the country, Sam might have waved him off and wished him good luck, but Theo Lockleigh was a man to nurture a grudge. He would not leave scores unsettled, and Sam intended to find his old friend and deadly enemy before he could do any lasting damage.

He carefully wiped the TV remote before replacing it on the little side table, then angled the chair just so. One of the techs turned the TV off at the mains.

This done, he glanced at his crew. 'Are we finished?'

A murmur of agreement and nods all around.

'Good.' Sam opened the tiled screen on his tablet, locating a view of the outer hallway and entrance. 'All clear.' He handed off the device, donned a grey fedora, and adjusted the tilt before issuing his final instructions. 'Two at a time, ladies and gentlemen, and tiptoe out on cats' paws – we wouldn't want the neighbours to think they have squatters to worry about.'

Chapter 22

Same day, eight p.m.

'SO NOW THEY'RE CALLING US CRIMINALS.'

Brock reached for a beer from Cap's fridge and handed another to his host.

'Technically, we *are*,' Cap reminded him. 'But this is a knee-jerk reaction. They're scrambling for something – anything – to make it look like they're not complete incompetents.'

'Anyway, I thought you wanted recognition,' Frosty added.

'You know what? I listened *very* hard,' Brock said, falling into snappish sarcasm. 'I didn't hear them say our name even once.'

'The logo was on-screen for the entire clip, Pandora pushed for us, and we're on every news media page across the country,' Frosty countered.

'Hashtag-WolfPack's *blown up* on social media,' Prozac offered. 'They love us!'

'It's nice to be liked,' Cap said gently, not wanting to quash his enthusiasm, 'but this isn't a popularity contest, so let's not get carried away.'

'I'm not saying it is,' Prozac said, looking hurt. 'There's the others – #justice4victims, #consequences4criminals, #cleanupthe-capital, #peoplepower – they're all trending as well.'

'Which is exactly what we want,' Cap soothed.

Mollified, Prozac went back to scrolling on his mobile phone.

'Pandora's doing all right, too,' Frosty said. 'She's at number one on the kickass podcasts hashtag right now. But fame makes people forget the important stuff – are we sure we're still on the same page?'

'I spoke to her an hour ago,' Cap said. 'She says she started *Pandora Unboxes* to hold the criminal justice system to account. Now she feels she has the audience figures to make that happen.'

Frosty nodded, content. 'Same page, same line,' she said, tossing a peanut and catching it with a snap of white teeth.

Pug gazed at her, fascinated. Frosty wasn't the sort of woman to play with her hair or touch her face or neck in unconscious gestures. That had been trained out of her in the army, but every man in the room was aware of her sexual attractiveness. When she noticed Pug blatantly ogling her, she laughed. 'God almighty, you're practically drooling, mate!'

She threw an unopened bag at him, and he caught it one-handed, grinning sheepishly, accepting the slap-down with good humour.

'Pandora has been invited onto LBC Radio, BBC London, and BBC radio 4,' Cap said, bringing them to order. 'And she intends to lead with our shared purpose – ordinary people wanting to feel safe on the streets.'

'She might want to ask why the Met is threatening us, given our "shared purpose".' Brock always managed to quote others' words like they were insincere or, worse, infantile.

'No doubt she will,' Cap said, refusing to rise to the bait. 'But I think we all know they're scared – of us, of our success – and of other people following our example.'

Brock responded with an irritated sneer.

Cap glanced around the room at the rest of his team. Sooner was standing at the end of the kitchen counter, a little apart, calm and silent, as was his habit, but Cap did not doubt that he was watching the others keenly, always ready to act if called upon. Frosty was her cool reserved self, Pug oblivious to most that went on, living in the moment like a kid, while Prozac, who they all thought of as 'the kid', worried about every word he said and suffered agonies over every choice they made.

'While we're on the subject of threat, we shouldn't overlook the risks we face from another quarter,' Cap said.

All except Brock looked at him. 'Making enemies in the police is one thing, but let's face it, disrupting gang activity is a far more dangerous business. So we need to protect our identities even more carefully from now on.'

Nods all round, and the hint of an eyeroll from Brock.

Cap quelled a sigh and said, 'Brock. The van?'

'Crushed. Gone.'

'Prozac, you've got some news for us about Emin?'

The youngest member of the pack put down his phone and sat up straight. 'I think I got a location.' He positively glowed with pride at the gasps of excitement that bit of intel prompted. Emin's home address was too heavily guarded for a direct assault, and they didn't have the resources to watch him twenty-four/seven to try an attack on one of the rare occasions he left the sanctuary of his house, so they'd targeted his work premises instead. And only Prozac had direct access to the police.

'Well, go on, mate,' Pug said. 'Don't keep us in suspenders!'

Brock snorted a laugh, and Pug squinted at him. 'Did I say something funny?'

'It's suspense, Pug,' Frosty said. 'Suspenders are what keep your stockings up.'

Faking confusion this time, Pug said, '*My* stockings – has one of you been spreading rumours?'

'D'you wanna hear this, or not?' Prozac demanded with unusual force, and Pug clamped his mouth shut, bugging his eyes in a comic pantomime of apology.

'Go ahead,' Cap said.

'Old warehouse, back end of Limehouse.'

'How sure are you?' Cap asked.

'Three days ago, I get wind of a big tech surveillance unit job coming up. High high-end kit. It's not really my job anymore, but I had a chat with a mate, and he's talking about this old place, used to be a backstreet garage in Limehouse.'

'What makes you think it's Emin?'

''Cos I'm loitering with intent outside the meeting room where the new gangs task force is having a conflab, and who should walk out at the end, but my old boss at the TSU, and he's talking to Rick Turner – who's working on the Emin case. So I go over to my mate in the canteen on a coffee break—'

'For fuck's *sake*,' Brock interrupted. 'Could you be more obvious?'

'I'm not *stupid* – I didn't ask him straight out,' Prozac said hotly, a red flush spreading from his collar to his cheeks. 'I just said, "Looks like they got Emin's new place sussed out." *He* says, "You working on the Limehouse gig?" and I say, "Reserve list – looks like a tricky one." And 'cos he thinks I'm already in on it, he starts moaning about the narrow road, only one way in, no line of sight from the main road. So I go looking, find it on a commercial estate agent's listing. It's just been let.'

Having given the kid his moment of glory, Cap took over. 'I checked Google Earth,' he said. 'It looks like it'll be hard to keep an eyeball on. But Emin's setting it up as a dark kitchen – Mexican food – and they're advertising for delivery staff.'

'Dream job for you, Pug,' Frosty said.

Missing the teasing tone, Pug said in all sincerity, 'If there's free food on offer, I'm your man.'

'I should say right out of the gate – torching this one will *not* be an option.' Cap picked up a tablet from the counter and showed them a bird's-eye view of the property. The adjacent apartment building would definitely rule out purging the place by fire.

123

As it circulated, he said, 'Other options?'

'Same as we did with the Blackfriars mob,' Brock said. 'Surprise attack when they're off guard.'

'It's high risk,' Sooner said. 'I guess they'd have the kitchen at the front of the building – by the main doors.' He took the tablet from Pug and turned it for them to see. 'There'll be folks in the kitchens who don't know it's a front. And Emin's crew will be heavily armed.'

'They're not gonna serve food *all night*, are they?' Brock said, raising his voice. 'We'll wait till the plebs get sent home, then move in – it's not bloody rocket science!'

'Okay, okay,' Cap said. 'We'll decide strategy when we've got intel on the layout, staffing and open hours – agreed?'

There were no dissenters, and he turned again to Prozac. 'Could you get any more out of your mate, maybe?'

'Not without making it obvious I'm *not* on the surveillance team.'

'What about Turner?'

Prozac grimaced. 'He's not exactly the chatty type.' He paused, frowning. 'He *was* asking about the Deptford fire, though.'

'When was this?' Brock cut in.

'Yesterday.'

'And you said nothing?'

'There's nothing *to* tell,' Prozac said, on the defensive. 'I offered to give him some gen – only as a way in – you know, to gain his confidence,' he added anxiously. 'But he wasn't interested. Said he wanted someone who was there when it happened.'

Cap and Frosty exchanged a look. They were the only two in the pack who'd actually been there as the buildings burned. As emergency responders, their names would be on work rotas, and they didn't need that kind of attention.

'Did he say why he was asking?' Cap said.

'Not *him*,' Prozac scoffed. 'But I *did* hear he got his arse kicked for it.'

'Why?'

Prozac shrugged. 'Poking his nose in, I suppose. The case is closed.'

'But he *has* been warned off?'

'Was practically limping when he came out of the boss's office, according to my source.'

Cap looked at Frosty and she tilted her head, 'It could be worse.' Switching her attention to Prozac, she added, 'Ear to the ground, kid.'

He nodded eagerly. 'Always, Frosty.'

'Oh, well, that's a relief. Can we get back to the Emin situation, now?' Brock demanded.

'As I pointed out, we need to know the layout,' Cap said.

'Maybe it isn't such a bad idea to get someone inside as a delivery rider,' Frosty chimed in.

Pug shot his hand up to volunteer.

'So, we're just gonna sit on our hands, like the police?' Brock shot a look at Prozac as if it was his fault. 'How long did they sit around doing fuck all about his last warehouse?' Prozac opened his mouth to answer, but Brock cut him off. 'And how many more people were harmed as a result?'

Cap stepped in. 'If we move in too early—'

'I'm not *saying* that, am I? Just that we move on him before he gets too bedded in. Show the public how easy it is for a snake like Emin to be up and running after a setback. I mean how long's it been since we torched the other place? Not much more than a week. We need to show the public, the police, *and* the Emins of this world that we won't let up till they stop.'

It was a rousing speech, and Cap had to admit to being halfway persuaded himself. He looked to Frosty, her military experience giving her the best overview in evaluating the potential risks of a tactical assault.

'They'd probably be less heavily armed, if they're not up to full speed,' she said. 'But we'd need entry and exit points, knowledge of anyone watching the street corners and the alleyway, opening hours, likely personnel – that kind of stuff.'

'Looks like I'm up, then,' Pug said, grinning. He ran his gym and boxing ring on a relaxed schedule, and since losing two of his rising stars to the Deptford fire, he'd cut back on training kids for competition, so his hours were as flexible as he decided to make them.

Cap asked everyone in turn, and they were all in, even Sooner – with the proviso that they did the groundwork.

Cap gave the go-ahead to Pug, and arranged for a training session for the full pack. He was about to wrap up, but Prozac looked like he wanted to add something, only he'd turned shy again.

'Go ahead, kid,' Cap encouraged.

'I was thinking – what Brock said about the police – calling us criminals, not giving us any credit. They can't ignore us if we livestream, can they?'

'Livestream from where?'

'I could link our bodycams to a website – I can set one up, easy – or I could livestream from Pandora's site. People'll see what we do as we do it.'

Cap shook his head, doubtful. 'It's risky – what if things go sideways?'

'We lock the viewers out – I could set it up as a single keystroke.'

Cap began to shake his head, but Brock spoke up – unexpectedly in Prozac's favour: 'We could've claimed Emin's old drug factory if we'd livestreamed, sent the link to the right people.'

'Floren as well,' Prozac said, and there was a murmur of agreement from the others.

Jason Floren had been their first joint venture, and it rankled every one of them that they hadn't been able to take his confession to the police.

'It's worth thinking about,' Cap said at last.

Chapter 23

A few days later

AS THE DARK KITCHEN BEGAN MAKING DELIVERIES, the real business behind it seemed to grind to a halt. Rick had fallen into a dull routine of twelve- or fourteen-hour shifts, reporting back at early-morning briefings, then crawling home to bed. New faces had begun to appear at the big roller door onto the backstreet, queuing outside before being taken inside one at a time. Rick photographed and video-recorded the delivery riders, who would be later identified by their moped and scooter registrations. Security was provided by known members of Emin's crew and although they were careful not to show it, every one of them was armed.

According to covert surveillance cameras inside the building, the length of the warehouse had been divided into three sections using quick-install panelling – kitchen with toilet facilities, office, and behind that, the drugs production line. The delivery guys were a small team – just five, so far – and they weren't allowed past the waiting area to the right of the kitchen.

The fact that Emin had thrown a lot of money into the set-up suggested that he intended to stay for the long haul – and that he expected to earn his investment back fast.

For now, though, all was quiet. Emin's second in command had not been near the warehouse since that first day, and the vans, colourfully branded with dancing burritos, seemed to be parked up outside the building more often than not. The delivery guys weren't exactly busy, either, although the NCA's surveillance cams inside the building recorded small quantities of drugs being packaged as food-to-go. Rick wondered if any of the riders knew what they were really carrying in their delivery bags – the NCA's surveillance crews had already logged one of them turning up at Emin's temporary home on three separate occasions.

Heading into Hammersmith Police Station after another uneventful night, Rick could barely keep his eyes open.

Then he saw the Border Force representative walk to the front of the room. The man looked calm, but there was an underlying tension and excitement in his carefully controlled demeanour and Rick felt an answering burst of adrenaline.

'We've had word from Interpol that a large consignment of heroin and cocaine is due to enter Dover Cargo Terminal imminently. Now, the UK delivery point is unknown, but they have good intel that it will be shipped onward from Dover through the London ports.'

'This could be it,' Ghosh said, the gleam of ambition unmistakable in his eyes.

Border Force, the Met's OCG Task Force, the NCA and Dover Police were immediately placed on high alert, and the Marine Policing Unit would be called on if the cargo was sent onward by boat. The multi-agency task force would coordinate resources to provide river and road surveillance, with the option of fixed-wing aircraft or helicopter eyes in the sky as needed.

Rick had driven to the station the afternoon before his shift started, so he picked up his car from the basement car park and began the short journey home, his mind abuzz with what might come next. He checked his rear-view frequently from habit and sensed, rather than saw, that he was being followed.

Extreme tiredness had given sounds and colours an unnatural sharpness on this spring morning, and at first, he dismissed the feeling as paranoia brought on by sleep deprivation. Still, the grey Audi two cars behind did seem to be hanging back – maybe even using the Hackney cab it was tailgating as cover – and it wouldn't do any harm to be sure.

On the approach to Putney Bridge, Rick made a cheeky lane change, darting left onto the New Kings Road. Its shallow curve exposed the Audi following after. Doubling back on himself, Rick took a couple more left turns into Fulham district's maze of narrow streets. His shadow slid into a parking space, allowing a van to overtake and shield him from view, but Rick caught him pulling out again.

Turning right at the next opportunity, Rick used his indicator to give the Audi plenty of warning, but once in the street, he made a fast three-point turn. Slowed by the van, the Audi accelerated into the side street, and found himself nose-to-nose with Rick's car.

Panicked, the driver slammed into reverse, engine screaming, backing up wildly the way he'd come.

A squeal of brakes and a shout of alarm.

Jesus, did he hit someone?

Rick pulled up to the junction and saw a cyclist sprawled in the road to his left. Reaching for his phone even as he flicked on the hazards, Rick tore out of his car, dialling triple nine and calling for an ambulance. As he crouched beside the cyclist, the Audi accelerated away.

Chapter 24

Forty hours later

TWO A.M. AND THE FOOD DELIVERY RIDERS WERE LONG GONE, the warehouse roller shutter firmly closed, and the access road had been silent for well over an hour. Even so, Rick felt as if a static charge was building inside him – like at any moment his skin would crackle and begin to spark electricity.

Intel had come in early the previous morning – Emin's drugs consignment was being shipped in a blue twenty-foot refrigerated container en route from Turkey. Emin had criminal interests in the UK, Turkey and across half of Europe, dealing in Turkish heroin and South American cocaine, and the consensus was that this shipment would carry both. Interpol's intel was that the drugs were not secreted in the imported goods but packed into compartments in the walls – apparently these so-called 'reefer' containers were popular with smugglers because of the extra space they offered inside the refrigeration units. The last Rick heard, the container had been transferred at Dover Cargo Terminal to a smaller vessel that had spent the day chugging around the Kent coast towards the Thames estuary.

Rick bent to retrieve a flask of stale coffee and a sandwich he'd picked up from a Sainsbury's local store on his tortuous journey in. The Audi driver who'd been tailing him still hadn't been identified, and he was taking no chances. He'd checked on the injured cyclist and learned that he'd been moved from ICU, but would be in hospital for some time.

The boat carrying the contraband had a scheduled stop at Gallions Reach in Woolwich, where Border Control expected the container would be offloaded onto a truck. Rick checked his watch: five more hours on his shift. He just hoped that whatever happened, he'd be around to see it.

Meal finished, he stood to stretch his legs. At that instant, the warehouse's roller shutter began to crank up. Four men ducked under the slowly rising door and strode to two box vans parked in the bay reserved for the warehouse. A fifth man appeared at the end of the alley – one of the lookouts who seemed to be present twenty-four/seven. He directed the reversing vans out onto the main road. Were they on their way to collect the shipment, or making way for a larger vehicle to park?

Zapping off a few images, Rick reported the activity via the Airwave network, knowing that the partner agencies in the operation would hear it, along with his Met Police colleagues.

Fifteen minutes later, he got a shout from the team watching the alleyway entrance – the vans had just passed them on the way back. Thankfully, Emin's lookouts had remained oblivious that they themselves were being watched.

Rick got ready to activate the videocam as a message came through that Emin had mobilised his forces. Two cars, each with three men – one of them his second in command – had set off from his temporary address in Dalston, heading south-east towards Docklands, likely en route to meet the cargo.

Rick focused on the two vans thirty-odd feet below him. They reversed into the bay and the driver's mate jumped down to open the doors. Rick's view was partly blocked by the vehicles, but he did get a few good shots of older women and teenaged boys being hustled inside. They looked frightened and disorientated – probably lower-echelon workers who would be tasked with splitting, weighing and packaging the drugs ready for sale or for dispersal.

He made a call, stating the number of people – twenty-five at his count. The vans left immediately – only the drivers this time – the other two went inside and the door rolled shut.

Twenty minutes on, surveillance reported that the two cars dispatched from Emin's bolthole had turned left, heading east towards Woolwich. It was looking more certain that they were on their way to escort the drugs shipment.

At four-thirty a.m., news came in that the boat had docked, and the container loaded onto a six-wheel trailer. The two cars Emin had sent were driving in convoy, one in front of the transporter, the other behind.

The plan would be to intercept the lorry on a sparsely populated industrial stretch of the A12 – not wanting to risk a gun battle on the streets of Limehouse. There were a few options where the roadway dipped into cuttings – effectively concrete canyons below the level of houses and apartment blocks – on the first leg of the journey from the docks. But they would need to coordinate the shipment take-down with the raid on Emin's new warehouse. Rick knew that armed units were close by, waiting for the order. Success or failure would hang on those units neutralising the threat from Emin's lookouts at either end of the alley before they could warn the men inside the building.

He couldn't rest, but he couldn't pace either, for fear of waking the residents sleeping in the first-floor flat beneath him, so he stood a short distance from the window, controlling his breathing and watching for any glimmer of light, any flicker of movement in the backstreet.

A sudden voice through his comms earpiece jolted him and he laughed softly at his attack of nerves. *Too much caffeine, too little sleep.*

A short, tense message from the team watching Emin's house in Dalston said that Emin himself had left with two guards in tow, heading south towards Limehouse, riding in a black Mercedes SUV with tinted windows. Rick made a note of the registration. It seemed that Emin wanted to be on site when the lorry arrived. At this time of the morning, he would get to the warehouse at just about the time the drugs convoy was expected. This shipment must mean a lot to him. As a rule, Emin kept his hands clean, delegating the dirty end of his business to trusted envoys, yet in the space of ten days he'd appeared in public talking to a major supplier, and now he was on his way to a warehouse with drugs already on-site – and a container-load more about to land on its doorstep. Bold risks – the actions of a desperate man. And although Rick hated to admit it, they probably had the Wolf Pack to thank for that.

The operational commander of armed interceptor teams chimed in that they were approaching one of the preferred take-down locations and traffic conditions were good, but Ghosh told them to wait which, as designated 'silver' level tactical commander on the operation, he was entitled to do. But he sounded tetchy, and that was not a good sign.

Five minutes later, the operational commander called in as they neared the second take-down point and Ghosh instructed him to keep his distance till the next, more dangerous location. He began to protest, but Superintendent Ghosh cut him off. 'We have a developing situation, here,' he snapped. 'You still have two more options. Stand by.'

While Ghosh had the authority to override the ops commander, he should be taking his lead from the officers who could see conditions on the ground. Rick groaned inwardly. He had the sinking feeling that his boss might delay the take-down till Emin was inside the drug factory.

Big mistake, Rick. A bird in the hand as they say . . .

The phantom voice of his older brother hadn't spoken up

for days, and Rick was surprised that Sam's steadying tone, half-mocking, half-chiding, had a soothing effect that he was grateful for.

'Yep,' he murmured. That decision could definitely turn around and bite Ghosh on the arse, but second-guessing the motivations of senior officers wasn't going to help the situation, so he stood by the videocam and kept his mouth shut.

Emin's SUV drove into the alleyway ten minutes later; they must've sailed through every traffic light on the route. There was still no order to stop the lorry, though, and watching Emin and his bodyguards disappear inside the building, Rick felt another moment of anxiety. He advised that the rollers had been left up.

A squawk of surprise on the comms, then the team watching the pedestrian end of the backstreet called in, demanding, 'Are we a go?'

Ghosh's voice blasted through Rick's earpiece: 'Negative! That's a negative, Tac-Two, you are *not* cleared to go. Please acknowledge.'

Puzzled, Rick drew closer to the window than he would normally dare, and immediately saw the cause of alarm. Identifying himself, he spoke into his radio: 'I see four – correction – five figures in tactical gear coming down the pedestrian access at the end of the street.'

Tac-Two confirmed his sighting, adding that they couldn't see Emin's lookout who was normally stationed at the narrow entryway.

Rick activated the videocam, but the tech unit guys hadn't set up a camera for the alley, so it wouldn't catch the assault team on camera until they were virtually at the entrance to the warehouse.

Ghosh repeated his order for Tac-Two to stay in place, then ordered the five to identify themselves.

No response.

He instructed all sections to acknowledge their position and report their status.

Meanwhile, the five unidentified figures continued at a crouch down the narrowest section of the alley.

Rick's first thought was, *These guys are textbook.* And when they didn't respond, *Jeez, tell me the Drugs Gangs Unit hasn't been kept in the dark about this operation!*

Tac-One reported that they were at their designated position. There was no movement at their end of the street, but a white van had drawn up half a block away. They were told to wait.

Time was wasting.

Rick saw that the five were carrying something. *Weapons?* Although the sky was beginning to lighten, the alley was still too dark to say for sure. Cursing softly, he snatched one of the still cameras from its tripod as the five figures split, three and two, either side of the walled space. His hands rock-steady now, Rick zoomed in on the tactical team and reeled off a few images.

Oh, hell . . .

He interrupted Ghosh's check of the units with an 'urgent' call.

'I have eyeball,' he said. 'I repeat, subjects are armed. Stand by.' He focused in on the weapons. 'Subjects carrying sub-machine guns. Possibly HK MP-fives, over.'

By now they were at the corner of the building. One of the five glanced up, and Rick saw that the front of his helmet was slightly lighter in colour.

What is that? A transfer or decal of some kind? Impossible to say from a distance of thirty feet or more.

He drew his elbows in to his sides to steady the shot and zoomed in, catching it perfectly.

Rick hit the emergency button on his radio, giving his call sign. 'It's the Wolf Pack. I repeat, the armed assault team is the Wolf Pack!'

Chapter 25

WHAT FOLLOWED, HAPPENED IN A CONFUSION of radio commands, counter-commands, and comms crosstalk.

The operational commander took the initiative and ordered his interceptor teams to force the drugs consignment to a halt. Ghosh tried to countermand. Rick watched as the armed personnel entered the unlit kitchen area of the warehouse. Seconds later, he heard the *crack, crack, crack!* of semiautomatic fire inside the building.

He hit the urgent button a second time. 'Shots fired!' he yelled. 'Please advise!'

He flung one of the windows open to better gauge what was going on, heard answering fire, and ducked instinctively. He was armed but couldn't risk using his weapon with so many civilians in close proximity.

Two unmarked police vehicles pulled across the end of the access road. A white van pulled in behind them, then screamed away, engine labouring in low gear. The steel door from the warehouse opened and four figures ran out.

Rick reported it and reeled off a few more snaps. Simultaneously, shouts from the pedestrianised end of the backstreet – police bellowing orders. Two shots rang out, followed by 'Officer down! Officer down!'

The warehouse shutter squealed, beginning to close, as two of Emin's men – armed and with murder in their eyes – ran out, shoving two of the female drugs packers ahead of them. The back of the first man's head exploded in a spray of blood and brain matter. He fell, taking a hostage with him, revealing one of the Wolf Pack, gun still aimed.

'Armed police!' Rick yelled through the open window. 'This is a POLICE OPERATION. Wolf Pack. Abort! ABORT MISSION!'

The militiaman lowered his carbine as the surviving hostage-taker swung his pistol towards Rick.

A loud bang – maybe two – and Rick felt a white-hot burn above his left eye; the next thing he knew, he was on the floor. He brought his hand to his eye and wiped away blood. He tried to get to his feet, but his legs wouldn't support him, and he ended up on the floor again. After that, boots on the ground, a lot of yelling. Sirens.

He must have passed out because it went quiet for a second. Then more yelling, the flicker of emergency lights. Sirens at both ends of the backstreet now. The sound of heavy boots in the corridor outside. A splintering crash – someone had kicked in the apartment door.

Rick's hand went to his gun, then he heard the roar of 'ARMED POLICE!'

The team knew that there was armed police surveillance in the apartment building, but adrenaline and gunfire did strange things to a person's reasoning, and Rick – armed and out of uniform – knew he might be seen as a threat. He raised his hands and waited, praying that whoever came through the door wasn't stoked enough to shoot him at first sight of the gun on his hip.

First through was built like a bull – huge shoulders, massive head, accentuated by his helmet and goggles.

'I'm job,' he said weakly. 'DS Rick Turner. My ID's in my—'

'DO NOT MOVE!' the man screamed.

'Okay, *okay*,' he said. 'Just don't shoot me.'

'I SAID STAY STILL!'

'I *am*,' Rick protested.

The next figure was shorter, bulky in their tac gear. A woman. She raised her voice. 'Stand down, Officer. He is who he says he is.'

Rick squinted at her, but he kept losing focus, and she seemed to understand, because she removed her helmet. It was the senior NCA agent, and he was suddenly embarrassed that he hadn't troubled to commit her name to memory.

She crouched beside him and checked his wound. 'He's in shock, possibly concussed. We need a medic.' She didn't bother to turn to the bull-headed man, but he spoke into his radio.

'You'll be okay,' she said. 'Can you sit up? Or are you comfy there?'

Rick tried hard to concentrate and realised that he'd slumped to one side.

'Give us a hand,' he said, and she helped him upright.

'Shit.' He began to struggle. 'Guns. I saw . . .'

'It's okay,' she said.

'No!' he tried to shove her away. 'People inside – weapons.' He couldn't get the words out and couldn't understand why. He tried to stand, but his legs turned to rubber and a sharp, sickening pain blasted through his temple.

Rick raised a hand to his head, and she grasped his wrist. 'Don't.'

He stared at her, seeing for the first time that there was blood on her hands and a shining slick of it on her tac gear.

'You're injured,' he gasped, feeling almost feverish. He had to get her help.

'It's not my blood,' she said. 'Listen to me. You've been shot. You need to stay calm – help is on the way.'

Suddenly overwhelmed by a wave of exhaustion, he said, ''Kay. Tired . . .' He felt his eyes begin to close.

'No-no-no! Stay awake.' He felt her fingers dig into his shoulders. 'Rick? Sergeant Turner – OPEN YOUR EYES.'

She was shouting and it hurt his head, so he made an effort, just to shut her up, and saw her face blur as she turned to the door.

The last thing he heard was her yelling, 'Where the *hell* is that medic?'

Chapter 26

SAM TURNER WAS ENJOYING AN EARLY BREAKFAST in his room at a pleasant hotel in Mayfair. His phone buzzed and, checking the screen, he saw that it was the message he'd been waiting for. Setting aside his plate, he slid his laptop across the table and opened a VPN before logging into a private chat-room. Two video clips were ready for him to download. While he watched the first, he rang his employee on his current very old-tech, basic-as-a-brick burner phone.

The shaky footage showed smoke pouring out of a crumbling industrial building.

'This is Emin's old factory?' Sam said.

'Captured two weeks ago on a mobile phone just minutes after the fire was set. The popular theory is the call to emergency services was made by whoever set the fire.'

The youth who'd filmed the video kept up a commentary, laughing and swearing as he swept the camera wildly right and left. Judging by the perspective, he must have been on the first or second floor of a building at the edge of an expanse of dark wasteland that lay between him and the burning structure. Figures streamed from the direction of the building across the uneven ground, crying out, stumbling, helping others up, running on.

A sudden flash was followed by an excited cry of 'Oh, my days!' and the image became distorted with blocky pixels of coloured light.

A moment later, sirens broke into the commentator's exclamations and a fire engine raced across the rough ground towards the building.

Noting the swirl of colours that came and went above the blaze, Sam said, 'They burned everything?'

'Tried to, according to sources.'

Interesting decision. 'Is the other recording any better?' he asked, beginning the second download.

'Much the same – but they started filming later. We didn't find anyone with footage before the fire broke out.'

Sam began watching the new offering. The factory was well ablaze in this clip, but whoever had filmed it had a steadier hand and a keener eye for detail, and Sam caught exactly what he'd been hoping to see about one minute in.

'This is perfect,' he said.

'Okay, Boss, as long as you're happy.' The voice at the other end of the line sounded puzzled, and Sam did not enlighten him.

He had, in fact, spotted a Ford van parked on an access road close to the amateur cinematographer's vantage point, some fifty metres from the burning building. The van's lights were off, and the meagre street lighting in the social housing complex was not good enough to gauge the colour, but it was certainly dark, and possibly blue. And there was no question about the registration plate. This was the van used by the vigilantes during the bank robbers' arrests – in all probability the same van he'd seen parked on the Deptford Waters development the night he'd shot Jason Floren. Sam experienced the satisfying glow of having a hunch prove right.

He let the video run, and his eye snagged at a familiar silhouette on the edge of the police cordon. It was Rick.

'Did our budding Spielberg share this with anyone?'

'TikTok.' Sam heard the disdain in his employee's voice. 'Just the first thirty seconds.'

That was helpful. Sam would like a few words in private with these vigilantes – not from any altruistic drive to prevent future harm – for Sam, the drive for self-preservation was always paramount. This fact-finding mission was entirely geared towards reducing the risks to Sam himself – to avoid a 'next time' scenario in which these self-styled 'gangbusters' posed a threat to him. Sam wasn't a gambling man; he believed in probability, and if his luck failed, he could end up in custody, or dead. And if the police remained ignorant of this recording, it would give him more time to locate the pack.

'Have them take the video down – and I'd like the phone, too.' He experienced a slight pang that he would be destroying footage that could prove helpful to his brother. But the Wolf Pack had already jeopardised his safety the night of the Floren hit, and his survival trumped Rick's career advancement. The sooner he found the vigilantes, the better.

Ending the call, Sam's next task was to ring a computer expert he had recently hired as a consultant. This was Dave Collins, a Serious Fraud Office finance investigator. Collins had no truck with texts or emails – they were what he called 'breadcrumbs' – and he'd followed too many of those trails and caught too many criminals in his role as a forensic accountant to take chances in that respect. Dave's computer skills and forensic accountancy genius had been crucial to Rick and Sam's success against very long odds last autumn.

Sam rang him, burner to burner.

'What d'you want? I'm in work!'

Sam lacked the emotional capacity to feel terror, but he knew it when he heard it in others, and he'd learned that this tech genius was constantly teetering on the edge of panic. He also knew that the big man preferred to work at night to avoid the beeps, clicks, chirrups, movement and chatter and that distressed him during normal work hours. At night, his workplace was dimly lit and blessedly quiet, and the frightening prospect of having to converse with colleagues was reduced to a minimum.

Sam checked his watch: it was coming up to six a.m.

'In the few minutes it takes you to reach the security gate, it'll be time to clock out,' he said, keeping his tone reassuring, not wanting to rattle the man further.

'I'll call you back.' The tech ended the call.

Sam stared at the phone in astonishment for a moment; those who knew him by reputation did not often hang up on him. But he shook his head and smiled, pouring a fresh cup of coffee and helping himself to a delightfully crisp and light croissant from the selection of pastries on offer while he waited.

It was seven minutes before Dave called back, and Sam surmised that he'd sought out a noisy corner in order to thwart nefarious attempts by unspecified organisations to listen in to their chat.

'Sorry I was rude. But you scared me.'

Sam apologised in return, hearing the misery of constant anxiety in Dave's voice.

'So, what did you want?' Dave asked.

'I'd like you to search for anything that looks like a non-lethal professional hit in the London boroughs over the last twelve months – and set up alerts to catch anything new as it occurs.'

'Okay.'

Sam didn't speak into the pause that followed, understanding that the big man needed time to process information and formulate questions without distraction.

'What does a professional hit look like?'

Sam reminded himself that the man he called his 'armchair ninja' didn't live in a world of inference and lateral thinking. His was a concrete, logical world of numbers, algorithms and absolutes. So he compiled an ad hoc checklist beginning with criminals as the targets. He included the efficient use of firearms and/or knives with minimal injuries or mess and few, if any, civilian injuries.

'I'm particularly interested in incidents where security cameras, alarms, recording equipment or other tech was disabled.'

'Like the Wolf Pack thing?'

'*Exactly* like the Wolf Pack thing,' Sam said.

The silence at the end of the line told him that his patterns expert had not yet decided to accept the commission.

'If you have any concerns, it's best you just tell me,' Sam said.

'You want me to find the Wolf Pack.'

'No, I want you to find incidents they were involved in.'

'You know I don't like breaking the rules, but they're trying to help people – they're not the bad guys.'

Sam wasn't really qualified to judge others on their morals, but he gave a neutral 'Um-hm' of encouragement.

'I don't want them to get into trouble because of something I do – I mean, what if they're the ones who got hurt in the first place?'

'You mean like *Daredevil*, or *Spider-Man*?'

'Don't make fun of me.'

'I'm not,' Sam said and meant it. 'I'm just trying to understand.'

He heard a long breath at the other end of the line – a release of tension. 'I was thinking more like *The Equalizer* or *The Punisher* – you know, not superheroes – real people who got hurt and just decided to fight back. What if they're like that?'

'What if they are?'

'I don't want them to get hurt again.'

'I promise you,' Sam said, 'I'll use the information you give me to save lives.'

It wasn't a lie: Sam's life might well be saved by having the information his expert was so uniquely equipped to ferret out, and he had no interest in punishing people for standing up for themselves. Those who'd suffered would be left in peace.

After a few more seconds, his tech ninja said, 'All right, I'll do it.'

'Good man!' Sam paused. 'One more thing – this has to be *completely* under the radar—' An odd chittering cut off his next words, and it took Sam a few moments to understand that he was hearing the unfamiliar sound of laughter from his techie.

'Under the radar is for amateurs, mate,' the big man said. 'It'll be like I wasn't even there.'

Signing off, Sam received an alert of his own. For many years, and from a discreet distance, he'd kept watch over his younger brother, and although they'd reconnected the previous autumn, Sam had found the habit impossible to break. Rick was investigating Emin, and Emin was back in the news, it seemed.

Sam opened the link from the alert and saw a mobile phone recording of Rick being wheeled into a hospital on a stretcher. The skin at the base of his skull prickled and Sam felt a stab of pain just below his heart. A paramedic was holding a bloodied pad of gauze over his brother's left eye, and Rick wasn't moving.

Chapter 27

RICK WAS FLOATING, SPINNING, ACTUALLY RELAXED for the first time in weeks.

Watching from the back window of his house, he saw five operatives in full assault gear, armed with semiautomatics. heading towards the side entrance gate. A surge of raw adrenaline set his pulse racing.

No. That's not right. They're in the alley – Emin's warehouse. You have to stop them – you have to tell the tac teams!

Noise billowed in and out, like the toll of a bell buffeted on the wind. He tried to make sense of the sounds: raised voices, beeps and clicks. Sirens.

They already know.

A whiff of chemicals. *Did they set fire to the place?*

Wait, no – that was two weeks ago – the other warehouse. This is Emin's new place. *Jesus, Rick, you're dreaming. You fell asleep on duty! Wake up!*

He balled his right fist and hit his leg, hard. The spinning became a violent rocking, and he began to fall.

A hard jolt.

Fully awake now, he opened his eyes. *So bright!* He reached to his hip for his gun.

No gun.

'Relax. It's okay . . .'

The sirens faded, distorted, and the beeping got louder, faster. Someone grabbed his hand.

Rick twisted his wrist and flicked, breaking the grip, forcing the restraining hand up and away.

'Hey, come on now . . .'

The light was blinding, and he screwed his eyes shut.

'*Sergeant Turner* – you're okay!'

'Gun!' Rick yelled, but his voice was weak, and he could barely hear himself. He tried to rise – the window – he had to get to the window. 'They have to stand down!' He coughed.

'*You* stand down, soldier.' A woman's voice, amused.

Exhausted, he sank back, panting.

The beeping subsided as he became calmer, and he willed his eyes to open.

'There you are!' Her tone was welcoming like he was a long-awaited guest who'd shown up at the last minute.

He began to form a question in his head, but she got there before him.

'You're in the hospital.'

The room was still spinning, but it was coming into focus now and Rick began to make sense of his surroundings. He was in a bay – one of many by the sound of what was going on around him – screened on three sides.

'A and E?' he asked.

'Bingo.'

The woman was still a blur, so he gave up on her and explored his arms and chest with his fingertips, discovering he was in a hospital gown, and there were wires trailing from him to a monitor on his right.

'How did I get here?'

'The usual way,' she said.

'But I was in Lime—' He stopped, remembering that the operation was supposed to be covert. 'I *wasn't* here.'

147

'And now you are.' She starred her hands, abracadabra-style. 'Ta-dah!'

'Hilarious,' he said. 'I need to know what happened between *there* and *here*. Did I pass out?'

'More like *blissed* out – just for a bit,' she reassured him. 'We needed to give you a CT scan and you were fighting the radiographer.'

'Oh, shit, I don't remember – is he okay?'

'*She's* fine, Mister Machismo. And so are you. No cranial damage and no signs of concussion *pro tem*.'

'Why don't I remember?'

'The sedative we gave you can cause mild amnesia.'

Rick groaned, plucking at the wires taped to his chest, and she said, 'Whoa!'

'You don't get it,' he said. 'I need to remember *everything*. My boss is gonna want to know what happened back there, and I feel like my brain's been shaken like a medicine bottle.'

'Well, your boss isn't in charge here – I am,' she said.

Rick really wanted to focus on the woman's face, she had such a nice voice.

'Well, thank you,' she said.

'Oh, God, did I say that out loud?'

'Yup. But technically, you're off your face right now, so I won't take it personally.'

What is she, a senior nurse?

'How about a doctor – sexist?' she demanded.

'Oh, f— I did it again, didn't I?'

She chuckled, 'I'm kidding. Senior Charge Nurse Verren,' she said, tapping her name badge.

The events of the last hour came back in a rush. Rick remembered hearing that first shot, the shout of 'Officer down!' and his heart picked up pace.

'Whoa, what just happened?' she said peering at the monitor next to his bed.

'Are they all right?' he asked.

'Who – the radiographer?'

Rick tried again. 'Someone was shot.'

'Yeah, genius, you were.'

'No, I mean . . .' His thoughts kept slipping away.

The nurse bent to look into his eyes. 'I'm going to check your pupil response rates, okay?' Then: 'Look straight ahead. Ready? Bright light.'

A flash of intense pain, and Rick flinched, holding his hand up. 'What are you *doing*?'

She lowered the pencil-thin torch. 'Checking for concussion.'

'You just said I wasn't concussed.'

'I said *pro tem*,' she said. 'Slow pupil response points to concussion – so does photophobia. Okay?'

He lowered his hand. 'Okay, but it hurts.'

'Noted. And I'll be quick.'

He winced as she shone the light, left, then moved it in a semicircle across his field of vision. Finally, she turned off the torch and slipped it into her pocket before picking up the chart at the end of his trolley to add a note.

'See, I'm fine,' Rick said.

She replied with a noncommittal 'Hm.'

'What I meant was—' He licked his lips. Hell, it was probably all over the news anyway, he might as well just say it. 'I heard someone shout "officer down". Did they bring him here? Is he okay?'

'Oh.' Suddenly he saw her clearly – brown hair scraped back and gelled severely in place, full lips, blue eyes. A look on her pale, oval face that he'd seen scores of times as a cop – stricken but trying to be professional. 'Oh, Sergeant . . .' She seemed to collect herself, straightened up, and began again. 'I'm sorry, I can't discuss other patients with you.'

'It's bad, isn't it?' He struggled fully upright to take a look around, hoping to see someone he knew.

'Like I said—'

'I've got to know,' he said, swinging his legs to the left of the trolley and coming up against a drip stand. A blood bag hung from it, and he realised for the first time that he was attached to it.

'What's this for?'

'It's blood. What d'you think it's for?'

She held both hands up, surrendering under his withering look. 'All right. Full facts, no gloss. The bullet grazed your forehead and skipped off your big bony brow. Now, while it doesn't seem to've caused any significant damage in here—' she tapped her temple '—it did slice off a chunk of skin.'

He brought his fingers up to his forehead and felt a pad of gauze and tape.

'And I hate to break this to you, Sergeant, but you're a bit of a bleeder,' she finished.

He offered a weak smile. 'You're not the first to say it.'

'*That*, I can believe. So, if you don't mind, we'll finish topping you up before you ride bare-arsed into the sunset – 'kay?'

He hesitated, felt around the back of his gown and pulled it closed over his exposed parts. 'Right, good plan.'

She grinned, helping him back onto the trolley.

As he settled against the pillows, Rick heard a scuffle of noise further down the line.

Then: 'Where the hell is he?'

Detective Superintendent Ghosh appeared in the bay a moment later and Rick shut his eyes, building his strength for what was coming.

'And who might you be?' the nurse demanded.

'I'm his boss.' Rick was glad he couldn't see the look on Ghosh's face.

'Good to know,' she said. 'I am Senior Charge Nurse Verren, and this is a restricted area.'

'I don't care if you're Florence bloody Nightingale – I need a word with him. Police business.'

'Sergeant Turner, are you all right with this?' Rick looked at her. She seemed ready to wrestle Ghosh to the ground if she had to.

Rick nodded, a wave of sickness washing over him, seeing the fury in Ghosh's face.

Without looking at her, Ghosh repeated, '*Police* business.'

She looked him up and down before quietly walking away.

'You had one job,' Ghosh said. 'Surveillance.'

'I was doing my job,' Rick said. 'I was in the best position to see what was going on, and I conveyed urgent intel, per protocol.'

'This isn't about you interrupting my trans*mission*,' Ghosh hissed, then lowered his voice to a hoarse whisper. 'You gave an order to those cowboys!'

'What? No—'

'"Abort! ABORT MISSION!" You even *named* them. Which makes me wonder if you know more than you've admitted to.'

'N-no,' Rick stammered, and the monitor registered a spike in his heart rate. 'The logo was in the footage they gave to the podcaster – the one about the Blackfriars mob arrests.'

Take it easy, Rick. He's more pissed off with himself than he is with you. His brother's phantom voice spoke as clearly as if he'd been sitting next to him. *He's just desperate to minimise his own role in the fuck-up.* Rick felt the sickness drain away, and his heart settled into its normal rhythm. He spoke with professional detachment, careful not to let his cold, hard dislike of the superintendent show.

'Two armed men dragged two terrified civilians out of the front entrance to the warehouse. Two militias followed – also armed. One member of the militia shoots a hostage-taker. Stands to reason the other's gonna return fire.' He realised he'd slipped into present tense, images of the hostages flashing across his vision, and took a moment to steady himself. 'I was on the second floor of an apartment building housing a dozen families – I had to try *something*.'

'So you addressed them as Wolf—' Ghosh checked himself. 'Under their self-styled name?'

151

'They're trained,' Rick said. 'Disciplined. I was counting on that. But if they'd made the mistake of thinking the police responders were Emin's men, it could have been a bloodbath.'

'*Could* have been?' Ghosh said, and Rick realised that he really didn't know what had happened after he'd shouted the warning.

'Was it?' he asked.

'Three hostages dead, two of Emin's crew – what would you call that?'

Not your doing, Rick, Sam counselled.

He swallowed. 'No police?'

Ghosh seemed thrown by the question.

'I heard shots,' Rick said. 'Then "officer down". Did he make it?'

Ghosh suddenly seemed to realise that they might be overheard through the flimsy curtaining around Rick's trolley. 'I'm afraid I can't discuss that here.'

'Sir—'

'Call me when they release you,' Ghosh said. 'I want you in for a full debriefing.'

'Sir, for God's sake—'

But Ghosh was already gone.

Nurse Verren appeared at his side a second later.

'He's a real charmer, isn't he?'

'You heard that?'

'Every word. What can I tell you – you're a bleeder, I'm a lurker.' She fussed around the monitor and checked the blood bag, twice taking a breath, then stopping herself with a shake of her head, as if she was engaged in an inner battle.

Finally, avoiding his eye, she said, 'From what I've heard, the casualties would've been much worse if you hadn't yelled out of that window.'

'And the cop – is he . . .?'

She shook her head. 'I'm sorry.'

'Shit . . .' Rick brought a hand to his face.

'But the three hostages who died were *inside* the building,' she said, firmly. 'The two "crew" who died were the shitheads who came out holding guns on hostages.' She sucked air through her teeth in a gesture of contempt.

Rick was pitched back into the apartment. Peering down from his vantage point, he saw, in an awful vivid flash, the terror on the hostages' faces – actually jerked at the sound of gunfire and the puff of blood as the gangster's head exploded. He let the mental footage play and then stared into the nurse's face, shocked by what he'd just remembered.

'*Two* shots,' he said.

'I'm not with you.'

'When I yelled down to the street, the second hostage-taker swung his gun on me – and I heard two shots.'

'So . . .?'

'I think the militia, vigilantes – whatever they are – shot the hostage-taker as he took aim at me.'

She shrugged. 'Well, one good turn deserves another.'

'I'm not sure my boss sees it that way.'

She leaned in. 'Would your boss risk taking a bullet to save lives? I'm surprised he risked messing up his nice Italian suit coming to A and E to see you – all this blood sloshing around.'

'To be fair,' Rick said, 'my ensemble was a ratty pair of jeans and a sweatshirt my girlfriend tried to give away to Oxfam – twice.'

'Aw, girlfriend?' she said, making a disappointed face, and Rick felt a pull of attraction he hadn't experienced in months.

'All over,' he said, adding, 'Aeons ago,' and for once he didn't feel the loss too keenly.

'Well, see ya later, Sergeant,' she said, signing his chart with a flourish.

'Rick,' he said.

She tilted her head.

'Nurse Verren, wasn't it?'

'Still is,' she said, smiling. 'But you can call me Vee.'

Chapter 28

Later that day

A SUBDUED WOLF PACK GATHERED AROUND Cap's TV with the volume set low, watching the aftermath of the incident they had created. Two police officers taken away in ambulances, white forensic tents covering a large area of the backstreet access to Emin's drug factory. Five confirmed dead at the scene, one police officer died later in hospital, an unknown number of civilians injured.

'We're not supposed to hurt innocent people!' Prozac was shaking violently, clasping his hands between his knees to try to still the tremors, failing absolutely. 'Fuck, a cop died!'

Pug looked ashen, too. Sooner looked pensive, Frosty pale and distant. Brock alone seemed angry that things hadn't gone their way.

'*We* didn't shoot him,' he said flatly.

'But it was our *fault*,' Prozac insisted.

'Nah, mate. That's on Emin.'

'Brock's right,' Cap said. 'There's an in-built risk in policing, especially at this level – he knew what he signed up for.'

'No, Cap. We spooked Emin's lot – they wouldn't even have known that cop was there if it wasn't for us,' Prozac said. 'It's our fault they got away. Our fault the drugs weren't seized. Our fault that cop is dead!'

'What you're saying is we went in blind,' Brock said. 'Bad intel. Who was in charge of that? Oh, yeah – that'd be you, shit-for-brains.'

Prozac began to shake his head.

'You told us there was one lookout either end of the access road, four guards inside – only two armed – and *no* civilians,' Brock went on, relentless. 'What did we get?'

Prozac shook his head again, refusing eye contact.

'Come on, Brock . . .' Pug – always unhappy to be caught in the middle of an argument.

Sooner looked tense, ready to intervene if he had to; Frosty alone seemed unmoved by the argument.

Brock was relentless. 'Shut up, Pug. I want to hear him say it.' He waited, head cocked. 'No? Okay, let me list it for you: four guards, all armed; Emin himself – tooled up; twenty-plus civilians. And how the *fuck* did you not know there was a multi-agency jamboree on the go as we rolled up?'

'Th–they must've kept it really quiet. I-it must have gone off fast – there was *no* chatter, *no* hint that something big was going down. I was listening – honest to God, I *swear*—'

Brock spoke over him, working himself into a fury.

'What were you doing while all this was going down – hm . . .?' He fell into a mincing imitation of Prozac: 'Giving Livi a little foot massage, 'cos the baby's been soooo colicky?'

Prozac surged to his feet, his cheeks afire. 'You leave my wife out of it.'

'Or what?'

Brock was taller than Prozac by a head and carried a good twenty pounds' weight advantage. Cap was tempted to let them get on with it, work their frustration out on each other. But Prozac wouldn't survive the humiliation, so he glanced at Sooner, who stepped between them, standing eyeball to eyeball with Brock. 'Be cool, man.'

For a second, Cap thought they might come to blows, but Brock retreated with a disgusted shake of his head. 'You should have been working intel, you *stupid* fucker!'

'Hey, let's not forget it was Prozac got us out of there,' Cap said. 'If he hadn't come around the back of the warehouse—'

'None of us would be here if that cop hadn't yelled out the window,' Frosty broke in, and they all looked at her in question. 'Unidentified militia types armed to the teeth and in full tac gear? It's a no-brainer.' She hadn't raised her voice, didn't seem angry or agitated. Maybe it was her stillness in all the turmoil that held them. Whatever it was, she had their full attention.

'We were supposed to get out of there via the main road,' she said. 'We'd already secured Emin's lookouts, so we assumed that was the safe route. If we'd tried getting out that way, we'd've been blasted to hell by the cops.'

Pug nodded, and Sooner jerked his chin in recognition. Cap started to agree with her, but she wasn't finished.

'We assumed the police would be satisfied with a surveillance detail on Emin's new factory. We assumed it would take Emin weeks or months to get up and running. And we assumed that Emin's crew would be lax, because there wouldn't be much to guard on-site – since we did *such a good job* taking his last factory down.' She looked around the group. 'We assumed *way* too much, and it got a cop killed.'

Pug bowed his head, and Sooner looked uncomfortable. Prozac should have been grateful that she'd made the argument for him, but the kid never was any good at reading the room. 'That's what *I've* been trying to say,' he whined.

'Shut the *fuck* up, Prozac,' Brock snarled. 'I won't tell you again.'

It was all about to kick off again, when Sooner said, 'Hey – that's us!' He was staring past them at the TV screen.

156

Cap snatched up the remote and rewound to the beginning of the section, turning up the volume as he did.

'London Metropolitan Police have taken the unusual step of releasing surveillance video taken at the scene of the multiple shooting – a warehouse in the Limehouse district of Tower Hamlets,' the news presenter said. 'A warning that viewers may find these images disturbing.'

They'd pixelated out the faces of the hostages and the gangsters, but it was obvious from the bang and the way he fell that the first man had been shot.

The surveillance guy's voice was loud and clear: 'This is a POLICE OPERATION. Wolf Pack. Abort! ABORT MISSION!'

Then two more bangs overlaying each other, and the second hostage-taker fell.

Staring in horror, Prozac rubbed his lower lip compulsively. 'Jesus, oh, sweet Jesus, they got us *shooting* people.'

The next shot was a close-up of the visor and helmet of the first shooter – this was Sooner. The blurring had been removed to show the Wolf Pack logo, and the newsreader introduced a clip of an assistant commissioner talking about the incident.

'A major inter-agency operation was disrupted by the actions of a group calling itself the "Wolf Pack",' he began. 'Their actions resulted in the escape of the chief suspect in an organised criminal gang, which is believed to be responsible for the shipping of tonnes of class-A drugs into the UK. Despite their irresponsible and dangerous intervention, London Metropolitan Police, the National Crime Agency, and Border Force UK seized cocaine with a potential street value of over a hundred million pounds en route to the warehouse.'

He went on to emphasise the dangers of vigilantism, enumerated the lives that were lost, the lives that were put at risk, one police officer dead, one seriously injured trying to stop a gunfight that might otherwise have caused massive civilian casualties.

One journalist said, 'We're hearing that three unarmed civilians died inside the building – can you give us any details as to how they died?'

He declined. 'That's part of an ongoing investigation. We know that the group calling itself the Wolf Pack went into the building heavily armed, and as you've seen on the video, we have two *on record* shooting and killing two men.'

'Who shot the police officers, Commissioner?' someone shouted out. 'Was it the Wolf Pack?'

He repeated the 'ongoing investigation' excuse, while the pack watched in shocked silence.

'They're saying *we* shot the cops,' Prozac said at last.

'We cannot let that stand,' Cap said.

'But we didn't kill them,' Prozac said, sounding like a lost child.

'You're contradicting yourself now, Prozac. Doesn't matter that we didn't pull the trigger,' Frosty said. 'It *is* partly our fault. And if we disclaim responsibility, we'd be doing exactly what the police do – failing to admit our mistakes.'

'We couldn't even if we wanted to,' Brock said. 'What is this – collective amnesia? The entire shitshow was *livestreamed* – and whose idea was that?' He glanced at Prozac, baring his teeth in a vicious grin.

'You pushed pretty hard for it, yourself, as I recall,' Cap said quietly.

Brock responded with a sneer. 'Yeah, well that was back when I thought Nerd Nuts here was up to doing his job.'

Prozac blinked rapidly. 'Oh, actually, I killed the livestream after the first shot was fired.' The other four snapped to him as if he'd screamed it through a megaphone.

'You did *what*?' Cap said.

'I *said* I'd kill the livestream if things went sideways.' He sounded almost tearful. 'I *told* you that!'

'You did,' Cap agreed, raising both hands in surrender. 'Yes, you did.' He took a breath and let it go. 'Okay, so you've got us going down the alley and breaching the warehouse. Is that it?'

'No.' Prozac sounded suddenly petulant. 'I have *all* of it, I just didn't *livestream* anything past the first shot.'

Cap saw a glimmer of hope that they might just get past this with their integrity intact, if a little bruised. 'Show me.'

'What – now?'

'Yes, *now*.' Cap clapped his hands. 'Jump to it.'

Pandora Hahn had rung him on his burner phone a dozen times since that morning and he'd declined each call. She'd turned to sending him texts, but he wasn't going to talk to her until he'd had the police reaction, and some way to respond that didn't amount to an admission of abject failure. Now, he knew the approach to take.

As Prozac set up his laptop, Cap explained: 'If we can show that we were nowhere near the alley when the police officer was killed, that's a good thing, yes?' He didn't wait for a reply. 'Say we also have Emin's crew shooting the three drug production-line workers. Say the bodycams caught Frosty shooting the hostage-taker before he had the chance to aim properly at the cop in the window . . .' He raised both shoulders.

Frosty and Sooner responded with a nod of understanding.

Pug had been frowning at him in intense concentration. Now, suddenly, his brow cleared. 'Then we're golden!' he exclaimed.

'I wouldn't go that far,' Cap said. 'But it will clear us of the worst allegations.'

'Well, let's hope Prozac didn't screw up that part of his job an' all,' Brock said. 'And what're are the rest of us supposed to do while you girls are managing the *social media*?'

Cap eyed Brock with detestation. *One of these days, you'll push me too far* . . . But he put on his game face and said, 'You, Frosty, Pug and Sooner will set about finding Emin.'

Brock scoffed. 'How're we supposed to do that? Didn't you hear what the assistant commissioner said? He escaped – and odds-on he hasn't gone back to any of the three London addresses we know about.'

'I didn't say it would be easy,' Cap said evenly.

'Mate, the Met's got thousands of detectives – they can call on Interpol, the NCA, Border Force – a whole raft of databases we got no access to. How're four of us supposed to—'

'You hunt down every known associate of Emin's gang,' Cap interrupted. 'You target the low-level pond life who *don't* have the luxury of escape plans and safe houses. You put pressure on them in ways the police *can't* till they give us Emin – or someone close to Emin – and we work it from there.'

Chapter 29

THEY KEPT RICK IN UNDER OBSERVATION, but the wards were rammed, so most of his stay was spent on a trolley in A&E. They moved him out of the 'serious injuries' bay into a 'minors' bay after the first eight hours, and from there, into a makeshift screened area in a corridor.

After another four hours, the constant noise and turmoil were making him antsy. By eleven p.m., the first wave of drunks came in. The singing drunks weren't so bad, the vomiting drunks harder to stomach, and when the fighting drunks started to turn up, Rick was ready to walk out in his hospital gown.

The next time a nurse checked his neurological signs, he told her he was going home.

'Well, you can't,' she said. 'You've got another—' she checked the chart '—seven hours before we can release you.'

'Not happening,' Rick said. 'Give me my clothes and whatever disclaimer form I need to sign. I'm off.'

She replaced the chart with unnecessary force and stamped away.

Ten minutes later, Charge Nurse Verren appeared at his side with a plastic bag Rick sincerely hoped contained his clothing.

'I hear you've been giving my colleagues a hard time.' The

161

flirty vibe of the morning had vanished. This evening, she was all business.

'I'm grateful and everything, but I just want to head home, get some kip.' He jerked his chin, indicating the bag. 'Is that my stuff?'

She placed it on the bed.

'Well, aren't you going to give me some privacy?'

'Willingly,' she said. 'But before I do . . .' She lifted his sweatshirt out and laid it on the covers. It was cut from waist to collar. Next came his trousers, sliced up all four leg seams.

'Oh.'

'Do you remember this happening, Sergeant Turner?' She was testing him again.

'I remember thinking that ripping my clothes to shreds was a bit over the top.'

'You'd been shot in the head,' she said flatly. 'We had to check for other bullet wounds.'

'I don't suppose there's anything I could buy or borrow . . .'

'It's the NHS, Rick. We don't have a gents' outfitters on the premises.'

A scuffle broke out in the bay next to his and Rick tensed, ready to intervene.

'Whoa, Hoss,' she said, softening a little. 'You're off duty, remember?'

She peeked into the next bay, where the patient had stopped struggling and instead set up a wailing at a volume to shatter toughened glass.

'I get it,' she said. 'By rights, you should've been admitted to a ward before lunchtime today, but you'll probably complete your twenty-four-hour obs right here. Welcome to your twenty-first-century National Health Service.'

'Vee, I've been working twelve- and fourteen-hour nights for over a week. I've been shot, had a verbal pounding from my boss, I'm sore and knackered, and I *really* need some sleep.'

She folded her arms and eyed him critically. 'Ideally, you should be under obs for another four hours at least. D'you have any family you can call?'

Rick thought of Sam. 'No,' he said.

'Well, I know there's no girlfriend, so – a trusted colleague, maybe?'

It was at times like this that Rick realised how few he did trust or rely on in the world. But there was someone – he'd been a friend and mentor to Rick since his first tentative steps in the CID. But he hadn't spoken to Jim Stott in nearly six months, and the circumstances of that last talk had been painful.

'My phone in there?'

She passed the bag to him, and he found it. It had been switched off, but the only messages awaiting him were from Detective Superintendent Ghosh. He scrolled through his contacts and hit the call icon for Stott.

'I'll give you a minute,' she said, 'but be sure to tell them they'll have to be willing to disturb your sleep every couple of hours for a little chat and to gaze into your baby blues.'

Rick raised his eyes to hers. 'Are you volunteering?'

She tipped back her head and laughed, then spun on her toes with a dancer's ease and vanished, pulling the curtain tightly across the foot of his trolley bed. He found himself straining to hear her footsteps in the corridor until they were swallowed in the noise and chatter of the department.

A few rings in, Rick heard Stott's familiar voice, sounding sharp and upbeat. Rick gave him a short summary – stuck in A&E – just for a quick once-over, ready to go home, except his clothes got messed up.

'Shit, are you okay son?' Stott was one of the few who'd always been able to see through Rick's bullshit.

'I'm *fine* – I can call an Uber. It's just they gave me a hospital gown with three of the ties missing and I'll probably get myself arrested the minute I step outside.'

'Mate, I would, but I'm not around.'

'Oh, I see,' Rick said, although he couldn't make sense of it – then he did. 'Oh, Jeez – sorry, mate – did you and Maddie—?'

'Nah, we're good – still working things out, you know, but we're getting there. I got this nice gig in Saudi—' He broke off as the wailing patient set off again.

'Bloody hell, Rick! Look, you got Maddie's number – why don't you give her a call?'

'It's eleven o'clock at night here,' Rick said, doubtful.

'She won't mind – give her chance to tell you about Billy – he's had an offer from one of the Oxford colleges. Won an essay prize – and he's up for a bursary an' all.'

Billy was their eldest, and Stott's financial problems had meant he'd come close to having to drop out of school last winter.

'Yeah, well, he inherited his brains from Maddie's side of the family,' Rick said, and Stott laughed.

'You always were a cheeky bleeder.'

'Funny you should say that—' Rick broke off as the wailing from the next bay abruptly rose to a scream. 'Sorry, Jim, I'm gonna have to go so I can stick my fingers in my ears.'

'All right,' Stott said. 'But promise me you'll call Maddie.'

'Yeah, I will, mate. Definitely.'

He ended the call and wrapped the pillow around his ears while the chaos swirled around him like a stormy ocean swell. He was roused from a doze sometime later by someone shaking his foot, and he opened his eyes to the amused face of Nurse Verren.

'It's stopped,' she said. 'You can come out, now.'

Rick cautiously uncovered his ears, relieved to find that the bay next to him was silent.

'Your friend's here,' she said.

Maybe the concussion was worse than he'd admit, because for one soaring moment, he thought Sam had turned up. Elation turned quickly to panic.

Is he mad? The place is crawling with cops.

'Someone called Stott?' she said, perhaps reading the anxiety in his face.

'Not possible,' Rick said shaking his head slowly to keep his brains from rattling. 'I just got off the phone with him. He's out of country.'

'Well, you're welcome to stay here, but *she* was quite insistent.'

A moment later, Maddie was standing at the foot of the trolley, looking pale, flustered, and sleep-dishevelled.

'Why didn't you *call*?' she demanded, hoisting a backpack from her shoulder and letting it drop at her feet.

He glanced at his phone. 'It's after midnight, Maddie.'

'You're kidding, aren't you? Jim would never have forgiven me if I hadn't come down here. And you the hero of the moment, too.'

Rick groaned. 'He went digging, didn't he?'

'Scratched the surface, more like,' she scoffed. 'You're all *over* the news – isn't he?'

She turned to Nurse Verren, but Vee had already faded discreetly away.

'I can't believe I didn't see it myself,' Maddie added crossly, as though she'd neglected her duties. 'It's just I've been so preoccupied . . .'

'You all right?' Rick asked, alarmed, wondering if Stotty hadn't misread the state of their marriage.

'Better than all right.' Maddie beamed that big, wide, infectious smile he'd missed so much over the last year and more. 'Jim's on a twelve-step programme – doing well.'

'Ah, I did wonder.'

'He didn't say? Well, he's still a bit shy about it.' She laughed. 'I bet he told you about Billy, though.'

'Said you'd tell me about it, then told me himself.'

'Typical.'

'So, what's got you so preoccupied?' he asked.

'Nothing much,' she said, still smiling. 'Only I'm Job again.'

'You applied for re-entry?' Rick asked, delighted for her.

She wrinkled her nose. 'Retraining. I've been out too long to just slide back in on the re-entry programme. But it's okay. New regime – the Met's looking for women who've had a bit of life experience.'

'About bloody time,' Rick said, and she seemed startled. 'Seriously – Stotty always said you were a brilliant detective – better than him.'

'Yeah, well.' Tears started in her eyes and she fussed over the backpack, digging around like she had a month's worth of survival kit jammed inside it.

'You wanted some clothes,' she said, when she'd regained her composure. 'Billy's about your height, now,' she added, like the proud mother she was.

Rick slid his arms in the sleeves, bracing himself for getting his very sore head through the collar, and she murmured, 'Sorry, Rick, I should've brought a shirt. Here, let me help with the . . .'

When they'd wrangled him into it, she handed him the joggers, and turned away with a smirk. 'You're on your own with those.'

Rick spent the rest of night on the Stotts' sofa, Maddie having absolutely refused to take him home. She woke him every two hours, per Nurse Verren's instructions, and performed the checks for signs of concussion assiduously. He finally drifted into a deep sleep at six a.m.

The sound of gunfire almost catapulted him off the sofa an hour later, sending sharp needles of pain from his forehead to his temple. He groaned, holding his head.

'Oh, sorry, Rick.' Billy was sitting on a La-Z-Boy recliner next to the sofa, dressed in school uniform. He lowered the volume with a little grimace.

Maddie poked her head around the door. 'I told you not to disturb him!'

'Yeah,' Billy said. 'Like I said – sorry.' He slid Rick a sly look, then back to the screen of his tablet. 'But – is that you?'

Rick held out his hand, not wanting to shift position or even move his head till the room had stopped spinning, and Billy handed him the tablet.

The Wolf Pack had uploaded a video to what looked like a hastily created website, WolfPack4Justice. It was playing in a loop – bodycam footage, as far as he could tell. They moved at speed down a narrow corridor constructed of panelling, by the looks of it. The shaky camera work accentuated Rick's dizziness and he swallowed, trying to make out the instructions and hear anything distinctive in the voices. But they used hand signals, military-style, and used code names when they spoke at all. 'Alpha One', 'Beta Two' and so on.

'Like wolf hierarchy,' Billy said.

The corridor opened up into the main body of Emin's ware-house – Rick recognised it from his reconnaissance trip – the office area a flimsy box tacked to one wall. Emin would be in there.

A shout of 'Cops!' and the office door slammed. Two men remained, blocking the doorway, and Rick remembered the hidden escape door from the office into the alley. The main floor space was laid out with tables end to end, weighing machines, pressers, plastic bags flying everywhere as the production-line workers scattered.

A distant shot, somewhere outside the building, then: 'Officer down!'

The camera shake made him sick, but Rick forced himself to watch.

The Wolf Pack began bellowing orders at two of Emin's men standing guard outside the shack-like office pod tacked on to one of the walls. The guards backed into the doorway, trying to force it open. It must have been locked against them, because they gave up on it, and surged forward.

More shouting – Rick couldn't make out what – and the frightened drug packers cried out, cowering from the onslaught, hiding under tables, fleeing to the walls. Then three broke away, running towards the front of the building.

Emin's bodyguards took deliberate aim and shot all three.

'Civilians down! Civilians down!' someone yelled.

The Wolf Pack point man yelled. 'Beta One, Beta Three, secure the escape route!'

Was that an American accent?

'Alpha One, protect the civilians!'

A glimpse of the Wolf decals on two helmets as he glanced towards the operatives.

The two shooters snatched a hostage each from under one of the tables.

'This is horrible – why would they put this online where anyone can see it?' This was Maddie – she must have crept into the room and now stood watching over Rick's shoulder.

'Alpha Two – with me.'

Rick couldn't see what happened at the office door – the point man's bodycam showing one of the vigilantes turning over tables. A brief switch to a different camera – presumably Alpha One's – as he shepherded the packers behind the upturned tables, guiding the women and boys towards sacks of chemical bulking agents, miming, 'Keep down.'

Then back to the point man's bodycam. He and Alpha Two, following Emin's men who were dragging hostages backwards, making their way back down the panelling corridor. The two militias kept up a steady flow of commands and cajoling.

'You don't want to do this. Lay down your weapons – we'll talk. Let the hostages go.'

Emin's men responded by firing off a couple of rounds, then Rick heard the grind of the warehouse door. Sirens, cars skidding to a halt at the end of the backstreet. The police had arrived.

The hostage-takers turned to the source of the noise; they must have known they were trapped.

Rick had seen what happened next from the apartment building. This time, he saw it from the vigilantes' viewpoint: a bang, and a hostage-taker's head vapourised.

Rick heard himself yell a warning, telling the Wolf Pack to stand down. He flashed to the moment as if it was still happening – this time, in slow motion. The second gunman swung his gun towards Rick, taking aim. Two shots – almost simultaneous. The gunman collapsed.

Next, a blur of movement and the sounds of hard breathing, boots pounding over cobblestones, sirens and police commands as background noise. The point man bounced off the brickwork in the alleyway. A white van pulled across in front of them, doors open. Their bodycams picked up two of the Wolf Pack holding on to leather ceiling straps inside the van, free hands outstretched.

'Move, move, move!'

The two shooters leapt, grasped an arm each, hauled themselves inside, then the screen went blank.

'Cooooo-wul,' Billy purred.

'Not cool, Bill,' Maddie chided. 'People died.'

'*Gangsters* died.'

'They shot Rick!'

Billy lowered his head, his cheeks flaming.

The website started the loop again, and Rick shut it down, setting the tablet aside with a shaking hand. 'Your mum's right, Bill. People died. Not just the gangsters – civilians. A cop, too,' he said quietly.

Billy started to apologise, and Rick raised a hand to stop him.

'But I don't think they shot the other police officer *or* the civilians, and it proves that they didn't shoot *me*, either. I think the Wolf Pack shooter fired just ahead of Emin's man.'

'You still got shot,' Maddie pointed out.

'But Emin's guy was probably going for body mass – it's what I'd do. He shot wild because the Wolf Packer dropped him before he could take full aim. I think that's why they put it online, Maddie.'

'Well, if they think *that's* vindication, they need their heads examining,' she scoffed. 'People *died* because of their stupid bravado.'

He didn't disagree, but watching the footage, he realised that the operation commanders had their own cameras inside the warehouse. They would have seen events from multiple viewpoints in clear, steady digital recordings. They must know that the pack hadn't shot the civilians. Why were they holding that back?

Because it suits their narrative, Rick. Sam, his phantom counsellor, sounded cynical – even a touch weary.

Chapter 30

One day after the drugs raid

THE POLICE CAME BACK FIGHTING, putting a spokesperson forward for every peak-time news bulletin on the London TV and radio stations – reserving the prime spot on BBC London and Radio 4's PM programme for the assistant commander who'd been saddled with the drugs bust from hell.

Everyone who spoke had been well rehearsed: they repeated the undeniable fact that the Wolf Pack's untimely interference had resulted in six fatalities, one of them a police officer. Four of the drug factory workers – identified only as 'warehouse personnel' by the Met – had been treated for minor injuries and many more for shock. Every London Met representative opened and closed their statements with the stats, including the quantity of drugs seized and their street value, going on to list the benefits of taking drugs off the streets in terms of public safety, in an attempt to put a positive spin on that disastrous night.

A couple of the more determined mouthpieces even managed to introduce what might have happened if it weren't for the 'quick thinking' and 'brave actions' of joint agency teams during their take-down of the drugs convoy. Again, citing the Wolf Pack's interference as causing danger to law enforcement and the public, they explained that the lorry driver carrying the massive drugs haul had tried to drive up the down-ramp at a junction in a bid to escape police interceptors.

The agreed sound bite for press and social media was 'Vigilantism threatens the rule of law'. And it was repeated in every police statement.

But interviewers and broadcasters pushed back hard. The police had implied by omission that it was the Wolf Pack who had shot the police officer and the three hostages who'd died, yet bodycam videos released by the vigilantes had proved them wrong – even dishonest. Rattled, the talking heads stuck to the sound bite, which did them no good at all. One London radio news programme even suggested that the pack had saved two hostages and the life of the officer who was shot trying to call off the Wolf Pack mission.

'*Mission*,' Prozac whispered, smiling faintly. 'They're calling it a *mission*.'

The assistant commissioner had snapped back, 'It was an assault. An assault on the rule of law, an assault on law-abiding citizens of this city – a *physical* assault on the Metropolitan Police officers, Border Force and National Crime Agency personnel who risked their lives that night. An already hazardous operation was made a hundred times more dangerous by the thoughtless, *amateur* intervention of a group with no legal or moral authority to take the action they did, and I believe that every right-thinking person in this country will agree with me.'

It was a strong comeback, but the public response was damning. Serious commentators and local politicians weighed in with opinion pieces, ordinary Londoners called local radio phone-ins, and social media mavens everywhere added comments, hashtag critiques and memes. The language and presentation were as varied as the age demographic, but they all agreed that the police had lost control of the streets. Some even praised the Wolf Pack for stepping in to fill the breach.

Watching the nine o'clock news at Cap's place, the Wolf Pack was ready to breathe a collective sigh of relief – until a 'Breaking News' screen crawler announced that the assistant commissioner was about to make a statement. The upshot: police had CCTV evidence linking the Wolf Pack to the murder of property developer Jason Floren in February.

Prozac had been chewing on his thumbnail. He stopped, his face grey with shock, and said, 'What? No . . .'

The others shushed him, and Cap rewound the news bulletin to get the full story.

The police had dug up images of their van – the same high-top Ford van they'd used in their citizens' arrests of the Blackfriars Bank mob – leaving 'the vicinity' as he put it, of Deptford Waters within seven minutes of the first responders arriving at the scene.

The pack only used stolen or cloned plates, so that wasn't an issue, but the cops had some kind of forensics nerd in. Showing images of the van snapped near the development and a second sequence of the vehicle fleeing the Tower Hamlets car park, she pointed out a crease on the sliding door and a dull patch on the paintwork over the wheel arches. Outlining the dull area over the front wheel with a digital pen, a stylised flame emerged and she explained that this was the remains of a vinyl graphic. Of course, there were new scratches and a big fat dent in the van's offside front panel after Prozac had crashed it into Gary Quinn's Qashqai in the car park, but that didn't distract the science nerd one bit.

She zoomed in on an empty crisp packet, squashed coffee cup, and drinks can on the dashboard of the dark van spotted near Floren's development on the night he was murdered and compared it to the van snapped after the bank mob arrests. Plenty more rubbish had accumulated over the three months since, but she focused on those three items, then made a convincing argument that their positions and orientation on the dash *precisely* matched the dashboard garbage in the van used at the car park in Tower Hamlets. There was no doubt in her mind that it was the same van the Wolf Pack had used on the night the police made the Blackfriars Bank arrests.

Pug uttered '*Shhiiiii-iiit*' in one, long, dying note.

Brock was already on his feet. 'We *prove* we didn't harm a single innocent victim and they come up with this fairy tale?'

'Yeah,' Pug said. '*We* didn't kill Floren.'

'There's no denying it's the same van,' Sooner said.

'And we were there the night he died, *and* when the Blackfriars mob were arrested,' Frosty added. 'Clever, how they changed the narrative, though – saying *they* arrested the bank mob.'

Cap's mouth felt dry; the bastard police had put them on the back foot – again. He ran his tongue around his teeth and said, 'I'll talk to the podcaster, get word out through her that this is a downright lie.'

''Course, she's gonna be highly cooperative after what went down in Limehouse,' Brock said.

'Brock, you just said yourself that we'd proved we didn't harm the packers.'

'Maybe I did – but we most definitely *caused* harm to come to them, didn't we?'

Cap was almost impressed that Brock was capable of making such a subtle distinction, but getting into a semantic argument with the man would not help. He delayed his response a fraction of a second too long, and Brock gave a snort of derision.

'Prozac and I proved that we didn't shoot police or the hostages,' Cap said, alarmed that he was in danger of losing his authority. 'What about you – what have *you* achieved in the last thirty-six hours?'

Brock raised both eyebrows. 'You asking for a status report, Cap'n?' he said, his tone mocking. He glanced around the room,

174

but no one was playing his game and he coloured slightly, the flush travelling from his angry brows to the dome of his pale, bald head.

Feeling more in control, Cap said, 'We need Emin's location – did you get it?'

Brock remained silent and Frosty spoke up. 'We got a couple of street names.'

'But street names don't necessarily link to street addresses,' Brock said.

Frosty asserted herself again. 'We really need Prozac to rummage through a couple of databases for us, get us some real names – and addresses – for those potential informants.'

Prozac was shaking his head – a tiny gesture, more like a tremor than a real headshake – and Brock said, 'Oh, what *now*?'

'I'm not – I-I won't hurt women and children,' Prozac stammered.

'No one asked you to.'

'No, but I don't wanna – you know – *cause* them to get hurt,' the kid said, throwing Brock's words back at him.

Brock's nostrils flared. 'Half their foot soldiers are under eighteen, mate,' he scoffed. 'But they still carry stonking great knives stuffed in their undies – and they wouldn't think twice to use them on you, or me, or anyone else who got in their way.'

'Don't care.'

Brock bared his teeth looking ready to grab him by the throat. 'Maybe I'll make you care.'

Prozac shook his head more violently, Brock made a feint towards him, and the kid threw his arms over his head.

Brock sucked his teeth. 'You need to take a pill, Prozac.'

He looked ready to say more, but Frosty said, 'I think Prozac's got a point.' She sighed. 'And though I hate to admit it, so does Brock.'

'Well, thank you, Your Majesty,' Brock sneered.

She ignored him, fixing her gaze on Cap. 'Handing Emin over

to the police would be the best way to make amends, but if we're drawn into terrorising the very people Emin is already victimising, it just makes us as bad as him – in fact, worse than him – 'cos we're *supposed* to be the good guys.'

Cap considered, admiring Frosty's clarity of thought. 'You're right. We won't regain the public's trust until we've exonerated ourselves of Floren's murder.'

'How do we do that?' Pug asked.

'We proved that we didn't shoot the cops; we can prove we didn't shoot Floren.'

'No,' Frosty said, way ahead of the rest, as usual. 'If we admit we were there the night he was killed, we just give the cops another stick to beat us with.'

'Not if we do it right,' Cap insisted.

She shook her head, exasperated. 'Cap, you saw how they twisted the evidence to make it look like we shot that cop in Limehouse – the hostages, even. They're not going to hold their hands up and say, "Okay, you got us – we lied to serve our agenda."'

'I agree. They've been passing the buck for so long they don't know when to say stop. So we give them another way to save face.'

She seemed intrigued. 'How would that work?'

Cap had been their leader from the beginning. He was group manager of the four fire stations called out to the Deptford fire, and he'd had contact with all of them in the aftermath. It was Cap who'd brought them together and until the disastrous mission in Limehouse he'd never had to explain his strategies in detail – nor had he faced such constant challenges and disparagement from Brock. Now, each time someone asked him to justify himself or questioned his reasoning, he felt his position as their leader slip another notch or two.

'You're going to have to trust me,' he said, calm, but uncompromising.

Frosty smiled, incredulous. 'Cap, you can't expect us to just walk away and let you—'

But he wasn't interested in persuading them, or listening to more arguments, allowing Brock to continue undermining his authority, clawing his way to the top with a thousand snide remarks.

He stood. 'Get out, the lot of you.'

'*What?*'

'Are you fucking *serious*?' Brock said.

'Get out of my house,' Cap said, lowering his voice to a soft growl.

Pug looked hurt and dismayed, like Mum and Dad were rowing and it was his fault; Frosty seemed stunned, and Prozac had drawn his shoulders down, his elbows in, making himself smaller, physically curling up – afraid, no doubt, that he would again become the outlet for Brock's frustrations.

Sooner was the first to make a move. 'Let's go,' he said.

'Or what?'

'Or I'll make you.'

Brock held Cap's gaze but not for long. 'Okay,' he said at last. 'His house, his rules. But d'you want us to keep looking for these shitheads, or not?'

It was a fair question.

Imposing control over his breathing and his tone, Cap said, 'Go home, be with your families if that's what makes you happy. Go back to work like this has nothing to do with you, if that's what you need.'

'That's it?' Brock said. 'You want us to lie low?'

Cap gave a brief nod. 'For now.'

'Till when?' Frosty asked.

'Till I contact you,' Cap said.

They drifted to the door, Sooner watching them file out, implacable and alert, like a nightclub bouncer expecting trouble to kick off at any moment.

Prozac was last, knowing his place in the hierarchy.

'Not you,' Cap said, and the kid ducked, turning frightened eyes on him as though he half expected to be struck a blow. 'Why?' he pleaded.

Cap favoured him with a grim smile. 'I've got a job for you.'

Chapter 31

The next morning, two a.m.

CAP SAT ON ONE SIDE OF PANDORA HAHN, Sooner on the other. Prozac was driving at speed in a newly acquired van towards an unnamed and – for Pandora at least – unknowable destination. Both Sooner and Cap were in full tactical gear – helmets and visors included – while Prozac was dressed more conventionally, a hoodie covering his body armour; scarf and beanie giving him sufficient anonymity without risking the chance of arousing police interest. Pandora was blindfolded.

Her preferred meeting place had been an empty community hall – more of a hut, really. Small, barred windows, corrugated concrete roof.

Checking it out on Google Earth, Prozac had said, 'Police ambush?'

Cap said, 'Unlikely.' Pandora was ambitious; tough, too. Showing up at the Blackfriars mob arrests with only a mobile phone and an unshakable belief in herself took courage. And hadn't she asked more testing questions than all the highly paid roving reporters with their professional recording equipment and support crews? But the police had demonstrated again and again that they would lie to save face; what if they'd convinced her that Floren's blood was on the Wolf Pack's hands?

At last, he spoke again: 'But we'll take no chances.'

So they'd proposed an alternative location – an unmonitored car park at the edge of a green space in south London. Off the main roads and out of range of Transport for London's CCTV and traffic cams, they would be safe there.

Prozac and Sooner had scouted out the place ahead of the agreed time and placed a couple of cameras to monitor activity prior to their return. Apart from a drunk weaving off the street into the car park to take a leak and a teenager on the roadway, trying car doors, the area had been deserted for an hour.

Pandora had turned into the tree-shrouded car park in a ten-year-old Mini Cooper hatchback. She seemed to be alone. Prozac flashed the van's lights, once, keeping the engine running and she got out, ducking to strap a messenger bag crosswise over her shoulder and locking the car after her. Alert to every movement and sound, Cap had stepped down from the van to meet her halfway. She really did seem to be alone, and Prozac would shout if he saw any unexpected action on the cameras.

Cap had said that he would be in tactical gear, and Pandora hadn't seemed unduly alarmed – had even extended her hand to greet him. As Cap reached out his gloved hand to shake hers, Prozac powered the van across the tarmac and Sooner slid open the side door.

Her eyes had widened as Cap grabbed her right wrist, pulling her in close, spinning her round, clamping his left hand over her mouth before she could scream. Between them, they manhandled her into the vehicle.

'Try to scream, I will gag you,' Cap had warned. 'Try to fight me, I will cuff you. Nod, if you understand.'

Her eyes were wet when he'd let go of her. She'd run a hand angrily over her face, spitting, 'Bastards!'

She'd protested at the blindfold, but complied when he'd explained, 'For our protection – and yours.'

Now, five minutes into their journey, her breathing still a little ragged, she gasped, 'You didn't need to do this.' Getting no response, she added, 'I'm a journalist – I protect my sources.'

'We'll see.' They had agreed that Cap would do all the talking – it was bad enough that she'd forced them to a meeting – the less she had to identify, the better. He tapped Prozac on the shoulder. 'Anything?'

Prozac shook his head.

'You can slow down; I think we're in the clear,' Cap said.

He and Sooner removed their helmets, retaining their balaclavas.

They reached their destination in fifty minutes: a barren stretch of post-industrial landscape that had been cleared for redevelopment almost two decades earlier, then abandoned after the world financial crash of the mid-Noughties.

Prozac bumped them over bricks and grass tussocks, finally coming to a stop dead centre of the space. Killing the lights but leaving the engine running, he pulled on a balaclava, climbed down from the cab, and opened the sliding door.

Pandora flinched at the sound, then steadied herself.

'I'm going to take the blindfold off, okay?' Cap said.

She nodded.

Blinking into the dark, she whispered, 'No landmarks, no locational clues, no traffic.'

Cap heard the tremor in her voice and respected her for keeping her fear under restraint. 'For our protection – and yours,' he repeated, his tone reassuring.

They were in a natural hollow. Nothing but dark, uneven terrain for a quarter of a mile in any direction, the lights of London concealed by the rim of the bowl.

Prozac was standing at the van door, carrying his favourite laptop and a digital audio recorder. He eyed Cap expectantly.

'Okay, come and get set up,' Cap said, hauling him in.

Pandora looked annoyed. 'I have my own kit.'

'That has been disabled. Temporarily,' Cap added, seeing her temper flare.

After a moment, she said, 'He'll record all of this?'

'Every word,' Cap promised. 'All right?'

She glared at him. The interior lights were dim, but he could see that her eyes were greenish, with hazel flecks. 'Seems I don't have a choice.'

'You really don't. Now, where d'you want to start?'

'The shootings in Limehouse.'

'What would you like to know?'

'I would have thought that was obvious,' she said. 'I want to know *why*.'

'I think we've made ourselves clear why we do this.'

'I'm not talking about your *manifesto*,' she spat. 'You shot and killed two men.' The aggression wasn't helpful, but she'd been badly frightened and was probably still riding the wave of an adrenaline spike, so Cap humoured her.

'We shot two gunmen to save three lives – the bodycam footage on the WolfPack4Justice website demonstrates that graphically.'

'*Graphically*,' she repeated. 'Apt word choice.' She pushed on: 'The police say you have no legal or moral authority. They say right-thinking people will see that.'

'Well . . . then, I suppose we'll have to agree to differ.'

She tilted her head, inviting him to go on.

'How can the justice system claim moral authority, when it allows dangerous criminals to blatantly commit crimes with no consequences? And when the state doesn't uphold its end of the bargain, it's natural that ordinary people will want to protect themselves.'

'Ordinary people? You wear body armour and carry semiautomatic weapons.'

'Only a fool brings a knife to a gunfight.' Cap took a breath of damp spring air and exhaled. He didn't want to come over as just another angry, ranting reactionary, and she'd made a fair point. 'I'm sorry – that sounded flippant. I know that I speak for all the of the Wolf Pack when I say we would *gladly* lay down our weapons if the police did the job they've sworn to do.'

'Wasn't that what they were *trying* to do when you blundered into their carefully planned operation?' He didn't answer and, her equilibrium restored, she asked the next question with what seemed like genuine curiosity: 'We don't even know who you *are* – how can anyone hold *you* to account? And if there's no accountability, surely the result is anarchy. Chaos.'

Cap was on surer ground here, and he took a moment to relax his shoulders and think through what he wanted to say.

'Look around you, Pandora,' he said. 'The streets of London are rife with crime. It's a daily challenge just to get to work and back without being subjected to aggression, intimidation, and even actual violence. What is *that* if not anarchy and chaos?'

She circled back. 'Six people were killed during the police raid that you disrupted. One was a police officer.'

'We deeply regret that,' Cap said. 'But look at the context: two of the men shot were holding guns on hostages; both the police officer who died and the officer who was wounded were shot by gangsters protecting a major criminal enterprise.

'We went after Emin and his drugs cartel because it seemed that law enforcement had given up on catching him.'

'But you were *wrong* – they hadn't given up – and because of you and your team of vigilantes, a suspected drug trafficker escaped. People died.'

This wasn't getting them anywhere, so Cap said, 'We're here to address new charges made against the Wolf Pack.'

'All right,' Pandora said. 'Let's talk about that. You say you're not a lynch mob, but you're wanted by the police for suspected involvement in the murder of a property developer named Jason Floren, last February. The police believe that you, the Wolf Pack, appointed yourselves judge, jury and executioners of a man who was *cleared* of any wrongdoing in the Deptford Waters arson killings. What do you say to that?' Her eyes darted over his face, as if she might penetrate the mask and memorise his features.

'The survivors have persistently claimed that Jason Floren had conspired with the owner of the properties to drive them out of their homes.'

'The police investigated. They found nothing to substantiate those claims.'

'Well, maybe they should've tried harder.' Cap turned to Prozac, who handed over the laptop with three video files ready to play.

The first was labelled 'Floren confession', the second, 'Floren killer?' and the third: 'Floren death?'

Glancing across to read the screen, she said, 'What's this?'

'There's only one way to find out, Pandora.' Cap handed her the laptop. 'Open the box.'

Chapter 32

Nine a.m., three days
after the Emin warehouse raid

UNABLE TO REST AT HOME AND BANNED from going out in the field, Rick was recuperating at his desk. Pandora Hahn had published a new *Pandora Unboxes* podcast an hour ago, and the content was sensational. Within minutes, it had gone viral, and the vigilante calling himself 'Alpha One' had been quoted extensively in local, national and international press. His voice had been digitally altered – by the Wolf Pack's technical expert, according to Pandora – her own recording equipment having been confiscated for the duration. She claimed to have thirty minutes of uncensored interview, although she'd used only short sections in this podcast.

Introducing it with a hair-raising account of being snatched off the street and taken to an unknown location, she outlined the content of her new episode, emphasising that it would deal with the Metropolitan Police's claims that the Wolf Pack were responsible for Jason Floren's murder.

'In this episode of *Pandora Unboxes* . . . *Hamstrung Law*, you will hear a chilling confession from murdered property developer

Jason Floren on the night he died. If you're able to watch the podcast, I would urge you to head over to my website because I am running *exclusive* video footage of the sequence of events leading up to the shooting of Mr Floren in February – video that the Wolf Pack claims clears them of all police charges.'

She went on to promise that the next episode would feature an in-depth discussion with the Wolf Pack's spokesman, addressing the causes as well as the moral dilemmas and dangers arising from vigilantism.

'This is material that no other journalist or news broadcaster has,' she said. 'You will hear this *only* on *Pandora Unboxes*. Interested? Then please "like" and subscribe to this podcast and join me tomorrow, when I'll be quizzing "Alpha One" of the Wolf Pack. I am Pandora Hahn, and you are listening to the *Pandora Unboxes* podcast.'

Rick had to admit the woman was slick, and she knew how to bait a hook.

She ran three clips over the course of the episode, beginning with a video of Jason Floren being set upon in the office of his show house at Deptford Waters by four armed, black-clad men wearing tactical gear, helmets and visors. Pandora described the key visuals for anyone listening to, rather than viewing, the episode.

The vigilantes had obviously cut some of the footage – the cut section presumably covering how they'd persuaded Floren to talk – resuming at the point when he'd confessed involvement in planning the arson attack on the flats. He'd admitted to having drawn diagrams for the slum landlord, indicating the 'most effective' places to start fires for 'devastating effect'.

Rick's phantom counsellor, spoke up at that moment, as he often did when issues arose in favour of the guilty: *I'm no lawyer, but I'm confident that confession would never have been permissible in a court of law.*

Maybe not, Rick thought. But Floren had provided a lot of detail, and it might have been enough to send investigators back for a second look.

The first clip ended with two of the vigilantes frog-marching Floren upstairs and securing him in the bathroom. Then, using the bodycam recording of the operative at the rear end of the group, all four left via the kitchen onto the patio, picking up a fifth member of the team who must have been keeping watch. The fifth person peered around the corner of the house, nodded, then took point, the others staying close, following all the way back from the show house to a dark high-top Ford van.

The van, Rick assumed.

As the last man climbed into the van, a sixth member of the team – the driver, also fully kitted out – was briefly visible. The tactical gear made it impossible to be certain that this was the same unit that took down the bank robbers, but judging by their build and style of approach, Rick would bet good money that it was. Pandora, at least, seemed convinced of it, and she'd had previous contact with them, so she should know.

Overdubbed onto the clip, the man calling himself Alpha One emphasised that they'd left Floren safely trussed up in the bath and called the police. Their intention had been to send Floren's confession to the police as they arrived on the development.

The man's distorted voice billowed, faded, and boomed, like a record played at variable speed, as he explained that the Wolf Pack had set up covert cameras to warn them of unexpected visitors to the site during their raid.

'Play the second file,' he said.

'This file was labelled "Floren Killer?"' Pandora said. 'It was filmed by a hidden camera on the development – what you see in this shot is the main access road into Deptford Waters.'

A moment later, a landscaper's van drove along the gentle curve of the roadway and into one of the empty bays. An elderly man in a waxed jacket and wide-brimmed hat lowered himself gingerly onto the gleaming tarmac and limped slowly around to the gate leading to the back of the show house.

On the video track, Pandora, asked, 'Who is this?'

'We don't know,' Alpha One said. 'We even considered moving in when the old guy made his way around to the back of the show house. We'd already called emergency services, but if he discovered Floren, he might release the bastard – and we did *not* want him to get away before the police arrived. Then something happened. You need to play the third clip.'

Pandora introduced the clip with a warning that some viewers might find what followed disturbing. 'And to give you a hint as to why, I should say that this video was labelled "Floren shooting?"' An ominous pause, then she added with a dramatic flourish, 'This file has not been edited, and I intend to let it run to the end.'

The sight-line of the final clip was different from the last, providing a wide-angle view of the show house frontage from the street, so they must have switched to a different camera. The development was still and quiet, except for the sound of a jet engine labouring overhead, no doubt taking off from London City Airport.

The lights were on in the front room of the house, which Floren had used as his office, Pandora explained. The camera picked up shadowy movement through the half-closed blinds, then it was gone.

Nothing for over a minute, but Pandora kept up a steady stream of information: the Wolf Pack continued to wait in the car park, not wanting to reveal themselves, 'or to put the old man in any danger – so they claim,' she added in a show of journalistic objectivity.

'According to the Wolf Pack's own account, Mr Floren was bound with tape to the bath taps,' she went on. 'And the bathroom is at the front of the house, so you need to focus on the first-floor window to the left of the front door.

'While you watch, notice that nobody enters or leaves the show house or the building next to it; the Wolf Pack operatives did *not* return to the house. This recording has been forensically verified – it is not a fake – it has *not* been digitally manipulated in any way.'

She waited a few seconds, then said, 'The clock on the recording shows that a total of seven and a half minutes has passed since the landscaper went around to the back of the show house. Then—'

Two grey-white flashes lit the frosted glass of the bathroom window – almost certainly the two shots that had ended Floren's life.

'Jeez!' Rick snatched up the remote and played the sequence again. This supported his theory: the assassin came in *after* the Wolf Pack had secured Floren. *Perhaps the shooter had removed the gag to be sure he'd got the right man?* He let the podcast play on and Pandora continued the narrative.

'In a moment, you'll hear sirens.'

On cue, the two-tone warning sirens of approaching police vehicles. Before the cars came into view, the van carrying the vigilantes pulled out of the bay and disappeared from shot.

'The police got there before we could act,' the vigilante said. 'We could see what was happening in real time on our covert cameras.' To prove it, Pandora let the video play on without sound, overlaying the visuals with commentary from her interview with Alpha One.

'When ambulances and a forensics team arrived,' he said, 'we knew something had gone badly wrong.'

'This was confirmed later when Floren's body was carried out,' Pandora went on. 'The shooting was labelled a professional hit. The strange thing is, the old man who drove the landscaper's van never reappeared. The show house's garden is enclosed by a six-foot fence, and there's a fifteen-foot drop on the other side.' Giving that a moment to sink in, she finished, 'The landscaper's van stayed on-site till the police took it away for forensic analysis, and the elderly landscaper has never been identified.'

Rick muted the podcast while Pandora ran through her promotional spiel. If the video footage was genuine, the 'old man' *had* to be the shooter. He'd abandoned the van, vaulted a six-foot fence and negotiated a dangerous drop, apparently without breaking his neck or alerting the police – and they must have arrived in under a minute after those muzzle flashes, so he moved *fast*. There wasn't a speck of trace evidence in that van, according to McGuinness, so this hitman was thorough. That kind of professionalism did not come cheap.

Chapter 33

RICK REPLAYED THE VIDEO CLIPS dozens of times. Using slow-motion and freeze-frame, he tried to pick out details from the sequences, hoping to catch the hint of a face behind the tinted visors, or idiosyncrasies of stance and gait in the Wolf Pack. The Met and NCA analysts would no doubt be looking at all of these things in the coming days, but Rick felt a strong, almost personal connection to the event as it unfolded, a need to discover who these people were. After two hours, all he'd gained was a headache, yet he couldn't help returning to the 'Floren killer' clip because realistically the only person he had any chance of identifying was the supposed landscaper.

The vigilantes must have skimped on the camera's tech specs – the image was grainy, even slightly blurred. Plus, the man had his head bowed, perhaps avoiding cameras. Of course, an old man taking care not to come a cropper on a wet night might well watch where he placed his feet. But if he'd played no part in the shooting, why had he disappeared? And more to the point, *how*? The scenario of an arthritic sixty-year-old with a bad hip leaping a six-foot fence just wasn't plausible.

And despite the overalls and battered hat, the old, waxed jacket and the limp, there was *something* about the man that made Rick think of Sam. Always a chameleon, Sam had an extraordinary ability to shrug on a new persona with each new set of clothes. Last autumn when they'd worked together, it seemed he'd had more costume changes than a Broadway show. But Sam hated heights – had almost got himself arrested on a teenage jaunt with Rick because he couldn't psych himself up to climb down from a high wall.

'I thought I told you I didn't want you rummaging about in cases outside your scope?'

Startled from his reminiscence, Rick quelled the urge to guiltily shut down the screen.

'Just watching Pandora's latest podcast, sir,' he said turning to face Detective Superintendent Ghosh. 'Got to say, there's a definite overlap with the Emin warehouse.'

Ghosh answered with a noncommittal 'Hm.'

'I was thinking maybe we should be working in tandem with the other inquiries.'

'That's something you need not concern yourself with.'

The superintendent's tone was ominous. Rick froze the frame and swung his chair around to face his boss. 'Sir?'

'You're supposed to be on sick leave,' Ghosh said. 'And – shocking though it may seem to you – the Met *can* function in your absence.'

'Couldn't rest. I thought I'd catch up on paperwork.'

'Well, you've been spotted,' Ghosh said, producing an image on his mobile phone of Rick entering the building, a white patch of gauze and wadding above his left eye.

Hell, is that blood on the dressing?

'It's on several local newsfeeds online,' Ghosh elaborated. 'It does *not* portray a good image of the Met's health and wellbeing policies, seeing a wounded officer pictured crawling into work looking like an extra on the latest zombie flick.'

'I came in upright,' Rick said, rather more sharply than he'd intended, and tried to soften his response by adding, 'I'll wear a beanie on the way out.'

'That's entirely up to you. There's an unmarked car waiting for you in the car park – I've arranged for someone to drop you at home. Don't keep him waiting.'

'Oh, thanks, but that's not necessary,' Rick said, deliberately misinterpreting the superintendent's dismissal as concern. 'I drove here – I'll head home when I've written my report.'

'*That* will wait,' Ghosh said, with an emphasis that brooked no argument.

The bastard was trying to sideline him under the guise of concern. *Well, you don't get off that easy, mate.*

'Won't it just stir up more interest if I'm ferried out of here under escort?'

Ghosh could be a smooth politician, and sometimes it was impossible to read any honest emotion behind the professional smile. At others, the man's barely suppressed rage surfaced, and he seemed to have very little control over it. Rick saw a flash of temper in the man's dark eyes now.

'Be that as it may,' Ghosh said. 'You are *complicating* the situation.'

'I'm not sure I—'

'Don't play the bloody innocent, Rick! It's all over the Web. Speculation about the officer who yelled a warning to the Wolf Pack. Who is he? Why did he shout "abort mission"? Some of the scrappier news media have already identified you by name. As for *what* you are, there are theories: a "modern-day gangbuster" in the mould of Detective Superintendent Wickstead, for instance – hunting down gangsters the old-fashioned way. Some say you knew about the raid – that you're one of them – that you might even be the leader of the bloody pack!'

'Sir, you can't think—'

'Frankly, right now I don't *know* what to think. But the social media crackpots think you're part of it. And you constantly poking around other people's business doesn't exactly inspire me with confidence.'

'Sir, I really wasn't—'

'I don't want to hear it,' Ghosh interrupted again. 'I want you out of the building in the next quarter hour, or I really will have you escorted out. Is that clear enough for you?'

'Yes, sir.'

Ghosh gave a curt nod. 'And don't come back until that dressing has been removed.'

'I'm due at the outpatient clinic later today,' Rick said. 'But that's just to check there's no infection so they can suture it. It might be a week before—'

'Not interested.' Ghosh checked his watch. 'Fourteen minutes.'

Joe Cossio peeked around the side of his computer screen and mimed 'Yikes!', but he waited till Ghosh was halfway down the corridor before saying aloud, 'He's all heart, isn't he?'

Rick shrugged. Bellyaching about the boss to Cossio would not be a wise move. He might as well pin a message to the staff noticeboard. With little time to spare, Rick needed to gather as much information as he could through official – if not sanctioned – channels.

Seeing that Rick was not inclined to chat, Cossio withdrew, and Rick called the switchboard from his desk phone and asked to be connected to Alan McGuinness.

He answered briskly, but Rick could almost *see* the detective's fair head duck when he realised who was at the other end of the line. He lowered his voice and, judging by the muffled tone, he'd cupped his hand over his mouth, too.

'Not a good time,' he murmured.

'Tell me about it,' Rick said.

'Oh, mate – sorry,' McGuinness said. 'How's the head?'

'Healing,' Rick said, then, taking advantage of the man's guilt. 'Have you watched the latest Pandora podcast?'

McGuinness groaned softly. 'Makes me almost glad they kicked me out of MIT.'

'The old guy – the landscaper – they never traced him?'

'We never even knew about him – all we had was the van left in one of the bays.'

'It's a crap recording. Didn't the murder investigation get *any* video of him?'

'I told you, the security cameras were out of action.' A pause, then: 'Why? D'you recognise him?'

MIT had lost a good cop when they'd got rid of McGuinness – the man was sharp.

'No,' Rick said, almost truthfully. He moved swiftly on. 'Pandora said the landscaper's van was taken away for forensic examination. You said there was no evidence in it, but was that no *usable* evidence or—'

'MO4 said it was "forensically clean" – which is rare, apparently. The fake graphics were cheap decals.'

'MIT didn't think it was odd that the killers had left a vehicle at the scene?'

'I wouldn't know, mate,' McGuinness said heavily. 'I was off the team by then.'

And after Ghosh's warning, Rick would not be able to risk asking anyone on the murder inquiry, so he wrapped up the call with small talk and a gripe about Ghosh sending him home, hanging up with a sigh of relief that McGuinness hadn't pressed him on potentially identifying the landscaper.

The phone rang immediately, and Rick picked up.

'DS Turner?' A woman's voice, familiar.

'Speaking,' he said.

'My name is Pandora Hahn, from—'

'I know who you are, Ms Hahn,' Rick said, with a stab of alarm. 'What do you want?'

'To talk.'

'You want Media and Communications,' he said. 'I can give you the number.'

'It's *you* I want to speak to,' she said.

'Yeah, not gonna happen.'

195

'Look, Sergeant, you must have seen what people are saying about you. I wanted to give you the opportunity to—'

Rick hung up, feeling more rattled than he should. It took him a moment to understand why. It was the video of the old landscaper: the more he kept circling back to it, the more he thought the limping man could be Sam. And Sam had used the fake decals trick during their joint operation last autumn. Could he be back in London? Rick had an emergency number; he could ring and find out. But the last thing he wanted was to bring his brother into this already messy picture.

Plus, Rick was still working through the trauma of what had happened a few months ago, still coming to terms with the fact that Sam – whom he'd been convinced for so long was dead – was a successful professional criminal who almost certainly listed contract killing as a key skill on his long résumé of lawbreaking. As the Met and the Wolf Pack had already discovered, Pandora Hahn had a way of winkling out the facts, of locating where the bodies were buried – and there were some that Rick fervently hoped would remain undisturbed.

Gathering his things ready to leave, he wondered if the Wolf Pack might have risked going back for the surveillance cameras they'd planted on Floren's development. It was doubtful. The CSIs collecting evidence at the scene can't have thought to look for CCTV that shouldn't have been there – otherwise the elderly landscaper would have been a major focus of attention. To be fair, they would have no reason to go looking. Having established that the security firm's CCTVs were down at the key time, the SIO on the case would have directed the forensic experts towards more promising lines of inquiry.

It was still early; his outpatient appointment wasn't until two p.m., and he really couldn't face an empty house. Maybe he was being paranoid, but after the Wolf Pack's recent revelations Rick wouldn't put it past Ghosh to sacrifice him to the media, and he wasn't going to be escorted off the premises in apparent disgrace.

He grabbed his car key from the drawer and headed for the basement.

Arriving at Deptford Waters at eleven a.m., he saw a neat, well-kept row of houses and bungalows. At the top end of the access road a high-rise block glinted in the spring sunshine. White curves broken up by sharper edges gave it an arty feel, and a landscaped park and play area at the base of it looked busy with families. Judging by the few cars that remained in the parking bays on a workday morning, the real estate did not come cheap, and Rick wondered if Floren's backers had found a way to wriggle out of their affordable housing pledge.

Rick drove to the end of the street to park so that he could get a leisurely look at the murder house. Gingerly pulling on a beanie hat to cover the dressing, he flinched as he caught the edge of the wound, and easing his fingers from under the hat gently, he sat for a moment till a wave of nausea passed. He'd been told not to constrict the wound, which probably meant wearing a woollen cap was out, but Ghosh would lose it if he was spotted and snapped on Floren's old turf. The wound throbbed and itched, and he hoped that wasn't a bad sign.

He walked back to the show house, phone in hand like the millennial he was and noticed that the frontage had been subtly altered at some time in the last few months – perhaps to dissociate the place from its grisly story – but it stood at the end of the row and was unmistakable. The construction site security cameras had been taken down – he assumed that families didn't like the thought of being observed as they went about their private lives.

Either the Wolf Pack's camera had been well hidden, or it was gone. He stood in front of the house for a minute, watching the *Pandora Unboxes* podcast footage and trying to work out the probable placement from the video of the old landscaper. The only possible place was some twenty feet away from the house. Turning, he peered into an island of bushes and trees behind him. A stout, mature specimen tree, topped to the shape of a helmet, had been planted in the centre. Rick was about to give up, when a small blue bird flew in through the branches. A frantic squabble of noise, then it emerged a few seconds later, carrying a white blob in its beak. Rick crossed to the tree and peered upwards.

An apex-design bird box was strapped to the trunk. Hidden among the burgeoning leaf growth, it was almost invisible now, but in February it would have had a clear line of sight to the show house, and it would be a simple task to hide a camera inside it.

Using his phone cam, he zoomed in and saw that the box had the usual access hole, but there was a second dark ring, near the apex. He magnified the image and saw that the circle was too small for a bird. It had a rim around the edge, and there was a hint of sheen to the centre. A camera lens, maybe?

Rick heard footsteps behind him – a man, he guessed by the weight and length of the stride. He went back to zapping off shots as though completely absorbed.

'What are you doing?' a male voice asked, and more petulantly when Rick didn't answer, '*Excuse* me – can I help you?'

Rick pasted a smile on his face and turned, asking excitedly, 'Is that a nest box up there?'

The man blinked at him, stupidly.

'Only, I just saw a bird fly in there – and there was this *amazing* racket.'

'You're a birder?' the man said.

'God no, I'm hopeless – but Izzy's mad about nature stuff. Would you happen to know? It was a blue one – tiny thing, with a yellow . . .' He patted his chest.

'Um,' was all the man could manage.

'Sorry,' Rick said, laughing at his apparent gaucheness, 'I must sound bonkers. It's just, we're having our first baby and thinking of moving out this way.' Rick was slightly alarmed that the lies rolled so easily off his tongue, but it seemed to be working and he went with it.

'We're in a rental in Newham right now.' He saw the slight twitch of the man's mouth and grimaced in agreement. 'Yeah, I know – it's a bit grim, but cheap, so we've got a good deposit ready. We had a whisper from the estate agent that something was coming up, so the plan was to come and do a recce. Izzy should've been with me, but her blood pressure's up a bit, and she had to stay home.' He paused and saw sympathy in the man's face.

'She was gutted, you know?' he said, laying it on a bit. 'So I thought I'd come over, take some snaps, cheer her up . . .'

He saw that the man's tension had drained away, and along with it, most of his interest.

'Oh, well, sorry for coming at you like that,' he said, already backing away. 'Only we've had trouble with ghouls, ever since that podcast.'

Rick wrinkled his brow. 'Why, has there been trouble? 'Cos—'

This put his inquisitor entirely on the defensive. 'No, no – it's a lovely place to live. Great family atmosphere, you know. And if your wife likes nature, there's even access to the canal towpath round the back.'

Rick beamed at him. 'Izzy's gonna love this! I gotta call her – cheers, mate!' He raised his hand in thanks as the man turned away, and Rick started back towards the car, already looking for Alan McGuinness's number in his contacts.

He'd given McGuinness a brief rundown by the time he'd slid behind the wheel.

'Shit, Rick,' McGuinness said. 'You do believe in living dangerously, don't you?'

'Who's it hurting?' Rick said.

'*You*, if Ghosh finds out.'

'Word's got around, has it?' Rick said.

McGuinness didn't answer immediately, but at last he said, 'Ah, what the hell – you're going to find out eventually. Cossio's been talking.'

So now everyone knows.

Shaking off his annoyance, Rick said, 'Look, this could give us an advantage over the Wolf Pack for the first time since they started messing us about. If it is their camera, it's been here since February,' Rick said. 'The recordings have probably been wiped or else they were uploaded straight to the cloud. But DNA, fingerprints . . .'

'How d'you expect me to get the info to the right person without dropping myself in it?' McGuinness demanded.

'I dunno,' Rick said. 'Talk to your mate at MIT – ask if they're planning to take a shufti at the development after the latest podcast.'

'And if they say no?'

Rick sighed. 'I suppose I'll have to find a way to get a photo to them anonymously.'

'Sarge, don't do that,' McGuinness said. 'They'll start asking questions and if your name comes out—'

'Okay . . .' Rick said, as though reluctant. What he'd say next would not get such a sympathetic reaction, so he spoke fast: 'You might want to have a word with DCI Steiner – see if the tech guys ever found out how our furry friends got audio at the car park during the Blackfriars mob arrests an' all.'

'All that's been checked,' McGuinness said.

'I'm saying it's probably worth a second look – if they missed a camera at Deptford, maybe they missed something at the car park.'

Chapter 34

AT THE HOSPITAL CLINIC, the nurse was a chatty Lancastrian. She told him as she cleaned and tidied up the area around the wound that it was healing nicely, and that it might not need stitching.

'So I can stop wearing the dressing?' he asked, eager to get back to work.

She pursed her lips. 'It's not all the way there, yet, chuck,' she said. 'And wounds open to the air usually scar worse' than the ones we keep nice and moist.'

Rick's stomach roiled at the thought of a 'nice, moist' wound. 'How about a plaster, then?' he asked. 'My boss is giving me a hard time – says I can't come back to work till the dressing's off.'

'What *I* wouldn't give to stay home under boss's orders.' She gave him a shrewd look. 'Put your feet up, get a bit of shut-eye – you look like you need it.'

'Thanks,' Rick said, with a wry smile.

'I speak as I find,' she said, laying the northern brogue on thick, for comic effect. 'Look, here's how it is: you've suffered a bullet wound to the head that took a chunk of skin almost clean off. You're lucky that it left a flap with enough healthy blood vessels to start the healing process so – fingers crossed – it'll reattach itself.'

201

Rick began to feel decidedly queasy.

'But it's a delicate process,' she went on, oblivious. 'The skin that's still attached to your skull is also damaged, and if you use sticky plaster to cover it, when you lift the dressing off to clean or replace it, you could tear off the flap of skin along with it.' She pinched air between her finger and thumb and moved her arm in a wide arc, graphically illustrating the action. 'So—'

'Okay,' Rick interrupted. 'No more. You convinced me.'

She chuckled. 'It's always strapping great men that come over all funny when you give 'em the gory details.'

She stood back and admired her handiwork. Satisfied, she binned the kit of saline and swabs from the trolley, stripped off her vinyl gloves and said, 'Sit tight, and I'll fetch a doctor – they'll tell you if it wants stitching.'

Rick waited for ten minutes. After another five, he dug his phone out of his pocket and saw that the unidentified man at Jason Floren's murder scene had become a hot topic.

#limpingman, #Florenkiller and #pandoraunboxes were all trending. Recalling the Deptford Waters development, Rick was touched by the rather sweet picture of family life and community watchfulness he'd witnessed there. What Floren had done was horrible, but he wondered if the man had tried to make some measure of reparation by building this beautiful oasis out of a grey corner of south London. Could there be redemption for a man like Floren?

After twenty minutes, beginning to think he'd been forgotten, Rick hopped off the bed and opened the door. A girl with a bandaged hand sat morosely next to an older woman – her mother, judging from the practised resentment on the kid's face. Rick looked right and left, but no nursing staff were around. As he began to retreat, he heard a click and zoomed in on the taciturn girl.

'Did you just take a picture of me?' Rick asked.

The kid didn't look up, but Rick saw her fingers darting over the virtual keyboard. With one final thumb tap, she glanced at Rick with a look of feigned innocence.

'I need you to delete that tweet,' Rick said.

'Tweet?' The girl sneered. 'Do I *look* like an angry old person?'

'Hey!' the mother exclaimed. 'I use Twitter.'

The look on the girl's face spoke volumes about their difficult relationship.

Rick appealed directly to the woman. 'Look, I'm just here for treatment – I can *really* do without the media attention.'

She looked at her daughter. 'Did you put that picture on Instagram?'

The girl gave her mother a pained look. '*Instagram?*'

'TikTok – whatever. Delete it.'

'Why?'

'Because. You wouldn't like it if someone took a picture of what's under that bandage.'

The girl blanched and then flushed, but she jammed the phone into her pocket defiantly.

Further down the corridor, a couple of older lads had reached for their phones. 'Oh my God, it's him,' one of them muttered. 'The Wolf Pack guy.'

Shit. Rick retreated fast, hoping that the mother would persuade her daughter to do the decent thing.

Within minutes, the images had been shared or stolen and posted as original across several platforms. The below-the-line comments ranged from criticisms of whoever had posted the picture to speculation that he'd been suspended on suspicion of conspiring with the Wolf Pack.

Rick closed the feed and sat for a moment with his eyes closed. This was a bloody nightmare.

The door opened and he panicked for a second, half expecting to see the two youths, trying their luck, but it was only the chatty nurse and the doctor. At last, having peered at him through a magnifying lens and issuing instructions that only vaguely acknowledged his presence, she left. The nurse redressed his wound – mercifully with a lighter dressing – and gave him instructions on what to do to aid the healing process, what to look out for in case of infection, and ending with advice on when to return for another check-up before the hospital discharged him to his GP practice.

Finally, she handed him a leaflet with helpful diagrams on dos and don'ts for a speedy recovery.

As he stood, Rick pulled a beanie from his pocket.

'Ah-ah-ah – no you don't,' she scolded. 'I've just spent the best part of twenty minutes cleaning you up!'

He stared at the inoffensive-looking hat. 'What's wrong with it?'

'When was the last time that raggedy thing was washed?'

'I've only had it a couple of months – it's practically new.'

She scoffed. 'You might as well dunk your head in a toilet bowl.'

Rick sighed. 'Okay, but I'm taking a hammering on the news feeds – some kid took a snap of me while you were gone. Now it's all over social media, and there's two lads outside just itching for me to poke my nose around the door.'

Her face darkened. 'Wait here.'

She came back less than a minute later. 'The corridor's clear, and if you follow me, I can take you a way that avoids the main clinic waiting area.' She didn't explain how she'd dealt with the two wannabe-paparazzi, and Rick didn't push it. He was just grateful to arrive back at his car without having been followed or photographed.

His mobile rang as he eased himself into the driving seat, and he answered without thinking.

'Pandora Hahn, from *Pandora Unboxes*.'

'Pandora, I swear, if this is about—' He stopped himself in time. An unguarded word quoted out of context right now could be the final nail in the coffin of his dying career.

'It isn't about the image of you at the hospital, or your possible suspension,' she said, filling in the blanks for him. 'At least, not directly. However, I have an eyewitness who states that on the night you were rushed to hospital with head wounds, you were harangued by a senior Met Police officer.'

Ghosh.

'I have *a* head wound,' Rick said. 'Singular.'

'Well done on ignoring the question,' she said. 'If the situation escalates, you should consider changing careers – you'd make a great politician.'

'And what would you call *that*?' Rick snapped back. 'The art of sarcastic journalism?'

She took a breath, held it, then exhaled loudly. 'Sorry. That was unprofessional. But I'm just looking for a little cooperation – we're on the same side, here.'

'What side is that?'

'Truth. Justice.'

Rick tugged his ear. 'Big words.'

'Not just words, Sergeant, I can promise you that. I think you have a right to tell your side. Don't get me wrong – I'll run the story either way – but I think it's only fair to offer you the chance to state your case.'

'My *case*? Are you accusing me of something, Ms Hahn?'

'I'm not, but others are. And as I said, I have an eyewitness who gave a detailed account of what they heard – and some of it is open to interpretation.'

'Most conversations are.'

'According to my witness, this wasn't a "conversation" – it was a bawling out. And some of what was said implied that a senior ranking officer suspected you of conspiring with a vigilante group.'

Remembering Ghosh, grinding his teeth, whispering, *You gave an order to those cowboys!* Rick saw how the entire rant could be interpreted as one accusation after another. His shoulders sagged.

God, can this get any worse?

Ghosh was a short fuse sitting on a big powder keg of suppressed anger. When he was in that kind of mood, he had no impulse control at all – what came out of his mouth could be destructive – ruinous, even. And hadn't Ghosh wondered very much out loud if Rick knew more than he'd admitted to?

'I *will* quote the senior officer,' she said, 'and it *will* look bad for you.'

'It looks bad already,' Rick said. 'What the hell d'you *want* from me?'

'Context,' she said simply.

'*Why?* You can't quote me – I'm close to losing my job already. The minute I go on record, I'm finished.'

'Then we talk *off* the record.'

That stopped Rick short. 'Seriously?'

'I'm absolutely serious. It's true what they say: context really is everything – in policing, in journalism – in everything.' She must have sensed his change of mood in his silence, because she pushed harder, repeating, '*Off* the record. No witnesses, just you and me. What d'you say – will you do it?'

Guilty instinct made Rick check his rear-view and side mirrors.

'I'll meet you,' he said. Hearing a gasp of excitement, he added quickly: 'But I get to choose the time and place.'

'O-kaaay,' she said. 'But it has to be public – and no blindfold.'

'What?'

'Joke,' Pandora said. 'Not a good one.' She laughed nervously, and he realised that the Wolf Pack had spooked her more than she'd made out. 'You can choose the place,' she began again. 'But it has to be in the next two hours – I plan to podcast this evening.'

It wouldn't be easy finding somewhere they could talk privately without being monitored: London was one of the most surveilled cities in the world, with almost as many cameras per square mile as Moscow. Rick was parked on a meter in a side street near the hospital; it had a couple of hours still on the clock, so it'd be easiest to just leave the car and walk along Whitechapel High Street till he found somewhere. But the clean white dressing would attract attention, so with a sigh, Rick took the hat out of his pocket, stretched it as wide as he could and lowered over his brow. Retrieving a hoodie from the boot, he swapped it for his jacket and pulled the hood up. If the chatty nurse saw him, she'd have a fit, but some snap-happy teen catching a shot of him meeting up with Pandora would be far more damaging.

By Aldgate East Station, he found the perfect place.

Pandora picked up on the first ring.

'Whitechapel Gallery.' He checked his watch. 'Three-thirty.'

'That doesn't give me much time,' she hedged.

'You mean you *didn't* head out to the hospital the minute that image got uploaded to the Web?'

She chuckled. 'Okay, you got me.'

'Meet me in the café.'

He spent the next half hour working out where the emergency exits were and sussing the safest place to sit. The room was square and well lit, with no dark corners to hide, so he decided on a window table, sitting with his back to the room.

She was prompt, taking a seat opposite him at precisely three-thirty. 'Well, this is nice,' she said.

'I'm here under protest, Ms Hahn,' Rick said. 'Not for a cosy chat.'

She tucked a stray lock of hair behind her ear and looked almost contrite. It was lighter than it had looked on TV, cut in a layered bob to soften a rather square chin. She seemed younger, too – more vulnerable than he'd expected.

A server, clearing the table next to theirs said, 'D'you know what you want, guys? We're still serving lunch if you want something light.'

They settled for coffee. Waiting a moment or two for the server to leave, Pandora said, 'Let's make a start, then.' She set her phone face-down on the table and Rick shook his head.

'It's not recording,' she said, on the defensive.

'You need to turn it off.'

A fleeting look of annoyance crossed her face, but she complied.

'*All* of this is off the record – even the fact that we're meeting,' Rick stressed.

She raised her gaze from her phone, meeting his with a frank, open look. Her eyes were greenish and deep set, her skin olive toned. 'Completely off the record,' she said, adding with a sharp mischievous gleam in her eye, 'But I'm hoping to change your mind on that score.'

He allowed himself a smile.

'So, how would you respond to the witness statement?'

Rick's smile broadened – it was an old trick, getting an interviewee to add details by holding back, implying that you know more than you really do.

'Depends on what they said.' She looked ready to argue, but he added, 'It's all in the detail.'

She glanced down at the table, and he had the sense that she was grounding herself.

By the time the coffee arrived, she'd provided a near word-for-word summary of what Ghosh had said to him on the night of the shootings.

Without confirming or denying the truth or accuracy of it, Rick asked who'd given her the information.

She answered him with a blank look.

'A nurse, perhaps?' Nurse Verren had admitted that she'd blatantly listened in on Ghosh's tirade in the emergency department.

'I'm a journalist,' Pandora said. 'I can't tell you my sources.'

'Did they name this supposed "senior officer"?'

'No.' She considered. 'But they did describe him.'

There weren't many Asian detective superintendents in the London Met, and she seemed to be implying that it wouldn't be hard to find out the name.

'They said that the man in question stood looming over the trolley and berated you as you fought the after-effects of a serious head injury.'

Nurse Verren. Got to be.

'Why would she tell you that – I mean what's her angle?' He was hoping she'd slip and reveal that her informant was a female nurse.

'Maybe they hate to see an injured man being bullied.' She emphasised 'they'. Fair enough.

'Or maybe they want their fifteen minutes of fame.'

'I don't think so,' Pandora said simply. 'They don't want to be named – they don't even want it known if they're male, or female. They said there were a lot of people milling around that night. Anyone might have heard what was said – they could even be a patient.'

'Okay. You clearly protect your sources. So, you'll have the journalistic integrity to keep this meeting confidential?'

'Well, of course,' she said, piqued. 'But it would be to your advantage to give your side.'

Rick looked into her face, returning her frank gaze. Finally, he broke eye contact and looked out across the street to the three-storey Edwardian terrace opposite: yellow London brick above, small shops in gunmetal grey below.

'*Off* the record,' he said. 'If your source is trying to help, she's only made things ten times worse. You might pass on that message.'

She inclined her head. 'If I see them again.'

Rick took a sip of coffee, undecided on whether to speak until the words started coming out of his mouth. 'That was a bloody night.'

She remained silent, giving him her full attention.

'Emotions were high – a police officer had been killed less than an hour earlier. Police are human, Ms Hahn – things are sometimes said in the heat of the moment.'

'Well,' she said, 'I must say that's very generous of you. If I'd been shot in the head and then – forgive the pun – brow-beaten by my boss, I think I'd be less forgiving.'

Rick suppressed a smile. It was hard not to like this forthright woman.

'My witness stated that you asked after your colleague and your guvnor didn't even have the decency to tell you that he'd died.'

Rick didn't comment.

'You addressed them as the Wolf Pack,' she said. 'How did you know to do that?'

Rick described the decals on their helmets.

'And what do you say to the accusation that you gave them an order – *and they complied*?'

Rick gave Pandora the same arguments he'd given Superintendent Ghosh: that they were clearly well trained, disciplined; it was worth a try, and thankfully, it worked.

Pandora nodded. 'That confirms what my source said. So you think they're professionally trained?'

'I'm not here to give you my opinions on a vigilante group, Ms Hahn.'

'Like you said – worth a try,' she said with a sheepish grin. 'But you don't have any idea who these people are?' Rick shot her a baleful look and she said, 'Come on – it's all off the record.'

'You're the one who's been in close contact with them,' he said. 'You tell me.'

'Off the record?' she said.

'If you like.'

'I haven't a clue. But you're right about them being disciplined – I was . . . with three of them for three hours – and the only one who spoke was the man calling himself Alpha One.' She seemed agitated, recalling her ordeal, and touched her face with the back of her hand, as if to cool it.

Rick saw a slight shadow under the makeup along her jawline.

'Are you all right?' he asked.

Startled by the question, she said, 'Why do you ask?'

'You were abducted by armed men; taken God knows where. And I see there's bruising.' He focused on her jawline, and he saw again that self-comforting gesture – her hand to her face again.

Seeing him watching, she folded her hands firmly on the table in front of her. 'I'm fine.'

They wrapped up a few minutes later, and she said again that she'd like to get his answers on record.

'Not a chance,' Rick said, standing and leaving a tenner on the table. 'That should cover the bill. Don't rush out on my account.'

She shot him a sardonic look. 'You needn't worry – I wasn't going to follow you.'

Rick paused. 'Be careful, Ms Hahn. They may be disciplined, but they're under intense pressure, and people who feel they have a righteous cause can lose perspective, abandon their training – lose all control – when things start to go against them.'

He pulled up the hood of his jacket, leaving her looking pale and shocked.

Chapter 35

BEFORE HE WENT HOME, Rick ducked inside the emergency department, hoping to find Senior Charge Nurse Verren, and was surprised to be told that she was on leave. Had been on the night of the shootings as well, but had come in anyway, which was typical of her according to the nurse he spoke to. When she went on to ask if he was the police officer everyone was talking about, Rick excused himself and returned to his car at a trot.

Maybe it was the incident with the TikToker at the hospital, but making his way home, he had the uncomfortable feeling of being watched. He thought about the Audi driver he'd confronted four days ago, just before things turned bad at Emin's Limehouse factory. He'd reported the incident, but the Audi plates he'd given to the attending officers belonged to a recently scrapped BMW. At the time, the task force had considered the possibility that Emin was on to their surveillance op. Needless to say, the car hadn't been found.

With a dozen ways to cross the river between Tower Bridge and Putney, Rick had plenty to choose from. He passed two, slowing deliberately and spurring irritated drivers to sound their horns and swerve past him at the first chance they got. After Waterloo Bridge, he pulled into a lay-by on the Victoria Embankment and observed the passing traffic. If he was being followed, they were good – or else they had a fleet of cars, following him in rotation. If he was right, whoever had organised tailing him would need substantial resources. Emin and his business associates would have that kind of money. But if Emin had known that the factory was being watched, surely he would never have gone ahead with the drugs delivery.

If it *wasn't* Emin, who else would go to the trouble and expense? Someone who'd bought in to the rumours and social media gossip, hoping he'd lead them to the Wolf Pack? That was a strong possibility – the broadsheets must be grinding their teeth over Pandora's monopoly on the vigilantes.

Yet how did his stalkers know where to find him? Rick was as sure as he could be that he hadn't been followed driving to work, nor on the journey to the outpatient clinic at the hospital. So it seemed likely that the TikToker's snapshot of him had given whoever it was a starting point to tail him; he just hoped that they hadn't followed him on foot from the hospital to the gallery.

With a sinking dread, Rick saw another possible scenario: London Met Police had the resources for exactly this kind of tracking, and over the last few days Ghosh had made it clear that he wasn't above using Rick as a scapegoat for his own mishandling of the warehouse raid.

Rick eased out into the traffic and turned left over Lambeth Bridge, taking right or left turns on a whim, doubling back – even crossing the Thames twice more – but he couldn't identify the following vehicles.

At home, he locked the car and walked back to the junction of his street. It was still early; the city workers wouldn't be home for another hour or so. A cold wind and gathering cloud threatened rain, and he saw only one young mum pushing a pram and an elderly man walking a dog. He peered at the cars parked at the roadside, but saw no shadowy forms huddled inside.

Frustrated, he returned to the house and dug out the scanner Sam had him buy last autumn when Rick had suspected he was being monitored at home. He swept every room for bugs, working methodically, checking cupboards, cubbyholes, wardrobes, lights, electrical sockets and smoke alarms. As an afterthought, he even stuck his head in the loft. There was nothing but a stack of plastic boxes containing Sam's old comic collection.

That left only the car itself.

His sports bag was clear, as was the jacket he'd thrown into the boot, but when Rick scanned the device across the rear bumper, he saw a sudden blip in the reading and the bars on the screen turned yellow. He moved in closer, scanning more slowly, lowering himself to a crouch. To the left of the exhaust pipe, he saw it: a small black box. Setting down the bug sweeper for a moment, Rick took out his phone and used its torch to get a clearer look. The box was attached by two magnetic disks as far as he could see. He snapped a few photos before getting to his feet.

Indoors again and feeling calmer now that he had something concrete to work with, Rick ran through the options again. Emin was an unlikely candidate as his stalker, and he had to admit that his suspicions of Met Police involvement edged into the realms of paranoia. Which left two more to consider: the news feeds, and Sam.

When Rick was fifteen, Sam had dropped out of his life so completely that Rick and his parents had been convinced he was dead. He'd stayed gone for thirteen years but had recently admitted that he'd kept tabs on Rick all that time. Inside the house again, he found the instructions for his router and changed the password before turning on his laptop. Using a VPN, he searched for the forum Sam had given him months ago in case he needed to make contact. Accessed via the Tor network, their internet activity would be difficult to trace.

As he typed his message, this last scenario seemed more and more like the only rational explanation. Rick wasn't sure if he should feel relieved or furious.

Chapter 36

SAM CHECKED HIS MESSAGES REGULARLY – the forum was his main conduit to work and a rich source of information; not to do so would be negligent. He had also set up push notifications for anything from Rick, so it was only minutes later that he received a ping on one of his untraceable phones. He had been listening to an update from his surveillance team leader, but he interrupted the speaker with an apology and a promise to call him back.

Rick's message was brief and to the point:

—Are you having me followed?

The question set off alarm bells. Sam typed swiftly:

—Why do you ask?

—Answer the question, Sam.

—No, I am not.

Sam added:

—*Are* you being followed?

He quickly deleted the question, typing instead:

—Are you *sure* you're being followed?

—Certain. Is it you?

—Are you all right? How's the head?

—Stop changing the damn subject!

The reply had come so fast that Sam could imagine Rick's fury as he typed.

—I didn't think I was, he answered, mildly.

No reply. Rick seemed to be waiting.

—I told you I'm not following you, and although I do keep you in the dark on many things, I do *not* lie to you, Rick.

The chat response ellipsis remained stubbornly motionless – Rick was not typing. *Okay* . . .

—Additionally, you were shot in the head a few days ago, and you seem agitated. Naturally, I'm concerned.

That got a fast response:

—I'm not paranoid FFS – someone is following me – tracking me!

—Well, which is it? Sam typed, knowing that the question would come across as sarcastic and disinterested, despite his growing alarm.

—Both.

Sam believed him, and the development was worrying. Of course, Rick's stalker could be linked to the shootings at Limehouse – Emin was more than capable of sending men after him, but Sam's intel said that the drug lord had suffered serious losses and was laying low in fear for his own life; pursuing a cop doing his job would not be high on his agenda right now. There again, Rick had become an unwilling social media icon since the Met's disastrous raid on Emin's new factory. This afternoon, the image of Rick, his head wound still swollen and seeping, had circulated globally. Rick was exposed, and exposure made him vulnerable. Of course, it *could* be a news company determined to get a picture or – better yet from their perspective – a story that would boost their following. It wasn't only Instagrammers and TikTokers who relied on advertising to pay their bills – even the news heavyweights needed their share of 'hits' in order to milk the corporate cash cow.

Rick typed:

—You there, Sam?

Sam watched the cursor blinking, knowing that there was a stronger, more dangerous possibility. It was tied into events that would be difficult to broach with his brother, and if Rick was to be persuaded of the real peril he was in, they would need to speak face to face. That, in itself, might be risky under current circumstances, but he couldn't see an alternative. Finally, he typed:

—We need to talk.

—What are you up to?

Ignoring the question, Sam typed:

—In person. Do you still have the burner we used to communicate last year?

A pause of twenty seconds, during which the chat ellipses moved in a steady arc, like fingers drumming a tabletop. Finally, the message came through:

—Yes.

He imagined that Rick had typed and then deleted an impulsive response.

—You really should have destroyed it. Sentimentality will get you killed in this game, Rick.

—Yeah, well it's not *my game*, is it?

Sam arched an eyebrow. He had a point.

—No matter. I'll ring you on that mobile in five minutes. Take a walk, though – if you're being tracked, you might also be bugged.

—I swept the house – it's clean, Rick snapped back. Then:

—You've got something to say, call and tell me.

Sam sighed.

—We need to meet. It's important.

—Call me.

—I can't do that. There are serious risks involved.

He waited.

—Rick?

No response: he'd gone.

217

Sam would not put his brother in greater jeopardy by talking to him in a setting that he couldn't control. He sat for a few moments, a frown creasing his habitually untroubled features. Finally, he picked up one of his basic burner phones and called the employee he'd been speaking to a few minutes earlier.

'Ready for the final instalment, guv?' the man asked.

'Not quite. This is a new commission. We'll be needing top-quality operatives.' He named two capable men he'd used last autumn when Rick had had his troubles with a gang boss named Unwin.

'Let me know if they're available for immediate deployment,' Sam said.

'What's the job?'

'As soon as I know they're free, I'll text you a number for them to contact me direct.' Sam would instruct those two personally. 'Surveillance may need to be stepped up – send me a few names – people we've used before. And if there's even a hint of activity at any of his old haunts, I want to hear about it immediately.'

'Will do.'

Next, Sam put in a call to Dave Collins. They'd never met – and hopefully never would – so there was no danger of Dave discovering that Rick and Sam were brothers. As far as he was concerned, they were friends, which apparently gave Sam special status in the trustworthy stakes.

'I'm calling about the Wolf Pack,' Sam said.

'I already sent you my report.' Collins sounded confused, on the brink of panic.

'You did, and it was good work. But now they've been involved in an incident that resulted in the death of a police officer and Rick getting shot.' He didn't expect an answer: the man he thought of as his armchair ninja would not see the need to reply, since everything Sam had said so far was correct.

'I need to know who these vigilantes are,' Sam said. 'They nearly got Rick killed, and that is unacceptable.'

'I'm with you there, mate.' The analyst spoke with unusual fierceness, and as Dave was a timid man practically incapable of eye contact, it was clear how much Rick meant to him.

'Where d'you want me to start?' Dave asked.

'With the incidents you identified as being likely Wolf Pack actions – starting with the most recent and working backwards.'

'Okaaaa-ay . . .'

'So first attenders, anyone who had a lot of interaction with the victims, crossover between different crimes, even. But we're looking for men with a specific skill set.'

'Or women,' Dave suggested.

'Or women,' Sam agreed, amused. The rules of social interaction did not come naturally to Dave, and Sam realised that this was a response he must have learned by rote. Knowing that there was a set of socially acceptable responses would no doubt have helped Dave to reduce the anxiety of being in a situation where he didn't know the correct behaviours. Sam had never experienced anxiety at not knowing the rules – he only cared about fitting in as far as it gave him the advantage. For Sam, pursuing his wants and needs as a child, there were simply things he got away with, and things he didn't, and he'd quickly identified and adopted strategies that played to his advantage and avoided the hated penalties and punishments.

'I only meant that they were disguised – so you couldn't be sure.'

Sam heard desperation in Dave's tone; he wanted to be useful, and Sam's silence had convinced him that he'd made a gaff.

'It's a good point,' Sam said. 'I can get the information to you and leave you to work on the analysis.'

Dave had an uncanny eye for patterns and anomalies – particularly where numbers were concerned. He could often see the problem just by glancing down a list or casting his eye over a spreadsheet. To him, it was as plain as a missing tooth in a perfect smile – ugly and jarring. He would always want to confirm his instinctive response with statistical checks, but he was invariably right.

After a moment's silence, Dave cleared his throat. 'About Rick – I've been thinking, maybe I should give him a call – see how he is?'

The big fellow had crushingly low self-esteem and assumed that any contact from him would, by default, be rated an intrusion. His armchair ninja was seeking an assurance that Rick would not reject his well-intentioned approach. He wanted *permission* to pick up the phone and make a simple call.

'I think Rick could really use a friend right now,' Sam said. 'But do me a favour and leave it until tomorrow, will you? I think he's had a tough day.' He had other reasons for wanting Rick left alone tonight, but Dave didn't need to know the details.

'There is *one* more thing, if you can spare the time,' Sam said. 'I'm considering investing a considerable sum of money in a business run by an old friend, but it's been a while since we were in touch, and I've since heard some disturbing rumours about the man. I believe he might be shielding his shadier deals behind shell companies,' he added in a disapproving tone. 'Now, I can't ask him outright, but you have a genius for discreet but thorough financial vetting, so I wondered if you could trace where any money is routed, and the sums involved.'

'Easy-peasy.' Dave knew his strengths and was not cursed with false modesty. 'You got names for any of the shell companies?'

'I'm afraid not,' Sam said. 'But I do have bank account details – I can send them over by text.'

'*No*,' Dave said, instantly alarmed. 'No texts. Send them via the forum.'

By this, he meant going through a VPN, then onward via Tor to an encrypted chatroom on a Deep Web forum he'd specified for their written communications. The Deep Web was even safer than the Dark Web and since Dave was using his skills and his privileged access as a senior financial investigator at the Serious Fraud Office for his unsanctioned dealings with Sam, his extreme caution was understandable.

'I'll do that,' Sam said. 'And I hate to pile on the pressure, but this is urgent.'

'Not a problem. Once I've set up the alerts, they'll run in the background. Soon as I know, you'll know.'

Chapter 37

RICK PEELED OFF HIS BEANIE HAT WHILE HE WAITED for Sam to call. It looked clean enough, but the wound on his forehead did feel hot after wearing the thing for the last couple of hours. He sniffed the fabric tentatively and recoiled – it definitely smelled ripe. The words of the Lancastrian nurse sounded loud and broad in his mind:

Might as well stick your head in the toilet!

He carried the thing between finger and thumb to the kitchen, washed and rinsed it, and left it to drip-dry over the back of a chair.

Keeping Sam's burner close by on charge while he made himself a microwave meal, he ate in the kitchen, then snagged a beer and took it through to the sitting room, where he brooded over what to do about the tracker on his car.

Musing over his online chat, he decided that Sam was telling the truth – he'd have no cause to put a tracker on his car. That settled, it was clear that whoever was stalking him was either keeping their distance or monitoring him remotely. He might use that to his advantage – park the car up somewhere and hop in a cab before whoever it was came to check why he'd stopped. Or he might leave the car parked at the kerbside near the house and sneak out the back way. He was on sick leave after all.

An hour later, Sam still hadn't rung, and Rick decided to see if Pandora had published her new podcast. Ignoring a disturbingly large number of notifications with his name in the header, and bypassing the social media platforms entirely, he went straight to her website.

She began by rehashing the widespread media speculation over Rick's warning to the Wolf Pack on the night of the shootings, then moved smoothly on to her new exclusive: an eyewitness at the hospital who'd claimed that Rick had been as good as accused of being a Wolf Packer by a senior officer.

'His exact words were: "You gave an order to those cowboys!"'

Rick groaned inwardly – she was just giving the conspiracy theorists more to work with.

'This is a high-ranking officer,' Pandora went on, 'talking to a detective who's just survived a bullet to the head – and is still coming round after treatment.'

Emphasising that she would not reveal her source, she added that she'd had corroboration of the accuracy of the account. Rick held his breath, but good as her word, she didn't even hint that he had provided that corroboration.

She rattled through the sequence of Rick's actions that evening before running a short clip from the video the Wolf Pack had sent her, and Rick heard himself bellowing: 'Armed police! This is a POLICE OPERATION. Wolf Pack. Abort! ABORT MISSION!'

'There's been a lot of speculation about those dozen words, and clearly this senior detective had put his own interpretation on it.' She paused, gazing in silence as if she was making eye contact with her eager followers on the other side of the screen.

'But let's unpack what Turner said: "This is a POLICE OPERATION." Clearly, he was trying to warn the Wolf Pack that they had blundered into a police action. Now, if Turner *was* a member of the Wolf Pack, wouldn't they already know about this operation? I mean, you would expect a vigilante to be in communication with his own team, wouldn't you? Yet, clearly they *didn't* know – because immediately after his warning, they withdrew. Is it even *plausible* that Sergeant Turner was part of this vigilante group?' She gave her followers time to reach their own conclusions.

'And what about the so-called "order" he gave? "ABORT MISSION!"?' She paused. 'How would *you* expect a police officer to address a pod of trained, armed men? "Hey, there, I'm a police officer. You need to stop – you're in the middle of a police raid?" As a journalist, I've witnessed a few police actions in person, and I've watched an awful lot more online during my research for *Pandora Unboxes . . . Hamstrung Law*. Police always use simple, powerful commands – such as "ABORT MISSION".

'Now you might ask yourself why didn't the multi-agency team involved in the operation *know* what was happening? To answer that question, you need to understand the layout of the warehouse and its location.'

She shifted to an aerial satellite view of the street.

'As you can see, the access road to the warehouse is in a narrow backstreet – more an alley than a street, really. There's a kind of dog-leg on the vehicle access approach from the main road, which means you have to advance about twenty yards down the alley before you can see the warehouse entrance. I know this, because I went to the location and checked it out today.'

To prove it, she showed an image of herself standing at the junction of the main road and the vehicle access to Emin's drug factory. A high wall was visible to the right of the image and a mid-rise apartment block on the left, but the warehouse itself was out of shot.

'The warehouse is slightly offset to the right,' she explained, pulling up another image that showed the street at the point it widened, with parking bays and truck access to it.

Highlighting a narrow passage to the left of its entrance, she said, 'The other end of the street is pedestrian access only

– protected from vehicles by concrete bollards. No one at *either* end of the street could have seen what was happening. *Only* the detective in the apartment building overlooking the warehouse had a good view of events – and that detective was DS Turner.'

Next, she played a video clip of the apartment building, panning up to the window where Rick had been stationed, zooming in on a bullet hole in the glass.

Rick's chest crunched in a quick spasm seeing blood spatter on the inside of the windowpane.

'The only *other* people who might have had a view of events as they unfolded that night were the families living in that same apartment building,' Pandora went on. 'But they were sleeping in their apartments, completely unaware that a police operation was in progress.'

She froze the video frame on the window spattered with red, its spider's web of cracks perfectly framing the bullet hole.

'A reasonable person might argue that those sleeping families were saved from random bullets by two distinct actions that night: DS Turner on the one hand, and – let's be totally honest here – the Wolf Pack on the other.

'Another question arises: since the police teams waiting to descend on the warehouse did not have a clear view of it, would they have had advance warning of the vigilantes going into the building? They had crews at both ends of the alley, and we know that the officer who died had been stationed at the pedestrianised end of the street. We can safely assume everyone involved in this operation was in radio contact with their team leaders – that's pretty standard stuff. But we *also* know that nobody tried to stop the Wolf Pack from entering the building. They accessed the warehouse from the pedestrianised end of the street, so the police officers on watch *must* have seen them approaching. Surely, they would have informed their bosses? How did their team leaders respond? And did Sergeant Turner warn his police colleagues of the danger?

'My source at the hospital heard Turner say that he'd "conveyed intel per protocol", which at least *implies* radio communication. And he *did* risk his own life warning the vigilantes about the police operation and – another undeniable fact – he *was* shot in the line of duty.'

She held the collective gaze of her growing number of followers. 'I spoke to the Met Police, but they didn't want to comment. Could it be that senior police *ignored* their surveillance crews' warnings?' She paused. 'I don't know. But I *do* know that the Wolf Pack stood down as soon as Sergeant Turner opened a window of the apartment building and shouted a warning. Does that mean that Detective Sergeant Turner is a member of the vigilante group?'

She waited for her followers to mull the question in their own minds before saying, 'I asked the Wolf Pack leader. This is the man calling himself "Alpha One" – the boss wolf, if you like – so you'd think he'd know. He denied it *categorically* – no hesitation, no hedging.' She tilted her head. 'It would be good to get a straight answer from the Met.'

She sighed. 'Okay, I can hear the sceptics out there, saying, "Of *course* the Wolf Pack will say Turner isn't on their team." In truth, we can't be certain that this detective has no links to the Wolf Pack – I don't have access to police recordings of communications between Turner and his senior officers on that night.'

She allowed that thought to lodge in her subscribers' minds. 'But in the circumstances,' she said, 'I think any reasonable person would applaud DS Turner's actions.'

Rick turned down the sound as she segued into a marketing spiel and thanked her sponsors. Sagging back in his chair, he let out a long, shaky breath. Smiling to himself, he thought if he was brought in front of a disciplinary board, he'd want Pandora Hahn as his advocate. But her brilliant arguments could just as easily rebound on him: social media squirrels would have no trouble unearthing Ghosh's identity and Rick knew that if Ghosh was volatile under threat, he could be explosive when he was backed into a corner.

He checked his watch; it was late, and it looked like Sam didn't intend to make that call. It seemed that finding out who was tracking him was a question for another day.

Chapter 38

Four days after the Emin warehouse raid

RICK SLEPT FITFULLY, TUMBLING BACK to the night of the shootings when he'd watched black-clad men breach Emin's warehouse with military precision.

Seconds later, he was awake, sweating, startled out of the dream by the sound of rifle shots. He rolled over and sank into light doze. He was lying on a hospital trolley, looking up at the nurse, Vee Verren. She was laughing.

'You can't really expect me to *kiss* you,' she said. 'I can't be certain you're not one of them.'

The next instant, Rick was sitting inside a van next to a man in tactical gear. Opposite him sat three more men. Fully kitted out: helmets on, visors down. The man beside him passed him a neatly stacked bundle. Rick knew this was Alpha One.

Taking the bundle, Rick was ready in seconds: padded jacket over Kevlar gilet, pistol in a pancake holster at his waist, helmet strapped and secure. Through the tinted rear windows, he recognised the backstreets of Limehouse.

'This is a bad idea,' Rick said.

'They'll be nervy, but it'll be all right. We just need to go in hard.'

'Seriously – it's an ambush.'

'We know,' Alpha One said. 'You told us, remember?'

Rick couldn't work out what was before and what was after; they seemed to swap places like binary stars, pulling apart then merging into one so that he couldn't tell one from the other. Finally, the best he could do was: 'People could get hurt.'

'That ship has *sailed*, Sergeant.'

He glanced across to the man who'd spoken; he was sitting on the bench seat opposite. But when Rick focused on him, he saw that it was Pandora Hahn. Her eyes were covered, and she looked badly scared.

He tried to reach across to help her but couldn't move.

'Why didn't you stop them?' Pandora demanded. 'I'll tell you why – you called those cowboys by name – you're one of them, you bastard!'

Suddenly aware that he was dreaming, Rick struggled to wake, but he couldn't open his eyes. He willed his limbs to move but they wouldn't obey him.

They were nearing the warehouse.

People will die.

Hearing his breath rattle in his chest, he tried to force a sound from his throat, but it closed and he couldn't breathe. Finally, with a tearing sound like the *rrrrrrriiip* of a Velcro fastener, he experienced a falling sensation and woke with a jarring thud as if he'd dropped from a height.

For a few seconds, he lay still, slowing his breathing and consoling himself that it was just a dream. Light seeped from under the curtains, and he checked his watch. It was one a.m.; the LED streetlights had created a false dawn. He thought again about how the morning light had kept Jess from her rest. A wave of loss rolled over him, and he waited for it to pass, knowing that the anger would follow, resigning himself to ride that wave.

A few minutes later, his breathing regulated, he began to drift off again.

In the instant between wakefulness and sleep, a quiet, slithering sound sent a spike of adrenaline to his heart. It seemed to come from the room below. The sliding doors to the patio?

Someone's in the house.

Easing off the bed, he trod softly to the wardrobe and reached inside, silently removing boxes from the top shelf and carefully lowering them to the floor until he found what he needed. A small metal safe with a combination lock.

The bedroom door was open a crack, and he swung it halfway, knowing that the hinge would creak if he pushed it further. On the landing, he listened. A cold draught rose to greet him; he hadn't heard the sliding doors a second time – the intruder must have left them open, keeping an escape route clear.

Padding barefoot down the stairs, he paused on the bottom riser. Was that a low chuckle he'd heard?

Weapon held in a double-handed grip at forty-five degrees, elbows pulled in close to his body, index finger just above the trigger guard, he checked left and right: the front door was secure; kitchen door closed; sitting-room door open. He and his father had knocked through the front room and dining rooms years ago to make one large sitting area, and this was the only way into it from inside the house. But Rick was sure he'd shut the door before he went to bed.

Holding the revolver in both hands, he swung the door open with his hip.

A man was sitting on his sofa at the far end of the room.

It was Sam.

Rick lowered the gun. 'Sam, what the *hell*?'

Sam glanced over the top of the Marvel comic he was reading – from a box of first editions he'd left behind thirteen years ago when he'd vanished out of Rick's life.

'You *did* dig them out of the attic!' he exclaimed with evident delight.

Rick broke out in a cold sweat. 'Jesus, Sam, I could've shot you!'

'You mean that thing's loaded?' Sam asked, glancing at the gun more in curiosity than alarm.

'It wouldn't be much use if it wasn't,' Rick said, fixing his brother with a dead look.

'I've been away for a while – did I miss some new legislation about UK police being armed?'

'Don't be facetious.'

Sam watched him set the gun down on the mantelshelf. 'Rick, did you steal that revolver from evidence?' he asked with mock disapproval.

'Of course not.'

'So . . .?'

'I confiscated it.'

'That could be dangerous.' He seemed serious. 'Look, I can get you a clean weapon, untraceable, no markings, no . . . dubious provenance.'

Sam was right about the gun's doubtful history – it *had* in fact been stolen from evidence – though not by Rick – and Rick had confiscated it to prevent the suicide of a friend. It had never found its way back where it belonged for the simple reason that he'd be at greater risk trying to return it than he was keeping it at home. But Rick wasn't remotely in the mood to explain all this to his brother. Instead, he moved across the room to shut the patio doors, then perched on the arm of a chair adjacent to Sam.

A compact black electronic device sat on the coffee table.

'What's that?' he asked.

'A signal jammer,' Sam said, as though it was obvious.

'I told you; I swept the house. There's no listening equipment, no hidden cameras.'

Sam carefully replaced the comic on top of the small stack on the coffee table and dropped Rick a wink. 'Can't be too careful.'

'How did you get in?'

231

Sam crinkled his brow, as if the question was obtuse. 'Have you forgotten – I used to live here – I have a key.'

Rick offered a sardonic smile. 'I changed the locks after what happened last autumn.'

With the merest lift of one shoulder Sam said, 'I didn't say it was the *original* key.' Then: 'How's the head?'

This was the second time he'd asked in the space of a few hours.

Rick sucked his teeth and said, 'It's *fine*,' although it had begun to itch abominably.

'Let me take a look.'

'No.'

'Seriously, Rick. I have experience with this kind of thing.'

He reached across, but Rick stood, batting his hand away. 'So does the nurse who patched me up.'

Sam rose from the sofa. He was a smidgen shorter than Rick, and his face had a softer, rounder look. But looks were deceiving. Keeping his distance, he scrutinised the dressing as if he could see through it with X-ray eyes. 'Did they explain *why* they didn't stitch it?'

'It's a hospital, Sam. They know what they're doing.'

Sam seemed unconvinced.

'Anyway, how did you know they didn't stitch it?'

'You're a social media sensation.'

There was the slightest dulling of his eyes when he said it – a sign of evasion, and Rick said, 'You told me you weren't having me followed.'

'I'm not – though that may have to change – we'll come to that. Just let me check; you don't want it to scar.'

Rick took half a step back.

'Did they at least give you antibiotics?' Sam asked. 'You *do* know you have to take the full course?'

'Jeez – I'm not fourteen anymore, Sam!'

'No, but gunshot wounds are nasty,' Sam said. 'They're the dog bite of weapon injuries. Fibres from your clothing get into a wound, carrying all kinds of bacteria with them.'

This time when Sam reached for the dressing, Rick parried and moved in, closing the gap between them, simultaneously grabbing Sam under the jaw, pivoting and bringing him backwards and down, so that he landed on the sofa with a thump.

He was surprised that Sam began to laugh.

'What's so damn funny?'

'Nothing . . . nothing.' Sam continued laughing. 'I was just thinking of the years of fun we might have had beating each other up if I hadn't cleared off when I did.'

'Well, that was kind of non-negotiable, wasn't it, Sam?' Rick said quietly, fighting mixed emotions. If Sam had stayed, he'd probably have been dead by now – killed in prison – and Rick didn't like to think how his own life might have turned out.

'Let's talk about the tracker,' Sam said.

'It's small; good kit, I'd say.'

'Never mind that – I'll have the tech specs checked later. What are you investigating at the moment?'

'You know I can't talk about ongoing criminal investigations – especially not with a wanted criminal.'

'All right,' Sam said. 'Let me tell you what I know: you're involved in the Emin drugs task force.'

Rick shrugged. 'That's a no-brainer.'

'Your surveillance role could well have made you a target.'

'It did,' Rick said. 'Literally.'

Sam sniffed. 'All right, keep your secrets if you must. But you might at least tell me how you knew you were being followed.'

''Cos I nearly caught the bastard.'

'Really?' Sam said, 'When?'

'A few days ago—' Rick broke off, thinking that in fact it was the day before things went pear-shaped at Emin's drugs factory in Limehouse.

'Just before you were shot,' Sam said, reading his mind. 'So, on a scale of one to ten, Emin as a likely candidate is what – a seven?'

'I dunno,' Rick admitted. 'Emin went ahead with the drug delivery, and he's usually careful.' He shrugged, uncomfortable that he couldn't make sense of it. 'It's a coincidence, and I don't like coincidences.'

Sam's look said he didn't, either. 'The poser is, why would they still be following you days *after* they got their rumps kicked at Limehouse?'

Rick agreed with him on that, and he saw a brightening in his brother's denim blue eyes: he knew, without Rick having said a word, that they were of the same mind.

'Tell me what happened.'

Rick went through the sequence of events: his suspicion that the grey Audi was following him; the tortuous journey around Fulham with the Audi in tow; catching the driver head-on in a backstreet; the driver's wild reversing that had ended with a cyclist lying injured in the road.

Sam seemed puzzled. 'You didn't follow him?'

'You must have missed the bit about the civilian casualty who was knocked off his bike,' Rick said dryly.

Sam answered with a neutral, 'Hm.' Then: 'Presumably your bosses followed up on the incident?'

'The Traffic Operational Command Unit deals with road incidents,' Rick said. 'But I reported it to my boss, who got it prioritised. The plates were fake – cloned from an old lady's Fiat Punto. I gave a description of the driver, but I only caught a glimpse of him, and the e-fit they made from my description is generic, to say the least.'

'You haven't seen this Audi since?'

Rick shook his head. 'And I've been extra vigilant. I thought maybe they'd taken the hint.'

'Can you get me a copy of the e-fit?'

Rick debated. The Traffic OCU had shelved the investigation – resources were just too tight – whereas Sam had both the resources and the motivation to settle this.

Finally, he went into the hallway and grabbed his backpack, handing Sam a slightly crumpled piece of paper from it.

Sam scrutinised it. 'Can I keep this?'

'Hold up.' Rick took it back and placed it flat on the table, snapping off a few images on his phone. 'All yours,' he said, sliding the paper over to Sam. 'What about the tracker?'

Sam keyed something into his own phone. 'My tech experts will establish if it's hackable – it'd be useful to be able to send your shadow off on a false trail. But leave it where it is for now. If you need to be somewhere incognito, leave the car at home or park it and—'

'Hop in a cab,' Rick finished for him. 'Yeah, thanks, Sam. I'd already thought of that.'

Sam gave him a look of genuine concern. 'I'm sorry you're going through this, Rick. I heard that you'd been sent home from work.'

'Been talking to your pocket police again?' Rick couldn't keep the bitterness out of his tone.

'Criminal contacts, mostly,' Sam said, clearly not taking offence.

'D'you lot have a professional guild, or something?'

'Did you think that criminals wouldn't share intel?' Sam shot back. 'Law enforcement does.'

'Yeah,' Rick said, 'to enforce the law.'

'Sometimes,' Sam agreed, with a comical moue.

'Who else have you been tapping for info?' Rick asked.

'The podcaster is thorough,' Sam said in a way that made Rick vaguely nervous.

'You've been following Pandora?'

'Not literally, of course. Although that wouldn't be the worst idea.'

'No, Sam. No! You can't go stalking journalists.'

'Even if she could lead us to the Wolf Pack? She seems to have a direct line to them.'

Rick answered with a baleful glance and Sam waved his hand

235

before his face. 'Oh, have it your way,' he murmured, sounding almost bored. 'I must say, though, I'm impressed – Ms Hahn makes a good argument – and in her latest effort she did a sterling job of rehabilitating you in the eyes of the public.'

'I think Ghosh will have the last say on that,' Rick said.

'Did you ever play Chinese Whispers as a kid, Rick?'

'No.' As a pre-teen Rick was too busy watching his back to play harmless games with other children.

'But you understand the principle: misheard or misinterpreted communications; the distortions of words as they're passed down the line. "Send reinforcements, we're going to advance." becomes: "Send three-and-fourpence, we're going to a dance."'

'Gotta say, that dates you, mate.'

Sam sat back in the sofa and Rick got a flash of him sitting exactly there over a decade ago, relaxed and cocky, his big brother who seemed to have all the answers.

'History is the wisest counsel – don't mock it,' Sam said. 'In this paranoid age of conspiracy theories and global mistrust, the simple act of trying to save lives becomes layered, twisted, a coded message. A political act.'

'Tell me about it.'

'Ms Hahn is like the runner on the front line who braves enemy fire to go back to the source and demand an explanation for such a trivial request. She demystifies, clarifies, and invites her subscribers to see the absurdity of the mangled message.'

'Okay, I get it – you're a fan,' Rick quipped. Sam began to make an exasperated protest and Rick held up his hands. 'And I'll try to be more optimistic.'

'That's all I ask.'

Rick gave his brother a sideways glance. Now was as good a time as any to bring up the Floren shooting.

'If you're watching the podcasts, you must have seen the Deptford Waters clips.'

Sam answered with a slight nod.

'What did you think of the vanishing landscaper?'

'The Vanishing Landscaper.' Sam tilted his head appreciatively. 'I like that. It has the ring of an urban myth about it, doesn't it?'

Rick picked up his laptop and clicked through a series of links to *Pandora Unboxes*, located the video clip entitled 'Floren Killer?' and then swivelled the screen so that Sam could see it.

'What am I looking at?' Sam seemed mildly puzzled.

'A recording of an unknown person at the scene of Jason Floren's murder last February,' Rick said. 'Floren was shot to death minutes later.'

'By this old fellow?' Sam asked, incredulous. 'I thought the police blamed the Wolf Pack – their van was caught on camera in the area, wasn't it?'

'The Met needed a distraction from the multiple screw-ups the Wolf Pack keep drawing to the public's attention,' Rick said. 'The *original* consensus was that Floren's murder was a professional hit.'

Sam shrugged. 'Those people are as professional as I've seen.'

'No,' Rick said. 'They aren't killers.'

Sam's eyebrows twitched. 'They killed two members of Emin's crew.'

'Because they were holding guns on hostages – and one of them took a pot-shot at me.'

Sam chuckled. 'Careful, Rick – now *you're* beginning to sound like a sympathiser.'

He's trying to wind you up because he's got something to hide. Just ask him. Is that you, Sam? Are you the 'old fellow' who turned up just before Floren was shot, then disappeared without a trace?

But he couldn't make himself say the words, focusing instead on the facts as he knew them: 'If the Wolf Pack killed Floren, his confession doesn't make sense.'

Sam cocked his head, waiting for an explanation.

'Like you said, they're professional. If they'd intended to kill Floren all along, they would have slipped away from Deptford leaving no trace,' Rick explained. 'But the whole *point* of their op was to record his confession. When Floren was murdered, they couldn't use the footage because it would look like a kangaroo trial followed by a lynching.'

'He *did* have innocent blood on his hands,' Sam observed coolly.

Another deflection. 'I wasn't trying to justify the hit, Sam – I'm saying that the Wolf Pack had no *motive* to kill him. With what they had on video, Floren would have gone to prison. The families would've had grounds for a civil suit.'

'If your Vanishing Landscaper is a lone hitman, then perhaps the families hired him,' Sam said.

'You think the families clubbed together and got someone to search the Dark Web for killers for hire?'

'It's been done,' Sam said. 'And you can hire a bargain-basement killer for a couple of hundred.'

'The police didn't even know of the bogus landscaper's existence until the Wolf Pack released this video,' Rick said, drawing Sam's attention to the screen again, watching for his reaction.

Sam seemed unaffected, only mildly interested on a professional level.

'Would a bargain-basement killer have been as careful as this guy?' Rick asked, dancing around the question he was afraid to ask.

'Careful in what way?' Sam said, as if he didn't know.

'The fake van. His disguise. The limp.'

'You're really convinced he's the killer?' Sam said with a quick glance at the screen.

'It fits, doesn't it? Unless you've got another explanation?'

Sam nodded. 'All right, let's see . . . A job done as cleanly as this one demands serious money. Do the families have that kind of buying power?'

Rick had to say no.

'And I don't see the average hitman deferring payment while the families take their class action case to court,' Sam said with a faint smile.

'What are the chances of tracing him?'

'From this?' Sam hit 'replay' on the video and peered closely at the screen for thirty seconds before making a pronouncement. 'Slim-to-nothing. It's terrible quality.' He froze the frame on a grainy, shadowy view of the back of the mystery man as if to emphasise the futility of even attempting an identification. 'But this isn't the security firm's CCTV footage, is it? The Wolf Pack gave it to Pandora,' he added almost to himself.

'I'm as sure as I can be that the Wolf Pack didn't kill Floren,' Rick said, feeling that he was being steered away from his question. 'So if the hit *wasn't* commissioned by the victims' families, you got to ask, who else would want Floren dead?'

'I really couldn't say,' Sam said, evasively.

'Well, it *is* kind of your province, Sam.'

'A hired assassin rarely knows *who* and it's often dangerous to ask *why*.'

'But you could find out why – I mean, if you wanted?'

'Possibly,' Sam said. 'But it won't help you find the Wolf Pack, so . . .' He raised one shoulder.

'What – you don't think it's worth the effort?' Rick asked.

'I was thinking more of the risk,' Sam said, indicating that they were circling dangerously close to that question Rick dared not ask. 'And the vigilantes are your biggest headache right now. Have you thought *what* they might be?'

'You're thinking military?' Rick said.

'Or police. The training is similar.'

It had occurred to him, but Rick kept pushing away the notion that fellow officers might be involved. 'Yeah,' he said at last with a sigh. 'Yeah, it is.'

Sam headed towards the sliding doors.

'You're going?'

'Lots to do,' he said. 'I'll look into the tracker – let you know what my techs find – and I'll consider the other thing.' He meant Rick's question about who would have wanted Floren dead, adding with a touch of humour, 'The police angle is more *your* province, though.'

Brooding over their conversation after he'd gone, Rick thought, *You should have asked. You should have asked straight out if he'd taken the contract on Floren.*

He returned to the video clip of the elderly landscaper. There was nothing that he could isolate, nothing to point to that was trademark Sam. The old man really did look like someone worn out by thirty-plus years of manual labour, working outdoors in punishing weather.

An insistent voice whispered in his head. *If he was genuine, why was he driving a van with faked decals – and where the hell did he disappear to when the police started pouring into the development?*

With a groan of frustration, Rick locked the patio doors and went to the kitchen to make coffee.

He found the process of measuring, filling and tamping the grounds into the filter a soothing ritual and, listening to the machine hiss and gurgle as it filled his espresso cup, he came to an acceptance. He'd spent too many years misjudging Sam, too much time miserable and alone, trapped in bitterness and recriminations that he couldn't share with anyone else – least of all his parents. He'd learned in the past months that trust was a slippery thing, often misplaced. And while Sam might be untrustworthy, he'd fought shoulder to shoulder with Rick last autumn.

At the end of it all, he'd challenged Rick to admit he'd had fun. Scary as it had been at the time, Rick *had* experienced a thrill working alongside Sam as equal partners in an impossible situation. It was selfish and wrong, but he couldn't risk losing the tenuous bonds they had so recently rebuilt.

Chapter 39

AFTER HE'D ARRANGED FOR REMOTE SURVEILLANCE on Rick with instructions not to interfere with the tracking device already placed on his car, Sam commissioned an additional team to monitor the whereabouts of the persistent podcaster. What Rick didn't know couldn't hurt him.

Impatient with himself, Sam shook his head. Ignorance was inherently dangerous. *Should I have told him who I believe is following him? Have I put him in more danger by saying nothing?* As a rule, Sam Turner did not second-guess himself. But Rick had always been the exception to the rule. His dilemma was that he didn't want his brother dragged into his mess if the reason he was being stalked came down to something simple – such as a drugs lord trying to get ahead of a police investigation. He needed to know who was paying to have Rick followed – then he would decide what to tell Rick.

As for the question of who would want Floren dead, Sam rarely asked *why* a person might have a price on their head – such questions were apt to make conspirators in murder a tad nervous. As for enquiring *who* had put up the money – *that* could be downright dangerous. But it paid to be sure of his facts, and he always researched the subject of the contract. Despite what

Rick might think, Sam was discerning in the choices he made; he may be *im*moral, but he liked to believe that he wasn't *a*moral. To Sam's mind, there were good kills and bad kills – the definitions of which were determined by a set of self-devised and sometimes ambiguously applied rules.

If the world would be improved by the absence of the target, he didn't think twice. But where the balance was more subtle then, like the goddess Maat of Egyptian mythology who balanced the hearts of the dead against a feather, Sam would weigh the target's dubious merit to humanity.

He had wondered when he'd committed to the Floren hit if the families of the arson victims had put up the money. He'd privately applauded their panache in taking out Jason Floren on the eve of his biggest business triumph. He'd revised his theory when Floren had told him about the armed men who'd extracted his confession. It seemed more likely that the crew he now knew as the Wolf Pack had been acting on behalf of the former residents of the glossy new development – justice, rather than vengeance being their aim. And prison might well have been a more fitting and painful punishment for Floren, but having undertaken to fulfil a contract, Sam felt professionally bound to see it through. So Floren had died. And Sam's near-miss with the police the night of the assassination had meant that he'd taken the money and, happy to get away unnoticed, never looked back.

Returning to his hotel, he looked again at Rick's e-fit of his stalker. He hadn't exaggerated when he'd said the likeness was generic. Although it had all the necessary components of a face, it was effectively featureless – except . . . Why had the skin around the outer corner of the left eye been shaded?

He sent a quick text to Rick, and the reply came through in seconds:

—Something off about the left eye. Looked pulled – scarring, maybe?

Sam generally avoided popular high-end mini-computer / mobile phones that most people used as too susceptible to hacking – so he retrieved a portable scanner from his backpack and connected it to his laptop, sending the scanned image to an account on the Dark Web, then onward to the operatives tasked with watching Rick.

Finally, he picked up a burner phone and called Dave Collins for an update.

'I haven't got much for you, Sam,' Dave said. 'Most of the burns victims at Deptford were taken to the Royal London – the hostages from the bank heist went there as well. But coincidence isn't the same thing as causality.'

'And my friend?' Sam asked.

'I've got alerts set up, but he hasn't made any transfer of assets, and the two bank accounts you gave me have been inactive for years.'

They would have been, Sam thought. *Meals and accommodation having been provided by His Majesty's Prison Belmarsh for the past decade.*

'Keep watching,' Sam said, 'and let me know of any change as soon as anything's flagged – day or night.'

'No problem.'

'I had a thought about the Wolf Pack by the way,' Dave went on. 'I'm checking Transport for London CCTV for the van they escaped in.'

'It was found – burned out,' Sam said, a little disorientated.

'Yeah, but if I can find a few locations where they might've stopped for traffic lights or petrol or what have you, we could get lucky and catch one of their faces.'

'Great idea!' Sam checked his watch. 'And talking of cameras, there's somewhere I need to be.'

Chapter 40

Early morning

RICK DOZED FOR A FEW HOURS but, plagued by nightmares, he gave up and took a shower before staggering downstairs. At six-forty-five, as he pondered brewing more coffee, his personal mobile rang, and checking the screen, he answered, grinning.

'Dave! Great to hear from you, mate. You been burning the midnight oil again?'

'No,' Dave said, taking him literally. 'I rang to see if you're okay.'

'Well, that's nice of you. So are you at work, or . . .?'

Flustered, Dave said, 'Oh, that's what you meant when you said—' He stopped himself with a mild curse and started again. 'Yes, I'm at work, but I'm due to finish in fifteen minutes. I've completed my work schedule for the night though, and I wanted to see if you're . . .'

He tailed off and Rick sensed that he was embarrassed that he'd overexplained and then begun to repeat himself.

'I don't suppose you'd be interested in grabbing breakfast somewhere?' Rick asked. 'I'm on enforced sick leave and I'm going stir-crazy.'

'Um, well, I always have breakfast at the caff near Vauxhall Railway Station.'

Dave had a flat in Vauxhall, a short underground ride from the Serious Fraud Office headquarters near Trafalgar Square. A creature of habit, he ate his meals in familiar places where he knew the system, the menus and the staff. Dave did not cope well with change.

'Not a problem,' Rick said. 'Just text me the address, I can be there in about half an hour.'

After reassuring Dave that it would be fine to go ahead and order before he arrived, Rick headed for the door, but catching a glimpse of himself in the hall mirror, he dodged back to the kitchen for his beanie. It was dry by now, if a little crumpled and he stretched it carefully, splaying his fingers to gently lower it over the dressing.

In a car parked in a lay-by a quarter of a mile away, one of Sam's operatives nudged the driver. 'He's on the move,' he said.

The driver, a large, heavily pumped individual with a neck like a grizzly bear, jerked wide awake with a snort, turning on the ignition in almost a reflex. But he waited, watching the satellite marker indicating Rick's car. Moments later, Rick's car passed the end of the road. A couple of minutes after that he said, 'Looks like he's heading east.'

'Well, come on, then,' his shorter, wiry partner said. 'Heigh-ho Silver an' all that.' He tapped the dashboard, but the bigger man remained stolidly immobile.

'Wait for it.'

A second later, a black Škoda zipped past the end of the road.

'Now I wonder where he's off to in such a hurry?' he said with a sly glance at his friend.

'All right, smart arse, hold back – we don't wanna spook him.'

'Hurry up or slow down – make up your mind, mate – which is it to be?'

The shorter man answered with a growl of impatience, and the two bickered pleasantly for the next twenty minutes, the driver keeping a sedate pace, chugging along just out of sight of Rick and his shadow.

At seven-twenty a.m., Rick's car stopped in a street just north of Vauxhall Park and didn't move on.

'I'm gonna close in,' the big man said.

They soon had the Škoda in their sights. Rick's car was already parked, and the Škoda driver pulled in a few yards ahead of it and jogged back, a compact camera in his hand.

Realising there was no sign of Rick, he stood for a moment glancing up and down the road, before turning full circle, muttering, '*Fuck!*'

'That's him all right. You ready?'

'Always,' his partner said.

'We're overlooked, so—'

'I'll be quick.'

The big man grinned, slowing to a halt next to their target. 'You all right, mate?'

'Do I *look* all right?'

'Not even a little bit,' he admitted.

His partner had nipped out of the passenger door and round to the back, opening the car boot.

'Can I help at all?' the driver persisted.

'You can fuck off.'

'Well, that's not a very nice way to talk,' the big fellow said mildly.

The driver had stopped at a slight angle to Rick's car, blocking the stalker from turning back the way he came.

'Do you wanna move?'

'Not really,' the big man said, smiling sweetly.

The stalker turned and stamped towards the rear of the car, swearing under his breath.

The boot lid obscured his view, so the big man didn't see what happened next, but he heard a surprised squawk followed by a tumbling sound and a slight dip at the rear of the car, then the boot was slammed shut. The driver's partner appeared at his side a second later.

'Got the camera?'

The small man raised his hand to reveal a Canon DSLR. As he swung into the car, the big man accelerated smoothly away.

Chapter 41

RICK WALKED BACK TO HIS CAR under a sky that threatened rain.

Dave Collins was obviously well known and liked by the staff, and he'd been contentedly ploughing through a full English when Rick pushed into the steamy and crowded café. A coffee appeared at his elbow a second after he'd sat down.

'Americano, milk on the side,' the server said, smartly.

Dave wasn't comfortable in social situations. Unsure of the boundaries and etiquette of informal settings, he found it hard to judge if he'd overstepped, so Rick understood the anxious glance the big man gave him.

'You're a bloody mind-reader,' he'd said, and Dave flushed with pleasure.

He was touched that Dave made the call at all, and knew that his friend had probably sweated over the timing. But once they got into chatting, Dave had relaxed, and was happy to let Rick burble on about work and the TikTok debacle as he ate steadily and companionably, offering only the occasional comment or murmur of sympathy. Now, refreshed with food in the company of a friend who was discreet and thoughtful, despite his awkwardness, Rick felt calmer.

His phone buzzed in his pocket, and he checked the screen. It was DC McGuinness.

'I thought you'd want to know – that tip-off you gave me about a camera in a bird box at Deptford Waters? No joy.'

'I got a picture of it, Alan,' Rick said, thinking sourly, *Another cover-up*. 'So if MIT is saying—'

'Hang on, I'm not saying there never *was* one – just that it's not there now.'

'How? It's been there for months, then suddenly overnight it's gone?'

'MIT sent two CSIs out to it first thing this morning and yeah, it's gone. The camera housing was still in place inside the nest box, like you said, and it looks like it was pointing towards the show house.'

Cursing himself for having given the game away to Sam, Rick asked, 'Any idea who took it down?'

'As it happens, a "concerned resident" came out of one of the houses further down the street and challenged the CSIs. He said this was the third time in two days that someone had been poking around that nest box.'

'Who were the other two?'

'A young guy thinking of buying in the area, and a council worker.'

Well, I know the house hunter was me, so the other one had to be Sam.

'This council worker,' Rick said, a question in his tone.

'Older guy. White, a bit portly, woolly hat – chirpy cockney type,' according to the witness. 'Agile as a monkey up and down the ladder.'

Either Sam had mastered his fear of heights, or he'd sent one of his crew to get the job done.

'Flashed council ID, but the feller didn't get a name – said he couldn't get a word in.'

Classic Sam. Bombard the mark with information, questions, idle chit-chat, till they can't think.

'Apparently, he said the council'd had a complaint about a camera pointing into the bedroom windows of one of the houses,' McGuinness went on. 'Concerned Resident says they've already taken those cameras down, but Council Guy says maybe they missed one. Next minute, he looks down from on high and says to Concerned Resident, words to the effect of: "You'll never guess what I just found".'

Rick could picture it. Sam giving it some, yapping about this bloomin' weather, and the council thinking he had nothing better to do with his time. *You'd think they'd at least've have sent a cherry-picker – I mean look at me, I'm not exactly built for climbing ladders. And at my age, I'm liable to—'* Then: *'Blow me! Would you take a butcher's at that?'*

Maybe the cockney rhyming slang was a bit over the top, but sometimes Sam pushed the limits just to see how far he could stretch credulity till it snapped.

'And in a jiffy he's scooted down the ladder, camera in hand,' Rick predicted. 'Of course, he didn't think to leave it alone and call in the police?'

'In fact, the concerned resident suggested he should do exactly that,' McGuinness said. 'But Council Guy gave him some guff about saving him a lot of trouble, took it away with him.'

'Thing about these noo cameras,' Sam would tell poor, gullible Concerned Resident, laying the accent on thick, *'you got your Wi-Fi capability – which means you can switch 'em on remotely from 'alfway raahnd the world if you've a mind to.'* Then with an expressive shudder: *'I don't know about you, mate, but I wouldn't want to risk my missus being ogled by some perve somewhere in the Balkans fiddling wiv his joystick.'*

'And I'm guessing the council has no record of sending anyone out to Deptford Waters,' Rick said.

'Correct.'

'What about the audio the Wolf Pack got at the car park?' Rick asked, meaning the scene of the Blackfriars arrests.

250

'You were right,' McGuinness said. 'When they went back, they realised there were a few too many smoke detectors on each floor – the extras were kitted out with audio devices. They're checking for trace, but it's not looking hopeful,' he finished.

Rick turned the corner into the quiet back street where he'd parked his car and stared in disbelief. 'Thanks, mate,' he said. 'Look, something's come up. I gotta go, but I owe you one.'

He finished the call and tried to decide if he should announce himself at what was obviously an ongoing crime scene, or quietly fade away and come back later in the hope that the police would leave before his parking fee ran out.

Chapter 42

SAM GAZED BENIGNLY AT THE MAN seated on a plastic chair in front of him, hands secured behind his back. They were in the basement of a disused and boarded-up pub on the corner of a street in Lambeth. The cellar still contained a few steel beer kegs and the walls and brick flooring, blackened with age and use, retained the faint reek of hops and stale beer.

Gavin and Noel had brought the captive in then returned to their assignment of watching Rick, and only Sam and Lawrence, a long-serving employee, remained.

Rick's stalker was in his early thirties, average height and build. Nondescript, as men who did his kind of work should be. Except for damage to his left eyelid – a burn, by the look of the scar tissue that seemed to drag the eyelid down on its outer rim. His skin had a greyish, unhealthy tint – possibly the result of a smoking habit – the first two fingers of his right hand were nicotine-stained. He licked his lips, trembling as Sam compared the image on his driver's licence with a copy of Rick's e-fit.

'Look, I don't know who you think I am, but—'

'It says right here who you are, John,' Sam said. 'And it's good to put a name to the face.' He glanced again at the police sketch. 'I understand that he'd only seen you for a second, but he's done

252

you proud – even caught that rabbit-in-the-headlights look,' Sam added warmly.

He passed the images to Lawrence, who placed them on a barrel next to John's house keys, camera and mobile phone, while Sam turned his attention to the man's wallet.

'Oyster card, credit cards, cash – no other form of ID. I don't believe you're a private investigator . . .'

The man took a breath and Sam raised a finger to warn him. 'I will check, so be careful how you answer.'

'I'm just minding my own business when your two thugs clock me and stick me in the boot of a car.'

Sam moved fast, bringing his face within an inch of the stalker. 'Don't lie to me.'

'But I didn't do anything!' the man wailed.

Sam straightened up, amused by the enormity of the lie. 'Seriously? You're wanted by the police for a hit-and-run incident that put a man in hospital. You're stalking a decorated Met Police detective. You placed a tracker on his car – all of which is *highly* illegal. Trust me, I know a thing or two about that.'

'Turn me over to the police then,' Rick's stalker said, the false bravado betrayed by the quaver in his voice. 'They can't prove I did anything.'

'You're missing the point, John. I don't need proof,' Sam said, almost purring. 'You see, as I already implied, I act outside the strict parameters of the law.'

'I don't get you.'

'Then I'll make it really simple for you,' Sam said. 'Do you know who I am?'

'I honestly don't – I-I'm sorry.'

'No apology necessary. I'm not asking out of narcissistic neediness. But it would save me time and effort, and you a *lot* of pain if you had the slightest notion what I'm capable of.' He waited for that notion to lodge itself in the man's scurrying thoughts.

'My real name doesn't matter – I go under various aliases – but

253

since I have your name, it's only fair that you have mine. They call me the Fixer.'

The man's Adam's apple bobbed and, registering the fear in his eyes, Sam said, 'Ah, I see that my moniker has come up.' He patted his captive's knee, which had started to jiggle uncontrollably.

John flinched, pressing himself back in the chair, and Sam said, 'Oh – you're following *him*, but you were supposed to be on the lookout for *me*? Didn't he give you an image?' He frowned in mock outrage at the oversight.

'It's not a very good one,' John said weakly.

Leaning over the man, Sam placed both hands on his shoulders. 'I think we're getting closer to a name, John – what d'you say?'

Panting in fear, now, John said, 'You don't know what he'll do to me.'

'If it's the man I think it is, then I know only too well,' Sam said solemnly, composing his features into an expression almost of concern.

'But if you *know* . . .' The tormented look on John's face said, *Why are you doing this to me?*

'I don't want to put words in your mouth; I want to hear it from you.'

John's response was to clamp his jaw shut.

'All I need is his name and a location,' Sam said patiently.

The stalker shook his head in great wide sweeps.

Sam glanced towards Lawrence, who picked up a folding table that was leaning against one of the beer kegs. He opened it out and put it next to Sam, returning to his own position a few feet away after he'd placed a metal toolbox on the tabletop.

Sam lifted out nose pliers, pincers, a hammer, nails, a small blowtorch, a taser and a cordless drill, laying them out in two orderly rows on the tabletop.

John began hyperventilating.

'You have legitimate concerns about what your employer might do to you if you talk,' Sam said, rummaging in the tool kit for one more item. 'But life is lived in the moment – every day, hour, minute and second is a succession of moments.' He brightened, having found what he wanted, and looked at John as he fitted a drill bit to the drill.

'In *this* moment, your greatest concern is not what your employer will do if you talk, but what *I* will do to you if you don't.'

Satisfied that the bit was secured, he returned it to the table.

'You have a simple choice: tell me what I need to know – or suffer excruciating pain.'

He held both hands out, tilting right and left to illustrate the dangerous balance of his captive's imminent decision-making. 'I'd hazard a guess that you have a low pain threshold, John. Am I right?'

John's eyes widened and he shook his head – a minuscule movement, more of a tremor, really, like the first subtle signs of a nascent neurological condition. But Sam recognised it as the first indicator that he was about to cave in.

'Shall we do a quick test – establish a baseline?'

The phone in Sam's pocket rang and he checked the number.

'I have to take this,' he said to Lawrence. 'If he makes a sound, gag him.'

He climbed the steps to the steel-reinforced door of the basement and entered the bar of the pub, closing the door behind him.

'Rick.'

'You sound tense. Did I catch you in the middle of something?'

'Nothing that won't wait.'

'Couple of questions,' Rick said. 'We'll start with an easy one.'

'This sounds fun; go ahead.'

'The CCTV footage we talked about last night,' Rick began.

'The Vanishing Landscaper – what about him?'

'The camera that recorded him was removed from Deptford Waters early this morning.'

'Oh, you sent your CSI techs for it – I thought you might,' Sam said.

'I *bet* you did. It was you, wasn't it?'

'You're going to have to be more specific,' Sam said. 'It was me who did what, exactly?'

'It was you on that clip; it was you who took the camera from Floren's new development.'

'Mm . . . if that's the easy question, what was the hard one?' Sam asked ruefully.

'I just got back to my car and a CSU van and a couple of marked police cars were blocking the road. Seems I'd stumbled on a crime scene – which, surprisingly, is a first for me. The CSIs are examining a black Škoda Supreme – does that mean anything to you?'

'It's an underrated vehicle . . .' Sam offered, suppressing the urge to ask Rick if he'd introduced himself to the police responders. If he had, things would only get more complicated. 'The V6 engine under the bonnet is not to be trifled with. It's termed a "sleeper car" because, like the sleeper spies of the Cold War, they can hide in plain sight until summoned by a single code word – or the metaphorical flip of a switch – to cause mayhem.'

'You make it sound so threatening, but if you're implying that the driver of the Škoda is some kind of sleeper, he must've dozed off – witnesses say he was grabbed off the street and thrown into a car boot in the time it takes to snap your fingers.'

'Distressing,' Sam said. 'Did they get a vehicle registration? A description?'

'As a matter of fact, yeah. He was driven off in a grey saloon—'

'There are a lot of those about,' Sam interrupted with a light laugh. 'Eyewitnesses – what *would* the police do without them?'

'*And* the assailant was a short man,' Rick continued. 'Wiry. Dark hair. Does that ring any bells?'

Alarm bells, Sam thought. Aloud, he said, 'I'll give it some thought.'

'Sam, stop messing me about. Did you snatch the guy who's been following me?'

'I've been otherwise occupied this morning,' Sam said truthfully.

'You *have* got him, though.'

Sam didn't answer.

'I swear, if you hurt him, we're finished. Sam, are you listening?'

Sam hung up, then dialled the two operatives who were following Rick.

'You neglected to mention that you were seen.'

A silence, then: 'I didn't know we had been.'

'Well, let's hope that you weren't photographed.' He knew it was hypocritical, given that he himself had spent an hour only that morning retrieving a video camera in case it contained footage of him, but that didn't cause Sam any guilty qualms. 'Where is Rick?'

'Vauxhall. On the street where we picked up the stalker.'

'Do you have him in sight?' he asked.

'Yes, Boss.'

'Has he spoken to police?'

'Not while we've been here. But he's been mingling with the locals, asking questions.'

Sam experienced an unfamiliar wave of relief. 'Stay on him. But make sure you are well under his radar – his antennae are twitching. And let me know if he gets up to anything unsettling.'

'Will do.'

Sam returned to the basement.

By now, John was ashen.

'Apparently your little altercation with my men was witnessed, but since your car was stolen and the number plates cloned, the police won't know who they're looking for.' He paused for a moment. 'Although they will check for prints. Criminal record?'

Rick's stalker stared blankly at him.

'John, keep up. Do you have a criminal record?'

'No, man – I'm just a driver . . .' The man's eyes were red-rimmed and teary.

'That being the case, you might disappear from the face of the earth, and no one would note your passing. Except your employer,'

Sam added after a moment's consideration. 'But only because you inconvenienced him, being caught in the act, so to speak.'

John's Adam's apple bobbed spasmodically, and his eyes darted towards the top of the stairs.

'All right, I'm on the system. A couple of drugs charges – nothing big. But the police are probably looking for me right now.'

Sam gazed on him compassionately. 'I hope you aren't banking on a dramatic rescue,' Sam said. 'They'll probably think that you just fell back into old habits. Now, where were we?' Sam stepped up to the table and studied the unpleasant-looking apparatus, finally selecting the drill.

At the first spin of the motor, John began gabbling.

'I – I don't know his name. Honest to *God*, I don't – I'd tell you if I knew. I've never even seen him – I s-swear. Word is, he used to be someone big on the East End – you know, a big fish – a-a kingpin. But he's been away.'

'Away,' Sam repeated. 'Abroad?'

'Banged up.'

'Who told you this?'

'The lads.'

'Names.'

'Seanie G, Errol, Rory Puck, and a guy they just call "No Mercy". They don't use surnames – I'm not lying.'

'Describe them,' Sam said.

'Seanie G's thirtyish, about five-eight, ginger – s-sneaky little bastard; Errol's black, my height, kind of skinny – he's more like thirty-five – carries a big-arsed hunting knife; Rory Puck is real quiet, hardly ever says a word, but there's a look in his eyes like he's gonna start screaming at any minute.' He paused. 'No Mercy is—' his breath came in a stuttering gasp '—scary. Kind of light-eyed, like a dog you wouldn't trust. And big – I mean *huge*. They say he crushed a man's skull with one hand one time, a-and I believe 'em. He's the one who gives the orders, but he's not the boss.'

'You never met any of the others?'

A single headshake.

'But there *are* others.'

'Errol said the boss runs a big business – lawyers, computer specialists, accountants and that.'

'Have you spoken to the boss?'

'Once – when I got the job. He said I was to follow this copper – only, he said "Detective Sergeant Turner".'

'You were recruited for this one task?'

He nodded and his teeth chattered.

'Who else is watching him?'

'Seanie G.'

'Did he tell you *why* you were following him?'

'Only that he was important. He said he'd usually use one of his regular crew, but he was trusting me. I'd get a bonus if I spotted you.'

'How did you land the job?' Seeing the man's eyebrows pucker, Sam added, 'I'm assuming you didn't see it advertised in the local jobcentre.'

'Sorry. Sorry, yeah – I got stopped for speeding. The cop said I'd lose my licence. But he said he knew someone who might be interested in someone with my driving skills.'

'Did this police officer have a name?'

John shot him a pathetic look of apology. 'I got a collar number . . .'

'That will do.'

John dictated the collar number and Sam tapped it into a text on his phone and sent it to a police contact for checking.

'Back to your employer,' he said without looking up. 'What did he sound like?'

'I dunno. Kind of . . . . oily? Posh – like that knob who used to be prime minister.'

'Eton-educated,' Sam said.

'Yeah, like that. Actually, he sounded a bit like you—' He flinched. 'No offence.'

'None taken,' Sam said. 'How did you contact him?'

'I didn't. He called me.'

'On *this* phone?' Sam pointed to John's mobile, lying on the nearest beer keg.

John's eyes darted from his mobile to Sam's face. 'Don't call him. Please don't – I'm begging you. He'll know. He'll know I grassed him up.'

'Calm yourself,' Sam said. 'We're just getting to know each other, establishing facts.' He handed the phone to Lawrence, who disappeared upstairs.

John watched the older man all the way, his eyes wide with terror. He looked more frightened than when he'd been threatened with the drill.

'How are you paid?' Sam asked.

His prisoner seemed not to hear, and Sam rapped twice on the table. 'Concentrate, John. How are you paid?'

'Cash. Always cash,' John said, still staring up at the door to the bar. 'I get a call from one of the lads and we meet. He's not gonna ring 'em, is he, mister? If he does, I'm as good as dead.'

'When and where?'

Bewildered, John crinkled his brow.

'When and where do you meet when a payment is made?'

'Different places – a pub, a car park, once in Regent's Park by the rose garden.'

'How very cloak and dagger,' Sam said, amused.

Lawrence appeared at the top of the stairs. He gave a brief nod, and Sam said, 'We have their contact details. Now I need to know the protocols: who you report to; how instructions are sent; how shift changes are managed between you and Seanie G; how to set up a meeting.'

John's face sagged and that strange, almost Parkinsonian tremor began again.

'I haven't time to argue,' Sam said sharply. 'And neither do you. You've told me who your boss is—'

'No! I never – I don't even know myself. Mister, *please*—'

Sam lifted a finger. 'It's sufficient that *I* know.' He paused. 'His name is Theodore Lockleigh.'

'Stop!' John begged. 'I don't wanna know! *I don't wanna know!*' If his hands hadn't been bound, Sam was sure he'd have clamped them over his ears.

'He *was* a mediocre lawyer – although having spent the last fourteen years in prison, he's finished in the legal business,' Sam carried on, relentless. 'He was a somewhat better criminal, and I imagine he's decided to pick up where he left off. But first, he's coming for me, and I resent that. You see, Theo is a sadist. You know what a sadist is?'

John's frightened face said that he had a good idea.

'Do as I ask, I can protect you,' Sam said.

'You can't. You can't . . .' John wept.

'If you tell me what I need to know – clearly and in detail – I can stop him once and for all,' Sam said. 'But the longer you're out of contact, the more suspect you become. And make no mistake, John – if Theo Lockleigh thinks you've betrayed him, he will cut out your liver and feed it to you.'

Chapter 43

RICK WANDERED OFF FOR COFFEE and returned to the crime scene ten minutes before his parking was due to expire. The Škoda had been winched onto a flatbed police recovery vehicle, and Rick hung around at the back of the few stragglers still watching the spectacle. Only one marked car remained, and that followed the truck as it moved off.

He was about to get into his own car when his mobile rang. It was Ghosh.

'Rick, where are you?'

'Out an' about,' Rick said. 'D'you want me to come in?'

'Are you signed off by the hospital?'

'Not officially.'

'Let me know when it *is* official and I'll consider bringing you back in,' Ghosh said dryly. 'Are you likely to be overheard?'

Rick considered getting into his car, but given that he had two trackers on it, he couldn't be sure it wasn't bugged, too, so he carried on past it and checked around for anyone paying particular notice to him. 'All clear,' he said.

'We've had the ballistics report in from the Limehouse shootings, and I thought you should know the results.'

Rick's heart rate kicked up a notch. 'Go ahead.'

'The bullet that hit you came from the hostage-taker's pistol. The bullet that took *him* down was from an HK MP-five.'

That was no surprise – Rick had said on the day that the Wolf Pack were toting HK weapons. And the Heckler and Koch sub-machine gun was a popular choice for police, military and security around the world.

'The bullet and the barrelling of the HK is a close match to ballistics in six other shootings,' Ghosh went on.

'Do we have any idea who owns it?'

'GDC Gang – standing for Guns, Drugs and Cash, so the gangs unit tell me. They operate out of Islington.'

'Doesn't exactly shout vigilante group, does it?' Rick said. 'So, do we round 'em up?'

'We can't do that,' Ghosh said. 'The gun has been logged into police evidence for eight months. Six gang members were arrested in a raid, four have already been convicted of drugs and firearms possession; two more trials are ongoing.'

'It was stolen from evidence?'

'It looks likely.'

'So, what happens now?'

'Internal inquiry, initially,' Ghosh said with a sigh. 'The weapon might have been taken while it was on-site at the local nick or in transit to long-term storage. Before the matter is passed on to the Directorate of Professional Standards, we need to know which.'

'How common is it that seized guns end up back on the street?' Rick asked.

'Actually, it's fairly rare.' Ghosh sounded relieved as he said it. 'Drugs and money are more likely to go missing. And even then, a lot of items turn up after a few months, having been misfiled or logged incorrectly – numbers jumbled up or whatever.'

'Yeah, but we're talking about an assault weapon, here, not a bag of weed,' Rick reminded him. 'Plus, I counted five entering Emin's warehouse that night, and they were *all* carrying.'

'Yes, we have the weapons on camera,' Ghosh said, his patience sounding stretched. 'But only one such weapon was seized in the GDC gang arrests. We focus on that, establish *when* it was most likely stolen, and work from there.'

'If there's anything I can—'

'Rick, I've got people on it. Just – get back to whatever you're doing and let me get on with the job.'

Like I'm stopping him.

Sam's counsellor voice spoke up in his head: *Well, you're not exactly giving him the full picture of 'whatever you're doing', so you might be seen as impeding the inquiry.*

Yeah, Rick thought, *and we both know why, don't we, Sam?*

Rick pocketed his phone and turned back the way he'd come. Something moved off to his left, just about registering in his peripheral vision, and he turned his head slightly. A man, walking with purpose down the pathway of one of the low-rise blocks of flats towards its main entrance. Short, dark-haired, lean build; he seemed vaguely familiar. By the time Rick drew level, he'd vanished inside.

Of course, there were a lot of short, dark-haired men in the city, but wasn't that the description the eyewitness had given of the abductor who'd toppled a man – Rick's stalker, no less – into the boot of a car?

Suddenly Rick knew he'd encountered the man before: the small man and his oppo, a giant who moved with the lightness of a dancer, had done something similar to Rick only last autumn. Admittedly Rick had been stunned and bundled into the back seat of a limo, but the humiliation of the memory still stung. He'd never found out their names, so Rick still thought of the two as Little and Large.

On an impulse, Rick walked up the pathway and rang the panel of bells one after another, and finally someone answered. 'What *now*?' a sleepy voice demanded.

'Meeting my mate in number four,' Rick said, checking the flat numbers.

'You better give him a ring then, ain'tcha?'

'I think his bell's on the blink,' Rick said.

'Not my problem, mate. And there's something dodgy about this – short-arse and now you ringing to be let in. Now piss off, or I'm calling the police.'

It wasn't worth the risk, so Rick moved on, lingering at the street corner for a while, but there was no sign of the small man or his gargantuan other half. With a slight shrug, he continued back to his car. At least now, he knew who Sam had put on his tail.

Cutting through an alley, he saw a traffic warden showing an interest in his car.

'Whoa, mate!' Rick called, jogging the rest of the distance. 'Sorry – I know I'm a couple of minutes over, but I'm here now,' he said, smiling.

The warden kept writing. 'Already booked it in. Can't help you.'

'Do us a favour, mate . . .'

He answered by slapping the fixed penalty notice to Rick's windscreen.

As the warden walked off in search of new victims, Rick took a breath and exhaled, letting his chin drop to his chest. So much for keeping a low profile.

Chapter 44

SAM WAS SCROLLING THROUGH dozens of images of Rick on the stalker's camera.

'You have been a busy bee!' he exclaimed. 'How many of these have you sent to your handler?'

'All of them,' John said miserably.

'Not to worry,' Sam said. 'I'm sure we can rustle something up.' He stopped at an image of Rick going into a red-brick building on a busy road. 'Where's this?'

'Whitechapel Gallery.'

'When?'

'Yesterday.' Sam cocked an eyebrow and John rushed to clarify: 'About three-ish? Just after? It'll be on the EXIF data.'

This was the metadata that recorded important information about an image, including the time, date and GPS coordinates of where it was taken.

Examining it more closely, Sam said, 'This might do.'

An hour later, he had an image of Rick entering the same building, and another of Sam himself apparently sneaking down a narrow alley leading to a staff entrance at the side of the building. The metadata had been faked to make it look like the image had been shot at six-ten p.m. that evening, which gave Sam's men two hours to set up an ambush if Lockleigh took the bait.

When all was in place, and John seated beside him, unbound, Sam sent a message to the man calling himself 'No Mercy' with the image of Rick attached. By now, it was twenty minutes past, and the gallery was locked and empty for the night.

The phone rang a second later and John leapt a foot in the air with a yell.

'Take a breath,' Sam said quietly. 'Do as we practised – everything will be fine.'

He hit the answer icon and switched to speaker.

'Why're you sending me this?' Sam recognised the voice immediately: even when he was still in his late teens, 'No Mercy' Mercer had always sounded like he was talking from the bottom of a deep and gritty well.

'The other guy went in just after him,' John said, his voice quaking. 'The Fixer.'

'You sound weird. What's up with you?'

'You said the Fixer's dangerous – what if he sees me?'

Sam gave him an encouraging thumbs-up.

'Christ, you're pathetic,' No Mercy growled. 'Where are you?'

'Whitechapel Gallery.'

'Got a picture of this bogeyman?'

'I *think* it's him, but he's different from the shot you gave me – older, you know? D'you want me to send it?'

'No, I want you to frame it and post it to your mum.'

'All right, all right, no need to be sarcastic,' John muttered, as Sam sent the second image.

'That's him,' his intermediary said. 'The boss said he'd prob'ly go in the back way if them two met up. He still there?'

'Unless there's some other way out I don't know about.'

'Stay sharp. Give us a shout if you see they're on the move.'

'No!'

'You *what*?'

'Sorry. Sorry . . . I just don't wanna be here when he comes out.'

267

'You better be, or I'm coming after you.' He cut the connection and John turned a terrified face to Sam.

'Brilliant work.' Sam grinned. 'You almost had *me* fooled.'

'But he wants me there.'

'Of course he does. He's not terribly bright, but he's had basic security precautions drummed into him.' Sam had anticipated the demand, and he and his captive were currently above a bar on a side street near the gallery, in a room jammed with boxes that smelled faintly of mould. 'He needs reassurance it's not a set-up.'

'Oh, God, you think he knows?'

John was becoming irritating, but Sam had vast reserves of patience he could call on if it meant getting his own way. 'No . . . he's just following protocol,' Sam soothed. 'He may look like a monster from a comic book, but all the threats and posturing are overcompensation. He's basically insecure – did you know he's afraid of spiders? And anyway, John, my men will be with you every step of the way. Not literally,' he added as John's eyes widened. 'I simply mean they'll be covering your back.'

'But I haven't got my car!' John's voice rose an octave. 'He's going to ask where it is!'

'That's not a problem,' Sam cajoled. 'He'll call you when he gets here. If he asks, you just tell him your target parked his car and left at a fair clip, so you had to abandon yours and follow on foot. Couldn't be simpler.'

The call from Mercer came at seven p.m.

John gave his handler a story about seeing the staff leave, but there was still no sign of Rick Turner or the Fixer.

'What, you mean they let them stay inside after closing?'

'I don't know, mate, I'm just telling you what I saw.'

'Meet me in the alley,' Mercer said. 'Show me which door the Fixer went through. Then you can leave.'

John threw Sam a panicked look and Sam splayed his hands, palms down, in a calming gesture.

'You still there, mate?'

'Yeah – just – I don't wanna share the bonus with Seanie. This is my catch, yeah?'

Sam gave him a smile of approval.

'All yours, mate – *if* he's still there when we go in.'

'We?'

A sound like boulders grinding over solid rock; Mercer was laughing. 'You didn't think I'd come on my own, did you?'

John gave a weak laugh. 'I'll be there in a tick.'

As Sam saw him onto the narrow street, he said, 'Don't think of running. My men will protect you, but only if you do as I've asked. Are we clear?'

With a jerky nod, John turned right, making his way reluctantly in the direction of the gallery. Sam turned left and left again, where Lawrence was waiting for him in an SUV half a block away. Two of Sam's operatives were positioned at vantage points opposite the gallery; two more were parked in a side street, waiting for the instruction to pounce on Mercer and his crew.

Sam had audio and visual from the entire team playing on a tablet in the SUV within thirty seconds. He knew that the two snipers with a view of the gallery would be ready to shoot if necessary.

'He's just appeared from the side road,' one of Sam's men said. 'Heading north-east towards the crossing.'

Traffic was still heavy on Whitechapel Road even at that time of night, producing a consistent background drone through the sniper's comms but most businesses were closed and shuttered so there were few pedestrians around, and with four lanes to cross plus two cycle lanes, it was the prudent option.

'I see him,' Sam said.

Standing at the lights waiting for them to change, John had his hands jammed in his pockets – no doubt to quell the violent shaking that seemed to have set in after Mercer's second phone call.

269

He waited until traffic was stopped both ways before stepping onto the crossing. A second later Sam saw a blur of movement to John's right.

A black motorbike careered around the corner. Two riders. Weaving between the chequered cycle lane barriers like a skier on a slalom, it drew level with John and the pillion passenger pointed.

Sam shouted, 'Gun!'

Two loud cracks, and John fell. Sam's snipers fired simultaneously, taking out the two men on the bike. It slid from under the riders, jarring to a halt when the back wheel impacted with one of the cycle lane bollards.

'Withdraw,' Sam said, knowing that his operatives would dismantle their kit and fade into the night before the police sirens even began to wail.

As for Lawrence, he had already guided the SUV down the street, heading north and then west, away from the carnage, blending with the evening traffic like thousands of other wealthy Londoners seeking their drama in the controlled setting of the theatres and cinemas of the West End.

Sam had held on to John's phone; now it buzzed in his hand. He tapped the screen to open the message:

—This round to me, I think.

Chapter 45

The same evening, nine p.m.

RICK AND SAM WERE SEATED IN what was quaintly described as a tavern but was in fact a fancy steakhouse inside a white stuccoed building in Fitzrovia. Complete with ornate Victorian covings, its walls were hung with more paintings than the National Gallery. The clientele was mixed in age, but they dressed conservatively, and the conversation was muted, seemingly set just below the level of the classical music playing in the background.

'What are we doing here?' Rick asked.

'You said you liked steak,' Sam said. He'd eaten his own ribeye with evident relish, clearing his plate and ordering a cheese board to follow.

Following his brother's instructions, Rick had been bounced around the underground from District to Central, Bakerloo and back to Central, hopping off at Oxford Circus and finishing his journey by taxi. And even that ended a quarter of a mile short of the restaurant.

Despite Sam's hearty appetite, Rick sensed a slight unease and that made him nervous. He set his half-finished meal aside and pushed his chair back a fraction, then looked Sam in the eye.

'You need to be straight with me, Sam,' he said.

'It *is* time we had a frank discussion,' Sam agreed.

Rick huffed a laugh. 'Oh, it's *way* past time.'

Sam dipped his head in acknowledgement. 'You know how it is, Rick: I tell you enough, but not so much that you'd feel compelled to do something rash about my involvement in any given situation.'

'Ah, my warped sense of justice,' Rick said. 'What can I say? It's a character flaw.'

Sam's mouth twitched and humour danced in his blue eyes. 'I'd better choose my words carefully, then.'

Rick relaxed in the chair, watching him.

'The man who was following you is dead.'

Rick sat forward, rage and horror surging through him. 'Sam, I *told* you—'

Sam raised both hands, palms down. 'I believe he was shot on Theo Lockleigh's orders.'

The news was so disorientating that Rick forgot to be angry. He stared at his brother. 'Lockleigh – *that's* who this is?'

'I believe so.'

'But Lockleigh's in prison.'

Sam shook his head. 'He's out, Rick.'

Rick felt winded. 'I can't believe I didn't know.'

'Released on licence.' Sam shrugged. 'Too many criminals, not enough space. The judicial system takes the naïve view that the old guard are a spent force, safe to let loose on an unsuspecting world. After all, where's the harm in recirculating a few old lags to make room for the young Turks?'

As the shock receded, Rick began to see the parts of the story that didn't fit. 'Why would Lockleigh shoot one of his own men?'

'To make an example of him. Theo somehow knew that your shadow was cooperating with me.'

'Like it's some big mystery. His abduction was on the *news*, Sam,' Rick growled. 'And just what did you do to get him to cooperate?'

'I gave him a choice – and before you ask, I didn't hurt him.'

'No, you left that to Lockleigh.' Rick ran a hand over his face. 'The poor bastard. He must've known that betraying Lockleigh was suicide – so whatever you did it must've been *really* bad.'

'John simply wasn't made for undercover work,' Sam said. 'I promise you; he gave up everything he knew without me having to lay a finger on him. I gave him a way to get out from under – and I'd planned to provide him with enough cash to get out of London and set up somewhere else.'

'After he helped you set up his boss.'

'Correct. Although he didn't know who his boss was,' Sam said evenly.

'Then what makes you so sure it's Theo Lockleigh?'

'He named the men he'd been working alongside: Errol, a skinny black guy, mid-thirties, carries "a big-arsed hunting knife"; No Mercy – a mountain of a man with weird, light eyes; Rory Puck—'

Rick sucked in a breath; he'd had personal dealings with Rory when he was about twelve or thirteen years old.

'I see you remember Rory.'

'I remember all of them,' Rick said, 'but Rory has a special place in my heart. Cracked two of my ribs over my unreasonable wish to keep my lunch money to feed myself.'

Sam nodded. 'That was when you first asked me about martial arts.'

'I didn't recognise the guy who was following me, though.'

'I imagine that Theo drafted in a couple of unknowns so that if you did happen to catch them in the act, you wouldn't make the connection.'

'He's trying to use me to get to you.'

Another nod.

Rick glanced around at the groups of businesspeople and tourists drinking and chatting, suddenly wondering if another stalker had been sent to shadow him.

'Don't worry, you weren't followed,' Sam said, reading his mind. 'I have two of my best operatives on you, and they didn't pick up a tail.'

'That would be Little and Large.'

Sam's eyebrows lifted in question, then his face cleared, and a smile played around the corners of his mouth. 'They do have more conventional names, but it's probably best you don't know them, and Little and Large is at least colourful.'

'Where did this happen?'

'The shooting?' Sam asked, like it was a minor detail in the conversation. 'On a crossing in Whitechapel.'

'How did it happen?'

'Fast.'

'Had him pegged out like a sacrificial goat, did you?'

'Not exactly.'

'I'm tired of this dancing around, Sam.' He shoved his chair back. 'Thanks for the meal.'

'Wait,' Sam said, extending a hand to stay him. He waited till Rick was settled in his chair again before going on.

'He'd phoned his handler – "No Mercy" Mercer, in case you're wondering – to tell him that you and I had met up. Mercer insisted that John be there when they moved in on us. I'd hoped to grab whoever came out, get Theo's location from them.'

'And John *knew* this was the plan?'

'You think he deserved to give "informed consent" when he'd been following you, knowing that the men he worked for were violent thugs? Knowing that the aim was to lead them to someone – me, as it happens – who was particularly disliked by these same thugs who terrified him? D'you think he asked them why they were so keen to find me, what they'd do with me if they did?'

'The man was a dupe, Sam. He didn't deserve this.'

'The minute my crew took him off the street, he was at risk. John knew that.'

Rick stared at his brother in disbelief. '*You're* the one who put him at risk in the first place – don't act like you did him a favour.'

'He put himself in jeopardy the moment he put a tracker on your car; I offered him a way out, which is more than Theo did.'

Rick shook his head. 'Yeah, I'm sure he's grateful.'

'You're missing the most important point here, Rick,' Sam said, overlooking the sarcasm. 'They shot John in broad daylight on a busy street. It's a message: they got to him, and they can get to you.'

Chapter 46

Next morning, eight a.m.,
five days after the Emin warehouse raid

FINDING HIS CUPBOARDS EMPTY, Rick tried a slow jog to the local Tesco Express, taking the tree-lined footpath of Putney Park Lane. The wound dressing was still a problem, but he found an old baseball cap that he could adjust to accommodate it and was there and back in under half an hour.

He'd picked up copies of the free newspapers and over coffee and toast, he saw that the shooting in Whitechapel was headline news in both the print press and local media online. They all seemed to be using the same police press release: Whitechapel Lane had been closed for an hour and a half while the police dealt with the crime scene but was opened again by nine p.m. and traffic was flowing freely this morning.

Witnesses said that they'd heard two shots, and police had apparently been able to secure dashcam footage from cars stopped at the traffic lights at the moment the victim – not named – was shot as he crossed the road. A handgun was recovered at the scene and was undergoing analysis.

The online media had more photos, so Rick ditched the print issues and dragged his laptop closer. BBC London was reporting live from Whitechapel. Their roving reporter was saying that the man who was shot had been pronounced dead at the scene. From eyewitness reports, it seemed that the bike riders had lost control of the bike – though that hadn't yet been confirmed by the police.

The reporter raised her voice over the sound of traffic. 'This is the junction this morning.' The wind blew in mischievous gusts, flipping her hair across her face and she clamped one hand over her head, fighting it as she made a quarter turn. The camera tech must have taken pity on her because they pulled back to catch the wider scene.

Rick halted, his coffee cup halfway to his lips. In the background was Whitechapel Gallery, where he'd met Pandora only two days ago. Why had Sam kept the location of the shooting from him – and why did he choose that exact location? All Rick could think was that it must have been information his stalker had provided to Sam, which meant that Lockleigh almost certainly had it, too. Did Lockleigh know that he'd spoken to the podcaster? Did Sam? He could ask, but the only thing he could rely on was that he wouldn't be able to trust the answer.

He chanced a quick call to DC Cossio, but even Gossip Guy seemed nervous of speaking out.

'And you call yourself the harbinger of Hammersmith,' Rick scoffed.

'Yeah, well, I know when to zip it.'

'Sounds like things are tense,' Rick said, just to keep him talking.

'That is putting it mildly. You should thank your lucky stars you don't have to deal with the drama.'

'Mate,' Rick said. 'You do know the only reason I'm not there is 'cos I got shot?'

'Oh, yeah, sorry, Sarge. But it's like an episode of *EastEnders* 'round here – dark mutterings in corners, people taking sides, finger-pointing, factions and blow-ups.'

'At least it's entertaining, yeah?' Cossio didn't seem to find that funny, so Rick added, 'Look, when d'you knock off? We'll go for beer; you can blow off some steam—'

'Not a chance.' The next second, the line was dead.

Rick had to admit, the news reports *were* scathing – another gang murder on London's streets being the popular theme – and perhaps he *should* be grateful, not having to face Superintendent Ghosh and DCI Steiner as they cast about to find anyone to blame but themselves, but he hated being so far from the action. He was due a final check-up at the hospital the following afternoon, and as soon as he was signed off, he'd be back at work.

Which left a day and a half still to get through, and he couldn't settle. After constant news-scrolling for fifty minutes, he limited himself to checking the news updates every hour, but that didn't help. Nothing had changed; neither the victim nor the shooters had been identified, and by now the Met with all its resources must surely have the victim's name. Rick saw only two reasons why the task force might withhold that information: because they were trying to locate his family, or to avoid alerting a suspect.

Even Pandora was uninformative: a post on her website saying only that she was 'looking into' the murder in Whitechapel, inviting anyone with information to email or DM her, and advising that she would contact her followers as soon as she had something new.

By mid-morning on the second day, he was ready to climb the walls. His clinic appointment wasn't until late afternoon, and after a jog and a shower, Rick was reduced to mowing the lawn to expend some nervous energy.

At just after eleven a.m., Sam rang him on the burner phone. 'Can you spare an hour?' he asked.

'I can spare three, if it'll get me out of the house,' Rick said.

Sam gave him precise instructions, and forty minutes later, he was standing in an expanse of polished concrete flooring in an open-plan apartment in a converted industrial building in Shoreditch. Exposed brick and reclaimed wood furnishings were the muscular theme, but by far the most striking aspect of the room was a four-by-five-metre free-standing canvas in the centre of the space.

The brothers stood side by side, staring at it, Rick with amused contempt. He shot Sam a glance, but it was impossible to tell what he might be thinking.

The work was plain matt black, bowed like a billowing sail, but the arresting quality was five great slashes sliced vertically in the canvas to reveal a vivid red underside, which glistened so that it almost looked wet, like a series of gaping wounds.

Sam slid him a sly glance, before performing one of his mind-reading tricks: 'What does it suggest to you?' he asked.

'If it's a Rorschach test, it doesn't leave much to the imagination,' Rick said.

'Mm. Subtlety was never Jost Bellingen's strong point.'

Rick bent to squint at the signature. It was dated 1973.

'Collectors do pay good money for his work, though,' Sam said. 'One of his shaped canvases went recently for thirty-eight million dollars.' He tilted his head to get a different perspective. 'Of course, this is relatively small, and stolen artworks are less saleable – dubious provenance and so on . . .' He stood back, examining it. 'Still, this one could fetch anywhere between fifteen and twenty million on the black market.'

Rick studied the art with increasing bemusement. 'Bellingen's collectors live in airport hangars, do they?' Sam chuckled, and Rick had to ask, 'D'you really like this?'

'God no,' Sam said. 'Bellingen was a con man – a glib charlatan with neither taste nor talent – even less imagination.' He paused. 'But I happen to know that Theo Lockleigh is a big fan and he's *desperate* to add this . . . item to his collection.'

Rick looked at the canvas with renewed interest. 'So . . . this is bait?'

'In a roundabout way,' Sam said. 'It'll have to go to auction on a Dark Web site, and I don't expect he'll show his face – that would be far too easy – but I believe it might just bring the white whale to the surface.'

'And if it doesn't?'

Sam shrugged. 'I'll make a good profit on it.'

'It's yours?'

Sam seemed astonished by the question. 'Who else's might it be?'

'First off, you said you didn't like it. Second, you told me once that rich people use brokers to buy stuff – especially if it's dodgy – and I imagine art brokering is the sort of work you're good at.'

'They do, and I am – good at it, I mean,' Sam said. 'But if I'd had to put someone else's asset up for sale I'd have to've first located the work, then persuaded the owner to sell before I could offer to set up the sale. That would've taken months to achieve – and I don't have the luxury of time. Anyway, people talk, and I wouldn't want anyone whispering my name.'

Rick assumed he meant his real name. 'So, how long have you owned it?'

'A while.'

Rick turned away from the painting. 'Why would you pay that kind of money for art you don't even like?'

'Theo has been collecting Bellingens for over twenty years. I thought it might come in handy as a bargaining chip one day.'

Rick laughed at the outrageous pragmaticism in his tone. 'Well, you always did believe in forward planning, but spending millions on crap art "just in case" is wild even for you.'

Sam smiled. 'I'll admit, there was an element of spiteful glee in knowing that I'd deprived Theo of the acquisition.' He scratched the back of his neck, apparently embarrassed by what he was about to say. 'But I'd forgotten about it until I saw my extremely valuable comics collection strewn across the coffee table the other night.'

Ignoring the dig, Rick shook his head. 'You forget about a tenner you left in your suit pockets a few months ago. You don't forget about a gargantuan artwork worth millions.'

Sam shrugged. 'It's been in storage.'

Rick laughed. 'You're unbelievable. Okay, let's pretend I accept that you bought it years ago, and it slipped your mind. How did you know Lockleigh was in the mood to buy right now? If he's only just got out of the clink, he must have other things on his mind.'

'*I* am on Theo Lockleigh's mind,' Sam said. 'Which is why I've been monitoring him ever since he was locked up.'

'You mean, ever since you got him locked up.'

Sam tilted his head. 'It was him or me – I much preferred that it was him.'

'So, you'll be watching his bank accounts during the auction, follow the money and hope it leads you to him?'

'Impossible,' Sam said. 'Theo's money is sheltered in shells within shells like Matryoshka dolls. Nope – I'll be following the goods.'

Rick was about to ask how, but he snagged on that Russian word. 'Matryoshka,' he said. 'Those little hollow dolls that fit one inside the other, getting smaller and smaller?'

Sam's eyebrow twitched. 'The very same.'

'Funny you should call them that – see, most people call them Babushka dolls.'

Sam gazed at him with bland curiosity.

'A friend of mine put me right on that.' Rick meant Dave Collins.

Sam's expression barely flickered, but it was enough for Rick and his shoulders dropped. 'Jeez, Sam . . . I told you to stay away from Dave.'

'Well, your armchair ninja's all grown up,' Sam said, an unusual irritation in his tone. 'He can make his own decisions.'

'You're right. What bothers me is how you dressed up the work so that Dave felt it was okay to do it. What did you tell him, Sam?'

Sam considered him placidly and after a few moments he seemed to come to a decision. 'I told him the truth: that I was thinking of entering into a transaction with an old friend, but I wasn't sure he could be trusted, so I needed Dave to vet his finances.'

Sam is all about plausibility, Rick thought. Often the grain of truth in a lie was what sold it to a mark. 'So you had Dave look for *shell* companies?'

'I gave Dave the details of a couple of Theo's secret bank accounts and asked him to keep an eye out for activity.'

Sam had told Rick recently that fifteen years ago, when he'd been Lockleigh's resident computer nerd, he'd set up accounts online to manage secure, anonymous payments. That was back when e-banking was a relatively new concept, and cryptocurrency still in its infancy.

'Lockleigh kept his old accounts?'

'He did. The CPS found some of his financial assets, but I made sure those two accounts were very well hidden. He'd have been mad to try to close them – risk attracting attention. But unfortunately, he changed his passwords as soon as he knew I'd betrayed him, so I haven't been able to gain access.'

Rick nodded towards the canvas. 'So you thought you'd pick his pockets with this monstrosity, instead, and he paid money from these accounts into one of the shell companies?'

'He *drained* one of the accounts dry, transferred the funds across to a shell,' Sam said. 'The identity of the company's real beneficial owner is hidden, but I can't imagine a world in which Theo Lockleigh would transfer his capital to benefit anyone but himself.'

'I'm guessing Dave kept looking till he found the next shell, maybe sheltered in the Virgin Islands or Jersey—'

'These were all in the US,' Sam said. 'It seems that South Dakota is quite the haven for dirty money these days.'

'Useful to know for squirrelling away your own ill-gotten gains,' Rick said dryly. 'I imagine Dave told you that your friend was probably not an honest broker, and you should steer clear.'

'He did!' Sam said, as if Rick's understanding of his friend's mentality was a revelation. 'Bless his heart.'

Rick glared at him. 'So you told him to drop it – didn't you?'

Sam sighed.

'Sam, Dave is not like you and me. He—'

'Oh, he's every bit as intelligent,' Sam cut in.

'That's not what I meant,' Rick said, indignant. 'He's smarter than anyone I know. I meant he's not *devious* like you and me. And faced with people like you and me, he's always on the back foot.'

Sam was watching him in what looked like disappointment. 'Well, you're just no fun anymore!' He held up a hand to silence Rick, laughter in his eyes. 'I thanked him for the advice and told him he could stop looking.'

Rick took a breath. Sam used to wind him up like this when they were kids; he should be wise to it by now. 'Good,' he said, after rethinking the outburst he'd been about to launch. 'So now you've got a rough idea of where Lockleigh's funnelling his money. But I still can't see how that'll help you net him. I mean, he didn't show up in person even when he thought he had you caught unawares in Whitechapel. How will you trace the goods to him?'

Sam grinned. 'In exactly the same way he tracked you.'

'You have a *tracker* on the artwork?'

'*In* it, technically.' He turned back to the canvas. 'This technique needs a very particular type of framing. For our purposes, it's the most beautiful aspect of this piece.' He led Rick around to the back of the stand.

The frame had a complicated structure of black powder-coated metal cross beams and struts supporting the canvas and holding the slashed sections in place.

'It's in the frame?' Rick asked.

'And you won't find the tiny hole that was made to accommodate it. That's been resealed and perfectly blended with the rest.' Sam ran a finger over the coating. 'The wonder of it is that the steel acts as a giant antenna. It'll light up like a beacon on the tracker.'

'What will you do when you find him?'

Sam tucked in his chin, fixing Rick with a look from under his brows. 'You don't really expect me to tell you?'

'Sam—'

'It's not open for discussion, Rick.'

'Listen – I know he's dangerous to you—'

'To both of us.'

'All right, to both of us. But just hear me out. Give me his location, I'll have him rearrested. He's caught with a stolen artwork in his possession, he's going back to finish his sentence – as well as facing a new prosecution.'

Sam gave him a long, thoughtful look and at last he said, 'I'll give it serious consideration.'

Chapter 47

Six days after the Emin warehouse raid

RICK HAD USED PUBLIC TRANSPORT for the 'art viewing' with Sam. It would take nearly an hour to get home, and then he'd have to trek back across the city to what he hoped would be his final appointment at the hospital, so he scouted out a decent café for lunch. Waiting for his order, he wondered how the investigation into his stalker's murder was going. Thinking about what Sam had done – the danger he'd put unsuspecting Londoners in – and what he might do to protect himself and his criminal pursuits in the future, Rick considered for the hundredth time if he should turn himself in, tell his bosses everything he knew.

He'd lied to so many people over the years: his parents, teachers, friends, girlfriends, colleagues and bosses. The lies weighed heavily on him, and the thought of unburdening himself sometimes became almost a craving. But what stopped him every time from making that devastating choice was the biggest lie – the one he'd told himself. The lies Sam told were nothing by comparison, and Rick owed his brother for every good thing that had happened to him since Sam had made it possible for the family to escape from the awful East End tenements of his childhood to the safe suburbs of Putney.

His phone rang.

'Can you get down here, now?' It was Ghosh.

Rick checked his watch. 'I'm across town, and I've got a hospital appointment at four-thirty.'

'It's what – one o'clock? This won't take long – you'll have plenty of time to get there after we've spoken.'

Rick couldn't very well refuse, so he went to the till and asked for the meal to go. Five minutes later, he was heading for the underground.

The mood at Hammersmith Police Station was subdued and unusually quiet. Rick stopped in at the office to pick up his mail and check for emails. Few were at their desks, and those who were spoke only in hushed tones. Joe Cossio angled his head past the edge of his computer monitor as though he was raising his head above a parapet to give Rick a cautious nod, and a couple of the admin staff asked how he was healing. Two minutes into scrolling through his emails, Rick's desk phone rang.

'You logged in ten minutes ago. Where the hell are you?'

It was Ghosh at his most irascible.

'I didn't know it was that urgent, Boss. I can come straight up if you want.'

'Yes,' Ghosh hissed. 'I do want.'

Rick replaced the receiver gingerly and, catching Cossio stealing another glimpse, he grimaced.

'I told you,' Cossio said. 'It's like Stalinist Russia in here – greet someone with a cheery, "Nice day!" they wanna know just what you *mean* by it. I swear, you don't know who it's safe to talk to.'

Rick tapped the side of his nose, logged out and snagged his jacket before heading up to the lion's den.

The superintendent was alone at a desk piled with folders.

His long, haughty face looked grey with strain and the look he gave Rick when he knocked at the door was far from friendly.

'Close it,' Ghosh said. He didn't invite Rick to sit and kept him waiting just long enough for Rick to take in the framed photographs of Ghosh with the Met Police Commissioner; Ghosh receiving an award; Ghosh with a former prime minister.

The superintendent placed three folders front and centre of the desk. 'A man was abducted near Vauxhall Park two days ago.'

Rick gave him the look of bland curiosity his brother had turned on him only hours earlier. 'I heard about that,' he said.

Ghosh watched him through half-closed eyes. 'Imagine my surprise when I was informed this morning that a serving Met Police officer's car was photographed at the scene.'

Rick composed his face and waited for a question.

'What were you doing at the scene of an abduction, Rick?'

'I drove over to see a mate.' No need to bring Dave Collins's name into this. 'We had breakfast at a caff near Vauxhall Bridge.'

'Lose track of time, did you?'

'Sorry?' Rick made sure it didn't show in his face, but he was thinking, *Oh, shit, the parking ticket.*

'You overstayed your welcome – got a fixed penalty notice.'

Rick nodded, mentally preparing during the slight delay. 'I saw a couple of TV cameras, and after what happened with the TikToker at the hospital, I didn't want to take the chance of ending up on the news again.'

'Laudable,' Ghosh said. 'And probably wise.'

'Why?'

'We'll come to that. What can you tell me about it?'

'Not a thing,' Rick said truthfully. 'I wasn't there when it happened.' Also true. 'Do we know who the victim is?' he added, before Ghosh could get his next question in.

'John Munot,' Ghosh said, watching for his reaction.

'The name's not familiar.' No lie, since Sam hadn't given him the poor sod's surname.

'Coincidental, though, isn't it?'

'It's that all right.'

Ghosh flipped a buff folder open just wide enough to retrieve a photo. 'This is the man.'

Rick stared down at the driver's licence photo of his stalker. 'That's the man who was following me.'

'Yes. The composite you put together with the e-fit officer wasn't bad at all. Almost like you know him.'

At least now he could see where Ghosh was heading.

'Well, do you?'

Just stay calm and take your time answering, counsellor Sam whispered in his ear.

'Know him? No, sir, I don't,' Rick said, thinking, *Shut up, Sam.*

'Would you care to speculate as to how Mr Munot ended up shot to death on a street corner in Whitechapel last night?'

Ah, here it is. Rick realised with a shock that Ghosh *had* withheld the dead man's name to avoid alerting a suspect – and that suspect might just be Rick himself.

He blinked as if in mild surprise and picked up the photo print-out. 'This is the guy? Has he got form? I mean, if we look into his associates, we might find a gang affiliation.'

'He had a couple of TWOCs as a fifteen-year-old – the first was his mother's car, for which he got a caution. On the second occasion he was fined and issued with two driving bans to run concurrently after he reached the driving legal age. He got into H by his early twenties – buying, not supplying,' Ghosh rattled off. 'Rehab in his mid-to-late twenties, then Uber driver for five years. No traffic offences, no criminal convictions in that time.'

'So, he'd know the streets, be up to following a car in heavy traffic,' Rick said. 'The TWOC conviction would be spent – and there's nothing else in his record to raise any red flags if he did happen to get stopped by police. He'd be an excellent choice for the covert surveillance of a cop – especially if the interested party was an OCG.'

'Always ready with a theory, aren't you?'

This isn't a fact-finding mission, it's a fault-finding mission, superego Sam intruded again.

Rick said coolly, 'To be fair, sir, you did invite me to speculate.'

The superintendent conceded the point with a dissatisfied twist of his mouth. 'It doesn't tell us anything we didn't already know, though, does it?'

'It *could*, if we looked into it,' Rick said with a flare of annoyance. Then subsided, acknowledging guiltily that since he was withholding all the answers Ghosh wanted, he had no right to take offence.

'Why didn't you report this two days ago, when it happened?' Ghosh demanded.

'I didn't see that there was anything to report, sir,' Rick said in a more civil tone. 'I saw an ongoing police incident, the situation was under control, so I left the crew to get on with their jobs. I can't tell you how many times I've chanced upon crime scenes in this city.'

He'd told Sam no more than a couple of hours ago that this was a first for him, but Ghosh didn't need to know that.

'There's a word for people like you,' Ghosh said, showing a flash of claws.

'People like me, sir?' Rick knew that Ghosh meant glib and plausible. He jutted his chin, challenging his boss to say it. But Ghosh lowered his eyes and sighed in a gesture of frustration; Rick had scored a minor victory.

'What's the online gossip on Munot's death?' Rick asked, pressing his advantage.

Ghosh raised one elegantly tailored shoulder. 'Social media tattle has chalked his death up as another gangland killing.'

'What about the shooters?' Rick asked. 'Do we know anything about them?'

'They were pronounced dead at the scene.'

'The news media said as much,' Rick said, thinking, *Now who's being evasive?*

'But they didn't say how the men died.'

Rick felt a spurt of alarm. 'It wasn't the crash?'

Watching him closely, Ghosh said, 'They were shot.'

Rick felt suddenly cold. *Sam, what have you done?* 'D-do we know who the bike riders were?' he stammered.

Feigning astonishment, Ghosh said, 'You mean you don't?'

What the hell? 'No, sir, I don't,' he said firmly.

'Perhaps this will refresh your memory.'

He sifted through the folders and placed two mugshots on the table, adding one after another, images of the bodies at the scene – a tangle of motorcycle and twisted limbs – and finally the post-mortem photographs. His eyes never left Rick's face and Rick made sure he would read nothing from his expression.

'This one is known as Seanie G – surname Green,' Rick said, tapping an image of the ginger terror of his school days. 'This is Rory MacKinnon.'

'Friends of yours?'

The room vanished, and Rick was a skinny twelve-year-old lying in the dirt of his old school playground, palms skinned, grit in the grazes. For a second, he couldn't breathe.

'*Sergeant Turner.*'

The harsh command in Ghosh's tone snapped him back to the present, and looking into the chief superintendent's dark eyes, Rick realised that Ghosh knew exactly who these dead men were – and what they meant to him.

'When I was a kid, Rory Puck broke my ribs,' Rick said, his voice hard. 'We called him "Puck", 'cos his weapon of choice was a two-pound ice-hockey puck. Seanie was more the type to stick the boot in when his bigger pals had already put you on the ground. So, no – not friends – not by any stretch of the imagination.' He shoved the images back to Ghosh, allowing him to see the anger.

The superintendent sucked his teeth.

Maybe he isn't sure if he believes me, or maybe he senses that the anger isn't entirely directed at him. Sam could have warned him; he must have known Ghosh would ask about these two at some point, yet he'd said nothing.

'You maintain that you don't know this Munot character?'

'I don't,' Rick said, bridling at the weasel-word 'maintain', and refusing to elaborate.

'Tell me about the other two.'

'I just did.'

'But there's more, isn't there?'

This was the kind of thing Rick himself did all the time as a cop: keep the suspect chatting; pose open questions; leave plenty of silences – give them time to implicate themselves.

'Is this an interrogation?' he asked. 'Do I need to call my union rep?'

'For the moment, this is between the two of us,' Ghosh said. 'It's your right to bring in your union, but then I'd have to widen the circle of knowledge.' The slight twitch of his shoulder said it all.

Interrogation one-oh-one, Rick thought. Never block legal representation – instead, offer the suspect a choice, but hint at dire consequences if they stopped cooperating. By now, Rick was in no doubt that he was a suspect. Widening the circle could mean that his boss would inform senior members of the task force of Rick's links to the dead men. Given the social media attention he had already been subjected to, adding in the ongoing speculation about his guilt or innocence regarding the Wolf Pack, Rick's reputation would be in shreds by the end of the week. But for now, Ghosh was saying, he and his superintendent were simply having a frank exchange of information. Bringing in a union rep would stir up the mud in the pool. And mud sticks.

Rick took a breath and forced his attention back to the images of the dead shooters.

'Those two worked for Theo Lockleigh – a shyster and loan shark on the estate where I grew up,' Rick began. This was a soft start: if Ghosh didn't know this already, it would only take a quick dip into his personal file to find out. 'I didn't mix with

291

them, kept my head down and studied. When we moved out of the area, I stayed out. But I did hear that when they left school, they became Lockleigh's bully boys and enforcers.'

'And you knew this even though you stayed out?'

'My brother was Lockleigh's right-hand man for a time.' Ghosh *must* know this – it was big news at the time, and then when Sam disappeared, the police were on their doorstep in Putney on and off for months.

'Your brother absconded from police protection.'

Rick held his gaze; he'd answer questions, but they both knew this wasn't a friendly chat and he didn't need Rick to confirm the facts on record.

'Wasn't he suspected of stabbing a man on the estate a week or so after he disappeared?'

That was a fact of record, as well.

'I wonder what that was about?'

You can wonder all you like.

His boss's hawk-like gaze never wavered from Rick's face. 'Did you know that your brother's blood was on the knife, as well?'

'No,' Rick said, truthfully – although it made sense, knowing what he now knew about the circumstances of that day.

Ghosh watched him, his eyes hooded once more. 'I understand that you had a bit of a name for turning up uninvited at unexplained deaths.' He paused, adding with a sneer, 'Looking for Sam, were you?'

'Yeah.' Knowing what the next question would be, and wanting to avoid telling a downright lie, he pre-empted it by adding, 'I never did find him at any of those scenes, but the upside is, me showing up at the Haskins death led to the Unwin case, and that was a big win – wasn't it, sir?'

It was for both of them, but Rick was gambling that in his present mood, his boss would not want to give him undue credit. True to form, Ghosh gave a slight shrug and said, 'Water under the bridge, Rick. We need to focus on the here and now.'

'Of course,' Rick said, and stood calmly waiting for him to get on with it.

Ghosh fell into a musing silence for some moments. 'So, Lockleigh sends two of his crew to shoot the man who was following you. Which suggests that Munot was working for a rival gang.'

Rick said nothing.

'And the rival gang must have shot those two in retaliation. But how would they *know* that Munot would be at that street corner at that precise time? If he was following you, it would make sense.' He looked suddenly into Rick's face. '*Were* you in Whitechapel when the shootings happened?'

'I was at home when that lot went down,' Rick said.

Ghosh seemed not to have heard. 'I mean, being on the spot at the exact instant Munot was shot – that seems planned. Does that seem planned to you?'

He was closer to the truth than he knew.

Rick nodded. 'It does. The question is, whose plan?'

'Perhaps Lockleigh didn't like the idea of you being followed.'

'And killed Munot as a *favour* to me? I told you, sir – I had nothing to do with Lockleigh – or his crew.'

'With the exception of Sam, your brother.'

'Sam was family – and he burned his boats with Lockleigh fourteen years ago when he informed against the bastard.' An idea occurred to him. 'When did Lockleigh get out?'

The question threw Ghosh out of his fake reverie. 'A couple of weeks ago – why?'

'He must be out on licence, so at the very least he should be reporting to his probation officer – he might even be e-tagged.'

Ghosh's eyebrows drew down. 'He's disappeared.'

'I'm guessing that tracing him is a priority?' Rick asked disingenuously, meeting his superintendent's angry gaze with an open, relaxed look.

'That is not your concern.' Ghosh began collecting up the images.

'Sir?' There was a finality in his tone that alarmed Rick.

'Until we have a clearer picture of what happened in Whitechapel, I'm afraid you will need to remain on leave.'

He hadn't been expecting that. He began to protest but Ghosh held up a finger to silence him.

'We'll call it sick leave – clearly you have a way to go before you're fully fit.'

'*Sir*, I—'

'I am decided on this point, Rick. I will not be persuaded otherwise. Your background – the um . . . links to Lockleigh – they're bound to come out when we name the shooters. Think of this as a PR exercise. The Met simply can't stand any more bad publicity.'

'I wasn't aware that the Met was in the business of selling,' Rick said, fighting to keep the bitterness out of his voice.

'Don't be naïve,' Ghosh shot back. 'We police by consent; appearances matter.'

There were a hundred things Rick could say about how misogyny and racism, sexual misconduct and generally piss-poor performance affected the appearance of the Met, but he held his tongue, saying mildly, 'My record speaks for itself.'

'No, Rick – right now, social media speaks on your behalf. And until that calms down, you are a liability. The fact is that you *do* have links to gangsters who work for a notorious criminal. Now, those links may be entirely innocent, but you haven't said anything in this office to convince me of that.'

What could he say – that he had no 'links' to Theo Lockleigh? That would be a patent lie. There was Sam, for a start, and if Rick couldn't say for sure that Lockleigh had Munot shot, he had a strong theory as to why his stalker was killed. As for Seanie G and Puck – Sam might not have pulled the trigger, but he'd given the word – Rick was certain of that.

Eyeing him coldly, his superintendent said, 'Close the door on the way out.'

As Rick turned, Ghosh called him back.

'This "friend" you met for breakfast – who was it?'

'Dave Collins,' Rick said. Lying would only make things worse.

'Ah, the forensic accountant.'

Rick nodded.

'When and where did you meet?'

Rick gave him a time and the address of the café, and Ghosh scribbled them onto a notepad. 'We'll be checking your alibi with him.'

Rick made a mental note to ring Dave on his burner phone as soon as he was out of the building – not to agree an alibi, but to warn his friend to prepare for the call. Dave Collins was terrified of Ghosh; he'd need to brace himself for the ordeal.

Chapter 48

By the time Rick reached the hospital for his clinic appointment, word was out on the Whitechapel assassins. The Met's Media and Communications Directorate must have released photographs of the dead bike riders shortly after he'd left the police station, and images of the men were featured on their witness appeals pages. Rick couldn't face the news media and, closing the browser, he slipped his phone into his inside pocket and retrieved the burner phone to text Sam, expecting a quick reply, but Sam remained uncharacteristically silent.

At the hospital, he was given the only good news of the day so far: he was healing well and could be discharged to his general practice. The doctor – a man, this time – shot Rick curious glances as he examined the wound.

'You're beginning to worry me, Doc,' Rick said.

'Sorry. It's just – you're the cop who got shot, aren't you?'

Sighing inwardly, Rick said, 'It's all in the notes.'

'Oh, I doubt it.' The doctor went off a moment later to print a letter for Rick to take to his local GP, while the nurse – the same chatty Lancastrian – prepared a lighter gauze dressing.

'What did he mean by that?'

'Relax, Sergeant. He's on your side,' she said. 'We all are. We've seen enough scapegoating in the NHS over the last few years to recognise it when it raises its ugly mush.'

A few minutes later, she tidied away and stripped off her gloves.

'Well, that's your last session with us – as long as you keep out of the line of fire,' she said chirpily.

'I just need that letter,' Rick said, though getting signed off as fit for work wouldn't do him much good, given recent developments.

Glancing over her shoulder, she said, 'He's probably got waylaid. Hang on a sec, I'll fetch it for you.'

She vanished and two minutes later the door opened, and another nurse stepped quickly inside.

'Well, if it isn't Senior Nurse Verren.'

'Vee,' she corrected. Today she was dressed in jeans and a close-fitting leather jacket. Her light brown hair was loose to her shoulders, and Rick felt that tug of attraction he'd experienced the night he was rolled into the hospital on an ambulance trolley.

'I take it you're still on leave.'

'That's some mad detective skills you got goin' on there,' she said. Then: 'Mandy asked me to give you this.' She handed him the promised letter and as he pocketed it, she produced a paper bag from inside her jacket, her blue eyes twinkling with merriment.

'What's this?'

'Peace offering.'

He crinkled his brow, puzzled.

'I probably shouldn't have told Pandora about your boss having a go at you when you were drugged and bloodied.'

'*Probably*? And it's the other way around,' he added with a theatrical scowl. 'The bloodying came first.'

'Yeah,' she said, grinning. 'Hashtag "wordordermatters".'

The fact that she'd told him without him having to ask made him feel suddenly lighter. He opened the bag and, laughing, pulled out a brand-new beanie.

'You lot *have* been talking about me.'

'Mandy got fairly graphic on the subject,' she said with a grimace. 'It's breathable cotton, and you should wash it every day.'

'Yes, Mum.'

'I'm serious,' she said, though she was smiling.

Rick peered into the bag. 'Aw . . . And you cut the tags off, so I can wear it now – that's *sweet*.'

'Don't push your luck, pal.'

As Rick eased the hat over the new dressing, she began again in a more sombre tone. 'I'm sorry about the suspension.'

'Social effing media!' Rick exclaimed. 'I suppose there's no point in denying it?'

'Nah – TikTok says you're suspended, you're suspended.' She sighed. 'It's a weird strategy – getting rid of cops who can do the job, promoting the politicians and the box-tickers.'

Surprised, he said, 'You think the Wolf Pack's justified in what they do?'

She gave him a long, hard look.

'A cop died, Vee,' Rick said. 'Hostages died.'

Tears sparkled in her eyes, and she palmed them away. 'Yeah,' she said.

Then, in a complete change of mood, she tilted her head, examining him with a critical gaze. 'Hey – you look almost presentable!'

Rick balled up the bag and with a note of alarm, she said, 'You might want to check the tag – in case you need help with the washing instructions.'

He fished out the tag; she'd written her phone number neatly in biro on the reverse. When he glanced up, the door was already closing after her.

'Wait!' He hopped off the examination table, retrieved his jacket and dashed outside, but she'd already gone.

Doesn't matter, he thought glancing down at the shiny triangle of card in his hand. *After all, I've got her number.*

Chapter 49

SAM GOT IN TOUCH AT AROUND NINE P.M. with an apology and a fresh set of instructions for a rendezvous. As always, he only gave the last leg of the journey after all the others had been safely completed.

An hour later, they were in an apartment in Maida Vale.

Sam poured Rick a glass of wine, which Rick ignored, and offered him a seat, which he accepted.

Relaxing into a chesterfield sofa, Rick glanced around the room with its preponderance of dark tan leather, subtle lighting, bookshelves crammed with law books, Turkish rugs and expensive-looking antiques; it couldn't be more different to the brutal style of the last place they'd met.

'Just how much London real estate d'you own?' he asked.

'Not much,' Sam said. 'I favour the European property market over the UK. The warehouse conversion is a rental, and this isn't mine.'

'So, this belongs to a friend?'

Sam must have caught something in Rick's expression, because he laughed. 'You needn't look so surprised – I have lots of friends. Not all are trustworthy – but at least it's never dull.' He took in the sumptuously appointed space. 'This being a case in point – it's owned by Theo Lockleigh.'

Rick surged from the chair. 'Are you *crazy*?'

'Don't fret,' Sam said. 'I have it under surveillance. He hasn't been anywhere near – and if he were to show up out of the blue, he'd set off a dozen alarms before he got within fifty yards of the building. It's actually the safest place we could be.'

'What, in the eye of the storm?' Rick said, although he did take a seat again.

'I read about your suspension. I'm truly sorry.'

'I *wasn't* sus—' Rick broke off. 'Never mind, it doesn't matter.' He composed himself and started again. 'I thought the shooters died in the crash. You could've had the decency to warn me, Sam.'

'The Met did hold back that detail, didn't they? I take it they kept you out of the loop?'

'Until my boss called me in for questioning.'

'It must have been a shock – but the less you know, the less you're liable.'

'Oh, well, it's good to know you were looking out for me, but the fact is you shot those men at a busy traffic junction – innocent people could've been hurt.'

'My men probably saved lives – think of the casualties if Theo's men had carried on riding through the traffic, blasting away.'

'Bollocks,' Rick scoffed. 'Shooting two of Lockleigh's core team does no one any good but you.'

'Well, that's just . . . cynical. Debatable, too. D'you think that Seanie G and Puck were paragons outside of the beatings and shootings, threats and intimidation they meted out for Theo? I'd wager that a good few souls will sleep easier knowing that those two are out of their lives – you among them.'

'Don't try to justify this by telling me they were bad men – you aren't qualified to make that judgement.'

'If not me, who *is*?' Sam looked genuinely amused.

'You're really arguing that you're doing society a favour?'

Sam chuckled. 'I'm far too wicked to start taking the moral

high ground at this late stage in my career. But I didn't kill John Munot, or Puck or Seanie G.'

Rick stared at his brother in disbelief: 'Have you completely lost touch with reality? Munot died because you used him as *bait*. Puck and Seanie were shot on your orders.'

'It's a workable theory,' Sam said. 'But you're a little short on proof.'

Rick shook his head. 'Why does it feel like this is all a big game to you?'

'I assure you, it isn't,' Sam said. 'Listen to me. Lockleigh was, is, and will *continue* to be a serious threat to us as long as he's around. Why d'you think I kept my distance all these years? Because it was better for you *and* me that way.'

'Piss off, Sam. You don't get to decide what's best for me.'

'Fair enough,' Sam said. 'But I think we can at least agree that if Lockleigh can't get to me, he'll come for you.'

'I can handle myself.'

'No one on this *earth* can handle a bullet in the back of the head.' Sam seemed shocked by the harshness of his own words. 'I apologise. That was uncalled-for.' After a few moments, he began again: 'Look – give me a few more days, I'll have this tidied away. Lockleigh will be a thing of the past.'

'What's *that* a euphemism for?' Rick took a breath and let it go – anger would never persuade Sam. 'At least let me help.'

'What did you have in mind?'

'Like I said, give me a location. I'll talk my boss round somehow – we'll scoop him up before he does any more damage.'

Sam shook his head. 'This is not your fight.'

'Except it kind of *is*, isn't it, Sam? Seanie G, Rory Puck – they're part of my history. And then there's you, steeped in all that criminality. I guess my boss thinks I learned more than a bit of street fighting from my big brother.'

'Surely he's just being cautious – given the social media storm raging right now.'

'He asked me where I was when Munot was shot. I'm *under suspicion*, Sam – he's checking my alibi – Lockleigh turns up dead, it'll be *me* the police come looking for.'

Sam sat back and thought for a moment. 'All right. I can let you know when we're ready to close in on the old scorpion – give you time to set something up. If you have people to back up your whereabouts—'

'No!' Rick exclaimed. 'You just don't get it, do you? I'm not asking for the chance to set up an alibi – I'm police; I can't cover for you while you wage war against old enemies.'

'I sympathise—' Sam broke off. 'Don't look at me like that; I *can* sympathise, and I do. I know your job is important to you Rick, and I don't want to jeopardise that. But I didn't start this war, and I have to fight it my own way.'

'And I'm supposed to let it happen?'

'I'll try to be discreet,' Sam said, side-stepping the question.

Rick choked out a bitter laugh. 'If what happened in Whitechapel is *discreet*, I fear for the city.'

'I'm sorry, Rick. I can't see any other way.'

'Sam, this has to stop.'

'It will – I give you my word.'

'I mean now.'

Sam fixed him with a solemn look. 'Lockleigh won't stop until he has me, or I stop him.'

'You've got money – more aliases than MI5 – you could go anywhere you want.' Rick heard the pleading tone in his voice and was furious with himself. Not that it had any effect – Sam was already shaking his head. 'I swear, Sam, if one more person gets hurt 'cos of you, I'm turning myself in.'

'Well, I hope you don't, because all the good work you've done – protecting people, upholding the law – will be undone.'

'You're unbelievable,' Rick said. 'If one scenario doesn't work for you, you just flip to another, don't you?' He shook his head. 'I should've told Ghosh when I had the chance. I was a coward not to.'

He took out his phone. Ghosh wouldn't take a call from him, but scrolling through his contacts list, he stopped at the ex-MIT detective, Alan McGuinness. *Yes, that's a man I could trust.*

'Rick,' Sam said. 'What're you doing?'

'You need to leave, bruv,' Rick said. 'Police'll be here any minute.'

Sam knocked the phone out of his hand. 'Don't,' he warned.

'Don't what? Don't do my job?'

'Rick, please—'

The phone had skittered across the carpet, lodging itself under a dresser against the wall, and Rick bent to pick it up. As he turned to face Sam, his brother was on him. A smooth and swift wrist grab and turn, and he had the phone in his hand. Rick was on the floor before he'd even seen it coming.

On his feet in a second, Rick muttered, 'Bastard.'

'Rick, stop.'

'No. *You* need to stop,' Rick snarled, jabbing towards Sam's brachial plexus, the bundle of nerves near his collarbone, aiming to incapacitate him.

But Sam blocked and parried, blocked and parried until, roaring in frustration, Rick rushed him.

Sam pivoted and shoved. Rick's momentum carried him hard onto the sofa. As he rolled, turning again to face his brother, Sam's hand came around from behind his back. He aimed a gun at Rick's chest.

'Well,' Rick said, his mind washed with calm and clarity. 'Now I know.' He spread his arms wide. 'Go ahead, mate – take your best shot.'

Sam had his back to the door. It opened, but he didn't flinch. Two men came in – the men Rick recognised them as Little and Large. Little moved behind Rick, binding his wrists with a zip tie. Rick couldn't see what the other was doing.

'I'm sorry, Rick,' Sam said. 'I really hoped it wouldn't come to this.' He nodded and something whipped fast over Rick's head. He couldn't breathe. The material was thick and dark. He felt the thing tighten around his face, then everything went black.

Chapter 50

Three days later, nine p.m.

PANDORA OPENED THE NEW EPISODE of her podcast with a warning: the video following her introduction contained graphic footage that some viewers might find upsetting. This, she explained, was exclusive dashcam footage of the shootings in Whitechapel.

Her podcast had attracted nationwide media attention, her ratings and followers were going stratospheric, and she'd gained enough advertising revenue to get herself a producer and some decent recording equipment on the back of it.

'I've been approached by journalists from the broadsheets asking me to "catch them up".' She gave the camera a knowing look. 'But I'm not falling for it. The rest of the media who have parachuted in on this story just want a story. I want *justice*.'

She went on to thank the subscriber who had provided the dashcam reel. 'They don't want to be named, but they did ask me to say that they would have handed the recording over to the police but didn't feel the Metropolitan Police could be trusted.' More direct eye contact. 'A sad sign of the loss of public faith in law enforcement.'

After a brief pause, she went on, 'Now, I'm about to show the dashcam recording. It is real, and it's shocking – so please, do use judgement before deciding if you want to see it.'

The video lasted no more than fifteen seconds. As it ended, the picture faded out, and an image of the victim came into focus on the screen.

'Five days ago, John Munot was targeted by two men on a motorcycle. He was shot to death in front of horrified onlookers in the early evening at a busy junction in Whitechapel.

'These facts are a matter of public record,' she went on. 'What many of you can't know is that Mr Munot bears a strong resemblance to an e-fit issued by police a week earlier.'

Munot's driver's licence photo slid to the left on the screen, and a police e-fit appeared next to it. 'This e-fit relates to a man wanted for questioning after an off-duty police officer witnessed a cyclist being knocked off his bicycle ten days ago in Fulham, an area of West London. The cyclist remains in hospital in a serious but stable condition.'

She felt slightly uncomfortable about the next slide, but it made good podcast material, and she was confident of her facts.

'The officer who reported the traffic incident was Detective Sergeant Rick Turner.' For her new followers, she explained Rick Turner's role in the recent gangland shootings in Limehouse, and – playing fair – adding details of his courageous attempts to avert the bloodbath that followed.

She urged those who had not seen the episode of *Pandora Unboxes* covering the Limehouse raid to catch up on it after the show.

'Two men are suspected of shooting Munot,' she said, supplying their names and their images. 'They died at the scene after their motorbike crashed, and the police revealed three days ago that both had been shot with high-powered rifles.

'Detective Sergeant Turner is still on leave, recovering from injuries sustained during the drugs raid in Limehouse that went so badly wrong. I tried contacting him by phone to ask if Munot was indeed the man who had caused the accident that put a cyclist in hospital, but he didn't want to talk to *Pandora Unboxes*.'

In fact, she'd texted and left messages on his voicemail and he hadn't replied, but she didn't think she was stretching the facts too far – time was pressing, and the broadsheets were hot on her heels.

'Let's take a closer look at the two men suspected of shooting Munot: Sean Green and Rory MacKinnon,' she went on.

Here, her producer had placed police mugshots of the two men side by side. The malevolence of one and incipient madness of the other were almost as disturbing as the dashcam reel that had just sent her podcast watch count soaring.

'My regular listeners will know that I do my research, which is one reason why I don't post daily updates. Sean Green and Rory MacKinnon's criminal behaviour began when they were just schoolboys. They went to the same school, lived in the same run-down social housing, committed crimes together – even went to prison together. But John Munot had no gangland connections I could find – in fact, for the past five years he has been an Uber driver, and in all that time, he was never even issued with a parking ticket. So why was he targeted by two known criminals?'

She stared into the camera as if lost for words.

'There are some things you can't know, and here's where you, *Pandora Unboxed* subscribers and listeners, play a vital role. You see, last week, I started a Patreon account.' A slide filled the screen showing the *Pandora Unboxed* page on Patreon.

'Patreon members get ad-free access to *Pandora Unboxed* – and premium members are also invited to exclusive online chats and Q&As with me, Pandora Hahn.'

She pointed her followers to the sub-links.

'I asked my Patreon members the same question. Why was John Munot targeted – shot dead – by two known gangland criminals? They came back with a different question which – well, to be frank with you – shocked me. Here it is: "Could there be a connection between a decorated London Metropolitan Police detective and these deaths?"'

She paused and the producer switched to a full-screen of Pandora herself. 'I want to give a special shout-out to my Patreon subscribers Kyra, Stu and Malissa, who came forward with the information that follows.'

A headshot of the detective sergeant appeared on-screen and the video stream of Pandora shrank to a small picture-in-picture inset at the bottom right.

'Fact one: Rick Turner grew up in social housing, sharing an apartment with his parents and older brother Samuel in a four-storey tenement in East London. Fact two: Rick Turner, Sean Green and Rory MacKinnon grew up on the same estate. Fact three: all three went to the same school, although Sean and Rory were a year or two older than Rick, and the Turner family moved away from the estate when Rick was in his early teens. While the young Rick Turner seems to have shunned the temptations of crime, his older brother, Samuel, went all-in.

'Samuel Turner, Sean Green, and Rory MacKinnon all worked for Theodore Lockleigh. He was a lawyer who for twenty-three years represented some of the most dangerous criminals in London's East End. Alongside his legal practice, Lockleigh ran a highly illegal loan shark business from that self-same social housing complex. Fourteen years ago, the police finally caught up with him, and he was jailed.'

Here she'd found a photograph of Lockleigh arriving at court looking suave in a well-cut suit and looking more like defending counsel than the accused. Her producer had split the screen so that her fans could see her when she delivered the next undisputed and gloriously compelling fact:

'The evidence that put Mr Lockleigh behind bars was provided by Samuel Turner – Detective Sergeant Rick Turner's brother.'

She and her producer had decided on a three-second pause to give that zinger the space it deserved. As they'd recorded that section, she'd felt a twinge of guilt that the new information might cast DS Turner in a bad light. But it *was* an undeniable fact that his brother was a criminal, and since Sam Turner had put another career criminal in jail, you might argue that she'd cast *both* of the brothers in a good light. Sitting in her car now, watching it play, hearing that electric pause, Pandora thrilled to the silence and, checking her social media, she saw that the comments, likes and shares were beginning to rocket, just as her new producer had promised they would.

'Samuel Turner vanished around the same time that Theodore Lockleigh went to trial,' the recording went on. 'He never resurfaced. Coincidentally, Theodore Lockleigh has just been released from prison on licence. This means that he has some of his prison term still to run, and he's allowed out of prison early only on specific licence terms. For someone with Lockleigh's history, that would certainly involve reporting to his supervising probation officer regularly and living at an address approved by his supervisor. But astonishingly, no one seems to know where he is. A reliable source told me that he has been recalled to prison for breach of licence, and the Metropolitan Police Service is about to issue a public appeal for information on his whereabouts. Is it a coincidence that, after years of obscurity, Sean Green and Rory MacKinnon exploded back on the scene just after their former boss was released from prison – and in such a dramatic way?' She took a breath.

'I don't know. But I'll keep digging, and if any listeners have information about the gangland activities of Theo Lockleigh before he was jailed fourteen years ago, *Pandora Unboxes* would be very interested to hear what you have to say.'

She listened with half an ear to her outro, her thanks to her one sponsor and her exhortations to like, subscribe and follow. Her Patreon page had a few more subscribers, too.

She tapped in replies to comments and questions, her thumbs flying over the virtual keyboard of her smartphone. The house she was watching was largely in darkness already. One light shone in the upstairs apartment. She would wait until the lights went out before heading home to her own tiny studio flat. Because Pandora Hahn, serious investigative journalist, conscientious and rigorous researcher, had found a small snag in something one of her informants had told her, and she'd plucked and picked at it till she'd freed the loose thread. And the more she pulled, the more the thread unravelled. Now she intended to follow that thread into the labyrinth, right to the minotaur's lair.

Chapter 51

Half past midnight, the same night

THE STEEL DOOR INTO THE BASEMENT OPENED and a man stood silhouetted in the meagre light of the pub's bar area. He flicked the lights on, and a few old-style strip lights flickered to life, bathing the space below in cold white light. He descended cautiously to the man seated on a mattress on the floor. One leg was shackled to an iron hoop driven deep into one of the age-blackened walls and he was handcuffed, but still the newly arrived man was wary. He was right to be.

He was fifty, maybe. Grey-haired, slightly built, diffident.

'Sergeant Turner,' he began. 'I'm sorry for all this,' He glanced around him at the dank conditions Rick had been kept in for the past three days. 'Do you remember me? My name is Lawrence, I'm Sam's—'

'Driver,' Rick interrupted. 'Yeah, I recognise you.'

This quiet man had chauffeured Sam last autumn in the final, fatal raid that had torn Rick's life, his future plans, and any chance of happiness to shreds. The others – ex-army, ex-police, paramilitaries – were of a type. Lawrence, courteous and softly spoken, was so unlike the rest of Sam's crew that he'd stood out.

The older man looked around him with something like dismay. 'Sam was hoping this would all be over by now.'

'By "this", you mean my abduction and illegal imprisonment?'

'You're angry. I get it—'

'Nah, mate,' Rick said. 'I got past anger two days ago. The stage I'm at now is ice-cold rage.'

'Yes,' Lawrence said softly. 'I can only imagine how you feel—'

'Come over here, mate – I'll *demonstrate*.'

Lawrence looked acutely embarrassed. 'I wouldn't normally have come here – stepping outside of my role – it's not something you do around Sam. But I thought you should know. Things didn't go to plan.'

'Tell me about it,' Rick said, jangling the chain attached to his leg.

For a second, Sam's chauffeur seemed stuck for words, but staring at the floor, he said softly, 'He was trying to protect you.'

'Yeah, that's Sam – protecting me by beating the shit out of me.' He had been beaten – first by Sam, although he admitted grudgingly that his brother had pulled his punches, let him down easy in their little tiff at Lockleigh's apartment. But he'd fought the two men guarding him repeatedly – and lost – till they'd resorted to chaining him up and staying well away.

Again, Lawrence seemed to be struggling, and for reasons he couldn't fathom, Rick felt sorry for him. 'You'd better tell me what's happened.'

'He's vanished.'

Despite all that Sam had done to him, Rick felt a stab of fear.

'When?' he managed.

'Just over an hour ago.'

'Circumstances,' Rick said. 'Details.'

'The auction took place yesterday at three p.m., BST. As expected, Lockleigh didn't show at the auction, and the winning bid was anonymous – brokered. The arrangement was that the Bellingen canvas would be held at a bonded warehouse, of sorts. It's all—'

'Dark Web, black-market stuff. I get it,' Rick said.

'Lockleigh was well organised – switched transport and used decoys, as Sam predicted, but we had the tracker. The canvas ended up on a trading estate just inside the M25 at Dartford.'

'I'm guessing you stayed close.'

A nod. 'Me, the boss, and a bodyguard in one car, three more in a van. The rest of us held back while two of the crew scouted the place out on foot.'

Rick huffed an incredulous laugh. 'He was planning to take back the canvas, wasn't he?'

Lawrence lifted one shoulder. 'Said it was a point of principle.'

Rick sighed, gestured for him to go on.

'As soon as the deliverers left, we drove onto the car park – it's a typical light industrial unit, part brick, part metal sidings. Sam went in with three men; me and the bodyguard were to wait and watch. There was no indication of an ambush, no shots fired, but it was taking too long, so we went in.' He swallowed. 'The place was empty. Sam was gone. We found the three who went in with him locked inside a meat storage locker – two shot, the other one knocked out.'

'The two who were shot?'

'One dead. The other two are being taken care of.'

Rick fixed him with a stony look. 'You need to clarify.'

'I-I mean medically taken care of. They're safe.'

'What about the canvas?'

'Gone.'

'Can you track it?'

He gave a slight shake of his head. 'Tracker's been deactivated.'

'Jesus,' Rick murmured. 'How'd they get out?' Lawrence looked confused and he said, 'What was the escape route? If your lot didn't see him—'

312

'They'd cut a hole in the steel panelling at the back. Must've done it before we'd even got there.'

'Shit . . .' Rick wiped a hand over his face. 'Why are you telling me this? I mean I'm trapped here.' Suddenly furious, he yanked ferociously at the chain. 'What the *fuck* am I supposed to do about it?'

'Sam has no second in command,' Lawrence said. 'He tends to trust in his . . .'

'Invincibility?' Rick supplied.

'I was going to say, "contingency plans",' the older man said with a faint smile. 'But I think you're closer to the mark.'

'So nobody's doing *anything*?'

'We don't know where he's been taken, and none of us has the authority to mobilise personnel.'

Still raging, Rick deliberately slowed his breathing and felt his heart rate follow suit; he had to be calm and rational when he asked the next question: 'Lawrence, I want the truth. Do you think Sam is already dead?'

The chauffeur looked hollowed out. 'I don't think Lockleigh would want to kill him right away.'

Jesus, Sam . . .

'How long d'you think he's got?'

A sigh. 'It depends how much he pisses Lockleigh off.'

'Sounds about right. Okay. Who's left?'

'Personnel?' Lawrence glanced up the steep steps to the bar area.

'What – Little and Large?' The chauffeur looked blank, and Rick added, 'Wiry short-arse and a big fucker built like a weightlifter, but deceptively light on his feet – *those two*, upstairs.'

Lawrence must have made the connection – a comedy duo of the Seventies and Eighties – because he nodded, with the ghost of a smile.

'They're good,' he said.

Feeling the bruising in his ribs and back, Rick ruefully agreed.

'And loyal. And we've got access to weapons and gadgets,' he went on eagerly.

'Useful to know,' Rick said. 'But it's gonna take more than four of us to tackle Lockleigh's mob. Those two must know people.'

Lawrence shook his head. 'That'd take funds – which we *don't* have.'

'They must know that Sam'd see them right after the event.'

The diffidence Rick had seen earlier in the man returned and he glanced away. 'Um, thing is, Sam doesn't like people using their initiative when it comes to spending his money.'

'This isn't a regular operation – this is Sam's *life*. *Talk* to them.'

Lawrence looked horrified by the prospect. 'You might think they're a couple of comedians, but they won't listen to me.'

Rick took a breath and let it out in one long, frustrated rush.

'You got a key to these?' He held up his manacled hands.

Lawrence took a set of keys from his pocket and extracted one from the bunch before handing it over gingerly.

Rick was out of the cuffs in a second, but looking down at the leg chain, he said, 'This presents a bigger challenge.'

The chauffeur frowned, then his brow cleared. 'I might have just the thing.' He disappeared behind a steel beer keg and came back with a metal tool kit. He set it on the keg and rummaged for a moment. 'Power drill?'

'Something quieter,' Rick said.

'Bolt cutters?'

They cut through the chain like butter.

'Now,' Rick said, 'are you armed?'

Lawrence swung back his jacket to reveal a holstered pistol on his waistband.

Rick held out his hand, but Lawrence stepped back, his hand on the butt of the gun.

'Lawrence. You want to help Sam, you gotta trust me.'

'I dunno. I mean, I *want* to—'

'You know who I am, don't you? I mean, who I *really* am.'

'He said you're a cop and he used to know you before and you're all right.'

'Before *what*? Before he was a crook? Lawrence, Sam's *always* been a crook.'

Lawrence raised his free hand to silence him. 'That's what he *told* me, but I guessed a while ago. I mean, Sam protects Sam – that's what he's like – but it's always been different with you. And I got to warn you, Rick, since nine o'clock tonight, *everyone* knows. It's all over the web that you're his brother.'

'Let me guess,' Rick said. 'Pandora.'

A curt nod.

For the first time in days, Rick was grateful he didn't have access to his phone to witness the carnage social media had wrought to his reputation.

'So . . .' he tried again, hand out, palm up.

After another brief hesitation, Lawrence unholstered his gun, and Rick had to steel himself not to flinch.

He handed Rick the weapon, butt first.

'Now, get those two down here,' Rick said. 'I'll handle the rest.'

Chapter 52

One a.m.

SAM'S BREATH STUTTERED, ECHOING UP into the high, vaulted rafters of the church. The Bellingen canvas was placed fifteen feet from him on herringbone parquet gritty with powdered plaster and brick and lit by a couple of high-power LED flashlights. Restoration work was in progress on the building and steel props supported a crumbling mezzanine of choir stalls that ran the length of the building on either side of the main aisle. Many of the windows had been vandalised, and thick plastic sheeting hung in their place, gently moving in and out like the bellows of a sleeping dragon. The altar had been removed, and scaffolding raised to access the glass rotunda in the former sanctuary.

Both men were sweating. Both out of breath. But Sam, alone, was in pain. Tethered by rope between two of the scaffolding poles, he hung his head, taking shallow sips of air to reduce the sharp stabs that accompanied every intake of breath. A broken rib, he thought.

Theo Lockleigh stood between him and the canvas. 'Beautiful, isn't it?' Lockleigh said.

Sam forced his head up. 'Doesn't leave much to the imagination,' he said, and was oddly cheered by repeating Rick's assessment of the daub.

'Yet you bought it.'

Sam shook his head, managing a faint smile. 'I *stole* it.' He was pleased to see Lockleigh's eyes spark with anger.

'Well, *I* paid for it, and I want my money back.'

'I didn't steal it from *you*, Theo!'

'You walked off with fourteen years of *my life*,' Lockleigh rasped.

'I suppose,' Sam said, between painful breaths, 'an apology won't suffice?'

'Not even close,' Lockleigh said, the corners of his mouth curling into the hint of a smile. He'd always appreciated Sam's chutzpah. 'But reimbursing the seventeen million I paid for this will go some way towards compensating me. I'll think of a few others to help you work off the debt by and by.'

Sam adjusted his stance and found a position of relative comfort. 'I had no idea that you missed me so much.' Breathing easier now, he went on, 'But, Theo, you have to learn to let go – the student outgrows his mentor.'

Lockleigh laughed and Sam heard danger in the sharpness of it.

'I taught you everything you know.' He paced left and right, looking Sam up and down. 'Your diction may have improved somewhat, and I gave you a little polish, taught you how to dress. But you were a guttersnipe then, and you remain a guttersnipe.'

'You taught me the basics that gave me access to your exclusive club,' Sam said, growing in confidence as the pain receded. 'It's disappointing, with your private education and your law degree, that you still don't realise that discernment – *taste* – is innate, it can't be learned.'

Lockleigh stepped up and backhanded him.

Sam's head whipped left, and blood flew from his nose, speckling his attacker. Lockleigh recoiled with an exclamation of disgust, and Sam snuffed more blood from his nostrils.

'The dealers and brokers don't care about your "art", Theo – they know most of it's dross. It's the *money* they respect.'

Lockleigh was wearing sap gloves, padded and weighted with powdered steel in the knuckles. Sam saw him pull the right glove tighter and he braced for the impact.

For a second he greyed out and his legs buckled. The strain of the ropes burned his wrists, yanking his shoulders at the sockets, and a sharp stab in his side made him cry out.

He regained his feet and forced himself upright. Something moved in the shadows – *Errol and 'No Mercy' Mercer*, Sam thought. Were any other members of Lockleigh's old crew still around, or had he brought in mercenaries especially for this sting operation? Sam knew that he and his men had taken down three in the ambush, but there had been more. How loyal were they? Might he turn their newness to his advantage? And what about Errol? They'd been friends, once.

'Want to know how I got Munot to cooperate?' he asked, willing control and strength into his tone. 'I gave him a way out. New identity, new life.'

Errol was smart; if he was there, he'd get the message.

'Didn't get very far, did he?' Lockleigh said. 'That's always been your problem, Sam – arrogance. You consistently underestimate the opposition.'

And you, Sam thought, *are like your choice in art. Heavy-handed, unsubtle*. Aloud, he said, 'Give a man a chance to better himself. If he's any kind of man, he'll take it.'

This again was for Errol.

It seemed that Lockleigh had little patience with the philosophical questions that used to entertain him, because he stepped in and hit Sam again. 'I want what's *mine*,' he roared.

Sam smiled, spat blood. 'Tell you what,' he said. 'Take that hideous thing away, and I'll give you whatever you want.'

Lockleigh worked on Sam some more, and after a few minutes, Sam heard a voice he recognised through the billowing and echoing sounds of his own grunts of pain, and the thump of Lockleigh's fists pummelling his body.

'Boss. *Boss*,' it said. 'He's tight as a clam – you'll just end up killing him.'

Errol. Sam could have wept in gratitude.

'Then he's no good to me.' Lockleigh, still out of breath, reached around to the small of his back and came out with a Glock-seventeen. 'I might as well kill him now.'

Sam raised his head and smiled, though it hurt every muscle in his face.

'Do you think I won't kill you?'

'I think you're greedy,' Sam murmured, his words slurred by the bruising in his mouth. 'I think you'll exhaust all other possibilities before you give up on seventeen *million* pounds.'

'Is it worth gambling your life on that?'

Sam laughed, coughed, groaned. 'We both know my life was forfeit the moment we left Dartford.'

Lockleigh ducked under the ropes that bound Sam. A second later he felt the barrel pressed hard into the base of his skull and he remembered his harsh warning to Rick: *No one on this earth can handle a bullet in the back of the head.*

'How many times have you done this to some luckless bastard who'd outlived his usefulness, Sam?' Lockleigh goaded. 'Dozens? Scores?'

'Oh, I lost count years ago,' Sam said, his jaw clenched to stop his teeth chattering.

The pressure vanished and, his breath coming in small creaking gasps, Sam waited for the next blow to fall.

Lockleigh's hand came around to his face and he flinched involuntarily.

'How about this one. Remember him?'

Lockleigh had a phone in his hand. Sam tried to focus on the image, but there was blood in his eyes. Blinking hard, his vision cleared, and he recognised Jason Floren. He was slumped sideways in a bathtub, bound to the bath taps by his wrists. His head was tilted back, and the two bullet wounds Sam had inflicted – chest and head – were clearly visible. Sam had made sure of that. Blood and brains had spattered the pristine wall tiles. The duct tape, which Sam had removed only minutes before taking the photograph, hung from Floren's cheek like a silvery flap of skin.

'You see, Sam,' Lockleigh whispered, his mouth close enough to Sam's ear that he could feel the warmth of his breath. 'You were working for me, and you didn't even know it.'

Sam turned and sank his teeth into Lockleigh's earlobe. Lockleigh howled, beating at him with the butt of the gun, finally catching him a blow across the bridge of his nose that made him let go.

Lockleigh fell onto his backside then scuttled away backwards clutching at his ear. Sam spat out blood and flesh.

'You *animal*!' Lockleigh screamed, levelling the gun at him. But Sam knew he wouldn't shoot. If he'd meant to use it, he would have shot Sam to get free of him. In all likelihood, the weapon wasn't even loaded. Exhausted and hurting though he was, Sam was comforted by the certainty that – at least for now – he was more valuable to Theo Lockleigh alive than dead.

A scuffle at the entrance to the church, the sound of boots crunching across the space, then whispering, like the prayers of the sorrowful and the penitent who must have worshipped in this church for over a century. Sam was transported to another time and place. Saw himself seated in a pew at his mother's funeral, watching Rick, his father, some old friends carrying her coffin on their shoulders. Rick, barely in his twenties at the time, pale, gaunt, staring straight ahead, carrying a burden Sam should have shared.

Lockleigh's voice intruded, breaking the hallucination. Sam snuffed, choked on blood and coughed. His former boss sounded angry, irritable, and Sam tried hard to focus through the waves of nausea and pain.

'I don't want to know where he *isn't*, I want to know where he *is*,' he demanded. 'You were supposed to be keeping tabs on him. I want him found.'

Rick, he thought. *They're talking about Rick.* As he allowed himself to sink into oblivion, his last thought was: *Fuck you, Theo. Rick is safe.*

Chapter 53

One a.m.

RICK HAD AGREED AN UNEASY TRUCE with Little and Large, who'd taken being held at gunpoint remarkably well, all things considered.

They'd relocated to the bar area of the old pub and were seated around a circular table, Lawrence having taken charge of the weapons, which he'd tucked under the bar. He'd also introduced them formally as Noel and Gavin, respectively.

'Okay,' Rick said. 'How do we find him?'

Gavin, the giant, said, 'The trading estate will have CCTV.'

'I can't go via official channels, for obvious reasons,' Rick said. 'And even if we could get hold of it unofficially, the police might be alerted. Then there's the problem of tracing the vehicles once we've identified them. I'm guessing you used fake plates on your transport?'

He nodded.

'So would Lockleigh.' After a silence, Rick said, 'Dartford's well outside Lockleigh's old manor, isn't it?' Nobody disagreed. 'D'you suppose he could be aiming to get Sam and the artwork onto a boat – ship out?'

'If he wants to leave the country, it'd take some planning,' Lawrence ventured.

'He's had *fourteen years* to plan it, mate,' Gavin snapped, and Rick saw the chauffeur's shoulders round and he slumped in his chair.

'Even if it was just the canvas he was moving, he'd need falsified Bills of Lading, import and export permissions, false passports,' Rick reasoned. 'But if we're agreed he wouldn't kill Sam straight away, he'd be taking an unwilling hostage as well. Does he have those resources?'

'He lost his foothold in East London while he was away,' Noel, the short man, said. 'But he raised the cash for the auction, so . . .'

Lawrence cleared his throat and the other two glared at him. 'I don't think he'll go abroad; I think he'll stay close.' He glanced nervously from Noel to Gavin. 'Sam said he's a hoarder, likes to gloat over new acquisitions—'

'Well, he can do *that* anywhere,' the irascible Gavin said.

'And he said Lockleigh's tied to London just now,' Lawrence added, more firmly.

'Tied to London, how?' Rick asked. 'I mean I doubt if he's reporting to his probation officer.'

'He's definitely not doing that,' Gavin said, shooting a glance at his oppo.

'The podcaster said he's absconded,' Noel explained.

Pandora again.

'All right. So, what's holding him here?'

'Properties, hard cash, valuables – that fucking canvas,' Noel said.

'He has an extensive art collection,' Lawrence added quietly.

'Do we know where he keeps it? No, scratch that – stupid question,' Rick said, interrupting himself. 'If he's kept his cash and valuables hidden from the CPS for fourteen years, we're not gonna find his stash in twenty-four hours.'

'He does have the Maida Vale apartment – and Sam's convinced he had more properties around London,' Lawrence offered.

'Someone's still watching the flat?' Rick asked.

'Yeah,' Gavin said. 'He's got some tech-heads who do that stuff for him.'

'And who gets notifications from them?'

'Uh . . .' Gavin scratched the stubble on his upper lip. 'That'd be Sam.'

Hell. 'What about his laptop? Did he leave it in the car?'

'Yes!' Lawrence half rose as if to rush off to find it, subsiding a second later. 'But it's password-protected.'

Rick took a breath and let it go. If all else failed, he'd try the tech-heads, see if they could hack it, but that would be a last, desperate measure.

'So it's back to searching for Lockleigh's properties.'

The other three looked helplessly at each other. It was Lawrence who spoke for all of them when he said, 'I wouldn't know where to start.'

'I know someone who might be able to help,' Rick said.

'Great. Give us an address, we'll bring him in,' Noel said.

'No. I'll do that. And we'll need decent Wi-Fi access. Lawrence, can you get us into the rental apartment in Shoreditch?'

'Yes,' Lawrence said.

'Good. You're with me. Noel, Gavin, you'll gather the weapons and ordnance we'll need.'

'Whoa, whoa, *whoa!*' The wiry man was on his feet before Rick had pushed his chair back. 'Sam said we was to stick with you.'

'Yeah, well, Sam isn't here, right now, is he?' Rick said levelly. 'Soon as we have a location, we need to be ready. So: vehicles, guns, ammo, tac gear, stun grenades, smoke bombs, RF jammers. And drones – can you get drones?'

Noel sneaked a look at Gavin like he thought maybe this might be fun.

'Yeah, we can get you all that,' Gavin said. 'Sam had it on standby, in case we needed it.'

'Okay. Let's go,' Rick said.

Lawrence disappeared behind the bar to gather their weapons while they swapped burner numbers. Watching them getting happily tooled up, Rick was torn, but he couldn't go against Lockleigh with a Casco baton, so he tamped down on his principles and said, 'I'm gonna need a firearm. Who's got a spare?'

Gavin secured his two weapons – one at his waist, the other in an ankle holster. 'I need my spare, man. We'll have plenty more when we rendezvous.'

Noel folded his arms. 'What he said.'

Lawrence said softly, 'Sam keeps a couple in the limo, in case of emergencies.'

''Course he does,' Rick sighed.

Lawrence drove while Rick made the call.

Dave Collins was at work. He knew that the forensic accountant would be anxious and to stem a volley of questions, he launched straight in.

'Dave, I know this is a bit of a weird time to call, but I'm in trouble and I need your help.'

'I already know that,' Dave said.

Surprised, Rick said, 'How d'you know?'

'I've been calling you every day for the last three days, straight after I finished work, but you didn't get back to me. You always get back to me. Plus, Sam told me.'

Rick's heart leapt. 'You've spoken to Sam?'

'Not for a few days. But he said you needed protecting. Shit—' He sounded dismayed. 'I probably shouldn't've told you that.'

'Well, I'm doing all right,' Rick said. 'It's Sam I'm worried about. He told me you've been helping him to suss out an old mate—'

'No-no-no, not here,' Dave sounded panicked. 'Not . . . here.' He sounded breathless with terror. 'We'll have to meet.'

'Thing is, this won't wait,' Rick said. 'D'you reckon you could nick off work early?'

'No need,' Dave said. 'It's my day off. I was just . . . Never mind – I can leave now.'

'You're gonna need some computing power.'

'Not a problem,' Dave said.

'And whatever you've already found for Sam.'

'Well, *obviously*.'

That was the closest to a sharp put-down that Rick had ever had from the numbers man, and he said, 'Sorry – I'm a bit agitated.'

'No worries.'

'I'm switching to speaker so I can scope out a route,' Rick said, knowing that Dave would hear the difference, and might freak out. 'I'm in Lambeth, but we're headed your way.'

'W-what – wait. Who's *we*?'

Please don't flake on me now, mate. 'Lawrence.' Rick heard the tension in his voice, and deliberately took it down a notch. 'Sam's driver – you'll like him, he's—'

'Yeah,' Dave said. 'Cool. Lawrence is all right.'

Wondering just how much off-the-books work Dave was doing for Sam, Rick stole a glance at Lawrence and could swear he was suppressing a smile.

'Okay,' he said, keeping up the momentum. 'Grab a taxi. We'll pick you up near Waterloo Bridge at Southbank . . .' Rick consulted Google Maps on his phone. 'Tell 'em to drop you at the lay-by outside King's College London Waterloo Campus.' He glanced at Lawrence, who nodded – he knew it.

Rick switched to street view. 'It's next door to the old Royal Waterloo Women's and Children's Hospital – big red-brick building, corner of Waterloo Bridge Road and Stamford Street.'

'I can be there in fifteen to twenty,' Dave said.

'Look for a black limo – we'll be waiting.'

Chapter 54

One-forty-five a.m.

DAVE COLLINS REACHED REPEATEDLY into a padded backpack, setting up an array of three laptops towards one end of a fifteen-foot-long table made of rough-hewn wood and tubular steel. Muttering to himself, he lowered the blinds opposite and dispensed with several of the dining chairs before dragging a kitchen stool across from the open-plan area. Designed for the more svelte elite of London's wealthy business class, the seat was inadequate for Dave's considerable girth, but he was able to rest one buttock on the stool. The bag, he kept at his feet. Rick took a seat at the narrow end of the table where he could catch a glimpse of the screens without hovering at his friend's shoulder and making him nervous. Lawrence brewed coffee for all of them and, discreet as ever, retired to the far end of the expanse of wood.

Dave's grey eyes darted from screen to screen as he set them up. Lawrence gave him the Wi-Fi password and he tapped it into the biggest laptop.

'Changing *that*,' Dave muttered, his thick fingers moving fast over the keyboard, entering a long sequence of letters, digits and symbols before repeating the process for the other two machines.

For now, it was just Rick, Lawrence and Dave occupying the vast space. Rick would break the news that they would soon be joined by two others only when he was sure that Dave was settled and feeling reasonably secure.

Finally, Dave leaned back with a nod of satisfaction, took a sip of coffee and with a quick, shy glance in Rick's direction, said, 'Right. What d'you want to know?'

'This old mate Sam wanted you to check out?' Rick began.

'Lazarus Theophilus,' Dave Collins shot back promptly.

Rick smiled and Dave said, 'What's funny?'

'Lazarus is a character from the Bible who rose from the dead.'

'Okay.'

He clearly didn't understand the significance, so Rick added, 'And the man we're looking for is Theo Lockleigh.'

'Oh . . . TL, LT,' Dave said. 'Alias. Right.'

'Sam didn't give you Lockleigh's name?'

Dave shook his head. 'Just this Lazarus Theophilus character.' *Sam's principle of 'the less you know, the less you're liable' in action.*

'He said Theophilus had set up the bank account as an under-the-radar thing a while back,' Dave went on. 'In case he ever needed to resurrect himself.' He stopped. 'Oh. Right, Lazarus.' He shook his head. 'But he'd heard that Theophilus might be up to no good, and Sam doesn't like doing business with dodgy types.'

'Yeah,' Rick said. *He probably even meant it when he said it.* 'Is there an address registered to the Theophilus account?'

Another shake of his head. 'It's an online thing. Offshore.' Dave rolled his eyes as if to say, *and you know what that means.* 'Sam wanted me to notify him if the account was accessed and follow the money if possible.'

'And?'

Dave riffled the keys on his laptop while he talked. 'Three days ago, Theophilus siphoned his assets into a shell company.'

'What sort of money are we talking about?'

'Just shy of twenty-six million euros.'

'Wow,' Rick said, playing dumb, although he'd had some of this from Sam. He didn't know if Sam had lied, for one thing, and he didn't want to miss anything his brother had held back, either.

Dave lifted one shoulder. 'The company's a shell – and it's registered in the Caymans – so I can't get much on it.'

Normally a query about a UK company could have been answered via the government's Companies House register in a few clicks of a mouse. But career criminals and super-wealthy tax evaders alike sheltered their money in these offshore havens, hiding the names of the real owners behind shell companies housed in empty offices and staffed by fake directors. The sole purpose of the shell corporations was to provide a smokescreen for the real owners to hide behind. And it worked: their money and illegal transactions were effectively invisible to both UK Revenue and Customs and international law enforcement.

'But I set up alerts for any activity from the shell company, just in case,' Dave went on. 'And yesterday, it makes a payment of three million British pounds to Dream Schemes Corporate Trust.'

The hairs on the back of Rick's neck stood up and his heart began a slow, steady thudding.

'And, like, five minutes later,' Dave said, oblivious, 'Lazarus Theophilus's bank account gets a top-up of exactly three million pounds.'

'That's bloody brilliant, mate,' Rick said.

'Oh, there's more,' the big man said, clearly enjoying himself. 'See, the trust manages a company called Dream Schemes Property Development. Up until very recently the director was named as Jason Floren, and the registered office was a business hub in Deptford. Which is important – 'cos as a *UK*-based company, it's obliged to register on the Companies House,' Dave went on. 'But the website shows Jason Floren as deceased as of last February.'

'Jason Floren was shot the night before the development was supposed to have its grand opening,' Rick said.

'Oh, you knew that?'

Rick nodded, picturing the video of the phantom landscaper limping into Jason Floren's show house on Deptford Waters just before he was shot. If it really *was* Sam who killed Floren, what the hell did this mean?

'Well, Floren was *de*registered as a director in March,' Dave said. 'At which point, an entity calling itself "Dream Schemes Corporate Trust" takes over.'

'Can they do that?' Rick asked, remembering his earlier conversation with DC McGuinness. 'I mean, just take over without going through probate an' all that?'

'Trusts are exempt from probate,' Dave said.

'And it looks like Lockleigh – under the alias of Theophilus – is the beneficiary?'

'*Looks* like it, but there's no way of checking. A trust is a private agreement between the settlor – the person who sets it up – and the beneficiary,' Dave explained. 'They can make up their own rules – have whatever terms they like – and they don't have to be registered or vetted by any of the financial services watchdogs.'

'Sounds like they're invisible,' Rick said. 'So how did they muscle in on Floren's property development company after he was killed?'

'A law firm in Dakota stepped in, had paperwork that proved their client was entitled to all assets formerly owned by Dream Schemes Property Development, including monies, sales, land, leases investment – the lot.'

'But they didn't have to *name* the person who actually benefits?'

'This trust is also lodged in Dakota,' Dave said. 'They don't have to name or register the settlor, trustees, *or* the beneficiaries. They could all be one and the same person – and you don't get dodgier than that.'

'Why are they allowed to get away with it?' Rick asked. 'Governments must be losing *billions* in revenue.'

'Maybe hundreds of billions,' Dave agreed. 'But trust funds are so complex and slippery that the authorities won't touch them. Under Dakota state law, trust administrators don't have to obey international law, so they can't be forced to disclose names or details of the trust agreement. You don't even have to disclose *payments* into a trust – they're completely opaque. It's impossible to get past that privacy wall, so law enforcement is toothless.'

'But *you* joined the dots, mate,' Rick said.

'That was pure luck,' Dave said with his habitual honesty. 'I decided to carry on monitoring Theophilus's bank accounts, so I happened to see the payment from Dream Schemes Trust.'

Rick shook his head, dizzied by the enormity of the financial exploitation. 'Have you told Sam all of this?'

Dave flushed, plucking anxiously at the front of his shirt. 'He said he'd got all he wanted on his mate after the twenty-six-million-euro transfer – I've been looking into this out of personal interest.'

'It's not a problem, Dave,' Rick said. 'This is helping.'

Dave perked up. 'Oh, well then you should know that at three-twelve yesterday afternoon, seventeen million British pounds was paid from Lockleigh's shell company in the Caymans to another shell company.'

Rick exchanged a look with Lawrence. *Just around the time the hammer would've come down on the Bellingen canvas.* A brief nod from Sam's chauffeur confirmed his assumption.

'All I got is a name for that one,' Dave went on. 'Poena Assets.'

This had to be Sam's shell company.

'It's registered in Wyoming,' Dave added. 'I don't think I'll get more than that – all those US cowboy states pride themselves on their corporate secrecy laws.'

'So, Sam doesn't know about Lockleigh's connection to Dream Schemes?' Rick asked.

'I only found out myself a few hours back.' Dave's voice went up in pitch. 'I tried to ring him, but—'

'Dave,' Rick said. 'I'm just trying to get the facts straight, that's all. And listen – this isn't your fault, but Sam is missing – and we need to find him fast.'

The accountant's shoulders dropped. 'Shit. That's what this is about? This Lockleigh, or Theophilus has got him?'

'We think so. Lockleigh is on the run, and we don't know how to find him. From what you've told us, we can't trace him via his bank accounts, the trust, or his shell companies. But the property development company is a real firm, and now we know that Lockleigh owns it, I'm wondering could we trace him through his registered office?'

'No,' Dave said, distressed. 'The new registered office is in Switzerland. No other properties are listed at Companies House.'

'What about properties they've got under development?' Dave seemed perplexed by the question and Rick added, 'Somewhere they might be hiding Sam.'

'I could check if Dream Schemes has any planning applications in,' Dave said, 'but you'd have to know which borough or council area the proposed development is in.'

Rick felt a pressure build in his chest; this was getting them nowhere. He took a breath and let it go slowly. 'Wait a minute.' He pulled out his phone and thumbed in a search. 'I'm looking at the Dream Schemes Property Development website. Says here they have "exciting developments in prospect".' He tapped through to the links. 'A restaurant in the West End, and a church conversion to flats in Camden.'

Dave turned to a second laptop. 'Go ahead.'

Rick gave him an address near Piccadilly. 'It says here that the work on the restaurant is under way.'

'Piccadilly is . . . Westminster council,' Dave murmured. 'This'll take me a minute.'

Dave fell silent as he accessed the planning department, and to distract himself, Rick opened Google Maps and searched for the building on his phone.

The street view was last updated two years ago, so that was no help. He went back to the Dream Schemes website for info on the church conversion. It didn't give a street address.

Returning to the map, Rick scrolled the area, but the screen was too small to get an overview. 'This is bloody useless.' He threw the phone down on the table in frustration and called across to Dave, 'Pass me one of those laptops, will you?'

From Dave's shocked look you might think that he'd demanded the keys to his house.

'Mate, Sam is missing, and I think really *bad* things are happening to him—' Rick had to stop to get control of himself. 'Look, I promise I won't mess with the settings – I just need to find this church—'

Dave fumbled in the backpack at his feet, keeping his eyes on Rick like he might reach across the table and snatch one of the valuable devices. He handed over a tablet from the bag. 'No access password,' he said. 'I don't keep anything sensitive on there. Wi-Fi password—'

'Jeez – slow *down*,' Rick begged.

Dave continued working on his laptop while Rick booted up the tablet and as soon as he was ready, rattled off the fifteen-digit password from memory.

'Planning went through on the restaurant eighteen months ago,' Dave said at last, then turning to the third laptop, he typed in the address and an additional search term. 'It's in use, now – though it's closed till ten tomorrow morning.'

'I don't see Lockleigh holding Sam at a functioning business premises,' Rick said, still sliding the map image, searching for the empty church. 'Too much risk.'

'Okay – well there's nothing else on the Dream Schemes website,' Dave said. 'So—'

'Hold up – I might have something.' Rick had found a church on the map. He switched to street view. The signage said it was a community centre.

He shook his head and went back to searching, sliding the map to search for large buildings. A quarter of a mile away, he found another church and again clicked to street view.

His heart seemed to stop for a full two seconds, then began again at a canter. 'Guys, I think this is it,' Rick said, his heart pounding so hard now that he could barely hear himself speak.

Chapter 55

Two-twenty a.m.

AFTER SAM CAME ROUND, Errol persuaded Lockleigh that he couldn't take any more pounding, and he'd changed tactics, working on Sam with a taser for a while. But his efforts were lacklustre, and he seemed to be filling time – waiting for news of Rick, maybe.

Sam couldn't currently see a way out of his present circumstances, but he knew he couldn't take much more punishment. Still, he'd talked his way out of deadly situations in the past, and he wasn't ready to give up just yet, so he straightened up, closing his fists around the ropes that bound him, focusing his attention away from the stabbing pain he felt with each breath.

'So, Dream Schemes is your business,' he said. 'Managing all of that from prison . . . That's impressive.'

Lockleigh had always been susceptible to flattery, and he bowed his head, accepting the compliment as his due. 'And you doing my dirty work – just like old times.'

'You paid me well,' Sam said, like it didn't matter. 'But I don't understand *why* you wanted Floren killed.'

'Floren was adding extras into the build that weren't on the original costings,' Lockleigh said.

'Skimming the books?' Sam kept his comments short to allow him to take shallow breaths.

'Worse. Dream Schemes was granted the contract to rebuild on the site of the old 1960s complex on condition that the arson victims and their families had the option to buy at a subsidised rate. We'd agreed between ourselves that he would offer the smallest of the high-rise flats.'

Sam smiled. 'I imagine that for an arson victim, a high-rise would be a living nightmare.'

'Precisely.' Lockleigh's tone said, *At last, someone who can see things from a business perspective.* 'Instead of which, Floren reserved the show house and *two* of the bungalows for former residents.'

'Ah,' Sam said, 'Signs of a guilty conscience. Unforgivable.'

'More than *signs*,' Lockleigh scoffed. 'The landlord set the blaze, but my contacts said that he'd begun to cooperate with police, and he was about to provide evidence of Floren's culpability.'

Through his pain, Sam recognised that Theo Lockleigh had fallen easily into old habits, sharing confidences, revealing rather more than he should to an untrustworthy manipulator like Sam – the old lag must have missed having an equal to confide in, he reflected.

'If the police had any flair at all, Floren might have confessed,' Lockleigh said. 'He might have exposed my entire operation.'

'He *did* confess,' Sam said. 'To the Wolf Pack. Surely you must have seen it?'

'I did.' Lockleigh's mouth twisted into a bitter smile. 'Entertaining, aren't they?'

Since he'd narrowly escaped detection at Deptford Waters, Sam found them only moderately so. 'I interrogated Floren myself,' he said aloud. 'He took the blame. He didn't betray you, Theo.'

'He'd already disobeyed me over the accommodation offer – and whether he named me or not, his confession would have exposed my company to a civil suit.'

Sam chuckled, then groaned at a jolt from his ribs. 'I should think a class action suit is back on the cards since the Wolf Pack released their video confession,' he wheezed.

Lockleigh smiled. 'My assets are now fully shielded in offshore accounts.' He leaned forward, staring into Sam's eyes. '*You* gave me time to organise that, Sam.'

He patted his cheek with the flat of his palm and Sam felt something shift under his right eye, sending knives of pain shooting into his skull.

Chapter 56

RICK'S FORMER JAILERS, NOEL AND GAVIN, came back at two-thirty.

'We've got everything you asked for, with a few extras,' Noel said. 'What've you got?'

'We think we know where he is,' Rick said.

'Think, or know?' Gavin said.

'Think,' Rick repeated, fixing the man with a level gaze. 'It's the best we can do for now.'

'Let's have a look then,' Noel said.

They gathered around the tablet and scrutinised a satellite image of an old Gothic church set back from the road, windows gone, hoardings wrapped around the entire building site, proclaiming 'Dream Schemes – Building your dream home.'

They pored over it for a few minutes, pointing out the danger spots, the pinch points, the possible routes of entry and exit.

The tall man sniffed and straightened up. 'Can't be done. Even if we took him with us—' he jerked his chin towards Lawrence '—we wouldn't have enough manpower.'

'Lockleigh won't be expecting us,' Rick said. 'We'd have the element of surprise.'

Gavin shook his head. 'Building works like that, they'll probably have security cameras, see us coming a mile off.'

With an apologetic glance to Lawrence, Rick said, 'Lawrence says you haven't got the cash to enlist more personnel. But I know there's someone Sam talks to when he needs equipment or muscle. What if I stand as guarantor on the funding?'

He ignored the chauffeur's intake of breath, keeping his focus on the two mercenaries. They exchanged looks and Noel rubbed his chin. Finally, the giant took responsibility.

'You can't trust him,' Gavin said.

'Why not?'

Noel spoke up. ''Cos Sam don't.'

Rick sighed. 'All right. I had to try.'

Rick had rehearsed his next ploy in his head over and over during the last hour. He took the holstered gun out of his waistband and ejected the clip before laying it on the table.

'What're you doing?'

Rick picked up his jacket. 'The only thing I *can* do – I'm calling this in.'

The two mercenaries shouted, 'No!' 'No *way*' simultaneously, and Lawrence stared at him horrified.

'I won't involve any of you,' Rick said evenly. 'You'll have plenty of time to get away. But I think you can all imagine what Theo Lockleigh is doing to Sam right now. I can't just stand by and let it happen.'

Noel was shaking his head. 'Sam'd be dead before the police set foot inside the building.'

'Not if I brief them carefully.'

Gavin gave a sceptical laugh.

'Sam is a wanted man,' Lawrence said. 'Even if he survives a police raid, he'd be arrested. If that happens, he'd be dead in three days, tops.'

'So what do we *do*?' Rick insisted.

'We could wait,' Noel suggested. 'Watch the place.'

'Haven't you been listening? We can't *wait*,' Rick spat.

'Aaaand we come full circle,' Noel said.

'We're agreed that we need more bodies, more firepower.'

Noel said, 'Yeah . . .'

Rick hesitated. Had he come to the point of revealing his plan too early?

Sam's voice rang loud in his head: *You're literally killing me here, bruv – get on with it!*

The effect was like a prod in the back. 'What if I could get you skilled, disciplined fighters – field-hardened and firearms trained?' he blurted out.

Gavin's brow crinkled and his mouth twisted into a smile. 'Got someone in mind, Boy Scout?'

Rick looked at each of the three men in turn. 'The Wolf Pack.'

An explosion of laughter and curses from the two hired guns.

'A vigilante group – are you *serious*?' Gavin spluttered. 'You do know that what we do makes *us* their target?'

'Not the way I'll spin it,' Rick said.

Gavin folded his arms. 'Go on then, let's hear it.'

'That's for their ears.' In reality, he hadn't quite worked out his pitch yet. 'If I can convince them, would you consider it?'

Noel and Gavin exchanged doubtful glances. 'What if they turn on us soon as they get a chance?' Gavin asked.

'Right now, the Wolf Pack is wanted by the law as well,' Rick said. 'And the way I'll put it to them, we'd be joining forces as vigilantes working for a common cause – justice.'

Noel was watching him through half-closed eyes, a smile twitching at the corners of his mouth. 'I kind of like it.'

'They've gone to ground, haven't they?' Gavin said. 'You got names, Rick? Addresses? 'Cos if you haven't, all I'm hearing is a bunch of ifs, ands, buts and maybes.'

'I think I might have a direct number for one of them.'

Chapter 57

PANDORA WOKE WITH A JOLT. Her laptop remained open, but like her, it had nodded off into sleep mode. It was trapped between her thigh and the car door, and she had a painful crick in her neck.

'Great surveillance technique, Pandora,' she muttered. Snapping the device closed and sliding it into its carrier, she gazed around her, bleary-eyed, trying to work out what had jarred her out of her doze.

Twenty yards away, Vee Verren stood at the front door of her maisonette. She double-locked it then trotted down the road, heading away. Pandora checked her watch. Three-fifteen a.m. Vee was supposed to be on annual leave – where could she be going at this hour?

As Pandora reached for the keys in the ignition, she noticed a shadow further down the street and grabbed her camera – one of her new acquisitions. She focused on the retreating figure and snapped a couple of images. She started the ignition as soon as the figure got into his car, but hesitated, torn between following the mystery man or Vee Verren.

The man's car was facing towards her, and she ducked low as he drove past. Then at the other end of the street, a dark van pulled across the junction, stopping at the corner. She held back, winding her window down to listen, heard a door slide open, a male voice, then the door again, closing. She started the ignition and steered slowly out from the kerb, keeping her headlights off, accelerating to the junction as the van moved away.

She'd been watching Nurse Verren for days, her mind refusing to let go of the small snag in her story about treating Rick Turner in the emergency department the night he was shot.

Vee had claimed to have been on duty on the night of Rick's shooting. She wasn't. Pandora always made a point of confirming stories wherever possible, and she'd treated several of Vee's co-workers to lunch or drinks in the past week. She wasn't the only one, it seemed – a man claiming to be from one of the local papers had been chatting up Vee's colleagues – early fifties, grey hair, soft-spoken. The description didn't ring any bells with Pandora, and she was worried it might be one of the broadsheets, sending in the big guns.

Vee's workmates seemed in awe of her – and they were happy to talk. They told Pandora that Vee had actually come in despite being on annual leave, but when she pressed for more details, she'd discovered that Vee had been telling her colleagues for weeks before this that she was planning to take a hiking trip in Northern Spain.

Eager to explain away the lie, one nurse had said that people sometimes *said* they'd be far away with no mobile access even if they'd planned a staycation, just to avoid being dragged in for extra shifts. Again, that was understandable. But if that was the case, why did Vee come running as soon as she heard about the Limehouse shootings? And she'd claimed that she'd heard about them on BBC London and dropped everything to come back in. But the farrago in Limehouse had been described as 'an incident' by BBC London – not a shooting. Pandora had checked.

The first mention of shootings was an hour after it happened – and the video of Rick Turner being carried into the hospital was shaky mobile phone footage from some drunk reveller who'd happened to be attending A&E at the time. Despite this, all the eyewitness accounts Pandora had gathered said that Vee Verren was at the hospital and caring for DS Turner shortly after he'd been wheeled in.

Having committed to following the van, Pandora settled into trailing it at a safe distance, only turning on her headlights when they'd merged onto a main road where she could duck behind a couple of other vehicles.

'Victoria Verren, what *are* you up to?' she murmured, feeling the excitement of the chase course through her veins.

Chapter 58

THE WOLF PACK MUSTERED AT PUG'S GYM, it being the most central place. Seated on unmatched chairs around a table behind the sparring ring, to lower the risk of being heard from outside the building, they waited for Frosty to begin. Sooner was impossible to read, Cap looked strained, Prozac more anxious than ever, Brock seething with pent-up energy. Pug alone looked pleased to see everyone. A single-storey structure, thrown together in the 1960s mode of doing things, the gym smelled of male sweat, chalk and old leather, and Frosty felt right at home.

As soon as she told them that she'd spoken to Turner, the arguments started.

'You talked to a copper about us?' Brock demanded.

'Jeez, Frosty! What the hell were you thinking?' She'd never seen Pug so outraged.

'To be clear, *he* came to *me* – to my flat. I did *not* invite him.'

'And he said he knew you were Wolf Pack?' Prozac asked.

'He talked like it was public knowledge. I admitted to nothing.'

'But he knows?' Cap said.

'He *thinks* he knows.'

'What did you say?' Brock demanded.

'Not much. Mostly, I listened,' she said pointedly.

344

But Brock wasn't ready to do that, yet. 'What if he was wired?' he said.

'He wasn't.'

Brock leered. 'Make him strip, did ya?'

She stared through him.

Pug sat, mouth open, staring from one to the other. Suddenly, he laughed, slapping his meaty boxer's hands together in a loud thunderclap. 'You did!' He turned to the others. 'She did it – she made him strip!'

Frosty snuffed air through her nose and tried to look pissed off, but Pug's laughter was infectious, and despite herself the corners of her mouth turned up, and even Sooner looked like he found it funny.

Cap raised his hand, asking for silence. 'What makes you think we can trust him?'

'He saved our arses at Limehouse, for one thing.'

Pug squinted at her. 'How d'you reckon that?'

'We went in blind – sorry, Prozac, but we did,' she added, seeing the hurt look on their techie's face. 'We had Emin's men tooled up and twitchy on one side, the police, NCA, Border Force, and God knows who else tooled up and gung-ho on the other – and we were *clueless*. Turner put himself in harm's way. Took a bullet for his trouble, too.'

In the silence that followed Frosty sensed a change of mood.

'What did he want?' Cap asked.

'Our help.'

Frosty recounted the story as Rick Turner had told it to her: an art collector had sold a valuable canvas online, delivered the canvas as agreed. But the buyer got greedy, kidnapped the seller, wanting to coerce him into refunding him the money.

Eyebrows raised, Cap said, 'Well, things must have gone sharply downhill at Sotheby's.'

She shot him an amused glance. 'I gather this was an under-the-counter type sale.'

'How does Turner know all this?'

'The seller's a friend.'

'Does he know who the buyer is?'

'Theodore Lockleigh,' she said.

'The gangster who had that man shot in Whitechapel?' Pug asked. She nodded.

'Be quite the coup if we brought him in,' Cap said.

Looking around the table, she saw that Sooner was considering it.

'Why can't he do it himself?' Brock wanted to know.

'Yeah,' Pug said. 'He's police.'

'Not for much longer, by the sounds of it,' Frosty said. 'He's suspended – thinks he's about to be given the boot.'

'That's a bit dramatic, isn't it?' Brock said.

Cap tilted his head. 'Criminal gangs practically running the capital, the mess at Limehouse. Us. It's one embarrassment after another for the Met, and if they're looking for a scapegoat, DS Turner must look like he's got horns and cloven hooves.'

Frosty nodded.

'He could call it in anonymously,' Brock said.

'And have a two-crew unit roll up just to do a quick check on a possible crank call – get themselves *and* the victim shot?'

'Wait a minute. Wait a minute,' Pug interrupted, his mind still stuck at the Whitechapel shootings. 'Didn't Pandora say that Turner's brother was one of Lockleigh's crew?'

'Samuel Turner's dead.' Everyone's eyes swivelled to Prozac and he immediately became defensive. 'Well, that's what they say. Happened way back. Got stabbed by one of Lockleigh's crew after he grassed them up.'

'So maybe this is just Turner out for revenge – getting us to do the job for him.' Brock again, obstinate to the end.

'It's a fair point,' Frosty said, 'but he told me that Lockleigh is one of the reasons he became a cop – he didn't think men like that should get away with it.'

'Pitching to join us, was he?' Brock asked.

'Matter of fact, I asked the same question,' she said, letting him see the glint in her eye. 'Know what he said? "You can't go on doing this."'

'"You" meaning *us*?' Brock spread his hands, gesturing to the rest of the pack. 'And yet, here he is, asking for our help.' He sniffed. 'Fuck him. This is his problem, not ours.'

'It's closer to home than you think,' Frosty said. 'Lockleigh had Floren shot.'

'I'm sorry,' Brock said. 'Did I miss something? Why should we care?'

'Because Lockleigh made us look like killers,' Cap said.

'That,' Frosty agreed. 'Plus, Turner has it on good authority that Floren was about to turn himself in. Maybe that's why he was killed.'

'Who gains by that?' Brock said. 'Frosty's shithead business partner's already banged up for torching the place – lost the land under a proceeds of crime seizure.'

'Did you know that the Deptford Waters development is now run by an offshore trust fund?' she asked.

They looked one to another. Apparently, nobody did.

'It's called Dream Schemes Corporate Trust, and it's filed in Dakota, USA, where the UK law can't touch it. Turner says he's got evidence that Lockleigh is the owner.'

'No,' Brock said. 'The landlord – *was* the owner, till the CPS confiscated it. It was him who took out the contract on Floren – it was revenge, pure and simple.'

'You asked who gains,' Frosty came back. 'Whoever owns Dream Schemes gains. Think about it, Brock – how many millions did Deptford Waters cost to build? The high-rise must've set him back what – thirty-five? Fifty million? If Floren had that kind of money, the company wouldn't just switch from his ownership to Dream Schemes Corporate Trust in the blink of an eye. It'd take months going through probate.'

Cap nodded. 'Years, maybe.'

Brock gave her a narrow look. 'So how did Lockleigh do it then?'

'Turner reckons the Dream Schemes Trust owned it all along.'

Brock rolled his eyes, and Frosty tried again.

'Look, I don't pretend to understand it, but Turner's got an expert working on it, and he's convinced that Lockleigh has always been the owner. Floren was just the frontman.'

Brock shrugged irritably, shook his head. 'How's Turner got all this if he's suspended?' Pug asked.

'The guy who sold the painting had Lockleigh checked out.'

Brock laughed. There was no humour in it. 'So, this "pal" of Turner's sold Lockleigh the painting, *knowing* all this, and we're supposed to ride to the rescue?'

'I don't *know* how much he knew,' she said. 'My guess is, he just checked that Lockleigh was good for the money.'

Prozac was hunched down in his chair, frowning at his hands in his lap. Cap leaned forward and rapped the table to get his attention.

Prozac jerked visibly. '*What?*'

'What's the word on Turner at the police station?'

'Like you said before. The higher-ups need a sacrifice – he's on the way out.'

Cap turned to Frosty. 'Do you think he's genuine?'

'I do.'

'What happens if we don't help?'

She shrugged. 'He goes in anyway, gets himself killed.'

'Thoughts?'

Prozac had sunk back into his defensive slump. 'We're in enough trouble as it is.'

Brock said, 'We've done all we can for the Deptford victims. We move on.'

'Pug?'

The boxer squirmed in his seat. 'I hate to see a toerag like Lockleigh end up on top.'

Cap turned last to Sooner. 'I haven't been with you all from the beginning,' Sooner said. He hadn't. But he'd seen how seriously they took their training, and as owner of the gun club, he'd had their full background and work history. It hadn't taken long to make the connection between this dedicated and disparate group of people and the Deptford fire. Brock had lost family; two of Pug's promising young boxers had perished in the flames. Cap, Frosty and Prozac were the professionals who'd seen at first hand the devastation the arson attack had caused. As soon as he understood what was driving them, Sooner had offered his services.

'But if Turner is right about Lockleigh, then the wrong man died at Deptford Waters. We need to finish the job.'

It was a long speech for the Oklahoman, and Frosty took it as a measure of the strength of his feeling.

Cap sighed. 'I think we can all agree that the job isn't finished. But as ever, the devil is in the detail. Frosty – treating this strictly as a hypothetical – what does Turner want from us?'

'He's got ordnance, but he needs boots on the ground,' she said.

'So he *does* want to join us!' Pug grinned, clearly feeling the need to lighten the mood.

'Join forces, is more like it,' Frosty said. 'He's got two military-trained associates, plus a driver and a tech-head. The victim is under armed guard, and the target site has security cameras. They need us to knock out security, and to assist in an armed assault on the site. Once they've got the hostage safe, we take Lockleigh, turn him over to the Met, take the credit.'

'Ooh, I like that!' Pug gazed excitedly from face to face. Brock scowled at him, and he clamped his lips together. Prozac cleared his throat but didn't speak.

Sooner lifted one shoulder and said: 'I guess it'd be a chance to make amends for Limehouse?' and Prozac glanced up with hope in his eyes.

Obviously hungry for the mission, Pug seemed to have trouble

349

sitting still. 'Well, I don't know about you guys, but I've been going crazy sitting around the gym since Cap sent us home.'

'Timescale?' Cap asked.

'Has to be tonight,' Frosty said.

This raised a chorus of protests – even Pug looked dismayed.

'I smell a set-up,' Brock said.

Frosty began to speak, but he shouted her down.

'Hear her out,' Cap said firmly, then to Frosty: 'Why the rush?'

'Turner thinks Lockleigh is torturing the art collector to get access to his money, and he won't stop till either he has the access codes to his bank account, or the guy is dead.'

That left a silence that nobody seemed to want to break.

After a full thirty seconds, Pug thunder-clapped his hands again. 'So, are we doing this or what?'

Chapter 59

FRUSTRATED WITH THE LACK OF PROGRESS in finding Rick, Lockleigh turned his attention again to Sam. The pain came in waves, rolling over him like a rising tide. He felt it in his chest, in the bruising of his kidneys, his thighs, in the burning pain in his shoulders from pulled ligaments and strained tendons, and in the dull throb in his face and head. He tasted blood in his mouth and his breathing was a painful creak. But Sam felt detached from it; almost like it was happening to someone else. He observed it building to a peak, then crashing, sapping him of strength and resolve as it receded.

'Boss. Rick Turner's car is on the move.'

Sound seemed to come in and out, first muffled, then booming, like someone shouting under water, and Sam thought he must have misheard. Rick *couldn't* be on the move – he was in a pub cellar, guarded by two of his most trusted people.

Rick is safe.

'Are you telling me he's been there this whole time?' Lockleigh demanded.

'We checked,' a voice from the far end of the church said. 'The place was empty.'

Sam missed Lockleigh's response, but another voice, higher in pitch, fearful – *the tech?* – chimed in. 'I swear, it's been parked up for days. Never moved an inch.'

'Well, now it *has*,' Lockleigh snapped.

A jumble of sounds, then: '*Where?*'

'East on the A205.'

Lockleigh pointed to someone in the darkness. '*You* – get after him.'

Errol spoke up. 'Want me to go with him boss? Young Rick can be a handful.' He was trying to sound casual, but Sam heard the strain in his voice. Perhaps remnants of their friendship had remained, even after all these years.

'No. I need you and Mercer here.' He gestured again. 'You – go with him.'

Sam wanted to see who was leaving, but his head was too heavy; he couldn't lift it.

He let himself drift, thinking, *Rick is safe.*

Time passed.

Sam heard a ringing in his ears. Lockleigh must have punctured an eardrum with his last assault. But it stopped abruptly and Lockleigh said, 'Tell me you've got him.'

Phone. He's talking on a mobile phone.

Lockleigh listened, then: 'He's doing what?' His laughter was distorted, hollow-sounding. 'All right, let him. He'll have to stop sometime. When he does, you grab him. Clear?'

Sam heard a slithering. Delirious, now, it sounded to him like the insinuating, treacherous approach of a snake. He jerked away dislodging the broken rib, so that it stabbed sharply into his flesh, and he cried out.

Lockleigh grabbed a handful of his hair, yanking his head up, and Sam saw a sliver of moon through the plain glass window at the far end of the church. Lockleigh gave an utterance of disgust and, cursing, let him go, wiping blood from his hand onto Sam's shirt.

'Mercer,' Lockleigh called. 'Hold his head up.'

Mercer's huge bulk emerged from the shadows. Sam felt a tug at the roots of his hair and found himself staring into Lockleigh's face, but he lost focus, and his eyes began to roll upwards.

'Don't you pass out on me!' Lockleigh threatened. 'Slap him.'

He didn't feel the slap, but he was fully conscious as Lockleigh said, 'Are you listening, Sam? Rick is circling – trying to lose the tail. But he's geotagged – he'll only succeed in making himself dizzy.'

It's a trick, he thought. Rick couldn't have got away from Noel and Gavin. *It's all right, he's safe.*

He must have passed out, because the next he was aware there was the sound of activity.

'Do you hear that, Sam?' Lockleigh said. 'Rick isn't *circling*, he's *spiralling*.' He must have switched to speakerphone, because the next Sam heard was: 'Boss, he seems to be heading towards you.'

No, he can't be. It's a lie. All a lie to get me to talk. Even if Rick had managed to get away from his guards, how could he know where to look? The pain affected his thinking. He couldn't imagine how Rick had got from a secure basement to this godforsaken place.

Then, in a hammer blow, it came to him: Dave Collins.

In the short time Sam had known Dave, he'd grown to appreciate the big man's thoroughness. Dave Collins was almost compulsive in his need to understand the entire network of connections in any investigation. He wasn't satisfied that the job was done until he'd – what did he call it? – 'joined all the dots'. Had he kept looking? Had he joined the dots between Lazarus Theophilus and Dream Schemes?

'He's not part of this, Theo,' Sam managed.

'I didn't *want* to involve him,' Lockleigh said. 'It's your intransigence that made this necessary.'

That was another lie, and Sam smiled weakly. 'Don't try to kid a kidder, Theo. You had someone following Rick the second you got out.'

Mercer jabbed him in the back, and he blacked out. After that, he faded in and out of consciousness for a while. Minutes? Hours?

Then, the words Sam feared most:

'He's here!' The man speaking to Lockleigh sounded incredulous. 'Brazen fucker's just parked right outside.'

Lockleigh turned to Sam, eyebrows raised. 'Looks like he *wants* to be involved.'

A yelp of consternation, then: 'Wait a minute, he's moving again.'

'Well, don't let him get away again. Stop him!' Lockleigh yelled.

'No. No. No . . .' Sam groaned.

'For God's sake, communicate, man!' Lockleigh commanded. 'What the hell is going on?'

'It's okay. All good, Boss.' The man sounded nervous. 'We have eyes on him.'

'Bring him in.'

'Theo,' Sam said, but his voice had no power. '*Theo.*'

Errol spoke up. 'Boss, he's trying to say something.'

Lockleigh turned again to Sam as if he'd almost forgotten him. 'What?' he said.

Sam mumbled, finding it hard to form the words.

'What are you *saying*?'

'You can have . . . the money.' Sam took small sips of air every few words, pushing himself to finish, to say it all. 'Apartment in Chelsea. Access details . . . are there.'

Lockleigh was staring avidly into his face. Sam saw in the wonder in his former mentor's mud-brown eyes that he understood what he was being offered.

'I would never have thought it possible,' Lockleigh murmured, almost to himself. 'Is *that* why you stuck around for the Unwin trial last year? For *him*?' He gave a soft gasp of amusement. 'Extraordinary.'

'Take me to Chelsea – you can have it. All of it,' Sam said, gathering his strength.

He saw a flicker in Lockleigh's eyes, a sharp glint in the murky depths.

'You can keep your promises,' Lockleigh said coldly. 'You'll give me the access codes eventually – no man holds out for a sequence of numbers.'

Theo Lockleigh had always been cruel, but prison had changed him, corrupting his surface sheen of urbane sophistication, exposing the base metal at his core. He repeated his original order to the men following Rick: 'Bring him in. I want to see this specimen that Sam Turner is so keen to protect.'

No response, and a few seconds later, Lockleigh said, 'What did I say about communicating? What's taking so long?'

'Nothing showing on the cameras, Boss. I'll try and get another angle.'

The tech again. Sam had seen this man only as a pale glow of laptop monitors near the church entrance, as he was dragged into the building. He heard panic in the man's tone. *The cameras are fritzed, but he's too afraid to say.*

Rick wasn't alone.

Lockleigh raised his voice to speak to someone at the church entrance. 'Find out where he is. Bring him here.'

Alert, now, Sam tallied the movements of Lockleigh's security personnel: Seanie G and Puck were long gone, and Sam's men had taken out another three at the storage facility in Dartford. He'd seen four unfamiliar faces in the van – all armed mercenaries. Lockleigh had sent two to follow Rick. He assumed that those two were disarmed or dead by now.

He'd just sent another mercenary to find Rick. Which left how many?

He panicked, unable to remember the sequence of events, then his mind cleared, and he had it: the tech expert, Errol, Mercer, one other hired gun, and Lockleigh himself.

If Rick had brought Noel and Gavin, that made three against four – discounting the technician. A tiny flicker of hope kindled in his chest, and he could have sworn he heard Rick's voice:

Stay alive long enough, we might just get you out of there, bruv.

Then Rick himself appeared at the end of the aisle, arms raised, and all hope failed. Sam heard the deadly sound of weapons being racked, but Lockleigh said, 'Easy . . . Hold your fire.'

Warrant card in one hand, Rick declared his name and police rank, and that he was unarmed.

'Rick, no . . .' Sam's voice broke.

'Where the fuck were you when he waltzed in unchallenged?' Lockleigh pointed to a blurred figure behind Rick.

'I—'

Lockleigh waved away the excuse. 'Never mind. Bring him here – and cuff him first.'

The man took hold of Rick's left wrist in his left hand but as he moved behind to slip on the plasticuffs, Rick followed, pivoting, grabbing his sidearm, jamming the barrel between the angle of the man's neck and jaw. The shock on the mercenary's face was a joy to behold.

Errol and Mercer raised their weapons again, and Rick nodded towards Lockleigh. 'Ah, ah, ah . . .'

A swarm of red bees had found a home on Lockleigh's chest. He murmured, 'What the—' clutching at the dots, until he realised what they were. All eyes turned to the mezzanine. Three mercenaries in full tac gear. Three semiautomatic rifles readied, cocked and raised.

Errol and Mercer lowered their handguns and Sam heard Errol whisper, '*Shit, shit, shit.*'

Two more – one exceptionally tall, one short – both helmeted like the rest, strode in.

Noel and Gavin, Sam thought, feeling almost giddy with relief.

Noel grabbed the tech by the scruff of the neck and swung him like a bowling ball. He fell, rolled, then scrambled to his feet again, scuttling ahead of them, his head bowed, arms held high, as they strode down the centre aisle, their boots crunching plaster and brick underfoot, weapons at the low ready position.

The church door closed with an echoing slam and two bolts rattled in place, before a final black-clad man appeared.

Rick secured the mercenary, finding and removing a knife and an ankle pistol before binding him to one of the steels supporting the mezzanine.

The tech kept moving ahead of the other two till he fell to his knees near the sacristy. The man who'd come in last was broad in the shoulders and carried himself like a bull about to charge. He heaved the canvas out of his way and Sam heard a yell of dismay as it fell backwards into the dirt.

'Was that really necessary?' Lockleigh demanded.

The big man punched him in the mouth, and he crumpled.

Sam felt Rick's arm around his back, supporting him.

'Brace yourself,' he whispered, before cutting through the first rope binding. Sam cried out at the tearing pain caused by the sudden release of tension on his pectoral muscles, but Rick held him, and he found his feet. 'Got it?' Rick said.

He could only manage a nod.

Rick cut the rope to his other wrist and, released, Sam leaned heavily on his brother.

Waiting until Errol and Mercer were bound, Rick said, 'Are we done here?' He'd directed the question to one of the figures up on the mezzanine. He got a nod in answer.

'Good luck,' Rick said, moving Sam towards the left-hand side of the sanctuary. Sam realised that he was intending to leave Lockleigh behind.

'We need him,' he wheezed.

'No,' Rick said. 'That's not the deal.'

Before Sam could protest, a siren wail went up and the three on the mezzanine turned.

'Squad car,' one man yelled. 'Everyone out.'

The big, bullish man jerked his head towards Lockleigh. 'I'm not leaving him.'

'Beta One, that's an order!'

Noel moved alongside Rick and slipped an arm under Sam's screaming shoulders. 'We gotta get him out of here.'

Rick and Noel hustled Sam through the vestry, waiting only long enough for Gavin to check ahead. They half-carried Sam to the boundary wall.

Sam saw the lights now, reflecting blue and red off the hoardings and plastic wreathing the upper reaches of the church.

'The door'll hold them for a minute, but we can't get out through the main gates,' Noel said.

Rick said, 'This way.' He led them to a narrow gap in the wall, where a small gate lay twisted off its hinges. It led onto what must have once been a graveyard.

Shouts, then gunfire.

They ducked low and Sam gave a muffled shout of pain.

The wall had been taken down to allow access, but the hoardings extended all the way for fifty yards on three side and the gates looked solid and secure. There was no way out.

A car engine roared, just the other side of the hoarding.

'Police?' Rick said.

Recognising the sound of the engine, Sam shook his head. 'Lawrence.'

The gates burst open a second later in a shower of splintered wood, and Sam's limo reversed at full acceleration into the space.

'Give him here,' Gavin said, picking Sam up like a child while Noel raced to open the doors. Rick fell in after the other three, yelling, 'Go, Go, Go!'

Chapter 60

LAWRENCE DROVE ACROSS TOWN, GAVIN RIDING SHOTGUN, Lawrence talking quietly into his headphones, making turns to avoid the major thoroughfares, taking them to a prearranged destination.

Noel and Rick helped Sam to find a position that eased the pain in his ribs, then Noel retreated to a corner of the limo and kept an eye on the rear window.

Sam tapped Rick on his knee to attract his attention. 'They were tracking your car. If the police find it—'

Rick shook his head. 'I pulled up outside the church to let them know I was there, then moved on – had them scrambling to follow. By the time they found me, we were waiting.'

'You and . . .?'

'Noel, Gavin, and one of the Wolf Pack.'

'Where . . . is it?' Sam was running out of stamina.

'The car? Relax,' Rick said. 'It's parked outside of the outer cordon. The police won't even notice it.'

Sam leaned back in his seat for a few seconds, closing his eyes.

'Don't fall asleep on me, mate,' Rick warned.

'You shouldn't have come,' Sam whispered. 'Too dangerous.'

'Yeah, well, you can deliver the lecture later.'

Sam recognised his brother's rough response for what it was – extreme emotion, barely controlled.

'Sam – open your eyes. *Sam – please.*'

Hearing the desperation in Rick's voice, he did as he was asked and groaned at the pain in his right eye.

Rick grasped his hand as he raised it to check the damage, and Sam felt a tremor in his brother's fingers.

'You'll be all right,' Rick said. 'Just leave it alone, okay?'

'How—' His breath failed him, and Rick supplied the rest:

'—did I find you? You can thank Dave.'

He nodded tiredly. 'And the Wolf Pack? Why would they . . .?'

'I persuaded them that Lockleigh was unfinished business.'

They slowed, and Lawrence steered the limo towards a set of heavy black gates under a Deco-style building.

'What is this?' Rick asked.

'A private clinic,' Noel said.

Lawrence wound down his window and spoke a few words into an intercom. The gate opened and they glided down into an underground garage.

A white-coated man and two nurses were waiting beside a trolley as they pulled up.

'We'll take it from here,' the white coat said.

'You can forget that,' Rick said. 'I'm going in.'

The man looked to Sam for a decision. He nodded and, between them, they got him onto the trolley and into a service lift. Gavin said he and Noel would sort the car, and Lawrence went with Rick.

The examination room looked much like any NHS clinic, but better lit and less scuffed around the edges.

Addressing Rick, the doctor said, 'We need to assess the patient. I understand your concern, but I do need you to leave, now.'

When Rick began to object, Sam said, 'It's all right, I trust them.'

Rick hesitated, then said, 'I'll be right outside the door,' and Sam smiled his thanks.

As Lawrence followed him, Sam called him back.

'Rick's car.'

'I had someone check it as soon as you asked Rick about it,' Lawrence said. 'It's on the move.'

Sam felt suddenly cold. 'Police?'

'I don't think so,' Lawrence said. 'It's heading towards the outskirts of the city.' He paused. 'There's something else you should know – Lockleigh hasn't been named as one of the men arrested.'

'Dead?' Sam asked.

'Unclear.'

Sam's breath came in creaking gasps. 'The car – it could be Theo.'

'We're low on personnel,' Lawrence said, 'but I could get Noel and Gavin to check it.'

Sam nodded. 'Tell them . . . extreme caution.'

'They know, Sam.'

Sam patted Lawrence's arm, too tired to say more.

'All finished, now?' the doctor demanded, a note of impatience in his voice.

Sam gave another weak nod.

'*Fantastic. Much* appreciated.' He turned his fierce gaze on Lawrence. 'Now clear out. I need to examine my patient.'

Chapter 61

RICK SAT BESIDE SAM'S BED, earbuds in, watching *Pandora Unboxes* on his phone. Every half-minute he checked his brother's vital signs on the monitor. The breaks to two of Sam's ribs were severe, and the doctor had performed rib-stabilisation surgery, rather than risk lacerations to his internal organs. His temp was lower and he seemed to be breathing easily, now, but his heart rate continued to fluctuate alarmingly. Rick had called the nursing staff half a dozen times in the last hour, but they didn't seem unduly alarmed, so he'd turned to the news as a distraction.

Pandora had released a new podcast. She introduced it with the usual recap and, sales pitch completed, she launched into her latest.

A video of a derelict church filled the screen, and Rick half rose from the chair. *It can't be.* But Dream Schemes' logo emblazoned across the hoardings meant there was no mistake – this was where Sam had been held the night before.

Rick mouthed, 'Shit . . .' lowering himself back into the seat to watch.

The road was quiet and there were no police lights. She must have been outside the church before the police arrived.

362

'I knew that something serious was about to happen,' she said over the footage, 'when I saw this.'

The videocam focused onto a dark, unmarked van, parked on the roadway at the northerly edge of the church. Four people piled out, all helmeted, armed, and in tactical gear. As the last person jumped down and did a quick recce, the Wolf Pack logo was visible on his helmet. The four piled over the hoardings at the side of the church, and she lost them.

'I didn't risk get any closer, in case the driver had stayed with the van,' she explained. 'But I *was* able to film this sequence.'

Moments later, three of the figures appeared again, climbing the scaffolding on the outside of the church. She remained quiet, and there wasn't a sound until a car pootled down the road, sweeping past the camera. The swoosh of its tyres and the gentle thrum of its engine were clearly audible.

'Yes,' she said at last. 'The audio was on for this entire sequence, but the Wolf Pack was absolutely silent – I was there, and straining to hear, as you can imagine, and I didn't hear a thing as they climbed the scaffolding.' She froze the recording here, and the picture-in-picture frame appeared.

Pandora stared out at her audience.

'That is when I called the police.' After a pause, she sighed. 'To be honest, I wasn't sure they'd taken me seriously, so I moved my car to the front of the building, intending to warn whoever came. But two minutes later, this happened.'

A new clip replaced the frozen image on the screen. Another three armed and black-clad figures appeared at the front gates of the development – two very large, one small. This would be Gavin, Noel and the bull-necked Wolf Packer who didn't want to leave Lockleigh to the police. They disappeared inside. Rick had already disarmed the last of the mercenaries by this time, having breached the fencing from the north side.

Pandora went on, 'Three minutes later . . .' *Can it really have been only three?* 'A police car pulled up at the main gates.'

The video footage bounced about after that, and Rick realised that Pandora had jumped out of her car and was running to intercept the police.

'You can't go in there unarmed!' she whispered.

The female officer ordered her to stay back, but Pandora kept talking. 'There are armed men in there!' she insisted.

The male said, 'She's bloody bonkers.' Then: 'Wait a minute – aren't you that podcaster? Look, if this is some kind of stunt—'

A sudden loud roar of an engine, then the crash of wooden gates being impacted. Lawrence, reversing onto the old graveyard.

Then swearing, a chaotic readjustment of the camera towards the sound, a swish of fabric on fabric as Pandora ran to the corner. All she got was a flash of taillights as Sam's limo hurtled off down the street.

Relieved, Rick suppressed a chuckle; he had to admit, the woman had nerves of steel.

Next, a van parked near the gates was swarmed by four armed men.

One of the cops yelled, 'Police, stop!'

They didn't even flinch but leapt into the van and it was off before the doors slid shut.

When the video finished, Pandora explained that the firm's security cameras had been put out of action. Doorbell cameras in the nearby streets were also knocked out.

She could be forgiven for the hint of self-satisfaction in her expression as she said, 'So the only video at the scene that night is what you've just seen right here on *Pandora Unboxes*.

'A stolen artwork, thought to be by Jost Bellingen, and worth an estimated twenty million pounds was found inside the church. Several men were arrested at the scene. Two are known associates of former gangland boss Theodore Lockleigh, who is currently at large, having breached the conditions of his early release from prison on licence. Lockleigh is a person of interest in a multiple shooting in Whitechapel last week. Two others – a computer technician and an ex-army veteran – were apparently discovered bound and secured inside the derelict church, and are being questioned by police. Three more men were found unconscious, locked inside a Dream Schemes van at the site. The police have not, as yet identified these three men.'

Rick saw a movement; Sam was stirring. He set the phone aside as Sam lifted his fingers to the pad over his right eye.

'How long have I been out?' He tried to sit up, and Rick was on his feet in a second, applying gentle pressure to his brother's shoulders.

'Whoa,' Rick said. 'You're held together by titanium plates right now, Sam. Give yourself a minute to heal.'

'How *long* have I been *out*?' Sam repeated, more insistently.

'Eight hours.'

The heart monitor spiked. 'Has Lawrence been back?'

'Sam, it's okay—'

'*Answer* me,' Sam said.

He seemed so agitated that Rick did – firmly and honestly: 'He came in an hour ago. Said to tell you it's all under control – whatever "it" is.'

Sam stopped struggling and sank back into the pillows. After a few moments, he said, 'For pity's sake, would you stop looking at the monitor like I'm flatlining?'

'Not funny,' Rick said.

'No,' Sam said, suddenly looking exhausted. 'I suppose not.'

He was silent for a few seconds, and Rick thought he'd drifted off again.

'So, what happened to my eye?'

'Isn't it obvious? Lockleigh used you as a punch bag,' Rick said, hearing a dangerous rasp in his voice. He moved towards the door, not wanting Sam to see him upset. 'I'll get the doctor – he'll explain.'

'No,' Sam said. 'Please, Rick – no doctors just yet. You tell me.'

Rick ran a hand over his face, wiping away tears before he turned back. Another glance at the monitor showed that Sam's

BP and heart rate were returning to normal, and taking a calming breath, he returned to the chair.

'They fractured your right eye socket. The doctor thinks it'll heal with cold compression and rest, but he can't be sure till the swelling's gone down.' Taking another shaky breath, he went on: 'They burst your left eardrum – only a small puncture – it should heal in a few weeks.' He went at a gallop, trying not to think how each injury had been inflicted on Sam – what he'd gone through in the hours until they'd found him. 'Your kidneys are bruised – ditto on the healing. But they broke two of your ribs really badly – that's where the titanium comes in.' He cleared his throat, thinking, *I'll fucking kill Lockleigh if I ever find him.* 'You're on antibiotics, saline, and morphine.'

He watched Sam as he explored the dressing over his ribs and discovered a tube and a small bag on the lower right-hand side.

'It's a drain,' Rick said. 'The doc says they'll probably take it out after twenty-four to forty-eight hours.'

Sam's hand slid to the sheet. 'Rick, I'm so sorry.'

'*You're* sorry?'

'You should never have been brought into this – you could've been killed.'

'Uh, Sam, have you forgotten you held a gun on me in Lockleigh's flat?' Rick felt again the jolt of horror he'd experienced when Sam pulled the gun.

Sam's eyes widened. 'Rick, the safety was on, I would never—'

His scepticism must have shown, because Sam looked stricken. 'You *must* know I was bluffing – why else would I have had Noel and Gavin waiting in the wings?'

Rick shrugged. 'Well, you had me fooled.'

'You know I always hope for the best and prepare for the worst.' Perhaps it was the pounding he'd taken, but Sam sounded as earnest as Rick had ever heard him, and a tear gathered at the corner of his good eye. 'I was trying to keep you safe, bruv,' he finished, almost in a whisper.

Rick shook his head. 'I keep telling you – I can take care of myself.'

Sam managed a weak smile. 'I know you can, Rick, but you're hobbled by your respect for the law.'

Rick laughed. 'One of these days, I'm gonna count up all the laws I've broken since you turned up last October.'

But Sam was brooding over something – it was as if he hadn't heard.

'What now?' Rick demanded.

'They were supposed to keep you out of this.'

'Don't you go blaming Little and Large – they were *very* clear you didn't want me involved.'

'They should've dealt with Lockleigh themselves.'

Rick scoffed. 'With *what*? Lockleigh had already taken out three of your crew, Lawrence said you couldn't trust your go-to guy in the circumstances, and *nobody* had clearance to make money decisions in your absence. We had to cobble together a small army with no contingency plans and zero cash.'

'I'll be sure to take that into consideration in future,' Sam said with a weary smile. 'But that's not what I meant. This isn't your fight, Rick.'

Rick tilted his head. 'Have you forgotten what happened four-teen years ago? Besides, a wise man once told me that when you're grown up, you get to make your own decisions.'

'Mind like a steel trap,' Sam said, smiling.

'Speaking of Dave,' Rick said in a bad segue. 'He was shocked to hear that you're a wanted man.'

'Sarcasm always was your fall-back under stress,' Sam said.

Sick or not, Rick wasn't letting him get away with that. 'He wanted to know what you're wanted for.'

'Oh, God, I *really* can't afford to lose my armchair ninja. What did you *say* to him, Rick?'

'I told him he'd have to ask you,' Rick said.

'Thank you,' Sam breathed.

'That wasn't an excuse for you to lie to him, Sam.'

'I never have.'

'Oh,' Rick said. 'So Lockleigh's an old mate?'

'He *was* . . .' Sam said with a comical wince, and Rick had to fight down a smile.

'I'm going to tell him not to believe a word you say.'

'That's probably sound advice,' Sam said soberly.

A small spike of contrary anger made Rick add, 'All this over that bloody canvas. I'm glad you didn't get it.'

'Now, why would you say that?' Sam looked almost hurt.

'The original owner was *murdered* during the theft, Sam.'

'Not by me.'

Rick opened his mouth to remonstrate, but Sam said, 'Seriously – that was nothing to do with me. And anyway, he was a *terrible* man.' In Sam's book, apparently that made it all right.

'If you didn't steal it, where d'you buy it?'

'Who said I bought it?'

'Unbelievable. You *stole* a stolen artwork?'

Smiling again, Sam said, 'Beautiful, isn't it? A truly victimless crime.'

Chapter 62

A month later, seven p.m.

RICK WAS WAITING IN HIS CAR near the hospital. He saw Vee Verren approach from fifty yards away. May had come in soft and warm, purring like a cat and, sleek, loose-limbed and confident, Vee was dressed in jeans and T-shirt, a backpack slung over one shoulder. Her brown hair was tied back, her shift having just finished, and she looked tired – even a little strained.

She opened the passenger door and slid in next to him. Fresh from the shower, she smelled wonderful.

'Electric car,' she said. 'Nice.'

'The ULEZ charges were killing me, so after my old banger disappeared, I decided to go all out.' At Sam's urging, he'd actually sold one of the vintage comics he'd hauled down from the attic and was surprised that it more than covered the cost.

'So,' she said. 'You wanted to talk?'

'Over a drink?' Rick suggested.

She debated. 'Why not.'

They drove to a bar under the arches near Brick Lane to avoid being spotted by Vee's work colleagues.

When they were seated with their drinks in a quiet booth, Rick began by saying how sorry he was to hear about Brock.

Brock – real name Carl Brody – had been found hours after the assault on the old church, shot dead at the side of country road just off the M25 in South Mimms. He was still in tac gear, his helmet dumped in a ditch nearby. The Wolf logo on the helmet was something of a giveaway.

Vee arched an eyebrow. 'You left it a while.'

'It seemed wise,' Rick said.

She tilted her head, accepting the logic.

It hadn't taken long for the Met to discover that Brock was related to one of the families devastated by the arson attack that had razed two blocks of flats to the ground in Deptford two years ago. Sympathies in the Twittersphere were divided, amateur sleuths had vied with the mainstream press to develop theories on who the rest of the pack were, and for a few weeks, the victims of the fire had been hounded.

'I shouldn't have dragged you into my mess,' he said.

'Lockleigh was our mess, too,' she said.

'It was the Deptford arson attack that brought you together?'

She seemed to think about whether she should answer, then gave a brief nod.

'I know that Brock had family who died in the fire, but what about the others?' She didn't answer. 'I'm thinking responders,' he said. 'First attenders – people like you who saw the human suffering.'

'Would knowing do you any good?' she asked.

He shrugged. 'Probably not. But one thing does bug me.'

She lifted her chin, inviting him to say it.

'How did you find the location of Emin's new factory in Limehouse so fast?' He'd been chewing on that one for a month. It had to be a police source.

She gave him a shrewd look. 'Settled on any names?'

'Just the one.'

370

At first, he'd wondered if Joe Cossio might be involved, but Gossip Guy was all surface. Then he'd remembered the quiet computer technician who'd been there on the day Rick had asked for the name of someone who was involved in the Deptford investigation. '*He* was,' Cossio had said, with a nod towards Timid Tim the techie.

Vee was watching him closely. 'Think he should be punished?' she asked.

Rick imagined the frightened kid sitting at a computer and scrolling through the texts and WhatsApp messages of desperate people trapped inside their burning flats. Or listening with cans clamped to his head to their last terrified voicemails to loved ones.

He shook his head. 'I think he's already in hell.'

She let out a long, slow sigh. 'You're not far wrong. Have you been watching *Pandora Unboxes*?'

How could he not? She'd established that Floren really was going to cooperate with the police.

'It's been worse for him since all that came out. If we hadn't been there that night, maybe Floren would've got away,' Vee went on. 'Had his chance to confess – given those families the justice they deserved.'

Rick felt his skin flush with guilt. 'I don't have much sympathy with the conspiracy theorists, but even the Met agrees that Floren's shooting was a professional hit. I'm certain Lockleigh set that up, and from what I know of him, he never gives up on a grudge. Floren was a dead man – it was just a question of when.'

She took a sip of beer. 'Maybe.'

Rick felt suddenly awkward. He glanced away, and then back. 'I wanted to say – to tell you – that I feel responsible for Brock. I—' A flash of pain creased her face and he stopped. 'I'm sorry, were you close?'

She gave a cough of laughter, then covered her mouth, shocked. Recovering her composure, she said, 'Well, that was . . .

371

inappropriate. It's been a tough day.' She frowned at the rim of her glass for a few seconds, before going on.

'Brock was a pain in *everyone's* arse. I think every single member of the pack had fantasised about beating the shit out of him at one time or another. He was a bully, a misogynist and a hothead. But he was also brave and relentless – always pushing us to do what we set out to do – to take risks the cops won't.' She shot him an apologetic look. 'I don't include you in that.'

She shrugged and sank into thoughtful silence.

'What happened at the church?' Rick asked. 'After we left, I mean.'

She sighed and passed a hand over her brow.

'You heard Cap – he told us to get out, to leave Lockleigh and his crew to the cops. But Brock wouldn't have it. Said Lockleigh was still in prison when he'd had Floren shot. Thought he'd just carry on making money on the backs of other people's misery like he did before – like he did at Deptford. You know he lost family in the Deptford fire?'

Rick nodded. 'He had a point.'

'Of course he did. And we all saw it,' she said. 'But we're not a lynch mob. And Lockleigh would have to answer for the Munot shooting.'

She stared at the scratched tabletop, her eyes dark.

'How did he get away?' Rick asked.

'Brock used Lockleigh as a shield. Like he thought we would've shot him!' She glanced into Rick's face as if appealing to him. 'None of us would do that.'

Her brow puckered. 'He dragged Lockleigh outside, same way you went, and Cap told us to beat it. The police had dispatched an unarmed unit to investigate – can you believe it?'

Rick nodded. 'They thought it was a crank call – I guess they've had a lot of that recently.'

'I suppose.' She let out a long breath. 'You've seen Pandora's footage. We got out. We had him, Rick. The police were there – we

could've left him for those two bobbies to take in. But Brock—'
She broke off. 'Crazy bastard. I dunno what he thought he was
going to *do* with him. *Shit . . .*' She ran a hand over her face.

'I'm guessing he wasn't thinking at all,' Rick said gently. 'Not
really.'

She sighed. 'And now Lockleigh's God knows where.'

Vee took a swallow of beer, a frown on her face. 'How he got
as far as South Mimms baffles me,' she said after a few moments.
'Brock had no transport.'

'Brock was on the ambush detail with me.' Rick gazed at her
steadily and at last, she seemed to make sense of what he was
telling her.

'Oh,' she said.

'I thought I'd dropped my car keys,' Rick said, 'but now I'm
wondering.'

'They never found your car?'

He shook his head. 'Which is why I feel responsible.'

She blinked, surprised. 'No – it's *my* fault that Pandora
was there. She told me after the shitstorm died down that
she'd been dogging my footsteps for days. She saw me being
picked up by the pack after you left my flat. That's how she
found the place.'

'So she knew you were in the church. Why didn't she name
you?'

'She says she can't *prove* I was there – I was in civvies when I
got in the van, in full kit by the time we arrived at the church.'

Rick nodded slowly, wondering if Pandora had seen him
leaving Vee's house.

'What about Brock – can he be traced to the rest of you?'

'We were careful.' She shrugged. 'But who knows?' They sipped
their beer in silence for a few moments. When he looked up again,
she was studying him.

'What?' he said.

'Just wondering. How did you know I was Wolf Pack?'

He might have said that growing up around Sam he'd learned to read the truth behind the words. Instead, he shrugged. 'Call it my copper's nose.'

'I'm serious,' she said. 'If I get hauled in for questioning, I need to know what gave me away.'

He feigned outrage. 'You want me to add assisting a known offender to my long list of criminal transgressions?'

'That one's already on your rap sheet, pal,' she shot back, smiling. 'We both know the "art collector" friend we helped you to liberate is actually the notorious Samuel Turner – wanted by the Met Police – and for all I know, half a dozen other police forces across Europe.'

Rick tilted his head. 'True enough.' Although half a dozen was probably an underestimate. 'Okay . . .' He took a breath and cast his mind back. 'You're lead nurse at the A&E department that treated the Deptford arson victims.'

He watched her closely. No response.

'You were on duty the night they brought the Blackfriars Bank hostages in.'

'Coincidence,' she said.

He wagged a finger at her. 'See – that's telling. You didn't bother to deny the first bit of evidence, but Blackfriars—' He clicked his fingers. 'You were straight in there with an excuse.'

'*Explanation*, surely?' she said, with a disapproving grimace.

'Really? Is it *coincidence* that you came in on your annual leave when I was shot?'

'Oh, I come in on my off-duties all the time,' she said, airily.

'You were supposed to be on holiday – in Spain.'

She lifted one shoulder. 'I changed my mind.'

'*And* you told Pandora about my boss having a go at me in the hospital the night I was shot.'

She set her features in an expression of mild interest. 'You sure about that?'

'You admitted it at the hospital clinic, when I came in for that last check-up.'

'Admitted to who – you? And where'd this happen? In the privacy of a clinic treatment room? Pfft!'

'CCTV,' he said, enjoying sparring with her. 'It may not be available in the treatment rooms, but it's on the corridors. I'll bet you're on digital record.'

'Who cares? I gave you a gift – and my number.' She twitched her eyebrows. 'Maybe I was just trying to get in your pants.'

'Oh, *that's* why you made me strip.' They were both smiling now. Rick hesitated for a second, wondering if he should be honest. *Ah, what the hell.*

'The crazy thing is, what *really* convinced me was that look you gave me. When you asked me did I think the Wolf Pack were justified, doing what they do.'

She frowned. 'I'm confused. Did you think I was trying to *recruit* you, or bed you?'

Rick frowned, trying to work it out for himself, and she eyed him speculatively.

'You don't *know*, do you?' Her eyes widened in delight, and Rick scratched his eyebrow.

'There's no good way to answer that question – either way, I look like a prick.'

She raised her glass, crowing, 'Yes, you *do*. It's what we call a no win—'

She stopped, as if a thought had just occurred to her, and her grin faded.

'It was a bold move, coming to my home. How *did* you get my address, by the way?'

It was a geolocation program Dave had access to. It had taken some cajoling to convince the big man – being highly illegal for him to use it outside of his duties – but he'd agreed to the smaller sin because Sam's life was in peril. Rick wasn't about to expose Dave, so he said, 'A little help from a friend.'

Vee nodded, accepting the evasion. 'You took a risk. I might've arrested you.'

'You might've *tried*.' Rick held her gaze, seeing humour and desire sparkle in her eyes.

'For the record,' she said, suddenly sombre, 'I'm not sure myself, anymore. After all the deaths and the hurt we've caused trying to do the right thing, it should be straightforward. I mean, were we ever justified?'

'I'm not in a moral position to answer the question,' Rick said, and she lifted her chin in acknowledgement. 'So, what're you going to do?'

'Keep our heads down, hope for the best.' She brought her glass to her lips and all he could think of was kissing her mouth. 'What about you?'

'I've taken extended leave,' he said.

She set the beer glass down untasted and stared at him. 'I know it must have been painful for you, breaking the law, going behind your colleagues' backs.'

He shook his head slowly. 'The truth is, I didn't hesitate. Never gave it a thought. When it came to protecting Sam, the law was . . .' he struggled to find the right word '. . . irrelevant.' He glanced into her eyes, almost afraid of what he might see in them. 'You're shocked. You should be – I am.'

She broke eye contact. 'Look, I'm in no position to judge. You saved lives, brought some awful men to justice.'

'Put a lot of lives in jeopardy, as well.'

'But you *will* go back?'

He thought about it. He'd spent the months since last autumn feeling he had no right to be in a police station – to even call himself a cop. After what he'd done back then he'd felt like an interloper amongst his peers – worse – a hypocrite. And he'd gone further, done far worse, to save Sam than he could ever have imagined himself doing.

Finally, he sighed. 'Honestly, Vee? I don't know if I can ever go back after what I've done.'

She stood to leave, and he gave a mental shrug. He deserved

nothing more. Then she plucked the beer glass from his hand and set it down firmly.

'What are you doing?' he said.

'You've been honest with me, so – in the spirit of reciprocation – I'll admit I don't know the answer myself.'

He stared at her, confused.

She held out her left hand, palm up. 'Recruit?' Then she raised her right: 'Or bed?' She left a few excruciating, delicious moments before adding, 'Shall we find out?'

Chapter 63

RICK ARRIVED HOME AT FOUR-THIRTY THE NEXT MORNING to find Sam in their sitting room, reading a vintage copy of *Daredevil*.

He glanced up. 'Did you kids have fun?'

Instantly boiling with rage, Rick said, 'Sam, if you're having Vee followed, I swear—'

'It's *you* they were following,' Sam said, as if that should reassure him.

'The same thing applies. You can tell Little and Large I'll kick their collective arses if I catch them.'

'I believe you would,' Sam said, and Rick was infuriated to realise that he was flattered.

'I'll call off the dogs,' Sam said. 'Scouts' honour. But before we set aside my egregious intrusions into your privacy, I should add that your Vee Verren is a keeper.'

'Sam!'

'Before you lay into me, remember, I'm still an invalid. And these checks were done before you – how shall I put it – *liaised* with Wolf Pack—'

'To save your arse.'

'Admittedly,' Sam said, 'to save my . . . hide. Your Vee's nickname

378

in the military was Frosty – did you know? She earned it from her reputation for coolness under fire.'

'Sam, I don't need you to vet my—'

'Girlfriends? Is *that* what you were about to say?'

'You're a *child*,' Rick said, slumping into a chair opposite. 'A dangerous, gun-wielding child.'

Sam laughed. 'I'll lay off. I promise,' he said. 'How is she holding up?'

He must have seen something in Rick's face because he back-pedalled. 'I know – none of my business. But the loss of her colleague must have hit hard.' Reading him again, reassessing, he added, 'Or perhaps not?'

Rick tilted his head. 'Apparently Brock was a "complicated" man.'

Frowning now, Sam said, 'You can understand his thirst for revenge, after what happened to his family. Theo was trying to force them out of their entitlement to be rehoused at Deptford – did you know?'

'I did.'

'The man has no conscience.'

Rick had never heard Sam talk like this.

'I suppose you're thinking, "Aren't you just like Lockleigh?"'

'No,' Rick said. 'Lockleigh revels in power – in the hurt and destruction he causes. I saw that in his face when he thought he had me trapped. He really would've tortured you by hurting me.'

Sam nodded. 'Taking a life is a thrill to men like Theo.'

Which implied that it wasn't like that for Sam. Rick could not have explained what an unexpected and emotional relief that was.

'I do wish I'd got that canvas back though,' Sam added, with roguish humour.

'Let it go,' Rick said, with a smile. 'By the way, the seventeen million Lockleigh paid you – Dave traced it to a company called Poena Assets.'

'Is that right?' Sam said, as if Rick had discovered something quite outside of his personal knowledge.

'It's Latin. I looked up what it meant.'

Sam gazed at him in expectation.

'It means penalty or punishment.'

Sam's expression did not change.

Rick pushed harder. 'So – did you get what you wanted – was he punished enough?'

'As the song goes, you can't always get what you want,' Sam said. 'As for Theo – time will tell.'

Rick sensed that the moment for confidences was past.

'So, you'll be returning to work soon,' Sam said brightly.

'I'm thinking of handing in my notice,' Rick said.

'Quitting the police – *why*?'

'Let's see,' Rick said. 'Setting aside what I did last autumn, in the last couple of months, I've harboured a criminal, obstructed a police investigation, aided and abetted a vigilante group. Carried illegal weapons with intent to use, failed to report an abduction—'

'Yours, or mine?' Sam interrupted, laughter dancing in his eyes.

Rick threw up his hands. 'I give up.'

'That's what I admire,' Sam said heartily. 'A man who knows when to admit defeat.'

The smile slowly faded from his face, and when he went on, it was in a more sober vein.

'But I believe you did try everything in your power to persuade your colleagues to reinvestigate Floren's killing. And I *know* that you prevented carnage at Emin's warehouse the night the Wolf Pack descended on it like clueless amateurs.'

'You weren't so picky when they stormed that church, were you?' Rick said, loyally.

The shadow of that night passed over Sam's face for a second, and Rick immediately regretted his words.

'I am grateful to them,' Sam said. 'But I'm more grateful to your friend Vee, for saving your life during the Emin shoot-out.'

'How do you—?' Rick shook his head. 'Never mind, I don't want to know.'

'She is a remarkable woman,' Sam said, and for once, Rick was sure that he was sincere.

Sam closed the comic and placed it carefully on to the table before he rose to leave.

'If you run short of money, you could sell a few more of these,' Sam said. 'You might start with *Daredevil*. I never did take to him – the man's too tormented by his conscience. Agonising over the morality of his actions deprives him of the power to act. It cripples him, and he could do *so much* good in the world.'

'You not gonna stay for breakfast?' Rick asked, deliberately ignoring the message in Sam's little homily.

'I have an early-morning meeting with an old friend,' Sam said. 'But I'll see you before I leave the country.'

Chapter 64

LAWRENCE CHAUFFEURED SAM north-eastwards from Putney to Lambeth in his usual unflappable manner, leaving Sam free to reflect on Rick's dilemma. He couldn't begin to guess how he would resolve it, since facility and personal advantage had always trumped morality in Sam's decision-making. *Almost always*, he corrected himself.

He'd meant what he'd said of Theo. He was cruel, and prison had apparently stripped him of his few saving graces. Sam owed Theo Lockleigh a lot – and Theo always called in his debts. But Sam was also guilty of the worst kind of betrayal, and he knew more than most that Lockleigh could carry a grudge from one decade to the next. He would never let this go. If he couldn't get to Sam, he would settle for Rick. While Theo Lockleigh breathed air, Rick was not safe – which was why, despite his promises, he continued and would continue to have Rick shadowed.

'Do we have everything we need?' he asked Lawrence as they turned into the alley at the back of the derelict pub.

'It's all there,' Lawrence said.

And so it was, resting on a trestle table: the laptop and mobile phone that would gain him access to Dream Schemes Corporate

Trust Fund and, seated on a dirty plastic chair and guarded by a distinctly moody-looking Gavin, was the key to both.

Sam looked down on a diminished Theo Lockleigh.

He hadn't been much mistreated, but his ear had healed badly. Lockleigh was a fastidious man, and the privations of being caged in a damp basement for thirty days had clearly been hard on him.

Lawrence had reported back to Sam nine hours after his rescue from Lockleigh's torture chamber. Rick had slipped away for breakfast, and they had the room quite to themselves.

'We have him,' Lawrence had said without preamble.

'The car?'

'Disposed of.'

Sam knew that Lawrence was rigorous in such matters, so he knew that the job would have been thoroughly done.

That was a month ago. Now Sam turned his attention to the man who had caused him so much pain. 'It's time we settled this once and for all,' he said.

'You won't get it,' Lockleigh said.

'Won't get what?' Sam asked, curious to know what Lockleigh imagined he found most important.

'My money.'

Sam frowned. 'I'm afraid you've misjudged me, Theo. It's Dream Schemes I want. "Building your dream home",' he said, quoting the firm's logo. 'It's a romantic notion, but perhaps you should have named it Phoenix Developments. Can't you see it? "Building from the ashes".'

'Oh, please,' Lockleigh spat. 'You're in no position to lecture *me* on morality.'

'"We in the Dream Schemes family are committed to delivering Jason's vision of creating premium homes that offer quality of life and personal wellbeing at affordable prices." That's verbatim from your website,' Sam went on as if he hadn't spoken. 'It's a lovely sentiment.'

'Don't tell me Floren's death is preying on your conscience.'

'What's done is done,' Sam said, and meant it. He moved to the table. 'Though I'll admit that I was affronted and humiliated to find I'd allowed myself to be manipulated – and by you, of all people.'

He opened the laptop, ready for use.

'D'you think I'm just going to hand over ownership?' Lockleigh demanded. 'D'you think I'm that *weak*?'

'No, Theo,' Sam said. 'No, I don't.' But he saw that a sweat had broken out on Lockleigh's brow.

He eyed Sam with contempt. 'Have you learned *nothing* in all these years? Even if *I* gave you access, the *lawyers* wouldn't just sign over the company registration.'

Sam returned his sneer with a benign smile. 'As the Americans so aptly put it, "If it ain't broke, don't fix it,"' he said. 'With things running so smoothly, I wouldn't dream of disturbing the status quo. *I* will be *you* – at least as far as your lawyers are concerned.' Then, briskly: 'All I need for full access is your biometrics.'

'My biom—' Lockleigh clenched his right hand, his eyes widening in alarm.

On the nod, Gavin dragged Lockleigh a couple of paces to a beer keg and clamped his hand flat on its surface.

Sam placed the steel toolbox on the trestle table and removed a bolt-cutter.

Lockleigh quailed. 'Sam, this isn't you.'

'You came after my brother.' A sudden, unexpected rage boiled in Sam's stomach. It rose into his chest, his throat, his brain, over-taking him entirely. He raised the cutters in his fist and roared into Lockleigh's face: 'MY BROTHER!'

Gavin held the stricken Lockleigh without any sign of emotion, but to the side of the two, Sam saw Lawrence. It was the shock on his old friend's face that brought him back to himself.

He straightened up, his breath coming raggedly, and gave himself time to regain control before saying, in an almost conversational tone, 'I'm thinking a thumb print.'

Lockleigh gave a frightened gasp, then: 'It's two-factor.' Then screeching the words: 'It's two-factor! Maiming me will get you nowhere – you'd need the number sequence as well.'

'Most helpful,' Sam said. He nodded to Gavin, who shoved the man back into the chair so hard that it distorted.

Lockleigh blinked at him stupidly. Grey now, sweating, he said, 'No,' but it was tentative. He was panting, terrified. 'No. I'll never do it.'

'Come now,' Sam said. 'Numbers are easy. No man holds out for a sequence of numbers.'

Lockleigh recognised his own words thrown back at him, and Sam read despair in his eyes. His capitulation was only hours away.

A Letter from M. K. Murphy

First of all, thanks for choosing *Blood Debt*. With so many books vying for attention, I'm grateful that you decided to come along on Rick and Sam's next escapade. I hope you found the journey challenging, intriguing and ultimately satisfying.

In *Dead Man Walking*, the first of the series, Rick Turner had to make some hard adjustments to his long-held assumptions and beliefs about his brother. I wanted to explore that further in *Blood Debt*, so I confronted Rick head-on with people who, like him, are trying to do the right thing but in doing so, break the law. Some of the decisions he is forced to make can't be neatly pigeonholed simply as 'right' or 'wrong', and it's these grey areas that I found most challenging and enjoyable to write. And as I wrote *Blood Debt*, working through the tangled web that Rick found himself ensnared in, I was heartened by the response from readers to the first in this series. I love to hear what readers think; it's like rocket fuel to my writing brain cells, and the kind comments of those who went to the trouble to get in touch via the contact page on my website got me over a few bumps in the road. Thank you!

If you've got this far, I'm guessing that you have followed Rick's new case to the end. After all Rick has done – the rules

he's broken and the crimes he has committed to keep Sam safe
– can he in all conscience justify returning to work as a police
officer sworn to enforce the law? As I started the book, I wasn't
sure how it would turn out; I didn't know how far Rick was
prepared to go. Even after outlining, which I do extensively, I
still wasn't sure. And when I finished the book, I wondered how
he could ever reconcile a return to policing. Should he quit the
police forever, I wondered. Do you have an opinion? Drop me
a line. Or perhaps I should create a poll on social media – with
no spoilers, of course!

As you will have learned, by the end of *Blood Debt*, Rick hasn't
decided. But this novel was completed last autumn, and I've had
a lot of time to think, so I do know, and I have decided. Rick's
next case (whether as police or private citizen), is ready, waiting
for me to take up my pen. Yet it might never see the light of day.
It may surprise you to hear that Rick's existence is very much
in your hands, dear readers. Because, however uncomfortable it
makes us feel, publishing is a hard-nosed business, and Rick and
Sam will only return if enough people buy the books, read the
books and ask for more from the Turner brothers. All of Sam's
wiles and all of Rick's determination are not on their own enough
to bring them back for another year, but you as readers hold the
power to make it happen. How? Well, if you enjoyed *Blood Debt*,
and want to ensure the brothers' return, please review and rate it
on your favourite book-buying platform; tell your friends; gift it
to your besties; talk about it in your reading groups.

Did you know that return is an anagram of Turner? Let's
campaign for #TurnerReturn.

Happy reading!

M. K. Murphy

Social media links:

Twitter/X: @murphynovels
Facebook: @murphynovels
Instagram: @murphynovels
Website: www.margaret-murphy.co.uk

I've written under my own name and three pseudonyms over the years, in genres ranging from domestic noir, through forensic, to detective fiction, and by some technical wizardry beyond my comprehension, my brilliant webmaster, Steve Bennett, has brought all of them under one virtual roof. Do have a good rootle through my backlist – you might find something you missed first time around!

Acknowledgements

As always, I'm deeply grateful for comments, suggestions, and advice on this manuscript at various points on its journey from 'What if . . .?' to 'THE END'. Felicity Blunt and Rosie Pierce gave their usual astute and penetrating opinions and suggestions, spurring me on to produce a cleaner, brighter and more compelling book, and they have continued to steer it through the sometimes rocky waters that a novel is subjected to at its launch. Thanks also to Tanja Goossens who brings my books to the notice of foreign publishers around the world – not forgetting the wider team at Curtis Brown who work so hard on my behalf. To my TV agent, Anna Weguelin – your enthusiasm and patience are administered in perfect balance and are much appreciated.

A special mention for Cat Camacho at HQ Digital, who stepped in as interim editor, despite already having more than enough on her desk to deal with day-to-day. Your editorial input has been invaluable and your enthusiasm for both *Dead Man Walking* and *Blood Debt* have been a cheering influence in a strange and highly demanding year. Writing is a fraught profession, so I'm grateful to fellow writer Daniel Sellers for sparing the time to read the type-script at both early draft and finished stages, providing welcome feedback. Finally, sincere thanks to my unofficial confessor and unpaid therapist, Annette Lawton, for being so liberal in sharing your superpower – unbridled laughter!

Dear Reader,

We hope you enjoyed reading this book. If you did, we'd be so appreciative if you left a review. It really helps us and the author to bring more books like this to you.

Here at HQ Digital we are dedicated to publishing fiction that will keep you turning the pages into the early hours. Don't want to miss a thing? To find out more about our books, promotions, discover exclusive content and enter competitions you can keep in touch in the following ways:

JOIN OUR COMMUNITY:

Sign up to our new email newsletter: http://smarturl.it/SignUpHQ

Read our new blog www.hqstories.co.uk

🐦 https://twitter.com/HQStories

𝐟 www.facebook.com/HQStories

BUDDING WRITER?

We're also looking for authors to join the HQ Digital family!

Find out more here:

https://www.hqstories.co.uk/want-to-write-for-us/

Thanks for reading, from the HQ Digital team